To Become a Priest—
a Love Story

To Become a Priest—
A Love Story

Den Adler

iUniverse, Inc.
New York Lincoln Shanghai

To Become a Priest—a Love Story

Copyright © 2007 by Den Adler

All rights reserved. No part of this book may be used or reproduced by any means, graphic, electronic, or mechanical, including photocopying, recording, taping or by any information storage retrieval system without the written permission of the publisher except in the case of brief quotations embodied in critical articles and reviews.

iUniverse books may be ordered through booksellers or by contacting:

iUniverse
2021 Pine Lake Road, Suite 100
Lincoln, NE 68512
www.iuniverse.com
1-800-Authors (1-800-288-4677)

Because of the dynamic nature of the Internet, any Web addresses or links contained in this book may have changed since publication and may no longer be valid.

This is a work of fiction. All of the characters, names, incidents, places, organizations, and dialogue in this novel are either the products of the author's imagination or are used fictitiously.

Cover design copyright Carol A. Herzig

Author photo copyright Carl Christiansen

ISBN: 978-0-595-44713-8 (pbk)
ISBN: 978-0-595-89034-7 (ebk)

Printed in the United States of America

For Judy and Eric

"We embraced a way of thinking
without knowing that it was only a way of thinking."

    Raymond Hedin,
        in *Married to the Church*

"I hope you are all well, still in love with life and its great meaning,
still mindful of your early days. And, too, that you forgive your old instructors.
Like yourselves, they are/were only human. Be good to one another."

    Father John Michael Murphy,
        in a St. Francis Seminary reunion booklet

"Once the torch is lit, it burns forever."

    Songwriter Jimmy Webb,
        to Terry Gross on National Public Radio's *Fresh Air*

Acknowledgments

Raymond Hedin wrote *Married to the Church*, his perceptive story about our seminary class, from which I got the idea for this novel. Ray read and commented on two versions of my manuscript and encouraged me to continue.

Another classmate and close friend read several versions of the novel, offered much insight and support, and finally pelted me with e-mails saying, "Stop revising and publish!" He preferred that I not name him and said a signed copy of the book is acknowledgment enough. I disagree but am complying with his wish, though the book feels incomplete without his name. He helped a *lot*.

Present and past members of the Wednesday Night Writers' Group gave me thoughtful feedback and support: Jo Ann Colby, Phyllis DeGioia, Teresa Elguezabal, Zach Elliott, Eileen Frank, Phillip Gaustad, John Halverson, David Heuss, Ingrid Kallick, Pamela Kosorek, Tom McKay, Jon Olson, Tim Strong, and Gypsy Thomas.

Others who read the manuscript and provided excellent suggestions and lots of encouragement include: Marshall J. Cook, Christine DeSmet, Rev. Erwin Matt, Helen Pelz, Barbara Tapovatz, Kathy Tapp, Ken Tapp, and Mary B. Williams.

Ann Allen, Bob Suter, and the late Veronica McBride, as well as seminary classmates Dick Kihslinger, Paul Plum, Dave Harrison, Dick Buggs, and the late John Bako, offered recollections or provided material important to the story.

Salzmann Library at St. Francis Seminary in St. Francis, Wisconsin, and the archives room of the *Catholic Herald* at the Bishop O'Connor Catholic Pastoral Center in Madison, Wisconsin, provided wonderful environments for research.

Carl Christiansen made my portrait, and Peggy Eagan edited it, but promised no miracles.

Carol A. Herzig tolerated my changing specifications and designed a beautiful cover.

And Judy, my wife, read the manuscript and solved endless word-processing riddles on our computers, as well as put up with my sleepless nights and many moods during this project. Without her, the story would have died.

Chapter 1

▼

The skinny girl with the ponytail stared back, and Danny Bates blushed. He knew, and he figured she knew too, that he shouldn't be staring at girls. Certainly not here on the sacred soil of Resurrection Seminary, and especially not this day, his first as a student for the Catholic priesthood.

Danny turned away and gazed at the seminary's main building. From the school catalog he knew Kleissman Hall was built in the 1890s, taking the shape of a Greek cross at the crest of a ridge a few hundred yards from Lake Michigan's southern Wisconsin shore. With its tall dome rising from the center of four wings, Kleissman reminded Danny of the state capitol in Madison.

He glanced again toward the girl, then away.

Custody of the eyes, Daniel. You must keep custody of your eyes. Sister Rosalie had said that a lot in eighth grade last year. She was right, of course. He wanted to become a priest. He had to stop looking at that girl.

A sudden breeze off the lake whipped around the old building and cooled Danny's face. He caught the scent of fresh-cut grass from the school's front lawn and from Bay View Park on the other side of Shoreline Road. Goose bumps peppered his arms. The weather guy on the radio during the drive to Southport was right: It felt cooler near the lake.

Danny pulled a tan jacket from the back seat of his family's green-and-white '53 Pontiac. He hoped his dad wouldn't trade this car; he wanted to drive it in a couple of years when he turned sixteen. He peeked again at the girl: his age, maybe younger, with dark-rimmed glasses framing darker eyes. She was grinning at a tall boy with a crewcut who said something to a man and a woman, then pulled a brown suitcase from the trunk of a turquoise-and-cream '56 Mercury.

Before the girl could catch him staring again, Danny looked toward the dozens of boys and their families lugging suitcases, bags and boxes into Kleissman Hall's two rear wings. He would spend six years here—four in high school and two in junior college—at Resurrection Seminary's so-called minor department. Then he'd move into the front wings—into the major seminary—and study philosophy for two years and theology for four.

It took twelve years to become a priest—almost as long as he'd been alive.

The girl was watching. Danny pretended to examine Kleissman's cream-city brick walls, framed at the corners with huge limestone blocks. The beauty of the masonry was marred by gray-and-black streaks from decades of sooty air, but age and looks didn't matter to Danny. On this Thursday, September 5, 1957, Resurrection Seminary became his school. He'd wanted to become a priest since his first communion in second grade, and entering the seminary was his first step toward that goal. Here, a hundred miles from home, he'd study Latin and theology, preparing himself to preach to those who'd look to him, the Reverend Daniel John Bates II, for spiritual guidance and the forgiveness of their sins.

The girl had moved to the other side of the Mercury and was talking with the boy. Danny hadn't even glanced at her for several minutes. That proved he still possessed the moral strength to turn his back on temptations of the flesh. He thanked God for that because the seminary catalog warned he'd have to fight those temptations all his life.

But then he looked the girl up and down twice more before guilt again turned him away. What was he doing? That girl could cost him his vocation. God might decide other boys would make more worthy priests, and Resurrection had a long list of kids, the catalog said, who would love to take his place.

Custody of the eyes.

The day before Christmas break last year, Sister Rosalie had kept him after school.

"Daniel, I've noticed you watching Kathy Sherman a lot."

Caught by a nun. "Yes, Sister." You didn't lie to Sister Rosalie.

"The eyes are windows to the soul, Daniel."

"Yes, Sister."

"A young man who's determined to answer God's call, who wishes to accept Our Lord's priceless vocation to the holy priesthood, will not place himself in the path of temptation. Do you understand, Daniel? That boy will practice custody of the eyes."

"Yes, Sister."

Well, then, that girl shouldn't be here. This is a seminary, for Pete's sake. *Guys* live here, guys who don't date and don't marry, guys who become priests. Girls bring nothing but temptation against the sacred goals that seminarians struggle toward: purity and celibacy and dedication to God.

Danny studied the girl once more. When she looked up at the boy, the tip of her light-brown ponytail brushed the back of her tanned neck. She had a small sharp nose, thin lips and a pointed chin. Pretty, but not perfect. Her ears stuck out a little too far.

The man said something to the boy, then pulled another suitcase from the trunk. The girl turned toward Danny. Her eyes were hidden by the glare off her glasses, and Danny recalled getting his glasses in seventh grade, one year after Kathy Sherman got hers. He swore to his mother that he'd never wear them outside the house.

"Be glad you're not a girl," she told him. "You know what they say: Guys don't make passes at girls who wear glasses."

He'd blushed. He knew because his cheeks got hot. It happened a lot, and he hated that because it let people know he felt embarrassed, and that was even more embarrassing. But, jeez, his mom shouldn't talk about passes. Besides, it wasn't true. As homely as he looked in *his* glasses, Kathy Sherman was stunning in hers, and all through eighth grade he wondered what it would be like to kiss her.

He never tried, of course. In fact, he had never kissed any girl, with glasses or without, and now he never would. He was a seminarian.

The girl leaned against the Mercury and folded her arms. Her ponytail curved up, around, down and out, like a big question mark. Her blue skirt covered her knees, and a yellow blouse draped her thin, straight body. Danny stared at her chest. It was flat.

Custody of the eyes.

He was blushing again. Had anyone caught him? He glanced toward his parents, the boy, the girl, and their parents, then let out a breath. No one had noticed. He was safe. But what kind of a seminarian was he? A guy who wanted to be a priest couldn't stare at a girl's breasts. Eight years of Catholic school had taught him sex was good, but only in marriage, and then only when it might produce a baby. Other than that, *any* sex—in thought, word, or deed—was a mortal sin. That meant you'd burn in hell for all eternity if you died without going to confession to wipe those sins from your soul. And—oh jeez, he was sorry—breast thoughts were sex thoughts, so perhaps he'd already committed a mortal sin.

Then it came to him: Impure thoughts weren't sinful if you didn't take deliberate pleasure in them, and how could he take pleasure in thinking about the girl's breasts if she hadn't grown any? Still, staring at her could be an occasion of sin. That's what the Church called doing something that would probably lead to sin.

And that was a sin, too.

A gut-clutching terror surged through him. He *couldn't* fall into mortal sin. Not here. Because not only would he go to hell if he died that night, he'd have to find a priest to hear his confession before receiving communion during the morning Mass. What could be more embarrassing than not going to communion at a seminary? The other students—and the priests—would know he was in a state of mortal sin. They'd know, too, that he'd been impure. It was probably the only serious sin a guy could commit in a place like this.

Worse, if any of the seminary priests found out he'd stared at a girl's breasts on his first day, they'd call his parents, tell him to pack up, and send him home.

Nobody that crude could be ordained a priest of God.

"C'mon, Danny," his mother said, "get your things and let's go."

He bent deep into the Pontiac's trunk and tugged at a battered brown suitcase, then led his parents up the worn stone steps and through a huge wooden door into the old building.

Near the center staircase on Kleissman Hall's third floor, a heavyset, gray-haired priest rested his elbows on a school desk whose varnish was cracking with age. He handed a curly-haired boy a small manila envelope, then called the next in line: the tall, crewcut kid Danny saw with the girl in the parking lot.

"Your name, please?"

"Patrick William Fernettan."

"So, Mr. Fernettan, welcome to Resurrection. I'm Father Salvatore Terry, the minor seminary rector." He paged through a notebook on his desk. "So. Here we are, freshman dormitory, first top bunk to the right, just inside the door."

The boy picked up his suitcase, and the girl giggled.

"A top bunk, Pat. You're scared of heights."

Mrs. Bates nudged Danny forward, and he looked from the girl to the priest. Father Terry was frowning.

"I asked your name, young man."

"Oh!" Danny tried not to get stuck in his higher voice. "Danny … um, Daniel John Bates the Second."

"Very good, Mr. Bates. You'll occupy the second top bunk to the right of the door, next to your classmate there, Mr. Fernettan."

When Danny entered the one-room dormitory, the girl—was she going to show up everywhere he went?—was watching Patrick and his mother stretch a sheet across the first top bunk. Along the walls between the beds, olive-green lockers awaited the contents of the luggage blocking the narrow aisles.

"They must have sixty beds in here," Danny's mother said.

His dad laughed. "Reminds me of my old army barracks."

An older guy—a student who had to shave—strolled toward them holding a clipboard. "Hello, I'm Kenny Keeton, the dorm prefect. Have you checked in with Father Terry?" Everyone nodded. Kenny introduced Danny and Patrick, and their parents introduced themselves. The girl bumped Patrick with her shoulder.

"Oh!" he said. "This is my sister, Jessie. We're twins."

The girl put out her hand. "Hi. I'm Jessica."

Danny shook Jessica's small hand, but only for a second. Her cool, smooth skin reminded him of hands he'd held last summer at the roller rink. One girl had a mean older brother who yelled halfway across the floor, "Bates! Ain't you headed for the priest factory? Thought you're s'posed to stay away from girls!"

Danny blushed from the memory. "Twins," he said. "I never met twins before." Oh, *that* was brilliant. But what else could he say?

"Not identical, though," Patrick said. "We're fraternal."

Jessica folded her arms. "Sororal."

Patrick shot her a look. "A sore what?"

"*Sororal* twins. It means sisterly, like fraternal means brotherly. It's in the dictionary. I looked it up."

"There are no such things as sororal twins," Patrick said.

Jessica stuck out her tongue. "That's 'cause men made up all the words." She put both hands on her hips. "Do I look brotherly? Besides, Mom said you never noticed we weren't identical till one night when we took a bath together."

Patrick looked away and Danny blushed. Did she say that in front of their parents?

Mr. Fernettan cleared his throat and turned to Danny's dad. "Um … do you live nearby?"

"No, northeast of Madison. A little town called Willow Run."

Jessica faced Danny. "You came all the way from Madison to *this* seminary? How come?"

"My pastor went here. He got 'em to let me in."

"I'm starting tomorrow at Holy Ghost High School," she said. "That's in Glendale, just north of Milwaukee. Pat would go there, too, if he wasn't coming here."

"And be a spook?" Pat said. "No thanks."

Danny looked from Pat to Jessica. "Spook?"

"Mean people—like my brother—call Holy Ghost kids spooks."

Pat grinned, then flung a suitcase onto his bunk. Jessica tipped her head toward Pat and winked at Danny. She did it a second time with a little smile, then stepped behind her father and leaned around to watch.

Danny got the hint. He moved back as Pat whipped open the top of his suitcase. Popcorn flowed out across Pat's bed, down to the lower bunk and onto the floor at Pat's feet.

"*Jessie!*" Pat glared at his sister.

"Jessica Marie," her mother said, "pick that up. *Now.* I'll find you a sack."

Jessica knelt and started gathering popcorn into piles on the lower bunk.

"We've got a bag," Danny said. He lifted his new black shoes from a large grocery sack and dropped to the floor next to the girl. "I think it'll all fit." He reached under the bed for a handful of puffy white kernels.

Jessica's thin back was heaving from laugh spasms. "Did you see Pat's face?" she whispered. "Jeez, I thought I'd die!"

Other seminarians edged closer to watch.

"Hey, you guys, treats!"

"What a waste of good popcorn!"

"We can still eat it. The floor is clean."

"Hey, Popcorn Girl, bring *us* some next time!"

Jessica grinned.

"Now look what you've done," her mother said. "You've made those boys act crazy their first day at the seminary."

Jessica turned serious.

"Are you in trouble?" Danny whispered.

"Sure," she said, "but not bad trouble."

The time came for their families to say goodbye, and Danny tensed. His parents were about to leave him. On their way to the parking lot, Mrs. Fernettan told his mother not to worry, that Milwaukee wasn't far from Southport and they were available if he needed anything.

Jessica poked her head between the two women. "And he can visit with Pat on weekends, right?"

Visit with Pat? At Jessica's? That would be fun. No, it wouldn't. What would he say to her? What if he saw her in her pajamas? What if she—or Pat or their parents—caught him staring at her? What if they told *his* parents?

His mom and dad would probably make him leave the seminary.

Around the dozens of cars in the parking lot, people hugged and kissed and laughed and cried and said goodbye. Danny and his dad shook hands.

"Take good care of yourself, boy."

"I will."

"Study hard," his mother said. "And write to us. A *lot*."

"I will." A raspy lump in his throat made it hard to talk.

Danny's mother stepped close and kissed his forehead. "Be good."

"I will."

His parents got into their Pontiac, rolled down the windows, said goodbye, waved, and drove slowly past Danny and the Fernettans. The car's exhaust stung Danny's nose and he stopped breathing until the breeze cleared the air. It seemed like a movie, watching his parents' car ease through the curve under the trees on Kleissman Hall's south side. He should stop them, tell them he'd changed his mind, pull open the back door and climb in for the ride back to Willow Run, back to his house and his friends, back to all the things he knew.

Instead, Danny kept waving, and the car and his parents disappeared behind the building. He shuffled up the walk, stopping near the door of the red-brick gymnasium to let the Fernettans say goodbye. And to keep his tears a secret.

The lump in his throat settled into his stomach the way it had the night he got lost at the county fair. A huge crowd had milled around him, but the faces were strange and he saw himself alone among the wild lights of the rides and the shouts and laughter of people he didn't know. He was only five, and you could forgive a little kid panicking. But now at thirteen—almost fourteen—it was time to grow up, time to act like a man.

Pat joined Danny as the Fernettans ducked into their car. Jessica lowered a window and shouted, "See you soon!" Then she waved from the back window as the Mercury pulled away.

The lump weighted Danny's stomach. He bet Pat didn't feel like that. Pat seemed a lot more grown up.

He had to become more like Pat.

That night in the gym, Danny joined Pat and a couple hundred other seminarians on wobbly wooden chairs set in long rows on the freshly waxed floor. They watched *Saturday's Hero*, and Danny stared at the images of John Derek and Donna Reed flashing across the ragged white screen above the stage. Donna Reed was pretty.

Custody of the eyes, Daniel.

Wait. Everyone expected guys to watch a girl in a movie, so why couldn't you look at one in person? Danny imagined Donna Reed in a ponytail, then Jessica Fernettan on the screen. He shut his eyes and Jessica disappeared. He was in his living room, lying on the couch, safe at home with his parents. He and his best friend, Eddie Schmertz, were on the phone cooking up things to do the last few days before starting their freshman year at Willow Run High School.

Someone coughed, and Danny stared again at the movie, peering through a forest of anonymous heads silhouetted against the screen. Maybe if he lifted weights and put on some muscle he'd feel more like John Derek, tough and confident. But tonight Danny Bates wanted only to curl up in his bed and cry. It was as if he didn't trust God to protect him, to give him the strength to handle whatever his years at the seminary might bring.

How, then, could he become a priest?

In three weeks they would all head home. He'd have a whole weekend to talk with Eddie and his other friends, to find out what life was like at Willow Run High.

He'd decide then if he wanted to come back to the seminary.

No, he had already decided that. He *had* to come back. He wanted to become a priest.

Chapter 2

At six-thirty the next morning, the clamor of the seminary bell drove Danny and his dorm mates from their beds. They stumbled down the hall to squint into washroom mirrors, hurried back to their lockers to dress, and herded themselves downstairs to the chapel for morning prayers, meditation, and Mass.

On this first morning they carried their missals—black prayer books with five colored ribbons to mark pages for the day's Mass—and guidebooks called *The Young Seminarian,* as well as other books for spiritual reading.

The Resurrection Seminary chapel had a high, arched ceiling similar to Sacred Heart's in Willow Run, but it was only half the size. The morning sun streamed through tall stained-glass windows, splashing deep reds, blues, greens and yellows across the wooden pews and onto the seminarians' shirts and trousers. Older students with deep voices led the morning prayers, and then the chapel fell silent for the period of meditation.

Danny's mind stayed blank. No one had explained how meditation worked. He wanted to watch how the upper classmen did it but, from his place in the front pew, he'd have to turn all the way around. The guys behind him would think he was odd. A few of his classmates were paging through prayer books or setting their missal ribbons. Across the aisle, two boys had fallen asleep, and their bobbing heads amused the sophomores behind them.

Danny paged through his stiff new *Young Seminarian*. Did reading count? He came across a prayer, "To Obtain the Grace of Preserving Chastity." Danny flipped the page before anyone could notice and assume he had a problem. But no one was watching, so he turned back to read the prayer. "Guardian of virgins, and holy father Joseph, to whose faithful custody Christ Jesus, Innocence itself, and Mary, Virgin of Virgins …"

He closed his eyes. His mind flashed from Mary to *Ave Maria* to Jessica Marie. A ponytailed girl waving from her car's back window. The sororal twin. The Popcorn Girl.

And he can visit with Pat on weekends, right?

In the silent chapel Danny imagined Jessica's voice as clearly as he'd heard it in the parking lot. This shouldn't happen to a seminarian. What was wrong with him?

The bell for Mass interrupted his dream, thank God. Wisps of smoke drifted through the chapel from newly-lit candles. The seminary spiritual director, Father Neil Pite, glanced at his congregation, turned toward the altar and recited, "*Introibo ad altare Dei.*" Danny knew the translation: "I will go in to the altar of God." Yes, he would, but not for twelve long years. This was only his first day.

But it was a *great* day, and he immersed himself in the joy of this Mass—this sacrifice—that he'd someday celebrate. He mouthed the prayers with the acolytes, enjoying the soft rhythm of the Church Latin. How many times had he recited these responses while serving Mass at Sacred Heart? *Ad Deum qui laetificat juventutem meam.* "To God who gives joy to my youth."

After Mass, the previous night's period of silence finally ended. At breakfast, Danny laughed with Pat and six classmates at a linen-covered table in the Kleissman Hall refectory. They gulped down rolls and cold cereal with milk and fruit set out by nuns dedicated to meeting the needs of these priests in training.

The boys went back to the dorms to make their beds, then returned to the chapel, where they were joined by the hundred day students who commuted to the seminary from their homes in Southport. On this first morning of the scholastic year, a solemn high Mass would dedicate their studies to the Holy Ghost, the third person of the Blessed Trinity and, Danny recalled, the patron of Jessica's high school. He glanced at his watch. Nine o'clock. She'd be in class by now, her first day of high school, like his.

But, jeez, he had to stop thinking about her in chapel.

After Mass, the seminarians filed into the gym for orientation, settling into the chairs no one had moved since last night's movie. Father Terry stood at the center of the stage behind a varnished lectern.

"Here at Resurrection," he said, "we are truly a family. That means the little charities we perform toward one another have great significance, possibly even the making or breaking of another young man's vocation. So. Keep in mind, then, that you, as seminarians, are set off from other young men your age in the outside world. You are truly different, and therefore you must *act* different from those young men. Keep in mind also that your friends and relatives already look to you as seminarians for examples of God's holiness, just as your parishioners will someday look to you as priests for guidance in their spiritual lives."

Danny folded his arms. Older people were supposed to set an example for younger ones, weren't they? He wasn't even fourteen. Why would his relatives look to *him*?

After Father Terry finished, Danny and his classmates scattered to their homerooms for religion class. That went okay until Father Dowd assigned homework. On the first day of school!

Then came Latin. Father "Woody" McDermott stood inside the classroom door as they found seats at old metal-and-wood desks. Father McDermott was short and thin, barely taller than Danny, with his hair combed back in a D.A. at the sides. Guys called it a duck's *tail* because seminarians weren't supposed to say *ass*. It was still morning, but Father McDermott's black whiskers made it look as if he'd forgotten to shave.

"This is first year Latin," he said. "If you're supposed to be somewhere else, you'd better run. You're late."

No one moved.

"In this class, you'll need two books, both by our Jesuit friend, Father Robert J. Henle. The maroon *Latin Grammar* you'll keep all through high school. The blue *Latin: First Year* you'll need only until next May when, God willing, you'll have mastered its contents and will thereby advance to *Latin: Second Year*. Makes sense, doesn't it?"

Danny paged through the blue book's translation exercises and lists of vocabularies. Few of the words were used at Mass. Why spend time learning a vocabulary you'll never need?

Father McDermott said, "For Monday ...," and several guys groaned. Were *all* the profs going to load them with homework this first weekend? "For Monday," he repeated, "memorize the first declension, using the noun *terra* at the top of page five. There are five declensions, all with different endings for their nouns and adjectives. You'll find Latin nouns more complicated than English, because the five declensions have six so-called cases that indicate the word's role in the sentence: subject, possessor, indirect object, direct object, et cetera."

Danny groaned inside. For years he had looked forward to learning Latin. He hadn't known it was going to be this tough. But he had to do it. He had to learn Latin to become a priest.

Chapter 3

▼

Sunday morning after breakfast, sophomore Jake Arbuten ran up the stairs behind Danny. "Hey, Bates. You got Woody for Latin?"

"Yeah." Danny frowned. Why would Arbuten care?

Jake was grinning. "Poor guy. Oh well, offer it up for the souls in purgatory."

"Offer what up? He was fine Friday."

"Haw," Jake said. "First day. Just warming up. Should tell ya, though, Woody hates people calling him Woody. It comes from Woodson, his real first name. But the catalog says he's the Reverend W. Riley McDermott. The other profs call him Ry."

"If he hates Woody, why call him that?"

"Just 'cause." Jake turned serious. "Look, Woody's weird. And *strict*. The guy starts every class sitting at his desk, looking real calm. But if you miss an answer he jumps up and stomps all over the room yelling at people. He never sits down again the rest of the period. You gotta keep him sitting as long as you can. Keep giving him the right answers."

That night in study hall, Danny wrote home. "Dear Mom and Dad, Everything's going pretty good. I'm making new friends and I spend a lot of time with Pat Fernettan, that tall kid in the next bunk whose family we met." He didn't mention the popcorn. His parents would remember, but he didn't want them suspecting he thought about Jessica. "Mom, you'll be glad to know I didn't go out for football, but Pat and me are going to play basketball this winter. If you see Eddie tell him I miss him (and you). See you in a couple of weeks."

He didn't write how much he missed them, especially at night when he couldn't talk to anyone and he lay awake thinking of home. Nor did he tell them Latin looked impossible. They'd worry. He saved those ideas—the ones nobody would understand—for his diary, which no one would ever read. He made sure of that, hiding it under a smelly old sock on the top shelf of his locker, way in back.

"Keep your books closed, please." Father W. Riley McDermott sat at his desk on Monday morning waiting for Danny and his classmates to sit down. "Last Friday I assigned the first declension for you to memorize. Let's see how you've done."

Danny had finished his homework during Saturday night's study hall, so he peeked at other parts of his Latin books on Sunday. Father McDermott was right: There were five declensions, all with different endings for their six cases: nominative, genitive, dative, accusative, ablative, and vocative, both singular and plural. Sixty word endings to memorize.

Plus vocabulary. Any idiot would know *fortuna* meant fortune, but some words were tricky. *Bellum* didn't mean bell or belly: It meant war. And Latin had no articles, so you could translate *bellum* as "war," "a war," or "the war."

The Church used Latin, according to Sister Rosalie, because its meanings were precise. How could anyone call three possible meanings precise?

Father McDermott called Steve Towan's name and told him to stand. Poor Steve.

"Decline *terra* for us, Mr. Towan, but first repeat the word and translate it. And don't pronounce it like *terrific*, say it like *terrarium*."

"Or *terrified*," Danny whispered.

Father McDermott glared across the room. "Whoever said that, please share your knowledge with the rest of us, or keep still." He paused, and his eyes darted from face to face.

Danny stared at his text.

Finally, the priest continued. "All right, Mr. Towan, the interruptions appear to have ended. *Terra*. Pronounce it, define it, decline it."

"*Terra*. Ah, *terra* means, ah, dirt, I guess, or the world. Yeah, I think *terra* means the world." Steve kept looking down at his desk.

"World or earth, Mr. Towan, that is correct. And our textbook tells us it means land, so I suppose it could mean dirt, too. We talk of being *on terra firma*, don't we, on solid ground. Thank you for adding to our vocabulary."

Danny scowled. *Yeah, thanks, Steve. Just what we need: a bigger vocabulary to memorize. Keep it simple, will ya? The book says* land. *Is that so hard?*

Father McDermott nodded toward Steve. "Now decline it for us, please, singular and plural."

Danny knew this. *Terra*, a word in the first declension, went: *terra, terrae, terrae, terram, terra* in the singular; *terrae, terrarum, terris, terras, terris* in the plural.

Steve stared at the maroon cover of the book containing the information he needed. He shut his eyes. "Ah, terrAH, terrAE, terrAE, terrAM, terrAH. That's the singular." Steve brightened. He was halfway through. "Ah, and the plural is …"

Father McDermott's old wooden chair scraped the hardwood floor as he pushed back from his desk.

Keep him sitting as long as you can. What did Steve do wrong? He declined terra *exactly the way it said in the book.*

"That is incorrect, Mr. Towan."

"But …," Steve said, almost to himself. Danny and his classmates shifted in their seats, examined their desktops or looked out the windows—anything to avoid catching the eye of Father McDermott.

"Mr. Towan, you placed the accents on the wrong syllables. Reciting a declension does not change the pronunciation of a word. Please try again."

"Okay," Steve said. He stared at his book.

"Anyone?" Father McDermott paced the room, glancing from one student to another.

"Terr-AH, terr-AE …," Steve said.

"*No!*" Father McDermott stomped the floor. "Place the accent on the *first* syllable, not the second. The *first* syllable, Mr. Towan." He paced the center aisle between the desks. "Would you care to try again?"

"Yes, Father. Ah … TERR-ah, TERR-ae, TERR-ae, terr-AM …"

"*No!*"

Steve's face turned red, but he started again. "TERR-am, TERR-ah."

"Good. Plurals?"

Steve stood tall, and Danny relaxed. "TERR-ae … TERR-ah-room … ah, terr-EES, terr-AHSS, terr-EES."

Father McDermott put his hands to his head. "No no no no *no!* Accents, accents, *accents!* Terr-AH-room, TERR-ees, et cetera. Do it."

"TERR-ae, terr-AH-room, TERR-ees, TERR-ahss, TERR-ees?"

"Yes, Mr. Towan, but don't say it as a question. Say it as though you're certain of it, even if, God forbid, you aren't. Once more, please."

Steve rolled his eyes a little. "Ah, it's terr-AH, terr ..., *no*, I mean ..."

Danny snickered. He slapped a hand over his mouth, but too late.

Father McDermott studied his seating chart. "Think this is funny, Mr., um, Bates? Perhaps *you* can recite this declension more fluently. Sit down, Mr. Towan. You showed tremendous improvement. Now, please decline *terra* for us, Mr. Bates, without the mistakes in Mr. Towan's recitation that you found so amusing."

"Um," Danny said. He looked at Steve, envied him.

"Mr. Towan cannot help you," Father McDermott said. "Decline *terra*, please."

"Yes, um ..."

"You've already said that, but *um* is not correct. As you will soon learn, *um* is a common ending in the *second* declension. Right now we're stuck on the *first* declension, aren't we, and there are no *um* endings here."

"Yes, Father," Danny said. They were all staring at him. If he squeezed himself tight, maybe he could crawl inside his desk and lower the lid.

"Look up when you recite, Mr. Bates. Look at me, or at your classmates, or at whomever you're addressing, but please don't gawk at your desk. Your desk couldn't care less if you get this correct. But we care, so look at us, please."

Danny looked up. The bell went off. He couldn't believe it. *Saved*. Thank God. His classmates slammed their books into piles. Some rose to go.

"*Stop!*" Father McDermott shouted. "That bell is *my* signal, not yours. Quickly, Mr. Bates, decline *terra* so we can end on a high note."

Danny glared at Woody. Yes, that's what he would call him. Now he knew what Arbuten meant. Woody was sarcastic. He'd embarrassed Steve, he'd embarrassed *him*. It was going to be a rotten year in Latin class.

"TERR-ah," Danny began—better slow and correct than fast and wrong—"TERR-ae ... TERR-ae ... TERR-am ... TERR-ah." He paused. "Um ..."

He stared at the floor, waiting for Woody to jump on him again.

But Woody smiled and headed for his desk. "Please continue. Plurals?"

The words appeared in his head, and Danny rattled them off: "TERR-ae, terr-AH-room, TERR-ees, TERR-ahss, TERR-ees."

"Excellent, Mr. Bates. Thank you for getting us out of here. For tomorrow, memorize the second declension. *Now* go!"

They filed out, squeezing through the door to escape.

"Jeez, fuss-EE," red-haired Pete Parensky whispered.

Several guys laughed, but not Steve Towan, who stopped Danny in the hall.

"Thanks a lot," he said. "I was getting it, but you had to laugh, you turd."

"Sorry, it slipped."

"Yeah? Well, I'll slip, too, next time *you* recite. We'll see how you do when I 'slip' and jab a pencil in your butt."

"Lord, make me an instrument of thy peace," Danny prayed inside the empty chapel that evening. He had stopped to visit the Blessed Sacrament—Christ present in the Eucharist—after walking with Pat and a few other classmates on the cinder track circling the football field. In a few minutes the bell would ring for study hall, ending the after-dinner recreation period and starting the night's silence.

He'd found a prayer of St. Francis of Assisi in his *Young Seminarian*. It asked God for all the things a priest or a seminarian needed.

"Lord, make me an instrument of thy peace," he said again. "Where there is hatred, let me sow love. Where there is injury, pardon."

Towan had walked with them around the track, but refused to say anything. Danny hoped he could convince him he didn't mean to laugh.

"Where there is doubt, faith; where there is despair, hope."

It was obvious he would never learn Latin. How could he become a priest? He stared at the altar. Trust in God. If God wanted him to be a priest, God would help.

In Latin class, he'd have to help a *lot*.

"Where there is darkness, light; and where there is sadness, joy. O Divine Master, grant that I may not so much seek to be consoled as to console; to be understood as to understand; to be loved as to love; for it is in giving that we receive; it is in pardoning that we are pardoned; and it is in dying that we are born to eternal life."

Danny bowed his head. He had asked for peace and understanding, for forgiveness and eternal life. What more should he pray for? He sat back in the pew and rubbed his knees. They got sore fast on the hardwood kneelers. At Sacred Heart the wood was padded. You could kneel forever if you wanted to.

The sanctuary lamp cast its flickering red light across the front of the chapel. The smell of beeswax candles and burned incense permeated the room. He ran his hand along the smooth wood of the pew. By himself in the quiet of the chapel, Danny felt at home. Somehow, with God's help, he'd make it to the priesthood.

After night prayers Danny and Pat stood at their lockers and put on their pajamas. They'd been slow brushing their teeth, and prefect Kenny Keeton had already turned out the lights and was patrolling the far end of the dorm.

"Pat!" Danny whispered.

Pat frowned and shook his head.

Danny edged closer. "I know we're not supposed to talk, but Kenny's way over there. Are you friends with Towan?"

Pat shook his head.

"You mean you're not friends or you don't want to talk?"

Pat hung his shirt on a hook. "Not during silence, okay?"

"But I need you to talk to Towan for me."

Keeton came up behind them. "Mr. Bates, you know there's no talking after night prayers, don't you?"

"Um, yeah. Sorry."

"That will be one demerit. Your first, I imagine?"

"Uh-huh." Jeez, a demerit already? Couldn't Keeton just give him a warning?

"And Fernettan, even if someone talks to you, the rule forbids answering. Now get to bed, both of you."

As soon as Keeton was out of sight, Danny whispered, "Towan's mad 'cause I laughed at him in class. Could you tell him I'm sorry?"

"Mr. Bates," Keeton said from the shadows, "I gave you a demerit a short time ago. What was it for?"

"Talking."

"Good, you remember. How long ago was that?"

Danny was blushing. Thank goodness it was dark. No one could see how red his face was. "Five minutes?"

"No, about thirty seconds ago. Now I have to give you another one. Two demerits inside of a minute. Do you know how many you can accumulate and still come back to Resurrection next year?"

"Sixty."

"Correct. At this rate you'll reach your limit within thirty minutes. You'll set a new record, Bates, here at Resurrection and probably at every seminary in God's great universe. Are you planning to set that record tonight?"

"No."

"Good. Then keep quiet."

Keeton turned away, but someone in the middle of the dorm yelled, "Hey, Kenny, make those guys shut up so we can sleep!"

"Quiet!" Keeton shouted. He shot Danny one last look.

So did Pat.

The next day, Woody sat hunched at his desk watching Danny and his classmates hurry to their seats. Most of them whipped open their grammars to the second declension for one final review before class. After the bell rang, Woody got up, swung the door shut with his foot and strolled past the first row of desks to stare out the window. Finally, he turned. In his long black cassock he seemed to float along the center aisle to Pete Parensky's desk.

"Mr. Parensky."

Pete's face turned pale. Above it, his red hair seemed to glow. "Yes, Father?"

"I should first inform you—for I'm sure you'll want to adjust your behavior accordingly—that you whisper very loudly."

Pete's face got whiter.

"At the end of class yesterday you suggested to your friends that I was fussy—'fuss-EE' is how you pronounced it, I believe—for requiring you to place the proper accent on your Latin declensions."

Pete hardly breathed. "Sorry, Father," he said to his desk.

Woody stepped back to the front of the room. "You don't have to be sorry for that, Mr. Parensky."

You don't have to be sorry? Danny figured Woody'd at least scold Pete, maybe give him a few demerits, even slap him with the dreaded P-52—probation, five demerits and two weeks confined to campus—the seminary's most severe punishment short of expulsion.

Woody stood behind his desk. "No, Mr. Parensky doesn't have to be sorry. I'm happy he noticed. I hope you *all* noticed, because Mr. Parensky was correct. I *am* fussy. I am *very* fussy. Yes, I am even fuss-EE."

Danny grinned. So did Pete, whose face regained some color.

"I am fussy enough to demand that you pronounce Latin words correctly. I am fussy enough to demand that you pay attention to detail. That includes here in your study of the Latin language and Roman culture, but it extends beyond this classroom, beyond this seminary, because I don't mean only in your schoolwork, I mean in every aspect of your lives."

Woody turned toward the window, then leaned over his desk. "Attention to detail can become boring, but it can also mean the difference between analyzing a situation carefully and coming to a good decision, versus looking at it sloppily and making a bad one."

One finger tapped the table to accent his words. "The sloppiness so evident these days in people's thoughts and actions can drive a person to distraction. In this class, at least, I will not allow you to be sloppy. I will remain fussy. I mean, fuss-EE."

Again Woody leaned over his desk. He seemed to stare directly at Danny. "I'm here to teach you Latin, but I will attempt more. I will try to teach you to avoid sloppy thinking. Learning Latin correctly will help you develop a habit of precise thought, not only this year but throughout your lives."

Danny sat back. Woody was the most sarcastic priest he'd ever met. Still, he seemed determined to make them learn. Was this the help God was going to give him?

Woody stood up. "Not that we all will come to the same conclusions. We won't. Human beings can study the same phenomena and—with clear thinking on all sides—come to differing, even opposing, answers."

What did he mean? The Church never wavered in what it taught. Those who came to opposing conclusions—Luther and Calvin and others—were heretics, excommunicated from the true faith and eternal life.

"I hope you will become fussy, too," Woody said. "I hope someday your parishioners—or possibly your students—will whisper behind *your* backs, 'He's so fuss-EE.'" He pulled out his chair and sat down. "Mr. Parensky, you insisted on the last word yesterday, so it would seem appropriate that you have the first word today." He leaned over his desk. "For review, Mr. Parensky, decline *silva* for us."

The color again drained from Pete's face. "*Silva?*"

"Yes, Mr. Parensky. You know this from yesterday, when we declined *terra*. Our knowledge is worthless if we can't apply it to other situations. Apply your knowledge of the first declension to a different word: *silva*."

"Okay," Pete said. And he did.

Woody stayed seated. "Excellent, Mr. Parensky. Now let's move on to the second declension, in which you can say *um* a lot." He glanced again at Danny, then grinned. "Except in Latin we pronounce it *oom*. As in *doom* if you don't get it right."

That night, restless in his bunk on a hot September night, Danny stared at the red exit light and thought back to Latin class. He recalled Woody's—no, Father McDermott's—little grin.

Oom. As in doom if you don't get it right.

Danny thanked God for having Father McDermott teach him Latin. Now he had no doubt: He would learn Latin, and he would become a priest.

Chapter 4

▼

Classes at Resurrection ended early on the third Friday of September so the seminarians could head home for the weekend. Danny and a dozen others hurried to downtown Southport to catch a bus to Madison.

An hour after he got home, he was with his Willow Run friends on a school bus rolling north for the Wildcats' football game at North Leeds. This was a different world: kids yelling back and forth, climbing over the seats and each other to visit friends, singing "Ninety-nine Bottles of Beer on the Wall." Danny sang too. No seminary priests or prefects could spring demerits on him here. But he missed Eddie Schmertz, who'd made the football team and was riding the players' bus. Eddie would suit up in his purple-and-white uniform, but he was only a freshman and wasn't expected to play.

Late in the first quarter, Danny spotted Kathy Sherman in the top row of bleachers with her friend Polly Edmonds. Kathy looked cute in her red coat and tam, and she smiled and waved. She hadn't been on the bus, so her parents, or Polly's, must have driven her to the game. Shoot.

By the fourth quarter, the Wildcats led 34-6, and the coach cleared his bench. Even skinny Eddie got in, running onto the field with a huge purple 78 on his white jersey. When North Leeds tried a draw play on third down, Eddie sidestepped a blocker and tackled the fullback by himself. Danny and the Willow Run freshmen stood and roared. Eddie was one of them, and he looked great.

During the ride home, Danny told kids around him about the seminary and its rules, about all-night silences and mandatory study halls.

"You can't say anything at all, all night?" asked a girl with short, straight hair.

"Unh-uh. Not after study hall starts, till breakfast the next morning."

"Is that supposed to make you holier or something?"

"I guess."

"I'd go nuts," the girl said. "Absolutely nuts."

Several times, Danny lost his train of thought when he saw kids making out in the back seats, but the others paid no attention. Later, when only boys were around, he described farting contests in the seminary dorms after lights were out. See, he wanted to say, we're more like you than you think.

"You can't talk but you can do *that*?" one boy asked.

"No, but we do it anyway," Danny said. He shouldn't feel so good about shocking them. It was the opposite of what Terry told them to do. But fooey. He wasn't at the seminary, he was home with his friends.

Back in Willow Run, Danny waited for Eddie to come out of the locker room, then they walked slowly up Third Street to Eddie's house.

"I had a lot of fun tonight," Danny said, "but I wish you'd been on our bus."

Eddie nodded. "Me, too, but if you hadn't gone to the seminary we could be teammates."

"I might not have made the team. You've got some pretty big guys."

Eddie laughed. "I'm smaller than you, and *I* made it. Anyway, we'll grow. I'm going out for end next year. You could be the quarterback. Wouldn't that be great? You passing to me, like last year at Sacred Heart."

"Yeah, but I still want to be a priest."

"Couldn't you stay here for high school, *then* go to the seminary?"

"I don't think so." Danny didn't tell him how tempting that sounded after going to the game. But he might lose his vocation if he went to a high school with girls.

Custody of the eyes. It was a lot easier at the seminary.

Eddie shrugged. "Well, you oughta at least *visit* our school someday. That would be fun—showing you around. Wouldn't you love sitting in class with Sherman again, even for one day?"

Danny tried to laugh. He would, but he wouldn't admit it. "Okay, I'll visit someday, but it's not gonna change my mind."

Saturday dawned warm and dry. Danny attended Mass at Sacred Heart, then walked home for breakfast. He was about to call Eddie when he remembered Eddie was visiting his grandma. So he mounted his white Schwinn and pedaled to the village park, where he stopped on the footbridge over Willow Run to watch the stream bubbling around smooth gray rocks someone had set to form a dam.

A mile north of town, at Rickmyer's airport, silver-and-red Piper Cubs glistened in the sun. Thick ropes anchored their wings to concrete blocks hidden in the tall grass. No one was around, so Danny eased open an unlocked door, caught the scent of the cockpit and considered climbing in, just to sit for a while in the black leather seat. Better yet, a pilot could drop by and take him for a ride.

A sharp breeze rocked the planes. Their wings bucked up and down as though struggling to pull free from the ropes, to climb into the sky and soar above Willow Run, maybe even Madison, over the state capitol and the four lakes.

"Guess we all feel roped down today," Danny said aloud. *Jeez, he was talking to airplanes!* Oh, so what. He was alone. Already his being a seminarian was splitting him from his old friends. Still, he wasn't as stuck as these planes. Not today. His bike freed him to pedal as far as he could before six o'clock. Then he had to be home for supper.

He rode past farms where gravel driveways led to white two-story houses and giant red barns. He pedaled between rolling fields, some with crops ready to harvest and others with grazing black-and-white cows staring at him across barbed-wire fences. Sometimes the road curved along the grassy bank of Willow Run, only a trickle there, pocked with small round rocks in the rainless autumn. At one turn, the current had carved a pool half hidden in the shade under some oaks. He stopped. He could strip off his clothes and skinnydip in the cool brown water.

No, the pool was right below the road. Sure as heck somebody'd see him and tell his parents, maybe even the pastor. Then Father Straud would tell Pite, and Pite would kick him out of the seminary for scandal. Or he'd drown, and people would ask why a seminarian was swimming naked in a pool that close to town, that close to the road.

Danny rode on toward Kathy Sherman's farm. Maybe this time he'd see her: Kathy with the gold-rimmed glasses and the curly blonde hair and the small, high breasts that he'd dared not let Sister Rosalie catch him staring at.

He'd ridden Rickmyer Road many times, but never saw Kathy. He panted up the steep hill a half mile past her farm, turned around, and sped down the hill past Kathy's. Again he didn't see her. Too bad, but okay, too. What would he say if he did?

Oh, is this *where you live, Kathy? I was just out getting some exercise.*

But maybe she'd take him on a tour of her farm, and in the dark of the barn's loft they'd sit on a hay bale and talk and laugh and stare at each other the way they had in eighth grade. Then, if he felt brave, he'd lean toward her for a kiss, expecting a slap or a scream, perhaps a scamper to another part of the barn.

Or maybe they'd walk together up Rickmyer Road, and at the little pool Kathy'd say "Let's go swimming" and he'd say "How can we without suits?" and she'd laugh and tumble down the bank and crawl under the barbed-wire fence. She'd yell "C'mon, hurry up!" and pull off her light-blue T-shirt and red shorts and stand there in her bra and panties under the big oak tree and then slip *them* off too and dive into the pond as though she'd done this forever.

The daydream was making Danny hard. He didn't want to go back to the seminary with his soul in mortal sin, so he rode faster, reciting the *Confiteor* from the Mass, a prayer he'd memorized in third grade when he trained to be an altar boy. "*Confiteor Deo omnipotenti, beatae Mariae, semper virgini,*" he shouted into the wind as he pedaled toward town. "I confess to almighty God, to blessed Mary, ever virgin," the Latin said. He'd do anything to avoid the shame of Father Pite's emergency confession line on Monday morning.

Back on the streets of Willow Run, Danny squinted into the late afternoon sun. He smelled fresh-cut grass and heard the steady chirr of an ancient reel lawnmower. Agnes Reuter was cutting the terrace in front of her yellow two-story house.

Danny straddled his bike at the curb. "Hi, Mrs. Reuter! How many cookies if I finish that for ya?"

"Too hot to bake today, Daniel. Maybe tonight when it cools. Come tomorrow noon and I'll give you cookies to take back to your friends at that priest place you go to. Agree?"

"Sure," Danny said. He pushed the kick stand down and headed for the lawnmower.

Mrs. Reuter had fed Danny and his friends peanut butter cookies since they were in first grade, even before. He'd heard people talk about Aggie Reuter— from Germany, they said—about how her husband didn't come back from the war in the Pacific and she seemed to go a little nuts. Why else would she stay in that big old house by herself, just her and a couple of black cats that stared out the window at people passing by.

And some said that's when Mrs. Reuter stopped going to church and became an atheist like the communists in Russia. Danny's mom suggested that Mrs. Reuter had better things to do than feed cookies to the neighbor kids, but Danny didn't think so, and he and his friends interrupted their games and ran to Mrs. Reuter's whenever someone said they were hungry.

Some days, though, she didn't answer their knocks. They knew she was home, somewhere in that huge house all by herself, unless you counted the cats, which Danny didn't. The kids decided she must be sick, and Danny led them in the

Lord's prayer even though Mrs. Reuter didn't believe in a God who could help her get well.

The next day, or the next, they'd find her out weeding her garden or shoveling snow off her steps. She'd smile and tell them to wait. "Let me see what I have in the kitchen." When she came back, sometimes the cookies were still warm. And Danny asked God to forgive Mrs. Reuter for being an atheist because she'd suffered enough from having her husband missing in the Pacific. Besides, she didn't act like a communist in Russia. She treated all the kids nice, even the little shy ones who hung back under the maple tree between the sidewalk and the curb and wouldn't climb the porch steps with the others. When Mrs. Reuter saw them she said, "Take these cookies to those children by the tree, and don't you dare eat any on the way."

Danny pushed the old lawnmower back and forth across Mrs. Reuter's lawn. The repetition numbed his brain into questioning why he had left Willow Run, the only town he'd lived in before he entered the seminary. He was giving up the fun he could have here for life under strict seminary rules, and sometimes he hated it. But that was the price of the priesthood, and all the priests he'd met at Sacred Heart said it was worth it. Besides, it didn't matter how much fun he had for a few years on this earth. He wanted to spend eternity in heaven, and for that, he was sure, he needed to become a priest.

He had already decided that in second grade, when he made his First Communion. A few years later, he was playing Mass in the little chapel he created in a corner of the basement, spending his allowance on rolls of Stark's candy wafers—the closest thing he could find for communion hosts—to place on the tongues of kids willing to sit through his sermons.

Still, Danny wondered: What would it be like to go to school here? To run around with his old friends and to make new ones, girls as well as boys? To go to a movie and hold hands with Kathy Sherman? To put on the Wildcats' purple and white and play on the same team as Eddie?

But he could choose only one: Willow Run High School or Resurrection Seminary. As Father Terry had said in chapel Friday morning before they left, "So, keep ever in mind, boys, you can not burn the candle at both ends."

Chapter 5

▼

In mid-February, at the Ash Wednesday Mass in the Resurrection chapel, Father Pite limped to the lectern. "As we start this holy season of Lent, I wish to remind you that, as seminarians, nothing is so important as a daily habit of prayer, voluntary submission to the seminary rule, and the willingness to sacrifice your own desires for the greater glory of God. On this first day of Lent, you have no doubt already promised Our Lord to give up some lawful pleasure—candy or desserts or what have you."

Pie, Danny thought. He'd give up pie.

"Perhaps," Pite said, "you will add an extra period of prayer to your day. These small sacrifices will surely harden you for the more difficult ones that lie ahead."

Danny blinked. No, tomorrow was Thursday, and Thursday was pie night. The nuns baked great pies and wouldn't appreciate seminarians giving up pie for Lent. Yeah, he'd give up candy instead. Then he could still have pie. For the nuns.

Pite pulled a handkerchief from the sleeve of his alb and wiped his forehead. "The month of March falls within this Lenten season, and March is, as you know, the month for vocations. When Our Lord bestows on a boy the grace of a vocation to his holy priesthood, he calls that boy to the most venerable career known to man. He invites that boy to the ultimate happiness, to a life more useful to his fellow man than any other, and to duties that contribute most to the greater honor and glory of God."

Pite stretched both arms wide toward the seminarians. "God has invited you to this happiness. Use this Lent, then, to establish your habits of prayer, obedience and sacrifice. They will serve you well during your years in the holy priesthood. And no, today is not too early to start. Remember: as the seminarian, so the priest."

Danny watched Pite head back to the altar. *As the seminarian, so the priest.* Could that be true? All these guys, the dumb ones and the mean ones and the pious ones: They'd stay that way as priests? He waited for Pite to return to the lectern to clarify what he said. Or to add *in many ways.* Pite had to know their sins and weaknesses. Some couldn't possibly become priests. Could they?

Maybe they were the ones who'd drop out.

He closed his eyes. What about him? Would he always stare at girls in shorts? Or dream of Jessie during meditation? Priests couldn't do that. Perhaps God was giving him a sign that he didn't belong here.

No. If he left, how would he explain it to his classmates? To Pat? To his parents? He stared at the tabernacle. With God's help he would overcome his weaknesses. All of them. And he would become a priest.

With April came spring: warm southern breezes, soft pastel greens on trees and bushes budding to cast their summer shade, waves lapping the Lake Michigan beaches beneath a bright sun. Most of the seminarians' requests for permission to go off-campus on weekend afternoons were to take walks, and most of their walks were to the lake.

On a day the temperature hit sixty, Danny and Pat walked down the seminary's front drive, crossed Shoreline Road into Bay View Park and gazed toward Southport and the lighthouse guarding its harbor. They tumbled down the grassy bluff and sat at the edge of the sand, watching gulls swoop along the shore.

Pat slipped off his shoes.

"What are you doing?" Danny said. "It's cold."

"Jessie went barefoot already last week. She says it's the only way to walk in the sand."

"Sometimes I think your sister is nuts," Danny said, but he pulled off his shoes and followed Pat over the sand to the lake. They skipped flat stones across the water, then rolled their pants to their knees and plodded along the beach. After the freezing winds of winter, the moist, fishy smell off the lake meant spring was finally here.

May turned to June, and the seminarians said farewell until September to guys who'd be back, goodbye forever to those who wouldn't.

Danny's last exam was Latin, and he looked forward to it. All year, Father McDermott had paced the classroom and made sarcastic remarks at their mistakes. But he had also answered their questions and made sense of noun declensions and verb conjugations. Danny had learned the Latin that first-year seminarians were expected to know.

Jake Arbuten had warned him that second-year Latin was twice as tough, but Danny told Jake he'd worry about that in September. And, he added, he hoped he got Father McDermott again.

Jake couldn't believe it.

An hour after Danny handed in his exam, he and his classmates were in their dorm packing, uncovering clothes from piles undisturbed since fall. Danny was trying to fold a shirt to fit into his suitcase.

"Like some help?" It was Jessica.

"I can do it," Danny said. "Are you here to pick up Pat?" *Jeez, stupid question.*

"Uh-huh." She watched him for a few seconds. "My mom can fold it for you if you don't want me to."

"I'll get it," he said. He shook the shirt open for a fresh try.

"Jeez, you guys. Talk about stubborn." Jessica walked away, then turned back. "Hey, guess what. My parents are going to ask yours if you can come to Door County with us this summer. We're gonna pick cherries."

"Pick cherries?" *Don't repeat what she says. It sounds stupid.*

"And we won't get back till late. That means you'll hafta stay overnight at our house!"

Overnight? He didn't know what to say.

She was grinning. "You will, won't you, go cherry picking with us?"

"Well, yeah. Okay, I guess. Sure. I've never been to Door County but yeah, I'd like to go. I like cherries. And I think my parents'll let me, sure." *Stop babbling.* As great as a trip to Door County sounded, spending a night in the same house as Jessica Fernettan was absolutely … something. Unbelievable. Exciting. Maybe that word he saw on a downtown book rack: *erotic*. That meant something about sex, something forbidden, something that priests, even future priests, weren't supposed to think about.

So maybe he shouldn't go. But his parents would expect him to because Pat was his best friend. They wouldn't care if Jessica was there because she was Pat's sister.

They wouldn't know, thank God, that Jessica was the main reason he wanted to go.

"Bates!" Pete Parensky called from across the dorm. "Green Pontiac out there."

Danny ran down the steps two at a time. He hugged his mom and shook hands with his dad. Yes, he was fine and, yes, he was all packed. Some of the guys had already left but Mr. and Mrs. Fernettan were still upstairs with Pat. And yes, they'd have time to say hi before carrying his stuff to the car and heading home to Willow Run.

Oh, yeah, they'd have time. Plenty of time. Time for Mr. and Mrs. Fernettan to ask if he could go to Door County with them. With Pat.

And, of course, with Jessica.

Chapter 6

On a hot, humid morning in late July, Danny set his battered brown suitcase next to the yellow curb at the Madison bus depot. He was headed for Pat's and a trip to Door County, and they'd have two days to talk about bike rides, classmates, and baseball games.

Jessica would be there, too, but Danny wasn't sure what he'd say to her. Would she walk around in her pajamas or nightgown or whatever she wore to bed? No, she'd wear a robe, but even then he'd blush. And when he saw she noticed, he'd blush even more.

She had sent him a letter the week before and he'd read it so many times he had it memorized, even the mistakes like "your" instead of "you're" that she wouldn't dare make if she took English at Resurrection.

Dear Danny,

Hi! How are things? Fine here. I'm going to a movie this afternoon with some girl friends but I thought I'd write and see how your doing and mail it on the way to the theater. Hope your fine. Are you saying your prayers and going to Mass every day? You'd better, because Pat is, as you probably would guess. I'm not, as you probably would guess too. I tell Pat to pray for me. Maybe you should too. OK? Then I can stay in bed and sleep! Write back, OK? Your not at Resurrection now so you can write to a girl, right? I can't wait for you to go to Door County and pick cherries with us. See you then! Love, Jessica. P.S. Pat would say hi if he knew I was writing to you but I didn't tell him because he would say it's against the seminary rules. But I'm not a seminarian! (Thank God for that!) P.P.S. Pat's looking forward to the trip too. He talks about you all the time. (I don't mind!) I'm glad you guys got to be good friends. Bye till then.

Jessica.

"Dear Jessica," Danny wrote the next day, then tore it up. Too mushy, even if that's how she wrote. Girls could get away with mushy.

"Jessica," he wrote, and flipped it into his waste basket. She was a friend, as much as a girl could be a seminarian's friend, and writing only "Jessica" sounded mean.

"Hi, Jess," he tried next, but that sounded dumb. So he gave up, not knowing how to start and not knowing what to say if he did.

The Fernettans met Danny at the bus station, then headed north to Door County, where orchard workers handed them tin buckets and directed them to a row of trees drooping with clusters of cherries.

"Pick only the red ones," Mrs. Fernettan said.

Danny tossed a few cherries into his bucket, then ate one off the stem, spitting out the seed and letting the tartness contract his mouth.

"Jeez, how can you eat them?" Jessica said, her face screwed up as though she'd eaten one herself.

"Try one. They're good. Did you try one, Pat?"

Pat studied the cherries in his hand, then tossed them into his bucket. "I'll wait until Mom bakes them in a pie."

"Me, too," Jessica said.

They filled their buckets under a hazy blue sky, then took them to the orchard crew to weigh.

Jessica pointed at Danny. "You should weigh him too. He ate at least a bucketful more."

They drove to Egg Harbor, where the boats were silhouetted against an orange sunset. In Sturgeon Bay they stopped for dinner at a supper club with dim lights and white cloth napkins and an amber-glass candle on each table.

"They have a wonderful fish boil here," Mrs. Fernettan said.

"Ew," Jessica, Pat, and Danny said at the same time.

"We want hamburgers," Jessica added.

"Ew," Mr. and Mrs. Fernettan said at the same time.

In the parking lot after dinner, Jessica refused to get into the car. "That hump on the floor gets in the way of my feet. I sat there on the way up. It's somebody else's turn."

"Pat, you sit there this time," Mr. Fernettan said.

Pat scowled. "She's the smallest. The smallest will be the least uncomfortable."

"I'll do it," Danny said.

"He's our guest," Mrs. Fernettan told her twins. "Will one of you please get in?"

"It's okay," Danny said. "I'm shorter than Pat." Actually, all of their classmates were shorter than Pat, and Pat had grown since school let out. So had Jessica: Danny had noticed two small mounds pushing out her green blouse when she stood in the breeze under the cherry trees.

He ducked into the back seat.

"Thank you," Mrs. Fernettan said. "Now will you two please get in?"

Pat sat at Danny's right, Jessica at his left. Before they were out of Door County, Pat's head slumped back on the seat.

The hump that bothered Jessica forced Danny to shift his feet from side to side.

"There's room over here," she said. "My feet aren't as big as Pat's."

He lifted his left foot across the hump. It landed on one of hers.

"Ouch! You crushed my toes. Take off your shoes."

Danny pulled his foot back onto the hump. His knee touched Jessica's, and he jerked it away.

"Take off your shoes," she said again. "It's more comfortable."

He pulled off his shoes and rested his feet on the hump until his legs ached. He shifted both feet to the left, and one foot touched Jessica's. She didn't say anything, nor did she move.

Danny edged his knee over until it touched hers again. She didn't move, and this time he left it there, touching so lightly that he could claim it was an accident if she said something. But she didn't, and he pushed closer until their thighs pressed together from their hips to their knees. His face was burning, but it was too dark for anyone to see.

Jessica kept her thigh tight against his, and he didn't want to move, even when his leg went numb. The only sound was the steady hum of the car.

"Wake us when we get home!" Jessica said.

Danny sat up straight.

"We will," Mrs. Fernettan said.

But Jessica didn't move her leg. Maybe she hadn't noticed. Or she felt sorry for him because she knew the middle was uncomfortable. But now his arm was tired. Maybe she'd let him put it around her.

No. Pat might be faking sleep.

Danny kept his arm at his side. He left his leg where it was, too, pressed against Jessica's as they rode through the rural Wisconsin night. At each street light in the small towns, he had a one-second glance at her, to see her closed eyes and small, straight nose and her thin lips and sharp chin before she disappeared again into the dark. He closed his eyes, too, and thought of falling asleep like Pat. But that would waste this chance to feel his thigh tight against Jessica's.

This had to be a sin. A mortal sin. And if Jessica felt the way he did, he had become an occasion of sin for her, unforgivable in a seminarian expected to lead other kids to purity by his good example.

But Danny kept his leg where it was.

"Anyone alive back there?"

Danny jerked upright at Mrs. Fernettan's voice.

"Uh-huh," Jessica said right away.

"Uh-huh," Danny said. *Oh jeez, don't turn around. I'm almost sitting on top of your daughter.*

"Pat's asleep," Jessica said.

Pat yawned. "Not any more. It got too noisy."

Mrs. Fernettan laughed. "You were all so quiet I thought you died."

"We did," Jessica said. "The fish boil killed us."

But she didn't move her leg. Why was it a mortal sin to sit close to a girl you liked?

Too soon they pulled into Fernettans' driveway. Jessica pushed open her door, climbed out, and stretched. Danny followed, but when he stepped onto the concrete his left leg buckled.

"You okay?" she asked.

"My leg's asleep." He waited for her to laugh.

Instead, she frowned. "Stretch it out and rub it for a while. That'll make the blood come back." She turned to her parents. "I told you that hump is bad."

"I'm sorry, Danny," Mrs. Fernettan said. "Is it feeling better?"

The leg still tingled, but he nodded. "Mm-hmm. It'll be okay."

Mrs. Fernettan started toward the house. "That orchard was dusty. You'd all better shower before bed."

"Me first," Jessica said.

Pat walked behind her through the front door. "You'll use up all the hot water. Us guys should go first, unless you agree to a five-minute limit."

"Five? No way. Fifteen!"

"Mom!" Pat said. "She's going to use up the hot water before Danny and I get a chance."

Jessica stuck out her tongue. "I heard guys need *cold* showers."

Pat glared at her. "Don't talk dirty."

Jessica set her bucket of cherries on the kitchen counter. "Showers aren't dirty."

"We know what you mean."

"Ha! You never know what I mean."

Mrs. Fernettan ran water over the cherries in her bucket. "Jessica, you'd be done by now if you'd stop arguing."

"No, she wouldn't," Pat said. "She said she's going to stay in there for fifteen minutes. She'll use all the hot water. Tell her five."

"Five, Jessica."

"Mom, I need ten. I'm all soaped up and shampooing at five."

"Eight then."

"Mom!" Pat yelled.

"Patrick, quiet. Girls need more time."

"Why?"

"Longer hair," Jessica said. "And we like to be cleaner than boys do."

Mrs. Fernettan pointed toward the bathroom. "Go, or it'll be morning and Danny'll have to go home with his Door County dirt. What'll his mother say?"

Jessica stopped at the bathroom door. "Nice souvenir?"

"*Get in the shower!*" her mother yelled. "Seven minutes."

"You said eight."

"*Hours* ago. Now you have seven."

"But Mom—"

"Six."

"Okay, okay, I'm going."

Moments later Danny heard the shower. He couldn't help imagining Jessica naked under the stream of hot water, hair plastered against her head, twin streams falling from the tips of her new breasts so pale beneath her brown shoulders, the smooth skin of her tanned back and her thighs, especially the one he sat against for two hours, and between them ...

No. He couldn't think about that. He had to prove to God that he was truly sorry for offending him by this sinful contact with a girl. With an act of perfect contrition he'd be back in a state of sanctifying grace and a fatal accident would send him to heaven.

But he kept hearing the shower, kept seeing Jessica beneath it. That proved he wasn't sorry. In fact, it added to his sins, mortal sins for which he'd burn in hell if he died before he got to confession. An accident could kill him. He had a shower to take, a car ride to the bus station, and bus and car rides home. He couldn't be certain of being in a state of grace. He'd have to watch himself every step until he got to confession tomorrow.

He dreaded that. How could he tell Father Straud this stuff? How could he convince him he was sorry if he wasn't sure himself?

The water stopped. Danny could see the shower door opening and Jessica stepping naked before the mirror, reaching for a deep-pink towel—how did he know it was pink?—and he wished he could see with his eyes what he saw in his mind.

No. He tried to shake the image from his head. He had risked eternity in hell for a few minutes of sitting close to Jessica and imagining her naked in the bathroom. He was a fool. A weak and right-now-damned-to-hell fool.

The image of her naked rushed back and Danny gave in. He wasn't sorry. Instead, he wanted to take the towel and dry her himself, gently, slowly, everywhere.

"Guys, I'm out!" She pounded at Pat's door. It was a Jessica Danny never imagined: soft and vulnerable, barefoot in a pink quilted robe with strands of wet, dark-brown hair hanging to her shoulders.

"After ten minutes and all the hot water," Pat said.

"Fastest shower I ever took, 'cause you guys need one so bad."

The water was still hot, and Danny savored its flow over his face and down his body. He should finish fast because Pat was waiting and because he couldn't stop thinking of Jessica in there naked like this under the water. Too bad you couldn't see the recent past of a place, a short trip back in time, ten minutes or so. To see Jessica there instead of him. Or *with* him. No, stop it. Wash and get out so Pat can shower and everyone can get to bed. Tomorrow he'd find a priest and confess his sins.

Danny looked down. He'd gotten hard from thinking about her. He ran his soapy right hand down across his belly and touched himself and imagined it was Jessica in the shower caressing him. Within seconds he came and he thought only to soap himself off and make sure everything disappeared down the drain so Pat and his parents and—Oh, God—Jessica wouldn't know what he'd done in their shower.

Now for sure he'd go to hell if he died tonight. He was so weak. *As the seminarian, so the priest.* You couldn't do this stuff and become a priest. He leaned against the wall of the shower, put his head down and let the water wash over him. He had failed again.

He turned off the water, dried himself and put on his pajamas. He checked the fly twice, brushed his teeth and dashed cold water over his face to cool his burning cheeks. He needed to get out of the bathroom so Pat wouldn't wonder why he took longer than Jessica. He hung up his towel, opened the door, and stepped from the steamy room.

"Your turn," he called to Pat. Then he lay down on Pat's guest bed, sinful and destined for hell if he died in his sleep.

Early the next afternoon, Danny looked up from the Wisconsin Avenue sidewalk at the face of Milwaukee's Gesu Church. "It's huge," he told Pat.

The idea to go to confession in Milwaukee came as Danny lay awake most of the night. Here, he could tell his sins to a priest who didn't know him, and he'd still have time to catch the late-afternoon bus to Madison.

Inside the dark, cavernous church, Danny wondered how the priest might react to what he said. He still worried about it, even after confessing impure thoughts and masturbation so many times. Today, though, he'd confess for the first time something he did with a girl.

But how to say it? "I sat next to a girl for two hours with our legs touching and I got aroused" took too long and didn't sound serious enough to be the mortal sin he knew he'd committed.

"I touched a girl" left out crucial information: where he touched her and with what and for how long. The priest might ask for details or, worse, assume Danny touched her between the legs, or at least on her breasts.

Maybe he should have. If the little contact he had with Jessica was a mortal sin that could send him to hell, how much worse could God punish him if he had made out like the kids on the Willow Run buses? In hell you burned for all eternity to pay for the brief sinful pleasures you stole on earth. Did God turn up the heat for each separate act? If not—and the priests and nuns who'd mentioned the subject suggested hell was hell with no difference in its intensity—why shouldn't a guy falling into sin anyway try to do as much as he could? Shoot. What he did with Jessica was an awfully feeble reason to spend eternity in hell.

People who tortured and killed someone would go to hell. And he'd go with them, merely for thinking of Jessica naked. It wasn't fair. His thoughts couldn't hurt her—she wouldn't even know, thank God—but that's what the Church taught. Mortal sin was a turning away from God, a refusal to follow his law, and an impure thought was as much against God's law as murder.

His turn. He tripped over the kneeler as he left the pew, and cringed at the sound echoing through the near-empty church. On his way to the confessional he passed an old man who'd just finished. The man looked content, at peace. Danny hoped he'd feel like that in a few minutes.

He pushed aside the heavy maroon curtain and ducked into the dark confessional. The priest was telling a woman on the other side to keep loving God and to say five Our Fathers and five Hail Marys. Shoot. Pat would take her place and probably hear what the priest told Danny. He should have let Pat go first. Too late now.

The priest slid the wooden panel aside and Danny made the sign of the cross. He could see the shadow of the priest through the white cloth hanging over the grill.

"Bless me, Father, for I have sinned." He should say he's a seminarian so the priest could give appropriate advice, but no rule said he had to, and he didn't. "It's been, ah, one week since my last confession. I, ah … I touched a girl, Father, one time. And I mas … I committed self abuse about five times. And I had impure thoughts a lot … ten times, maybe. Or twenty. I don't remember them all, Father. And I disobeyed my parents about five times. I am sorry for these and all the sins of my past life."

Silence.

Say something, Father. But—oh, damn—please don't ask for details.

From the other side came a creak. Pat, maybe, shifting on the kneeler, impatient for Danny to finish. Or—oh God no—reacting to what he heard.

Father, please hurry.

"Okay," the priest finally said, "you know how important it is to stay pure in the sight of almighty God. We will continue to be tempted, but not beyond our strength to say no. For your penance say ten Our Fathers and ten Hail Marys. Now make a good act of contrition."

That was *it*? Danny couldn't believe it. "O My God, I am heartily sorry for having offended Thee …" He watched the shadow of the priest's raised hand granting him absolution and paused in his act of contrition to listen to the words: "*Dominus noster Jesus Christus te absolvat…. Deinde ego te absolvo a peccatis tuis, in nomine Patris, et Filii, et Spritus Sancti. Amen.*"

Relief flowed into his body like hot cocoa on a cold winter day. He didn't care anymore if Pat had heard, and he finished his act of contrition: "I firmly resolve with the help of thy grace to confess my sins, to do penance and to amend my life. Amen."

"Now go in peace and sin no more," the priest said.

It wasn't necessary. He'd never sin again. No pleasure with any girl, even Jessica, could match this blissful immersion into God's sanctifying grace. It guaranteed him heaven for all eternity, no matter what happened to him here on earth.

In September he'd return to Resurrection and continue his journey to the priesthood. Then, after he was ordained, he'd help other people achieve this same great feeling and, eventually, their eternal reward.

The world had so many temptations, and it was difficult to stay in God's grace. He himself had sinned many times at Resurrection, despite having it easy with daily Mass and twice-daily prayer times and constant reminders of God's laws. Kids out in the world, like Eddie Schmertz, didn't have this advantage. Summer vacation had given him a taste of what they faced. He couldn't blame them for failing.

When he became a priest would never, ever, yell at or embarrass a penitent who came to him. Ever.

At the rear of the church, Danny knelt to say his Our Fathers and Hail Marys. Pat joined him, and when they finished they stepped from the dark silence of the old church into the sunlit noise of the city.

But Danny didn't notice. He was at peace.

Chapter 7

▼

On the first day of the 1958-1959 school year, Danny watched Jessica lug one of Pat's suitcases into the sophomore dorm.

"Hey, Popcorn Girl," someone yelled, "anything to eat in there?"

She dropped the suitcase and marched over to Danny, who was hanging the last of his clothes in his locker. "Summer's over. We only saw you once." She leaned against his bunk. "Know what I wanna know? If you guys quit the seminary, will you stay friends? You hardly saw each other this summer."

Danny closed his suitcase. He tried not to stare, but Jessica's blue blouse showed she'd grown a lot since spring. "Sure. But we want to be priests. We're not going to quit."

"You'd hardly know you're friends. One time all summer."

"Next summer we'll get together more."

She headed back to Pat's suitcase. Danny watched her.

Before the seminarians gathered in the gym for the first night's movie, Danny slipped into the chapel. It was empty and quiet, and smelled of fresh floor wax. He studied the candle flickering inside the red sanctuary lamp, then the white curtain hiding the tabernacle.

"Well, I'm back," he prayed. "Thank you for getting me through the summer. Help me to study hard and stay pure this year so I can stay and become one of your priests."

Temptations hit less hard and less often here than they did at home. And here he could escape to the chapel and pray until the impure thoughts went away.

They always came back though, vivid images of Kathy or Jessica or nameless girls his mind created every night before he fell asleep.

Jessica was his best friend's sister. It was disgusting the way he thought of her that night at her house. Thank God she didn't know, or she'd run from him the way she would from a wild animal sneaking up to destroy her. He *could* destroy her morally. He'd proven that on the ride back from Door County. She might not have noticed how close he sat, but next time his weakness could stain her with mortal sin, and he'd never forgive himself if she lost her soul because of him. Even if God forgave him. And God might not, because how could an all-just God allow a guy into heaven who caused a girl to be damned to hell?

On Saturday, Danny, Pat, and Joe Trainor lay on the grass atop the bluff in Bay View Park, listening to the rhythm of the waves against the beach. They rolled down the bluff, picked themselves up off the sand and searched for flat stones to skip across the water. They counted the hops.

"Three!"

"Four!"

"Five!"

"Liar."

"That last little hop, didn't you see it?"

"No."

They stared at other high-school boys and girls holding hands. One couple wrapped their arms around each other and kissed.

Joe—most of the guys called him Train—glanced at his watch. "Thirty seconds."

"Jeez."

"Forty-five."

"How do they breathe?"

"Maybe they don't."

"Think they know we're watching?"

"They don't care."

"Would you?"

"One minute."

"C'mon, let's go. They aren't ever gonna stop."

Pat and Train strolled along the beach toward Southport, but Danny hung back. The guy had his black hair combed into a D.A., and the girl wore hers up in yellow curls. Kissing like that, the Church said, was a mortal sin when people weren't married. Why, then, did it look so natural, like something those kids were supposed to do?

A business-size envelope came in Danny's mail the following Wednesday. A picture postcard was hidden inside a folded sheet of paper.

"Door County, Wisconsin," the card read, and its front showed cherry trees blossoming in the spring. The trees they'd picked from? Probably not, but similar. Danny closed his eyes and saw Jessica's shorts inching up the backs of her thighs as she stretched for cherries on a high branch.

He turned the card over. "In memory of our trip here. Hope for lots more! I'll send you more cards, since you can't escape that place and see things yourself. Somebody has to show you what you're missing. Love, Jessica."

She shouldn't write *love*. They were only sophomores. Friends. Plus he was a seminarian. He couldn't show the card to anyone.

Danny had stared at girls in two-piece swim suits and peeked at naked natives in his uncle's *National Geographics*, but he'd never seen a live girl naked. How, then, did his brain dream up the full-color movies that played in his head every night?

He tried switching his thoughts to basketball or camping or bike riding. But one night after he climbed into bed, his bike-riding fantasy discovered a group of girls skinny dipping in a stream much like Willow Run along Rickmyer Road. Huge bushes hid the creek—and the girls—from the road as it flowed through a field where no one went after the farmer cultivated his corn.

He shouldn't stop, of course, but he couldn't ride on and risk the girls getting seen by guys who might bother them. So in his daydream Danny stood guard, not to watch but to keep others away. The girls came to trust him and stepped out of the pond for water from his canteen and candy from his bike bag. He couldn't *not* see them, but that was their fault, not his, and they didn't seem to mind when he stared.

One girl stepped on a stick and cried when her foot bled. The others said blood made them dizzy and asked Danny to wash the girl's foot and wrap it in a clean handkerchief. When he put his arm around her to help her hop to her clothes, her breast rubbed against his chest, but it wasn't a sin because it wasn't his fault. He'd happened to ride by and stopped to help.

By then Danny's erection poked out of his pajamas and he slipped his hand beneath the blanket for a second, for a minute, and then he was no longer a knight on a white bike protecting the girls. He was a depraved sinner destined for hell, and he lay awake the rest of the night waiting for morning and the shame of another emergency confession line.

Each weekday morning at six thirty, Father Pite limped down the central staircase from his third-floor room, pulled a portable confessional from along the chapel wall, and heard confessions until it was time to vest for the seven o'clock Mass.

Fifteen minutes before the wake-up bell at six thirty, Danny rolled out of bed, washed, dressed and raced to the chapel. If he got to Father Pite early enough, he might be sitting in his pew before Pat and the others came into chapel.

In a little over a year, Danny had become a regular in Pite's line. So had his classmates Billy Gogarin and Matt Mohrical. Billy was a tough-looking kid in a crewcut, but Matt looked so innocent that Danny couldn't believe he was capable of conjuring up fantasies vivid enough to call sinful. They stood in line two or three mornings a week, staring at the floor while two hundred fellow seminarians streamed into the chapel for morning prayers.

Danny pulled open the chapel door. In the soft glow from two lights, more than a dozen seminarians were already in line waiting to confess their sins of the night. "O God, please let Father Pite go fast," he prayed, trying to quiet the panic in his gut.

The boys in line shifted their feet and glanced at the confessional. If Pite didn't get to them, they'd be in mortal sin for another day, and they'd have to slink back to their pews in front of their schoolmates. They wouldn't be able to receive communion. And everyone would know why.

As soon as one boy finished, the next in line replaced him. Pite must have noticed the line, because he was offering little counsel before giving absolution. Still, there were too many, and the two boys before Danny and four others who'd joined the line after him didn't get to confess.

At communion time, he sat back in the pew as his classmates stepped past him on their way to the altar rail. He pulled his feet as far back as he could to avoid tripping anyone. Across the aisle, Billy Gogarin, who'd been three places behind him in line, knelt by himself too. Danny tried to not feel glad that someone else had joined him in his shame.

But what did the others think, those who never had this weakness or had overcome it? Most never stood in the morning confession line, so Father Pite was right: Anyone could remain pure once he formed the will to stay strong. So Danny could too.

He'd have to if he was going to reach his goal.

One morning a few weeks later, Father Pite waited at the communion rail for the seminarians to settle into chapel. "Gentlemen, I have sad news. Last night at eight fifty-two our time, on October 8, 1958, His Holiness Pope Pius the Twelfth died of a stroke after twenty years as successor to St. Peter."

Several seminarians gasped. Pius had been pope since before most of them were born.

"Let us, in our prayers this morning," Father Pite said, "pray for the repose of his soul and for God's grace to descend on the Sacred College of Cardinals as they meet to choose a new leader for our holy Church."

Danny looked around. Did others feel a twinge of nervousness? For the first time in their lives, the Church was without a leader.

"Dear Danny, here's a picture of my school," Jessica wrote two weeks later on a postcard. It showed a yellow-brick building with blue panels between the windows. "One of the seniors is going to wear a sheet at our football game on Halloween. He's our new mascot, the Holy Ghost ghost. Pat says we should call him 'Spook.' I wish you were going here. We'd be classmates! We do have religion classes, you know, and I'll bet our school's a lot like yours except we go home every night, and of course we have girls and you don't. That makes me feel sorry for your school. Love, Jessica."

Would she ever stop signing them *love*? But it was nice to see what her school looked like. He imagined her walking with her books through the front door, but suddenly he realized boys would be watching her. Something tightened deep in his gut. He didn't want guys at Jessica's school staring at her, not the way he checked the curve of her calves and tried to decipher the shape of her breasts. But she was there and he was here, and he could do nothing to stop them. Damn.

"Your school looks nice and new," he wrote back. "But I like old buildings like we have. I think about the guys who studied here in the past and became priests, like Father Straud, my pastor. I think I'd feel strange going to school with girls again."

At lunch on Tuesday, October 28, Father Terry called for attention. "It was announced an hour ago in Rome that we have a new pope after three days of balloting: Angelo Cardinal Roncalli, the Patriarch of Venice. He's seventy-six years old, and he's taken the name Pope John the Twenty-Third."

"That's pretty old for a pope," Pete Parensky whispered. "Bet it won't be long before they have to pick another one."

Danny bit into a peanut butter sandwich. If the Holy Ghost directed the cardinals in choosing the new pope, why didn't they decide on one during the first ballot? Did God have trouble making up his mind?

On a cold Monday in December, Danny's Sophomore basketball team trailed the favored Juniors by two points with ten seconds to go. Bobby Lippen, the Juniors' best ball handler, was dribbling to run out the clock. Suddenly Matt Mohrical dove for the ball and swiped it ahead to Billy Gogarin, who raced down the court for the tying basket. Later, with the game still tied near the end of overtime, Pat Fernettan swished a shot to win it.

"A miracle!" Train shouted in the locker room. "Matt stealing the ball like that, we should call him 'Miracle' Mohrical. And Pat hitting that basket at the end? 'Nothin' But Net' Fernettan. And we got 'Go-Go' Gogarin too."

The overtime, however, had pushed the game past the recreation period, so the players skipped their showers and came to the chapel still sweating. Father Terry waited for them outside the door. Danny expected a scolding about their uncombed hair, but Terry kept saying "Come on, hurry up" without looking at anyone.

Before they started the rosary, Father Pite limped out of the sacristy. Pite usually smiled, but that evening his mouth was tight and he stared past them as he walked to the lectern. "I have terrible news tonight, gentlemen." His voice was raspy and he kept looking down as though he had written what he wanted to say across the sanctuary floor. "This afternoon, in Chicago, at a Catholic grade school called Our Lady of the Angels, a fire broke out."

The chapel fell silent. Some of the Resurrection guys came from Chicago.

"A fire broke out in the school," Pite said so softly that everyone leaned forward to hear. "News reports say many children were injured, possibly even killed, in the fire. They don't know how many yet." The priest paused again and, for the first time, looked up. "All we can do this afternoon is remember in our prayers those people in Chicago, the children and their parents, the firemen, everyone involved in this terrible tragedy, even our former archbishop Cardinal Meyer who recently left us for Chicago. Please pray for them." Father Pite left the lectern and walked down the center aisle and entered a pew at the back of the chapel.

No one moved. Pite had to know more than he told them. *They don't know how many yet.* Danny bet there were a lot.

One of the theology students started the rosary, declaring a "special intention" for the victims, their families, and the firemen. It was hard to concentrate on the prayers. The victims were mostly kids. What was it like, trapped in a burning building, smelling smoke and watching the flames come at you? What should you do? Scream? Jump out a window? Pray?

One Saturday night when Danny was seven, lightning struck St. Mary of the Lake church north of Madison. Sunday morning, after Mass at Sacred Heart, his dad drove them to see what the fire had done. The steeple, the roof, the windows and doors were gone. Thick smoke curled out of the stone walls. The church looked as if it had been bombed in a war.

Wars were started by men, but lightning was controlled by God. God had destroyed his own house, a beautiful old church that people prayed in and celebrated their baptisms and weddings and funerals in.

That was two months after Danny made his first communion on a sunny spring morning. He had watched Father Krimek, his favorite assistant at Sacred Heart. Father Krimek was funny and friendly, and he kept his summer sermons short so the kids could play ball. It was on his first communion day that Danny decided to become a priest like Father Krimek. But the St. Mary's fire made him wonder if there truly was a God, because why would God do something so dumb?

But the nuns at Sacred Heart School insisted that faith was a mystery. Humans could not understand the mind of God. We had to submit to his will and fight our doubts. So Danny never told anyone about his. Who could he tell? He was seven years old.

First that church, now a school. An all-powerful God could have stopped those fires. People prayed for protection from such things. Every morning, from his *Young Seminarian,* Danny prayed, "O Holy Virgin, Mother of God, my Mother and Patroness, I place myself under thy protection, I throw myself with confidence into the arms of thy compassion." Well, if something that terrible happened in a school dedicated to Mary herself, where the kids recited daily prayers, what difference would it make if he never prayed again?

Did God love those kids he let burn? It didn't make sense, but a seminarian had to believe that God did love them. So Danny moved his fingers along the black beads of his rosary and decided once again to ignore his doubts.

On the first day of Christmas vacation, Jessica stood in the fluffy new snow next to her parents' Mercury. Danny opened the car door but she didn't move.

She was staring at Kleissmann Hall. "It's old, like that school that burned in Chicago."

"Kleissman's not going to burn," Danny said.

She kept staring. "The newspapers have stories about firetrap schools. That looks like one."

Pat came over. "Don't worry. We have lots of escapes. See? There and there and there. And the same on the other side."

Jessica started crying. "The school that burned had escapes, too, but the kids couldn't get to them. Those ninety kids that died weren't even as old as we are."

"I know," Danny said.

"I know," Pat said.

She shivered and wrapped her arms around herself. "Jeez, you guys. How can you feel safe in there?"

"The priests live in the building with us," Pat said.

"Those Chicago kids felt safe with those nuns too, I'll bet, but three of 'em died with the kids. So don't tell *me* the priests will keep you safe."

Danny couldn't think of anything to say. In the days after the Holy Angels fire he'd checked the fire escapes outside all his classrooms.

And in the dorm, guys had gathered at the fire-escape door and spoke of basketball, but their eyes studied the steel steps outside.

Jessica turned to Pat. "So where was God when those kids burned?"

Pat looked at her, but didn't say anything.

"Well? Didn't they say their prayers or something?"

"I don't know. I—"

"If you become a priest you'll have to explain this stuff. So practice explaining it to me."

"We can't know what God's plan is," Pat said.

Jessica threw out her arms. "God's *plan*? You mean God *plans* to burn little kids in their school? That was a Catholic school, with Catholic kids and Catholic nuns, not some old public school filled with little pagans. So what difference does it make, huh?" She started crying again and ducked into the back seat of the car.

"We'll ask the priests when we get back in January," Danny said.

"Yeah," Pat said. "Then we'll tell you what they say."

Danny leaned toward her window. "We're only sophomores. It's a long time till we study theology."

Jessica wiped her eyes. "The guy in the *Catholic Herald Citizen* studied theology, I'll bet. He said those who keep asking 'why' are forgetting this is God's world, not ours. And God's ways aren't our ways. Well, if God's way is to burn little kids, then God's *mean*."

Danny agreed, but he couldn't admit it. "We'll ask the priests."

Pat nodded. "Yes. We will."

But when they came back to the seminary after Christmas break Danny didn't ask, and neither did Pat. How could they without sounding as though they had doubts about their faith?

A few weeks later, on the first Sunday of February in 1959, Father Terry stood behind the lectern in the chapel. "I have news from Rome."

The seminarians had heard rumors.

"By now you are aware," Terry said, "that, in last fall's election, the College of Cardinals couldn't agree on a pope through the first two ballots, so they compromised on an older man, Cardinal Roncalli, as a so-called interim pope to lead the Church for a short time."

Terry smiled. "So. The dear cardinals may have gotten more than they bargained for. John the Twenty-Third has already created twenty-three new cardinals, and last Sunday in his first public address he said he will convene an ecumenical council to study reunion with the Eastern church that broke away from Rome in 1054."

The priest paused. "You've probably never heard of such a council. Certainly you won't recall the last one. It occurred in 1870. An ecumenical council is a meeting of all the church's cardinals, archbishops and bishops. Fifteen hundred or more are expected to attend this one."

Father Terry smiled again. "So. We don't know when the council will start, but this new pope is starting to surprise people. I think, with this council, we'll see some interesting changes in the coming years."

Why was Terry smiling? The Church couldn't change. Its doctrine reflected God's will. Its teachings were forever. In matters of faith and morals, the Church was infallible. It could never make a mistake. No ecumenical council could change that.

On a warm day early in June, the seminarians attended Mass before their final exams. Father Terry gave the sermon.

"Before you leave here for the summer months, I must remind you of Canon 124, the law pertaining to young men studying for the priesthood. It states, 'During the days of vacation the ecclesiastical student shall not descend to the common plane of the layman, but should preserve an internal and external sanctity of life demanded by his holy vocation. They should by the sanctity of their lives give edification to the laity, and promote the honor of the Church.' So, I hope all of you will take that to heart, and we look forward to seeing you back here in September."

He'd try, Danny promised. He'd try very hard.

Chapter 8

▼

It was Eddie Schmertz calling. "Wanna go swimming tonight?"

"Sure," Danny said. "Where?" *Where?* Anywhere would do this hot August day when he felt so bored he wished he could go back to the seminary.

Eddie talked fast. "My folks know Kathy Sherman's mom and dad, and they invited us to Kathy's uncle's cottage on Lake Mendota. Kathy's gonna have a girlfriend there so I get to bring somebody too. I thought maybe you'd like to come."

Kathy Sherman, it was said, wore a red swim suit. "Yeah," Danny said.

After Polly Edmonds and Kathy jumped off the pier into chest-deep water, Eddie and Danny tossed around a sponge ball that the girls tried to intercept. They played keepaway for a while, then paddled around in the warm water.

Danny tossed a sprig of seaweed toward Kathy. "Haven't seen you much this summer."

She flung it back. "I'm in church every week. Don't you see me?"

"Not when I can say hi."

Polly was lying across Eddie's arms, and he was carrying her through the water.

Danny edged closer to Kathy. "Here," he said. He stretched out his arms and Kathy lay back in them the way Polly did in Eddie's. Danny couldn't believe it: His right arm circled Kathy's bare back and his left arm and hand were under her knees against her smooth wet skin.

Eddie and Polly drifted to the far side of the pier where the dark hid them.

Kathy squinted their way. "I'll bet they're kissing."

"Maybe." Danny's heart jumped. Did she think they should too?

She wiggled a little and he let her down. She pulled him by the hand. "Let's go see."

They waded toward the pier and heard smooching sounds but it was too dark to see more than the outline of a pair of heads. Danny put his arm around Kathy's waist. He ached to kiss her, but he was a seminarian. A junior next month, almost sixteen years old. Kissing might have been all right a year or two ago when he was only thirteen or fourteen and too young to act mature, but now he was older—*too* old to kiss a girl.

Kathy grinned. She put her arms around his neck, but Danny ducked away.

What was he doing? She *wanted* to kiss. He should kiss her.

I remind you of Canon 124: During the days of vacation the ecclesiastical student should not descend to the common plane of the layman.

No. He was a seminarian, an *ecclesiastical student*, a man set apart from the world. He was forbidden the fun other boys and girls had, and dared not scandalize them by ignoring the sacredness of his vocation. He was under orders from God to provide a good example to Eddie and Polly and Kathy by overcoming everything inside of him that screamed *Kiss her, you fool!*

So he didn't.

A week later, two days before Danny left for Southport, Eddie stopped by. "The swimming party was fun, wasn't it?"

"I guess," Danny said.

Eddie frowned. "But you know what? Kathy's going steady with Brett Cooper."

Cooper? The guy was a jerk! And going steady was a sin. It said so in the pamphlets on the literature rack near the seminary chapel. Going steady was an occasion of sin that led to all sorts of mortal sins against purity. Kathy was a Catholic. How could she go steady?

Eddie talked faster. "You oughta quit the seminary. Come back to Willow Run. A lotta guys say Kathy'd break up with Coop if you asked her out."

"C'mon, you know I can't do that if I'm going to be a priest."

But Danny wished, and after Eddie left he slammed the door to his room. He dropped a Sousa march onto his hi-fi and lay face down on his bed. He cursed himself for being a seminarian, for being too old to kiss a girl who wanted him to kiss her. And for still liking her after she committed a mortal sin by going steady with that jerk Cooper. Danny started to cry, and he pushed his face deep into the pillow so his parents wouldn't hear. Damn! Why did he have to be different?

Why did he have to go to a school a hundred miles away where he couldn't do a damned thing to change Kathy Sherman's mind?

On October 7, one month into their junior year, Pat and Joe Trainor took Danny into Southport. "We're going to Foxie's for malts," Pat said. "It's your birthday. Train and I'll buy."

At the counter Pat and Train toasted Danny for turning sixteen, then discussed how picky the state examiners were for drivers' licenses. The bell above the front door jingled.

Train looked first. "Popcorn Girl!"

Jessica walked toward them in a dark green jacket over a flowery pink dress. She headed straight for Danny, said "happy birthday" and threw her arms around his neck from the back. Something soft brushed his left cheek. A kiss? He wasn't sure, but he blushed.

"Hi, guys," she said.

"How'd you get here?" Pat asked.

"I told mom I needed the car for a friend's birthday, that I'll be home for dinner."

"You lied?"

"Danny's a friend, today's his birthday, and I'll get home on time."

"I'll bet you didn't tell her it was Danny's party."

Jessica rolled her eyes. "If I said, 'Mom, can I drive our car to Southport and crash a seminary party,' do you think I'd have gotten it? Besides, how much trouble can a girl get into in a couple of hours?"

Pat stared at her. "Any girl, or you?"

Jessica stuck out her tongue.

Train moved to the next seat, and Jessica sat between him and Danny.

"Now you're sixteen too," she said. "You can get your license and drive down to see us next summer."

"Oh, sure," Danny said. "You couldn't tell your mom you wanted the car to come here, but you think I'll get ours for a trip to Milwaukee?"

"Try," she said. She slipped him a folded piece of paper. "Read this later," she whispered, "when you're alone."

At the dorm, Danny headed for the only private place in the seminary, a bathroom stall. He lowered his trousers, though he didn't have to go, sat on the toilet and pulled Jessica's note from his pocket. "Call me Saturday afternoon. Alone. Very important. J."

That was all it said.

After lunch on Saturday, Danny walked south along Shoreline Road, around a curve and under the Chicago and NorthWestern railroad bridge, to a small pizza place with a few Formica-topped booths along the side wall. Back in March, his basketball team had celebrated their intramural league championship there, and he remembered a pay phone in the corner near the door.

An older kid was using the phone, so Danny sat at the edge of a booth. The pizza workers watched, and he read their minds: *Is this guy going to order or just sit there taking up space?* Maybe he should look for another phone, but where?

As soon as Danny decided to buy a pizza slice, the kid hung up and walked out. Danny put his wallet away. The phone jingled as his dime dropped.

"Hello?"

Shoot! "Hi, Mrs. Fernettan." He tried to sound casual, as though he called the Fernettans every week. "This is Danny Bates. How are you?" He'd better talk to her a while before he asked for Jessica.

"We're fine, Danny. Is Patrick okay? He's not here, you know. He's at the seminary. Didn't you see him? There's nothing wrong, is there?"

Oh, great, he had her worried. "No, Ma'am, Pat's fine. Actually, I called because I need to ask Jessie something. Is she home?"

"Oh! Yes, Jessica's here. Just a minute, I'll get her. Patrick's okay, though?"

"Uh-huh. Saw him at lunch."

"Is he with you?"

"Um ... no, not right now. He went for a walk with some other guys. To the airport. To watch planes or something."

"Mom, who is it?" Jessica's voice.

"Danny Bates, dear. Actually, he's calling for you. Here, I'll let you talk. Goodbye, Danny."

"Bye, Mrs. Fern—"

"Danny?"

"Jess? I called like you said."

"Yes ... I had fun at your party the other day."

"Me too." *That's all she wanted?*

"Danny, this'll sound kinda weird, but ... well, would you take me to our prom? It's going to be on May sixth. I know that's a long time away but I looked at Pat's schedule. Our prom's the night you guys go home for the weekend, so you won't be stuck at the seminary. Can you believe it?"

Believe what, that her prom is the first night of a weekend home or that she's asking him to take her? "Um, I don't know, I—"

"You think seminarians never go out, don't you? Well, my friend Joanie came to homecoming last year with a senior from St. Francis, that seminary here in Milwaukee."

"He could've gotten kicked out."

"Oh, yeah?" Jessica's voice got very high. "A priest from our school talked to him and Joanie heard the priest say he was going to tell somebody he knew at St. Francis. But Sam's still there, in college now. He and Joanie even went out some more times last summer."

"Maybe the priest didn't tell."

She sighed loud enough for him to hear. "Look, they do not kick guys out for going on dates. If you still don't believe me, ask Pat about Train."

"Train?"

"Yeah. Ask Pat. He knows all about it. You don't have to give me an answer right away 'cause it's early, but pretty soon, 'cause there's a guy been asking me. He's nice, but I'd rather go with you. Our class only gets one prom, you know, so it's important."

"But …" Danny didn't know what to say. How could he go to her prom? His parents knew the rule about girls. So did her parents. Everybody did. Besides, how would he get home? And what would the guys say? What would the priests say? But what did Pat know about Train?

Jessica's voice was calmer. "Remember, you don't have to tell me right away. Call when you decide. And we won't tell anyone I asked *you*. We'll say *you* asked *me*."

"What would I wear?" *He wasn't going. Why was he asking?*

"A suit."

"I thought guys wore tuxedos."

"Not all of 'em. Some wear suits. Or sport coats. They look nice."

"Mine's getting too small."

"Hey, wear a cassock. Or borrow some overalls from a farmer in Willow Run if you want to. I don't care."

"But I've never danced."

"Nobody'll know that except me, and I won't tell anyone, not even Joanie. You'll only dance with me, and it won't matter how we look 'cause it'll be dark. Besides, everyone'll be too nervous about how *they* look to worry about us."

"How will I get home?" *Why ask? He wasn't going.*

She sighed again. "I'll get Pat to invite you to stay over. You can take the bus home. That part's worked out. All you have to do is say yes."

That night after dinner, Pat shook his head. "Is this your idea, or hers?"
"Well, we—"
"She asked *you*, didn't she."
Danny nodded.
"Do you want to go?"
"Kinda, but I don't know what to do at a prom."
"We're not supposed to know."
"Jessie said Train goes out."
Pat looked around. "It wasn't that big a deal. He went to the Catholic Action Convention in Milwaukee and met a girl from Kenosha. They went to the dance. Terry was a chaperone and caught him."
Danny tried to imagine it. What if Terry had caught *him* with Kathy Sherman last summer? "What did he do?"
"Nothing," Pat said. "He never said a word, at the dance or back here."
"He could've kicked him out!"
"Well, he didn't. That's probably why Jess figures you can go to her prom. But don't. Maybe Train was lucky, like Terry didn't recognize him or something."
"Well, I should let her know. She said some guy's been asking her."
"Jason Torgleman, one of the guys she's gone out with. I told him to ask her because she's gone out with him more than once, so she must like him. The trouble is, Jessie gets so sarcastic that she scares guys off. Did she say she won't go with him?"
"No, just that she'd rather go with me and wants to tell him soon so he has time to ask someone else."
"How sweet of her," Pat said. "I'll run home tomorrow and tell her to go with Jase."

Sunday night, Pat met Danny in the library. "She still wants you to take her. I told her she's nuts, but she promised to go straight home and skip the parties afterward."
"So now what?"
"Now you have to decide."
"Can I stay at your house that night?"
"I suppose. I don't want anything to do with it, but I owe her a favor and she wants this, so I said okay. My parents said you can stay, but they're wondering

why we're planning stuff already for May. I have no idea what they'll say when they find out you're Jessie's prom date. I'll probably get grounded."

"Not Jessie?"

"Her too."

"Does she know that?"

"Oh, yeah. I told you, she's nuts. And so are you if you agree to go."

A few weeks later, Pat and Danny strolled against the cold wind along the cinder path.

"The pope's calling that new council the Second Vatican Council," Pat said.

Danny pulled his hat over his ears. "I hate November. The grass is dead, the leaves are down, and there's no snow to make things pretty."

"Don't you care about anything but the weather? This council is important. It'll be in Rome, at St. Peter's. But it won't start before '62."

"We'll be in college," Danny said. "Besides, the Church can't change. Why is everyone getting so excited?"

They headed inside. "Well, one thing isn't changing," Pat said. "The pope said Latin will be the official language of the council. Oh, speaking of language, Jessie said some naughty words last weekend because I didn't remind you to call her."

"Wouldn't have mattered. I couldn't decide what to say."

"Say no."

"I want to stay friends."

"She'll be disappointed, not mad."

"I suppose I should call. Then she can tell that other guy okay."

"Too late. She told him no."

"But *I'm* going to say no."

"She says then she won't go."

Danny paused. "Going to her prom might be fun, though. In fact, we should have one *here*. We could chip in to send the priests and nuns out to dinner and a movie, decorate the gym and invite girls from that convent in Southport. Our class would host the first-ever Resurrection Seminary prom. Great idea, huh?"

"Terry wouldn't leave. He'd know something was up."

"But think of it: a prom in our gym. Our class would make history."

Pat laughed. "Our class would *be* history."

Danny pulled off his hat. "Like me, I suppose, if I take Jess to her prom."

CHAPTER 9

▼

Shortly after Thanksgiving, at a Mass celebrating the feast of Saint Francis Xavier, Father Pite was singing the Latin: "*Signa autem eos, qui crediderent, haec sequentur.*" Danny followed the translation in his missal: "And these signs shall follow them that believe: In my name, they shall cast out devils; they shall speak with new tongues; they shall take up serpents; and if they drink any deadly thing, it shall not hurt them; they shall lay their hands upon the sick, and they shall recover."

But Danny didn't know anyone, not even a priest, who showed these signs. Earlier, he'd laughed with Train and Pat at a story about a religious fanatic bitten by a snake he'd "taken up" to prove his faith. The story was no longer funny. The poor guy had taken Christ's words literally, and why not? Who decided which verses we were to follow and which we could ignore? Could we ignore *any*? If not, why did Jesus order his followers to do things that would kill them?

A few days later, Danny read that Jesus cursed a fig tree because it had no figs. But it wasn't the season for figs. The tree was following God's plan—the natural law. It was *supposed* to be barren. Christ's anger seemed childish, like a temper tantrum.

Was he the only one at Resurrection wondering about this stuff? There was no one to ask. If the priests found out he had these doubts, they'd ship him out.

God had given him this vocation. *Vocation*, from the Latin *vocare*, to call. God had called him; he had to come. He couldn't say no to God.

But there had to be answers. It was only a matter of time—perhaps when he studied philosophy and theology—before he discovered them.

The Saturday before the seminarians headed home for Christmas, Danny decided to give Jessica his answer about her prom. She'd asked him back in October. He shouldn't take her, of course, but going out with her would be fun, and the seminary probably wouldn't kick him out even if he did get caught.

But Father Terry had warned them against going out with girls. "Burning the candle at both ends," he called it. And that quotation from canon law: *The ecclesiastical student should not descend to the common plane of the layman.*

Shoot.

After lunch, Danny trudged back to the pizza place he had phoned Jessica from in October. He pushed his cold hands deep into his pockets as the wind whipped snow down the neck of his coat. The gray day matched his mood. This time he didn't care what the pizza guys thought. Dialing halfway around on the second-to-last number, Danny's numb finger slipped from the hole. He slammed the phone onto its hook and waited for his dime to jingle down to the return. He could still change his mind: He could tell Jessica yes.

The scent of pasta and sausage tempted him. One slice would give him time to think, to come up with a way to say yes without disobeying the rule.

No. Danny pulled his dime from the cup and dialed.

"Hello, Fernettan's." Jessica's voice.

Danny's legs turned to rubber. He looked for a place to sit but the cord wouldn't stretch to the nearest booth, so he propped himself against the wall. "Jessie?" *Of course* it was Jessie; it wasn't her mom.

"Danny, is that you?"

"Uh-huh."

Silence. Say *something.* "Jessie, I can't."

She sucked in a breath as though he had poked her in the side. "Danny, it's my prom."

"I'm a seminarian, Jess." A sting started deep in his throat. He should tell her he didn't mean it, that he was playing a stupid joke, that yes, he would take her to her prom. They'd dance till the band quit and maybe they'd hug and kiss good night and they'd remember being together at her prom forever like she said.

But the rule said no, so Danny kept quiet and Jessica did too, and *this* had to be a sin, refusing to take her to her prom after she told him how important it was. Telling her no was mean, and that made it a sin, a bigger sin than those so-called sins of the flesh like impure thoughts or making out or even masturbating, that solitary sin the seminary retreat masters and spiritual directors kept railing against.

This sin was against charity, the greatest virtue, St. Paul said. A sin against the greatest virtue had to be the greatest sin, didn't it? But the Church seldom spoke of sins like this that caused people pain.

"Danny."

He braced himself.

"Listen to me. You have to get out of that place. The seminary's killing your feelings. And it's trying to kill our friendship. We're not doing anything wrong. We're just being friends."

She paused. He should say something, but he didn't know what and his throat hurt worse. "I thought you'd see through it by now," she said. "Pat hasn't yet, but I figured you were ahead of him. Don't you see the stupidity in what they're saying? Jeez, you guys, they're brainwashing you! My prom's at a Catholic high school. Proms aren't a sin. Even Pat says so."

Danny tried to clear his throat. "But he says I shouldn't go."

"Of course he does. He follows the rules, all of 'em, even the ones he thinks are dumb. You really gotta get out of there. I wasn't going to say anything till next year 'cause I know you guys want to graduate together. But you have to get out right now." She paused. "I know why you won't take me to the prom: Those priests tell you guys that boys and girls going out together always fall into sin."

"No they don't. But it could endanger my vocation."

Jessica took a deep breath. "Please get out of there before they mess up your mind even worse. Do you hear me?"

"Uh-huh."

She didn't say anything for several seconds. "But you won't, will you? You'll stay and stay and stay until it's too damned late. Jeez, you guys. I gotta go."

"I want to be a priest," Danny said, but he hardly heard himself. There was a click, then the dial tone. He set the phone on its hook, then shuffled toward the pizza-place door, where he pulled his coat tight around his neck for the walk back to the seminary.

He'd been good. He'd followed the rule. He hadn't descended to the common plane of the layman. So, damn it, why did he feel so shitty?

On Christmas eve, at midnight Mass in Sacred Heart Church, Danny and the other altar boys led Father Straud into a sanctuary radiant with candles, Christmas lights and poinsettia. Danny asked God to rid him of a sinful pride at the congregation's eyes feasting on him, the parish seminarian home on leave from his priestly training. Several people had stopped him downtown to beg for his prayers. A few pressed money into his hand. He tried to give it back, promising to pray for them anyway.

Kathy Sherman appeared at the altar rail to receive communion, and Danny eased the gold patin under her chin a moment before Father Straud placed the white wafer on her tongue. Had she quit going steady? Had she confessed it? Did she remember the swimming party, how he carried her through the water that warm August night, his hands slipping ever so briefly across her smooth skin?

You should have kissed her, you fool!

Danny forced his attention back to Sacred Heart and to Mrs. Montpelier's double chin, which left no room for the paten.

When the Mass was over, everyone faced the resplendent altar, and the four-part choir burst into "Joy to the World." The music echoed through the old church, and the contradictions and doubts about his faith no longer mattered. Chills ran down his back at the beauty of this sacred night, celebrated by millions of Christians for so many centuries.

On January 6, the feast of the Epiphany, the seminarians returned to Resurrection for their annual retreat: three days of silence, meditation, and inspirational talks from the retreat master, this year a short, heavy, balding guy with a black goatee.

"In the words of Jesus, I do not come to bring peace," he shouted at their first meeting. His name was Father Dolos, and God had placed within his throat a voice that thundered off the hard plaster walls so Danny swore he heard every word two or three times.

"At retreat we look into ourselves. We discover where we fall short in God's eyes, then pull ourselves back to him if we have fallen from his favor. *Woe* to us who have fallen and refuse to return to God's grace. I must tell you this most unpleasant story about a young man similar to yourselves, a seminarian who was loved and admired by all the parishioners back home."

Father Dolos pushed himself away from the lectern. He looked them in the eye as he talked, starting in front, moving back and forth from the first pew to the second, from the second to the third, and on toward the back of the chapel.

"This fine young man whom everyone loved, however, had a terrible secret. He had fallen into the sinful habit of masturbation, the *abuse* of his own body condemned by almighty God, for which the boy many times asked forgiveness in the confessional."

The retreat master paced behind the altar rail, raising his hands and throwing them down as he ranted. "One night while taking a shower, this boy, this priest in training, touched himself again in a most sinful way. He sullied once again, as he had so often, the *temple* of the Holy Spirit that God had entrusted to his care. Then, while in a state of mortal sin, the boy slipped and fell as he exited the stall."

Father Dolos dropped his head. "This fine young man *fell* as he departed the shower in which he had sinned. He *fell*, and he smashed his head against the sink in such a way that he died immediately. *Immediately*! Do you know what that *means*? That means he went straight to hell, *condemned* to suffer the pains of hellfire for all eternity. That's forever, my friends."

Head down, Father Dolos shuffled back to the lectern. "They had a funeral, of course, for the young man, a wonderful service at which priests from the boy's parish and from the seminary grieved at the tragic accident that cut short such a promising vocation. 'He'd have made a wonderful priest,' they all said. Of course, they had no way of knowing the utter tragedy that had befallen that seminarian: At that very moment, that young man was *burning* in hell."

The priest again raised his arms. "My friends, do not risk becoming like that young man. The flesh tempts us all, but God is kind: He will give us the grace to overcome whatever temptations come our way. We must accept that grace. Use these three days to examine *your* conscience as to how receptive you are to God's grace and, if necessary, to overcome once and for all any habit of sin you have fallen into. Because sometimes, as in the case of our young seminarian friend, we have no time for confession or even an act of perfect contrition after we sin. Then it will be that we find ourselves condemned—yes, *condemned*—to eternal hellfire."

Father Dolos turned toward the altar. "Now," he said, "let us pray for the grace to make a successful retreat. And, to prepare our bodies for our work tomorrow, let us all retire for a good night's sleep."

Danny rolled over in bed that night and checked his watch. Ten after two in the morning. He lay on his side staring at the red exit light over the door. After Father Dolos's story, he feared hell more than ever. Could he resist sinning again? How many times had he started over, only to fail once more? How many times would God put up with it?

He sat up. Wait. How did Dolos know what the boy did? How did he know God condemned him to hell? He *couldn't* know that. No one could. Dolos had made up the story to scare them.

Besides, how could a just and merciful God ignore the good things a kid did? How could he condemn him only for masturbating, something that didn't hurt anyone? If a guy was good to people, God, in his final judgment, would credit him for that.

Or would he? If Dolos was right—and the Church insisted he was—you could do all sorts of good works but God would still send you to hell if you took pleasure in even *thinking* about a naked girl, much less touching her—or yourself.

It made no sense.

But the next morning Dolos seemed to read Danny's mind. "God's law doesn't make sense, does it? Sure it does, when you remember *why* God gave us the gift of sex: to perpetuate the human race and to thereby provide members for his holy Church. The reward God grants parents for their great sacrifices in raising children is the gift of sexual pleasure. It is *so* important that they alone receive this reward that God forbids *any* sexual pleasure to those outside the sacred bonds of holy matrimony."

Okay, maybe it did make sense. Except God's sixth commandment mentioned only adultery. Who added the rest?

In his final talk, Dolos urged the seminarians to be charitable to each other, but he didn't say God would condemn them to hell if they weren't. Maybe he figured guys in a seminary weren't as tempted to be mean as they were to take pleasure in sex. And Dolos reminded them that it didn't matter if you were weak or tired or worried or in love: *Any* sin of impurity was a mortal sin. Do it, say it, even *think* it, and you're damned for all eternity. God doesn't grant parole.

So Danny said another act of contrition. He prayed for chastity and for a happy death with time to confess his sins before he died. He prayed for the grace to never again commit the sin of self abuse, that despicable, unmanly sin, as Dolos called it. Danny prayed, as the retreat master suggested, for strength to overcome the many and powerful occasions of sin that Satan would place in his way to tempt him away from the priesthood.

That night Danny lay awake again. He had no doubt that the most certain way to save his soul was to become a priest. And then he could help others save their souls too. But to do that he had to quit doing the things that might lead him astray. He had to stop thinking about Jessica and Kathy and other girls. Starting now.

Chapter 10

Three months later, after dinner on a cool April evening toward the end of their junior year, Pat pulled Danny aside at the refectory door. "This will sound strange, but would you go to Holy Ghost's prom with me next month?"

Danny started down the hall. "April Fool's was two weeks ago."

Pat caught up and reached for Danny's arm. "No, really. Would you?"

"Sorry. Jess asked me first and I told her no. You'd be my second choice, though."

"Come on, I'm serious," Pat said. "Listen. Jessie had a friend in sixth grade. Lorie. She moved to Green Bay but they kept in touch. Last week Lorie and her mother had a fight and she—Lorie's mom—dragged her to their parish priest. He suggested they get away from each other for a while, so Lorie called Jess and she got Mom to let her—Lorie—visit the first weekend in May. That's Jessie's prom."

Father McDermott walked by. Pat kept still until the priest disappeared around a corner. "Jess told Mom Lorie'd like to go to the prom and, since she doesn't know any guys here, suggested it would be nice if I took her."

"*You?*" Danny laughed. "Your mom told her no, right?"

"She said *yes*. When I called home last night, Jess answered and the first thing she said was, 'Lorie's coming.' 'So what,' I said. She started laughing. Then Mom got on the phone and told me it would be an act of Christian charity if I escorted Lorie to Jessie's prom."

"Your *mom?*"

"I told her I couldn't do that, but she insisted it's not a real date, just a favor for my sister and her friend. I told her I have no idea what to do at a prom, but Mom said she'd help with the details—like getting the corsage and stuff."

They headed toward the track around the football field.

"Isn't she worried about your vocation?" Danny asked.

"I guess not, probably because Lorie's kind of homely. Back in sixth grade I told Jessie that and she tattled. Mom said I was cruel. She—Mom—remembers stuff like that. She told me taking Lorie to Jessie's prom would atone for what I said plus God would reward me for my charity."

"Charity, taking a girl to a prom?"

"I told her God never intended charity to be that difficult, and she said I'm still cruel and need to do penance."

"So you're going."

"That's why I need you to come. If I take Lorie and you take Jess, we can do my mom's act of Christian charity together. Jessie suggested it."

"But I *want* to take Jess. It wouldn't be charity for me! Hey, maybe you could take Jess and *I'll* take Lorie."

Pat laughed. "Oh, Jess would be thrilled. Besides, Mom says taking her isn't really a date for you either, because you're like a member of the family."

"But you told me *not* to take her."

"Everything's changed. I don't want to go alone, okay?"

Two nights later, Danny had a dream. He and Jessica were marching with the prom court toward the Holy Ghost dance in a Quonset airplane hangar draped with orange-and-black crepe paper. Outside, on the runway, kids formed two lines to cheer the king and queen's grand entrance. But the cheers turned to hoots when Danny and Jessica walked by. He was wearing a black cassock and biretta borrowed from Father Pite.

"Hey, priest! You here to say Mass?"

"Stick around! You can hear our confessions after we make out all night."

"Aw, he ain't a priest yet, just a priestling."

Jessica tugged at his arm. "I told you a dozen times: sport coat and slacks, sport coat and slacks. Nobody in history has gone to a prom in a priest's black dress and funny-looking hat."

The music started. The band leader, dressed as an altar boy in cassock and surplice, swung a smoking censer toward the crowd. He directed everyone to form a circle. They shoved Danny to the center where a tall boy in a white tuxedo whipped the biretta off Danny's head and flung it toward the crowd. Danny jumped to catch it, but missed, and a game of keepaway developed as Jessica's classmates tossed the biretta around the circle and Danny tried to grab it. The band played faster and faster, and the game became a dance with kids jumping up and down and throwing the biretta in time to the music.

"The priest can dance!" someone yelled. "Dance, priest, dance!"

Jessica stepped into the circle, spinning wildly so her black dress lifted, exposing her thighs to the crowd clapping in time to the music. She danced closer to Danny, slinking around him as though she were going to rub against him, but every time she got close she stopped, pointed to the cassock and screamed, "Eek, is that a *dress*?" Then she laughed and danced away.

Where was Pat? Pat got him into this; the least he could do is help him out of it. The circle closed in, and Jessica's classmates were grabbing Danny and pushing him back and forth between them. They started to tear at his cassock and he realized he had nothing on underneath. He tried to run but tripped on the hem and fell. He rolled over and looked up at the laughing faces. There, bending over him with the others, was Pat. Pat, dressed in white slacks and a red sport coat with a white carnation pinned to his lapel. Pat, his friend, laughing the hardest of them all.

The laughter woke him, and Danny sat up. Sweat soaked his pajamas.

Upstairs in Pat's room on prom night, Danny buttoned the front of his black slacks and reached for his gray sport coat. "Jeez, I'm shaking."

"*You're* shaking?" Pat pulled on his black suit coat. "You're with a girl who likes you. I'm with one I don't even know. And did you see her? She's *beautiful*."

Danny grinned. "There goes your act of Christian charity."

Mrs. Fernettan called them downstairs. "I realize they don't teach you this at the seminary, so I bought corsages for you to pin on the girls."

"*Us*?!?"

"Of course, you. I'll stand right beside you to make sure you don't poke them."

Pat's hands trembled as he pressed the corsage to the top of Lorie's forest-green dress.

"Lift the cloth away slightly," Mrs. Fernettan said. "Keep the pin between your thumb and forefinger … There, now poke it through her dress … yes. Now push the pin a half-inch or so and poke it back through her dress to the outside again … Like that … Great! That's all there is to it. Danny, your turn!"

The yellow satin top of Jessica's dress accented the pastels of green, blue, pink and yellow in her skirt. Her light-brown, shoulder-length hair fell in gentle curls to her shoulders. She looked too pretty to touch, but Danny stepped closer. Behind Jessica, Lorie was examining her corsage and Pat's face was dripping sweat. Danny took the pin from Mrs. Fernettan. Its point pricked his thumb.

"Ow!"

Jessica giggled. "Testing it?"

He licked his thumb. "Didn't hurt, just surprised me." He moved closer and inserted the pin into Jessica's shiny yellow bodice.

"Ouch!" She jumped back.

Danny dropped the corsage. "Oh God! I'm sorry."

Jessica pulled her top away and looked inside. "Jeez, am I bleeding?"

Danny blushed at the pain he caused and at Jessica's show of skin.

Her mother stepped between them. "Jessica Marie, stop it. He didn't touch you. Another trick like that will get you a real poke, from *me* if not from him."

"Sorry, I got nervous," she said, and flashed the smile Danny had come to see.

At Holy Ghost High School, Danny and Jessica, Pat and Lorie joined the line at the gymnasium door. Jessica was right: Some guys wore tuxedos but many, including Pat and him, wore dark suits or sport coats.

But the girls, with their hair fixed up, looked stunning in dresses of all colors. And the gym was a world Danny had never seen: Soft lighting accented streams of crepe paper forming a low ceiling over the polished floor. Around it, tables and chairs were filling with smiling couples, their faces reflecting light from flickering candles set in tall red glasses.

"Jeez," Danny whispered to Pat, "those look like a bunch of sanctuary lamps."

Jessica grinned. "Like how we decorated it?"

"Mm-hmm," Danny said. "Pretty." It was more than pretty, but he couldn't find the word he wanted. It was so beautiful—the decorated gym, Jessica and Lorie and the other girls dressed up—that he was glad he'd come. He looked toward the dance floor and imagined shuffling around it with Jessica in his arms.

Was this really going to happen?

Three hours later, Jessica and Danny swayed slowly to "Yellow Bird." It was the night's last dance. He wanted the song to go on forever so they'd never have to break apart. Each dance, she had moved tighter against him. It had to be a sin, but he didn't care. He loved it, loved Jessica, and perhaps loving her made it less a sin or no sin at all. Or maybe a worse sin. But he'd never done anything like this and he didn't want to stop.

The song ended and the gym lights came up. Behind the blue-and-white crepe paper, cotton nets hung from orange hoops bolted to white backboards. The magic was gone.

Pat came up to them, his eyes dull, his mouth down. "Ready to go?"

"I guess," Jessica said. "Where's Lorie?"

Pat shrugged. "I haven't seen her since the first dance."

Jessica raised an eyebrow. "What? Well, *I* see her." She bolted across the floor.

Pat leaned toward Danny. "Lorie doesn't like me."

"How do you know?"

"During the first dance, I kept stepping on her feet and bumping into her. Afterward, she said she'd be right back, but I never saw her again. Until now."

They caught up to Jessica. Lorie was telling her, "You can come, too. The guys don't care. Lots of kids are going to hit all the parties."

"We're not going to a party," Jessica said. "I told you that."

"But Tony and Bob and Bill and … and one other guy all invited us." Lorie reached toward Jessica with a slip of paper. "I have the addresses."

Jessica shoved Lorie's hand aside. "I promised my parents we'd be home a half hour after the dance. We gotta get going."

"Go ahead," Lorie said. "I'm going to the parties."

Jessica stepped toward her. "We came together and we're leaving together."

"Like hell. I'll do what I want. And that doesn't include hanging around with you duds all night. I'll bet you don't even have beer in your trunk."

Danny, Pat and Jessica stared at her.

Lorie stuck out her face toward Jessica. "You don't, do you? Hey, prom's for getting plastered and staying out all night, and that's what I'm going to do. So you guys go on home to beddy-bye. I'll see you in the morning." She turned away.

"Hey!" Jessica caught Lorie's dress at the shoulder.

"Hey, yourself! Let go!"

Kids gathered around.

Pat stepped toward the girls. "Let's go outside and talk about what we're going to do."

"You go outside," Lorie said. "I've got a ride with some guys."

"No, you don't," Jessica said. "You're with Pat."

"Pat? Who dances like I'm a broom that he holds three feet away and still steps all over my feet?"

"You bitch!" Jessica yelled. She grabbed a handful of Lorie's hair.

Lorie screeched and kids yelled "Fight!" Pat held Jessica around the waist and pulled her back, but her hand was entwined in Lorie's hair and Lorie staggered forward, bent over and screaming at Jessica to let go.

Pat was yelling too. "Let go, Jess, let go," he said over and over.

Finally, she did.

Lorie backed away sobbing and rubbing her head. She started again toward Jessica. "You nut case!"

Two boys hurried over and grabbed her.

Jessica strained to break free of Pat. "And you're a slut, you ... you *whore*!"

A tall teacher with a graying crew cut broke through the circle of kids. "Fernettan, shut up!" He turned to Lorie. "Who are you?"

"I'm from Green Bay."

"Your *name*," the teacher said.

"Lorie Brown."

"Are you here with someone?"

Lorie pointed at Pat, who still held Jessica.

"And who are you?"

"Patrick Fernettan. Jessie's brother."

"And you brought *her*?" the teacher asked, pointing at Lorie.

Pat nodded.

"It was a mistake!" Jessica yelled.

The teacher looked at Danny. "And you?"

Oh, God, don't let him find out I'm a seminarian. "Daniel Bates, from Willow Run."

"Where? Never mind. Are *you* here with someone?"

"Jessie." Danny pointed at her.

The teacher rolled his eyes. "*You* brought these people here, Fernettan?"

Jessica wiggled free of Pat's grasp. "Yes, and I'm sorry, Mr. Williams. About *her*, anyway. She can go to hell for all I care."

"Same to you," Lorie said. She brought a hand up with its middle finger raised, but one of the boys yanked her arm down.

Mr. Williams looked around. "Do you have a ride, Miss Brown?"

"Yeah, with these guys." Lorie glanced left, then right, toward the boys at her side.

They nodded.

He turned to Pat. "Is that all right with you?"

Jessica bolted forward. "No! She's supposed to—"

Danny grabbed her arm.

"It's fine," Pat said.

"No it's not!" Jessica yelled. "She's gotta—"

"Come on, Jess, let's go." Pat put a hand on her shoulder and pulled her around. He turned to Mr. Williams. "Thank you for your help, sir. C'mon, Danny."

No one said anything during their ten-minute ride. Pat turned into the Fernettans' driveway, stopped the car, and disappeared inside the front door.

Danny reached for his door handle, but Jessica caught his arm. "I'm sorry. Lorie was such a bitch to him."

"He'll be okay," Danny said.

She tightened her grip. "Did you see his face? He's … he's …, I don't know the word."

"Depressed. He didn't expect this."

"I've never seen him this down. And it's my fault."

"Lorie's, not yours. You stood up for him."

"I had to. I set him up with her."

"You tried to be nice when she needed help."

Jessica looked away. "Not really."

"Pat told me how you invited her here after she and her mom had a fight."

"I made that up."

Danny looked at her. "Made *what* up?"

"The whole thing. I had to, or my parents wouldn't have let her come, not with you here."

"But I said I *wasn't* coming."

"I never told 'em. I kept hoping you'd change your mind."

"But I didn't … I wouldn't have … if Pat hadn't—"

"I know. That's why I dreamed up the fight, priest and all, 'cause my parents would never go against a priest's advice."

Danny frowned. "But why—"

"I figured if Pat took Lorie, he'd want you along, and then you'd take me. I told Mom Pat should take Lorie 'cause she didn't know any guys." Jessica tried to laugh. "It didn't take her long, though, did it? Every guy in the class invited her to a party."

Danny didn't know what to say. Jessica had tricked them—her mom and dad, Pat, and him—just so he'd take her to the prom. After he told her no.

She had her hand on his arm. "Do you hate me?"

He took her hand. "No. But that was dumb." He looked toward the house. "We should go in. Pat'll be wondering—"

"But you don't love me."

"I don't love *anybody*. Not a girl, I mean. I'm a seminarian."

"Stop saying that."

"Stop ignoring it."

Her eyes were wet. He thought she was going to cry. "Look, I do like you. I probably shouldn't even say that because I still want to be a priest. Pretty weird, huh."

"No," she said. "Pretty awful."

Danny reached for the door. "I'd better go talk to Pat."

Jessica pressed closer. "In a minute, okay? It was a nice prom, wasn't it? Up to the last part anyway."

He put his arm around her. "Yeah, it was nice." He'd shock her if he admitted the best part was dancing close during the slow songs.

She put a hand to his chin. "No matter what happened at the end, and even if you do become a priest, I'll always remember tonight." She kissed him lightly, for a second, then pulled back.

"I will too," he said. He wrapped his arms around her the way he had on the dance floor and kissed her back, softly at first, then hard and long in a way he'd only imagined, the way the Church called "prolonged and passionate," the way that was always a mortal sin. Maybe God wouldn't mind too much if he kissed her just once on this special night.

He lost track of how long they held that one kiss, but he was shaking when they stopped.

"We'd better go in," he said. But Jessica had no trouble pulling him back to her.

"Man, I am such a fool," Pat said twenty minutes later when Danny stepped into the bedroom. Pat's eyes were red.

"No you're not," Danny said. "Jessie's right. Lorie's a bitch."

Pat stared at the floor. "I shouldn't have gone. What a joke, me at a prom, trying to dance. I don't blame her for running away."

They went downstairs. Jessica was opening a cream soda in the kitchen.

"What did you tell your parents?" Danny asked.

"The truth. That Lorie took off to some parties and said she'd get here in the morning."

Pat opened the refrigerator. "I hope Mom doesn't think it's my fault."

"She asked if you made a pass and scared the poor girl off."

"*What?*"

Jessica kept a straight face. "Mom knows you're not as angelic as you act."

"You told her I didn't, right?"

"I said it was too dark to tell."

Pat threw a pot holder. Jessica ducked.

"Dad called Lorie's parents," she said. "They're driving down to take her home when she gets in."

Pat pulled a Coke from the refrigerator, then put it back. "I'm going for a walk."

"Me too," Danny said.

Jessica took another swig. "I'll stay and listen to records and let you guys handle tonight's *post morten.*"

"*Post mort*em!" Pat yelled. "*Em*, not en! How many times have I told you not to speak Latin when you don't know it. Jeez. You try to show off and you just sound stupid!"

Jessica grinned, and Danny got it. Her absurd comments had drained the tightness from Pat's face.

"Yeah, let's walk," Danny said. "It's time for the *post morten.*"

Pat shook his head, but a thin smile lifted the corners of his mouth.

They walked two blocks in silence, then Pat said, "I can't explain this, but I felt embarrassed about being good tonight."

Danny nodded. "Me too. When Lorie called us duds, I wanted to yell, 'Oh, yeah? We have a whole *trunkful* of booze and we're going to drink it all ourselves and get soused!'"

Pat laughed. "I wanted to say that too. *Something* to show those Holy Ghost brats that us guys from the seminary could be even worse than they are."

"We should have," Danny said. "Even if we lied, we should have."

They walked another block, and Pat picked up a fallen branch and tested his weight against it. "Good walking stick.... Know what? Those feelings don't make sense."

"What do you mean?"

"Think about it. If we're good and they're bad, shouldn't *we* feel proud and *they* feel ashamed?"

Danny shrugged. "I get sick of having to set a good example. Sometimes, like tonight, *descending to the common plane of the layman* looks like fun. Jeez, other kids must wonder what the heck's wrong with us."

Pat tapped the huge trunk of an oak with his branch. "And now *we're* wondering what's wrong with us."

"I'm still not as different from my friends in Willow Run as the seminary wants me to be," Danny said. "Sometimes I feel like a phony, trying to pretend I'm better."

"Do you ever think of quitting?"

"Sometimes I think I'll never make it to the priesthood. Then I figure I may as well drop out. But not this year. I want to graduate together."

"There are times," Pat said, "when I feel I'm not worthy to be a priest. I get these thoughts … like tonight—jeez, don't tell Jessie—I actually thought about making out with Lorie, even going to those parties and drinking beer. To be like the other kids, you know? Just for tonight." He tossed his stick onto the terrace near the curb.

Danny picked it up. "We all get tempted, but at least you don't give in like I do sometimes. I need to go to confession. Jess and I danced … kinda close."

Damn, why'd he say that? Pat was her brother. He didn't dare mention the kissing in the car. Thank God that was all they did.

Pat's voice was soft. "When I watched, I got jealous."

"That I was dancing with your sister?"

"That you were dancing at all."

"But dancing like that's a mortal sin!"

"They say *everything* is a sin. You and Jessie looked like a natural couple when you danced. You looked … nice."

"But we shouldn't have. I'm—"

"You've liked each other for a long time."

"What about the rule? 'Seminarians may not keep company with, nor correspond with girls or attend mixed parties, dances, etc. Failure to obey this important rule may result in expulsion from the seminary.' I could get *expelled*."

Pat swung himself around a small tree and headed back toward the house. "We both could, but we won't. Train proved that. Ha! I never even read that rule. I figured I'd never go out. Then tonight I … well, this sounds stupid, but I really liked Lorie at first."

Danny woke soon after six that morning to shouts and slamming doors. One voice was Lorie's. The front door banged shut and the voices got muffled. Three doors slammed, then a car raced away. Mr. and Mrs. Fernettan whispered in the hall, the door to their bedroom closed, and the house was quiet.

In the next bed, Pat stirred.

"You awake?" Danny whispered.

"Uh-huh."

"I think Lorie's gone."

"Yeah."

Danny turned toward Pat. "Maybe I'll say a prayer for her."

Pat lay on his back, staring at the ceiling. "I already did."

The next afternoon, on the bus to Madison, Danny stretched against his seat. He was tired, but didn't want to sleep. He tried to remember the prom, everything about it. He had more physical contact that night with Jessica Fernettan than he'd had with all the girls in his whole life. And he'd liked it.

But he liked the idea of becoming a priest, too. It seemed a part of who he was. He'd heard people in Willow Run: *There goes Danny Bates, home from the seminary. He's going to be a priest.*

Maybe. But even if he decided to quit, he couldn't this year. Not if he wanted to graduate with Pat and Train and the rest of the guys. So he still had time to figure out what God wanted him to do.

The sign for the Lake Mills exit zipped by. Danny turned from the window and closed his eyes. He was back in Holy Ghost's gym staring at Jessica Fernettan across the red candle at the center of their table. The band started a familiar song, and he guided her to the dance floor where they clutched each other as tight as they could.

And "Yellow Bird" played on and on and on.

Chapter 11

▼

On the third day of classes in the fall of 1960, Danny tore open an envelope from Jessica. She'd sent a postcard of Milwaukee viewed from high above the city.

"Remember when we met three years ago?" she wrote. "We were freshmen, now we're seniors already. Can you meet me in Bay View Park Saturday afternoon? Weather's supposed to be great and we only saw each other twice last summer. I'll be there by 1. Love, Jessica."

At lunch on Saturday, Danny left half of his sandwich on the plate and passed his Jell-O across the table to Train. Then he ran from the refectory. At Shoreline Road he spotted Jessica in a sleeveless white blouse and blue shorts sitting on a bench along the path to the lake. Together they stumbled down the bluff to the beach. No one else was in sight, and they stood and grinned at each other for several seconds. Then Danny started across the sand.

"Hey!" Jessica balanced herself on one leg. "Take off your shoes. It's the best way to walk across the sand."

"Pat said you stepped on some glass and had to get a tetanus shot and couldn't walk for three days."

"*Two* days. Last spring. I'm more careful now. Hey, race you to that piece of driftwood."

She flew along the beach close to the water, her feet barely touching the sand before kicking back into the air. A wave washed across her path and she splashed through it, not slowing. When she stopped next to the driftwood, Danny was still watching.

She laughed. "What are you waiting for? C'mon!"

He stepped into the dry sand and wiggled his toes so the grains edged up between them. Then he ran to her, forgetting the seminary, its walls and its rules, forgetting everything but this warm sunny afternoon when he and Jessica could breathe fresh air and listen to the waves while running barefoot across the sand.

"Isn't this great?" she said. "I'll bet the only way to feel freer is to take *everything* off!" He blushed, and she laughed. "Like the Greeks. They ran nude in the Olympics. You're taking Greek this year. I'll bet you already know where *gymnasium* comes from. It means *exercise naked*, right? Can you imagine, running along the beach like this totally free, feeling the wind all over your body?"

He was still blushing, but he dropped several steps behind her to imagine, as she suggested, a naked Jessica sprinting across the sand.

Later, they sat in the grass next to their shoes and leaned back against the bluff. To their right was Southport and its harbor, to their left only parkland and a sandy beach.

"When I look that way," Jessica said, "there's nothing around—no buildings, no people—just sand and water and us. And clouds. Do you ever see things in the clouds?"

"Airplanes. The airport's a couple miles away."

She poked him. "Not airplanes. Clouds. Don't their shapes ever remind you of something?"

He turned toward the city. "Like that big one up there? That one looks like … like an airplane."

She rolled on top of him and wrapped her fingers around his neck "Not airplanes! Animals, plants, people, even *nothing*. But not airplanes!"

They laughed together, then she bent slowly and kissed him. He wanted another of the long kisses they shared in the car after her prom, and his arms drew her down. She stretched out on top of him and they kissed again and he squeezed her as tight as he dared. This was better than prom, lying together in the cool grass under the sky. Alone.

And that was odd. He'd never seen this park empty on a Saturday afternoon. God seemed to want them alone together. To tempt him? It was working. Pressed against her, kissing longer and harder than they had before, Danny dismissed the idea that God didn't want them doing this because God had obviously set it up, and—

"Wait, somebody's up there! Get off! Get off!" He pushed Jessica onto the grass and sat up. "Somebody's coming! Maybe some of the guys! It might be Pat!"

"Danny, for Pete's sake, there's no one around."

"Yes, there is. I heard somebody." He pointed toward the top of the bluff. "Up there."

She laughed. "Gulls flying over."

"No." He climbed the bluff on all fours and peeked over the top. Two people in their early twenties sat talking on a bench next to the trail. He skidded back down the bluff. "Told you. There are people up there."

She lay back staring at the sky. "Pat? With a committee of your classmates?"

"No, a guy and a girl sitting on a bench."

Jessica propped herself on one elbow. "Wow. A guy and a girl. On a bench. In a park. On a pretty fall day. Imagine."

He blushed. "C'mon, Jess—"

"C'mon, Jess," she mimicked. "You've watched kids neck here. What makes you think seeing us would bother *them*?"

"I don't care about them, but I can't let the guys see me—us—like that!"

She tickled his cheek with a long blade of grass. "It won't matter if you come to Madison with me next year. We could do this all the time."

He lay still. "Your school doesn't say kissing like this is a sin?"

"Sure they do, but I don't believe it. Kissing's nice. Why would it be a sin?"

"Because God created sex for married people, for—"

"We weren't having sex, we were necking. The sixth commandment forbids adultery, but the pope has tossed in everything else that people like."

He pulled her down to him. "Let's not argue."

"All right. But someday we have to talk."

A few months later, on a Saturday in January shortly after retreat, Danny hiked into Southport to confess to a priest who didn't know him.

"You committed self abuse three times in one day?" the priest said in a thunderous whisper. "You can't be sorry."

It had finally happened: He had sinned so many times the Church decided he couldn't be forgiven. Now he wouldn't get to decide whether or not to stay at the seminary. They'd kick him out. He tried once more. "I am sorry, Father. Really."

"But you keep committing the same sin. How can you say you're sorry?" The priest paused, and Danny wondered if he should go.

"Well," the priest finally said, "you haven't convinced me, but I'll give you conditional absolution. If you *are* sorry God will forgive you. Now go and this time sin no more. *Prove* you're sorry."

Danny returned to Resurrection and sinned no more—for three days. "O God," he prayed that night, "I *am* sorry. You know I'm sorry. Please don't let the priests think I'm not. I want to stay at Resurrection. I want to be one of your priests."

He confessed the next morning.
Father Pite spoke slowly. "I don't question your sincerity, Daniel, but I must be honest. Your inability to conquer these temptations may be a sign that God hasn't called you to the priesthood. You've tried. No one can fault you for that. But I believe it's time for you to consider a different calling in which you can faithfully serve God on this earth. Certainly you can't enter the major seminary with a sinful habit like yours."

Danny wiped his eyes before the tears rolled down his cheeks. "Maybe I'll do better at the major."

"That's not likely. It's much more rigorous than the minor."

"I have to go, Father. I'm feeling sick." He ran to the bathroom and knelt next to the toilet. The nausea drifted away, but he had failed. The Church no longer wanted him. Pite would write to Father Straud, telling him that Daniel Bates was no longer welcome at Resurrection.

No, that wouldn't happen. Pite was bound to secrecy by the seal of the confessional. He could advise a guy to leave, but he couldn't make him go, nor stop him from coming back. And, damn it, he would be back. He would overcome his habit of sin, be a model seminarian and work hard to become a great priest. He'd prove Pite wrong.

On the first day of February, Danny stood next to Eddie Schmertz in the Willow Run High School cafeteria.

"Wanna go to English, or come with me to phy ed?" Eddie asked. They waited behind three girls to stack their lunch trays at the window in the school's cafeteria.

For four years, at football and basketball games, Eddie had urged Danny to visit Willow Run High. "Come see where you would have wound up if you hadn't run off to the seminary."

"I will," Danny had said every time. He wanted to see what high school was like for his old friends. And, he admitted, to see what he had given up. Then, at a basketball game over Christmas break, Eddie reminded him it that it was now or never: They were in their last year of high school.

"So which one?" Eddie said. "I'm gonna be late."

"At the seminary, we have English, but not phy ed," Danny said. "I'll come with you."

"Great! We got dancing today."

Danny laughed. "In school? That's weird."

The fourth-period phy-ed class gathered near the gym's north wall along a set of bleachers. Danny presented his visitor's pass to Mrs. Kinner, who wore her gray hair in a tight bun. She nodded, turned and instructed the students to pair up. Danny climbed into the bleachers to watch, but Kathy Sherman came over and asked him to be her partner.

Eddie had told him Kathy was still going steady with Brett Cooper. Danny looked around, but Coop wasn't in class. He stepped from the bleachers and followed Kathy onto the floor.

Mrs. Kinner introduced the waltz. When the music came over the tinny sound system, Danny placed his hand on the back of Kathy's blue dress. As they moved he became so aware of his contact with her breasts and thighs that he couldn't follow Mrs. Kinner's count. Within a minute he stepped on Kathy's feet, kicked her on the shin—lightly, he hoped, though she said *ouch*—then stepped on his own left foot.

"Sorry," he said. "I don't dance too well."

"Not today anyway. How'd you do last year at that girl's prom?"

Danny's face got hot. He knew he was blushing, and Kathy could see it.

Kathy laughed. "Hey, you can't keep secrets in a small town. Especially when another seminarian has a cousin here and—"

"Who?"

"I'm not telling."

"If I find out, I'll—"

Mrs. Kinner was shouting. "Miss Sherman and partner, would you care to stop now that the music has ended?" Then, to Eddie Schmertz, "Your visitor seems very enthused about this class." Eddie and the other kids laughed.

Danny blushed more. He should have gone to English.

Mrs. Kinner demonstrated another dance—the foxtrot—and started the next record. The other kids paired up.

Kathy put out her arms. "Try again?"

"Okay, but let's pay attention this time."

She moved in, smiling. "You're not supposed to go out with people of our gender, are you?"

"No."

"Some kids say you're going to quit the seminary."

"I only went to one prom."

"When I saw you here today, I thought maybe you had already left."

"No, just visiting."

"To see what you missed?"

"Or to see if I really missed it."

"Did you?"

"The seminary's different. We live in big dorms, though we have day students, too. They live at home."

"Do *they* go out?"

"I don't know."

"I'll bet they do.... So you're really going to become a priest?"

"Uh-huh."

"That girl's going to be upset. She has a name ... a nickname ... Popcorn Girl! The one you took to prom, right? Will she be at your graduation?"

"Of course. Her brother's my classmate."

"Are you going to hers?"

"I don't know."

The music stopped. Kathy held Danny's hand a second longer than she had to before they walked off the gym floor. "This class was fun today. Know what? I bet you *will* go to that girl's graduation. And when she gets her diploma you'll get all teary and afterward you'll kiss her congratulations."

He blushed again.

Kathy grinned. "Hey, there's nothing wrong with kissing someone you like, even if you do become a priest."

The bell rang. Eddie yelled "Chemistry?" from near the door, and Danny nodded and ran to catch up. They didn't offer chemistry at the seminary either.

Kathy waved, then headed for the exit with Polly Edmonds.

Eddie held open a hallway door for Danny. "Boy, Coop's gonna be pissed. You danced with Sherman the whole period!"

"*Everybody* danced with someone the whole period."

"Not the same person. The rest of us switched partners after each dance. Man, wait till Coop hears. Maybe you oughta head back to the seminary right now."

"All we did was talk. Where's chemistry?"

Eddie grinned. "Wouldn't you rather go to home ec and watch Sherman cook something?"

"No, I'd rather go to chemistry and watch you blow up something."

Eddie swung his chemistry book toward Danny's head. "You're lying. Isn't that a sin too?"

Chapter 12

▼

After class on a sunny day in mid-May, the seminarians picked up their 1961 yearbooks at the seminary bookstore, then gathered near the gym to exchange autographs.

Joe Trainor wrote a farewell.

"You're leaving?" Danny said.

"It's not for me. Graduation's a good time to go. How 'bout you?"

"Coming back. We're gonna miss you."

"I'll miss you, too," Train said. "Worst part is, I gotta tell my dad. He's always wanted me to be a priest. I feel like I'm letting him down."

"You gotta do what you think is best. Maybe your dad'll surprise you. Hope so, anyway."

That evening Danny and Pat autographed each other's yearbooks.

"Pat, we've become best friends and you were an indispensable help to me these past four years. I hope we can assist at each other's First Solemn Mass in 1969. Eight years to go! Had fun playing basketball with you these four years, especially taking the championship this year! Good luck and God bless you always." How should he sign it? "Danny" seemed too kiddish for a high-school graduate. Okay, he'd do it this way: "Dan Bates."

They handed each other their books and drifted off by themselves.

"Dear Dan," Pat had written. *Dan*, not *Danny*. How had he known? "You have made senior year (and the others) a lot more pleasant, and God has blessed us with a friendship that helped me make it through these four years. We've survived some strange times together: Latin, Greek, Jessie, even a prom! We've made it one-third of the way, and with God's help we will make it another eight to become priests together, though unfortunately in different dioceses. But your friendship will be as important to me then as it is now. May God continue to bless you. Actually, God bless us both! Pat Fernettan."

Dan scanned his classmates' autographs. For Pat and him and the others coming back, not much would change. They'd be *called* college men, but they'd still live in the same old building under the same old rules. For Train and the others who were leaving, much would change: jobs, colleges, new places to live, new friends.

It sounded exciting. Maybe he should try it. But leaving, even for a year, would bring more temptations. Then, even if he returned to Resurrection, he wouldn't be ordained the same year as Pat and his other classmates.

In the early evening of Wednesday, the last day in May, the Resurrection Minor Seminary High School Class of 1961 stood outside the old gym, slipping into maroon gowns and helping each other straighten their caps. An orange sun peeked through the trees in the campus woods as smiling parents, relatives, and friends milled around.

Dan kept an eye on Jessica. She looked sweet in a white dress with a pattern of burgundy flowers and green leaves. This was where he'd spotted her on his first day at the seminary. Now they were leaving high school. In the fall, she'd move to Madison to study nursing at the University of Wisconsin, but he'd still be here. Something—Jealousy? Embarrassment?—ate at his gut. Jessica was leaving him behind.

But this is what he had to do to become a priest, and he had made that choice. Dan concentrated on the smiles of his parents and classmates and began to feel the joy of this night.

During the ceremony the ushers kept the gymnasium doors propped open, but the warm air inside didn't stir. Father Ry McDermott encouraged the graduates to follow their dreams and to attend to details. Father Salvatore Terry said they were the best class he'd seen pass through Resurrection's hallowed halls. The archbishop handed them maroon folders with their diplomas inside. Four years. One third of the way. Dan glanced at Pat, and together they grinned.

The graduates led their guests from the gym to the chapel, where an acolyte swinging a censer sweetened the air with incense while the archbishop presided at a solemn benediction service. Finally, after Father Terry locked the Eucharist in the tabernacle, everyone picked up songbooks and began Dan's favorite hymn,

To Christ the King. The chapel rang with their voices: "Holy God, we praise thy name; Lord of all, we bow before thee."

The sound pulsed off the hard plaster walls. Dan would remember this forever, singing this triumphant song with his family and friends. He turned toward his parents and smiled as they shared his night. This had to be a preview of the great day of ordination, perhaps even of the final, glorious resurrection.

The voices grew louder for the hymn's refrain: "Fill the heavens with sweet accord; Holy, holy, holy Lord." On the last note Dan glanced back. Jessica, her light-brown hair falling to her shoulders, stood with her parents five rows behind him.

But she wasn't singing. She was gripping the pew in front of her with both hands, and she was standing there. Just standing there, staring at him.

Chapter 13

▼

Dan lugged his battered brown suitcase across the seminary parking lot toward the north-wing entrance. His first day of college.

"Hey, Bates!" Train was standing at the south-wing door. "You get to use this one now!"

Dan changed direction. "Old habit." From the open window of the basement rec room a few feet away, Pat Boone's *Moody River* drifted across the back lawn.

"So," Train said, "you said you'd be back, and here you are!"

Dan grinned. "And you said you wouldn't be, but here *you* are."

"No, no, no. I start next week at Southport State. Just dropped by to give you guys a pep talk. And to climb the college stairway once in my life. Pat's already up there, by the way. Jessie too. You know, a lotta guys bet you'd be with her in Madison."

"Well, they lost." He rubbed his right forearm. "Packed too much again. How'd it go with your dad?"

"Tough. I put it off a few days, then blurted it out: 'Dad, I'm quitting the seminary.' All he said was, 'Well, you tried it.' It was like he expected it or something. But I hated disappointing him." He picked up Dan's suitcase. "Jeez!" He set it down. "Why didn't you pack two, for Pete's sake, divide the load? I'll probably never find out why he was so set on my being a priest. Maybe he couldn't, so he thought I should. Anyway, I'm out of here, Dad accepts it and everything's fine, except I'll miss you guys."

"You're not far away," Dan said. "Come watch us play basketball and see how bad we are without you in—"

The wooden door banged open and Jessica stepped outside. Her red sweatshirt had a white Bucky Badger guarding her left breast. "So you did come back. Shit.... And now I suppose you'll scold me for saying that here."

"It's better not to say it anywhere."

"Pat said all summer you'd be back, but I still hoped. Damn."

Dan tried to smile but his face froze. Twice Pat had phoned to say Jessica kept yelling that they were out of their gourds for locking themselves behind seminary walls. He couldn't think of anything to say to her, so he turned to Train. "Guess I'd better go up."

Train picked up the suitcase again but Jessica stepped between Dan and the door. "Damn it, have you looked at your school catalog?" She didn't wait for his answer. "I read Pat's. They've got you guys taking Latin five days a week. *Latin*, a dead-duck language, every damned day!"

He slid past her and pulled open the door. "Priests have to know Latin."

Train banged the suitcase against the door frame as he stepped through. "Shit!"

"He said it too," Jessica said. "Aren't you going to bawl *him* out?"

Dan grinned. "I didn't bawl you out."

She didn't smile back. "Listen, you can still get into the U. I know you can."

Train was halfway up the stairs. Dan held the door. "When do you start classes?"

"Next week." Jessica stepped into the doorway. "You're ignoring everything I say, aren't you?" She moved toward the stairs. "Will you come to Madison and visit me?"

Dan touched her arm. "The first day I get back there."

"Stay away from her," Pat told him two weeks later while they packed for their weekend home. "Let her make new friends. That's the only way she'll stop pestering you to quit. Her attitude's gotten so bad I feel like she's a threat to *my* vocation. I refuse to talk to her about this place anymore." He turned away, then added, "As bad as she is for my vocation, she's a worse threat to yours. Don't go see her."

Dan snapped the latch on his suitcase. "I'll be careful."

Elizabeth Waters Hall sprawled along Observatory Drive on a wooded hillside overlooking Lake Mendota, the largest of Madison's four lakes. Dan drove slowly past the white-stone dormitory up the hill until he found a place to park across from an old observatory with a silver dome. Below him, along the lake's shoreline, red-orange maples speckled the still-green woods beneath a blue sky.

Inside Jessica's dorm, Dan stood motionless next to a phone booth as laughing girls hurried through the room. His eyes followed a red-haired girl in shorts until she disappeared behind a door marked "Residents Only."

He felt a tug at his sleeve.

"Here I am," Jessica said. "Didn't you see me come in?"

He shook his head.

She glanced toward the door. "Who were you looking at?"

Dan blushed. "I've never been in a girl's dorm before."

"Well, don't make it so obvious. Wait here, I'll drop my books in my room and give you a tour of the campus." She swept through the door.

He kept his eyes on the floor, the walls, the ceiling, on anything except the girls parading past him. *Custody of the eyes.*

Minutes later Jessica bounced across the room, her ponytail swinging side to side. "We'll save Observatory Hill for after dark. You *can* stay after dark, can't you?"

He nodded. After four years under the seminary rule, staying out late seemed beyond freedom. Here there were no bells calling a halt to his free time, no mandatory lights out, no nighttime silence. Maybe heaven was like this.

They walked past the Carillon Tower to the front of Bascom Hall. From the hilltop, they could see the full length of State Street to the white-granite dome of the state capitol a mile away.

Jessica moved to the side of a statue of a sitting Abraham Lincoln. "There's an old legend that Abe stands whenever a virgin walks by."

Dan blushed again. *Damn!* Pat never blushed. Maybe that was because he lived all his life with Jessica.

They crossed Park Street and entered the Memorial Union. She led him to the Rathskeller, a low, dim room painted orange and brown with German proverbs set in ornate letters across the walls. Students sat at thick wooden tables, eating and drinking, reading and talking and laughing.

"If you came to the U, we could study here," she said.

This was so different from the seminary. And she was right. He could be here.

At the ice-cream counter he ordered triple-scoop sugar cones—chocolate swirl for Jessica and peach for him. Made right here on campus, she said. They stopped talking but still couldn't lick fast enough to prevent the ice cream from dripping down the cones across their fingers. He hurried back to the counter for napkins.

"Too late," she said. With her left index finger she wiped a splotch of white liquid from her right breast. Dan pretended to watch two guys arguing about Christopher Columbus.

"He didn't discover a damned thing," one said. "There were people already here."

"Just Indians."

"You're a fuckin' bigot, Dixon."

Dan blushed at the public obscenity, but Jessica didn't react.

"Lucky it was all vanilla," she said. "The chocolate would stain."

They dodged cars to cross Langdon Street, then circled the fountain on the library mall. She scooped a handful of water toward the back of his neck.

He ducked too late. "That's cold!"

Her laugh carried across the lawns and sidewalks of the mall. Heads turned, and Dan wasn't surprised. He kept hearing that laugh during his morning meditations at school, the free laugh of a girl so different from him, the somber seminarian who followed foolish rules toward a priesthood still eight years away.

"You'd love it here," she said. "You'd take a while getting used to all this freedom, but you'd like it. And so would Pat."

At Pat's name, Dan heard his friend's voice as though he were walking with them.

As bad as she is for my vocation, she's an even worse threat to yours.

Dan and Jessica strolled beneath giant oaks along Langdon Street, looking at the fraternity and sorority houses.

"Care for pizza?" she asked. "Paisans is best. C'mon."

They passed the Old Red Gym with its silhouette of a turreted castle, then again crossed the library mall. At the fountain, he stooped toward the water, but she grabbed his hand and yanked him away.

"Don't even think about it."

They ran across the four lanes of University Avenue before the stoplight turned green, then ducked into a single-story building with a yellow stucco front. A dozen students stood in a crooked line, talking and laughing.

"Wait here." She disappeared into the crowd, then returned a minute later. "It's under your name."

"What is?"

"Our reservation. They'll call your name and I can pretend you live here."

The line edged forward. Finally a thin, balding man with wire-rimmed glasses picked up menus and said, "Bates party of two, this way, please." He led them down a dimly lit aisle, past a waitress balancing a huge tray of pizzas, to the last in a line of wooden booths. They squeezed in on opposite sides of the table.

"Romantic, isn't it?" Jessica said. "Dark and private with high walls between the booths. It's almost like having the place to ourselves."

"Mm-hmm." He could stare at her here without anyone seeing him.

She put down her menu. "Sausage and mushrooms?"

"Sure."

"You don't have to agree. Pick whatever you want. They'll make it half and half."

He scanned the choices. "Okay, pepperoni."

"Yeah, I'll have that, too," she said.

Dan closed his menu. "You don't have to agree. Pick whatever you want. They'll make it half and half."

She kicked him.

The waiter took their order and disappeared toward the kitchen. Jessica reached across the table and stroked the back of Dan's hand. He pulled it away.

She beat her fist on the table. "*C'mon*! This is Madison, not Southport or Willow Run. Nobody cares what we do here."

He knew that in his head, but in his gut he was sitting in the seminary chapel with Terry insisting they not lower themselves to the common plane of the layman.

After dinner, Jessica led Dan toward the lake shore path west of the Memorial Union, but they paused on the terrace to watch a dozen sailboats gliding across a red-orange sunset.

"I'm so glad you came," she said. "I do love it here, but I needed a break. Some of my classes are tough. Like algebra. I don't understand it, but I gotta pass it."

"Maybe I should leave so you can study."

"I'll study after you imprison yourself again. And you have ten seconds."

"Before I have to leave?"

"No. *Jeez*. To take my hand, or I'm gonna grab yours and this time I won't let you pull away." He reached for her and she intertwined her fingers with his. "Is this so bad?"

Her cool palm pressed his and he ached to feel as much of her smooth skin as he could, but he fought the idea. They walked the path in silence as the sky darkened and waves lapped at the rocks between them and the water. A cool breeze stirred the lake and the swells became more insistent, splashing up at them through the tangled roots of willow trees leaning out over the water.

She stopped and laid her head on his chest. "It's getting colder."

"Maybe we should go inside."

She pulled closer. "There are nicer ways to get warm."

He hadn't held her since last summer at the beach, and before that at her prom. Now it was dark and they were alone. He wanted to squeeze her, but he held back. He couldn't explain why even to himself.

"You know," she said, "if you came here to school we could do this every night." She looked up. "But you won't, will you?"

"No."

"I hate your being a seminarian."

"But if I hadn't gone to Resurrection we'd have never met."

"Maybe here."

He laughed. "With thirty-thousand students? Besides, it wouldn't have been till now. We'd have missed knowing each other in high school."

She tugged at his hand. "C'mon, it's time I show you Observatory Hill."

"I saw it. That's where I'm parked."

"That was in daylight. It's a lot prettier at night. There's even an old song about it, called *It's Dark on Observatory Hill*. Going up there is a tradition, and I know the seminary loves traditions!"

"Yes," Dan said, "but I'm not sure I should—"

"Well, *I'm* sure, Danny Bates." Jessica pulled him toward a path leading up the hill. "C'mon!"

This time, he didn't resist.

The next afternoon in Willow Run, Dan joined Father Straud's confession line during Sacred Heart's regular Saturday hours.

He tried to disguise his voice. "I kissed and hugged a girl for over an hour, Father."

Stroud's voice turned cold. "Did you touch this girl in a sinful manner?"

"No, Father."

"Was this kissing prolonged and passionate?"

"Yes, Father."

"You must stop playing with fire. Besides defiling the temples of the Holy Ghost that God has entrusted to you and this girl, you are endangering your immortal souls. Do you wish to be responsible for this girl's failure to reach heaven?"

A rhetorical question? Dan waited.

"Well, *do* you?"

"No, Father."

"Then you must stop this dangerous course immediately. Your, um, natural instincts will lead you further and further away from Almighty God toward even more despicable sins. Keep in mind, however, that God's grace will enable you to overcome these, um, baser instincts, and in that way you may help both yourself and this girl toward the true happiness of purity."

Straud then gave him absolution.

Dan was back at Resurrection when the postcard arrived. Jessica had slipped it inside a white envelope with "Jess Fernettan" above the return address. The card showed the west wing of Liz Waters Hall from Observatory Hill, with Picnic Point and Lake Mendota in the background.

"Remember here? It was so much fun showing you the campus, especially this spot that night! Please come again—soon. (Please come again—PERMANENTLY!) Passed my algebra test—barely. I'd probably do better at Latin. (YOU could tutor me!) Love, Jessica."

In study hall that night, Dan wrote in his diary:

> Good thing Jess's letters break the boredom once in a while. Otherwise this journal gets so repetitious that I might as well stop writing it. I leave big gaps already—it's been two weeks since I wrote last time. But it seems I'm always having to make the same old decision: stay here or quit. Maybe I wouldn't think about it so much if Jess didn't keep bugging me about it. But she knows I can leave anytime before I get ordained so till then nothing's settled, and she keeps trying. And it gets tempting. I think I'd love the UW. Especially with her there. But some days—no, most days—I really want to be a priest. Especially during the liturgy or other times I feel so close to God during a quiet prayer time. But other times ... Well, I don't know sometimes. Funny. I used to hide this notebook and worry about somebody finding it. Ha! They'd probably throw it away out of sheer boredom.

"Hey, Pat!" Dan was following several seminarians up the stairs after dinner. "I found a neat book about a Scottish priest at McCutchan's Book Store!"

Pat let him catch up. "What was a Scottish priest doing at McCutchan's?"

"Very funny. It's called *Keys of the Kingdom*, and it starts with a snotty monsignor named Sleeth—great name, huh?—who wants to send this Father Chisholm to an old folks' home and put Chisholm's adopted son in an orphanage."

"The priest had a son?"

"Yeah, adopted in China. Why is part of the story when he—the priest, I mean—was younger. What's neat is how he thinks for himself and acts on his own conscience and his love of people, even when the Church orders him to do something different."

Pat held the hall door. "How can it be a good book if he disobeys the Church?"

"I can't explain it. But it's the first time I've felt any hope of being free as a priest ... I mean, being able to follow my own conscience against some of the stupid things the Church says."

"It sounds dangerous."

"I'll let you borrow it. I think you'll like it too."

On Christmas Eve in Willow Run, at Sacred Heart's midnight Mass, Dan served as master of ceremonies, assisting the three priests wearing the parish's finest white vestments with red and gold trim. He moved easily through his duties, turning Father Straud's missal to a certain page and deflecting the back of his chasuble over the sedelia at the *Gloria in Excelsis Deo*.

Too bad Jessica wasn't there. If she saw him wrapped up in the liturgy like this, doing what he hoped to do in his life, she might stop trying to get him to quit.

Kathy Sherman came to communion. Eddie Schmertz had told him Kathy married Brett Cooper and they moved away from Willow Run. He glanced at her as she turned to enter her pew. She smiled, and he hoped Eddie was wrong.

Pete Parensky met Dan outside the dormitory door when Dan arrived after the holiday break. "Bates, what's the matter with Pat?"

Dan tried to see past Pete into the dorm. "I don't know. Is he sick?"

"He was moping around. Took him half an hour to unpack that little suitcase of his. And he hasn't said a word all night, except he was going for a walk. He's still not back."

Dan waited in the hallway outside the chapel before the start of their three-day retreat. Pat finally came around the corner, and he looked worse than he had on prom night.

Dan hurried down the hall. "You okay?"

"I'm fine."

"You don't look fine."

"It's nothing you can do anything about."

"Tell me anyway."

"You won't like it. Are you sure you want to know?"

Dan wasn't, but he nodded.

Pat's eyes glistened. "My dear sister and your friend Jessica announced yesterday that she's left the Church. She says there is no God. She's an atheist."

Chapter 14

▼

The hallway spun. The nearest place to sit was a pew inside the chapel ten yards away, so Dan braced himself against the wall.

Jess, an atheist? Impossible. Pat had misunderstood. She teased a lot, cruelly sometimes, and this time she'd gone too far. "Pat, it's a joke. She's always looking for ways to get you."

"That's what I thought. But she says kids at the U who don't believe in God make more sense than we do." Pat reached for Dan's arm. "Can a guy with an atheist sister still become a priest?"

"Of course." Dan's question was tougher: Could a priest, or a seminarian, have an atheist friend? Then he remembered his favorite book. "In *Keys of the Kingdom*, Father Chisholm's best friend was an atheist. We hate the sin, not the sinner, remember?"

Father Terry's voice interrupted: "Are you gentlemen planning to join us this evening?"

They edged toward the chapel door. "Talk to the retreat master," Dan said. "I'll bet he's seen this before."

But Pat's questions haunted Dan during the retreat. In the novel, Father Chisholm's atheist friend was another guy, not a girl. Jessica was Pat's sister, so Pat could ask a priest for help, but Dan was only a friend.

Um, Father, I still want to be a priest, but could you tell me how I can stay friends with a Catholic girl who's become an atheist?

No, there was no one he could ask.

Before he started Mass on the last Sunday in February, Father Terry stood at the communion rail and cleared his throat to get their attention. "We've been told to announce in all seminaries today that the Holy Father has reconfirmed Latin as the official language of the Church. He says, and I quote, 'Latin remains for us a source of doctrinal clarity and certainty. It is above all an instrument of mutual understanding,' unquote.

"The holy father insists that we admit no one to philosophical or theological studies who does not know Latin perfectly. So. We will therefore begin re-emphasizing our curriculum in Latin to prepare you for the major seminary."

A low murmur echoed through the chapel, and Dan lowered his head.

A dead-duck language, Jessica had called it. Jessica. The atheist. Well, she was right about this. Language was supposed to be a tool for communication, so why not teach and learn in a language one understood? There was no way they'd become proficient enough in Latin to pick up the nuances of philosophy and theology. The seminary would either have to ignore the pope's order or kick out his entire class.

In March, Dan tore open a letter from Jessica. It was on a light-blue sheet of paper.

> Dear Danny,
>
> Pat told me you guys are sad because I lost my faith. I didn't lose it, I gave it up because it doesn't make sense. And now things are so much more clear. I don't have to look for ways to defend my religion against its contradictions and lack of logic.
>
> I used to believe in a god, so I understand how you and Pat (and other relatives and friends) wish I would again. Faith does provide a lot of comfort during times of trouble and, despite what I just said, it is difficult giving that up. After all, I've counted on it, like you guys, all my life. But now I realize the basis for that comfort doesn't exist, and I no longer feel it.
>
> I'm sorry you and Pat (and Mom and Dad and the others) are so upset about this, because I'm happier than ever. I'm free to consider all ideas, and I can accept or reject them based on how much sense they make instead of how they fit Church doctrine. No, I don't have all the answers, but I believe everyone can find bits and pieces of them in our search for truth. It's so arrogant for some people to insist that we all believe the same way they do about things no one can see or prove. Here at the U I'm dis-

covering all sorts of wonderful teachers and other students I can learn from. And that's another reason why I wish you'd come here.

Please think about it.

Love, Jessica.

He read the letter four times, studying the familiar slant to the letters and the huge upper loop of the *J*. Jessica had written it, all right. She had rejected God.

The next afternoon Dan and Pat hiked through the seminary woods, where the few remaining patches of snow were disappearing on a fifty-degree day.

Pat had gotten a similar letter. "I told her I'm praying she gets over her anger at God or the Church or whatever she's mad about and comes to her senses. Our parents are really upset. I told her to consider them, if not us."

Dan stepped over a tree root half hidden by snow at the side of the trail. "Do you really think we should consider other people's feelings when we decide what's true?"

"Of course," Pat said. "Especially those of our parents. They raised us and paid our tuition to Catholic schools. It's not fair to say, in effect, 'You're nuts.'"

"Jessie didn't say that. Not to me, anyway. I think she believes she's right."

"She can't be right. She doesn't believe in God! And damn it, if I can't convince my own sister there's a God who loves us, how can I convince anyone else? I mean, jeez, she's a fallen-away Catholic. She's going straight to hell." Pat turned away.

Dan pulled a straight, five-foot branch from under wet leaves, broke some twigs off the sides, and jabbed it against the ground to test its strength. "God won't send Jessie to hell. She's like my friend Mrs. Reuter. Neither of 'em believes in God but they're kind to people. That's what really matters, isn't it?"

"But how can she turn her back on us and all the things we believe in?"

"If she really believes there's no God, what else can she do?"

Pat leaned against a huge oak at the edge of the path. "How can she not believe? She went to a Catholic high school!"

"I go here, but there are days I feel like it's all a big, complicated fairy tale."

"God's a fairy tale?"

"No. I mean I can see how he might not seem real to some people, so they stop believing in him. I don't think that means he's going to send 'em to hell."

Pat brushed pieces of bark from his shoulders and headed back toward the dorm. "You keep defending her, but with the way our parents raised us Jess has no reason to deny there's a God. And I'm going to tell her that."

Apparently he did. A week later Dan got another letter, this one in the wild script of someone trying to yell from Madison to Southport.

> Don't psychoanalyze me to figure out why I quit. Yes, I'm angry about things in your Church. Its cruel treatment of women for one. I could handle that if there was some basis for believing what it said, but there isn't, so I left. If you came here you could read ideas the Church doesn't want you to see, by people you'll never hear of there, all sorts of 'freethinkers' who've lived moral lives *without* believing in a god.
>
> Like Zona Gale. She graduated from here in 1895 and was a pacifist during World War I. When she was 5, her mother told her some kids think Santa Claus brings presents down the chimney. Zona said, 'You can't make me believe any such stuff as that.' At *five*! I wish I'd have been like that. And there's Elizabeth Cady Stanton and Susan B. Anthony and Susan H. Wixom. But not only women. You probably won't find anything by Robert Green Ingersoll in your library, but *you should* so you can consider different ideas.
>
> Pat begged me not to fall into a life of sin. Jeez, you guys. Will you *please* think things through before going off half cocked? There's a lot more to morality than your stupid list of commandments and those add-ons the Church demands that people follow. I have no intention of treating people cruelly, unfairly, or even unkindly. (Because I'm not like the Church!) But I *will* live my life without having to worry about going to hell for it.
>
> Jessica.

Dan put the letter down. What did she mean, *live without having to worry about going to hell?* Did she think she could do anything she wanted because nothing was a sin anymore?

That night Dan pushed aside his half-eaten chicken dinner and gave Meer Mohrical his apple pie.

Before study hall on Good Friday evening, Dan sat alone in the last pew of the seminary chapel. In commemoration of Christ's death, the tabernacle was empty and the sanctuary lamp extinguished. The chapel seemed dead, as dead as he was … spiritually.

He had sinned terribly.

How could anyone, especially a candidate for the priesthood, give in to lust on the day of Christ's death? How could he confess to a priest that he had sinned that way *today*?

It was over. He would leave the seminary. Perhaps enter a monastery. Become a monk. He'd have to add poverty to the vows of celibacy and obedience, but that didn't seem so bad. Life on earth was short; eternity was forever.

Dan sat back in the pew. He had to find a priest. *Damn*. Committing a mortal sin on Good Friday proved beyond hope that he'd never be worthy of becoming a priest. He wiped his eyes. He felt so sorry, for himself, for his parents, for the people whose souls he would have saved.

And he had only himself to blame.

Dan didn't tell Pat—didn't tell anyone—until the night they returned from their weekend home in early May.

Pat stared. His face reminded Dan of the night Pat announced Jessica had left the Church. "But I was sure you were going to the major with us."

"I was too. But I decided I don't a vocation." It was a lie. Or, if he no longer had one, it was because he'd lost it. But there was no way to admit why he was leaving. Anything Pat and the guys imagined would be less embarrassing than the truth.

"Pat told me the great news!" Jessica wrote a week later. "Of course he's upset, but I'm glad! Danny, you have no idea of the world that's waiting for you out here. Ideas! Freedom! Different kinds of people! It's so great! You guys don't even *know* what's out here. Come to the U, Danny. You'll be free to be what you want to be, free to do what you want to do."

No. He wouldn't. He still wanted to be a priest, to do God's work with people. Leaving wasn't his decision. He had failed.

This time he didn't write back.

On the last Friday of May 1962, Dan completed his final exam, climbed the stairs to the dorm, said his goodbyes, then carried his suitcase outside and tossed it into his parents' new Pontiac. He took a last look around the campus, at the woods where he'd walked with Pat, at the gym where they'd won so many basketball games, at Kleissman Hall where he'd lived for five years.

Dan's eyes stung. He glanced at the dome, then turned away. It reminded him of his failure. He nodded toward his parents, somber and silent inside the car. His dad started the engine.

Daniel John Bates II, ex-seminarian, ducked into the back seat for his last ride out of Resurrection Seminary.

Chapter 15

Dan dreaded facing the people at home, though most of them didn't know he had left Resurrection because he'd have come home for the summer anyway. But, by September, when he should have returned to Southport, everyone would know.

He even avoided Mrs. Reuter, who always made him feel good when he stopped by to tell her how he was doing. But one cloudy day in his third week at home she caught him riding his bike past her house.

"Daniel! Stop!"

He did.

She stood at the curb, frowning. "I knew you were home, but you haven't come by to tell me how things have gone for you. Is everything all right?"

He couldn't think of a lie he was willing to tell her, so he told the truth. "I've left the seminary. I won't be going back." Even as he said it, it didn't sound right.

Mrs. Reuter studied his face. "You appear sad, Daniel."

She did too—in her eyes—and it surprised him, though he hadn't expected her to shout with joy the way Jessica must have.

"That must have been very difficult, to do that after all these years," she said. She glanced up and down the street. "Do not worry what people think, Daniel. Oh, you probably will—we all do—but try not to. It's not their business." She smiled and touched his arm. "Just do now what is right for you." She stepped back. "So, what does comes next? A job? A different school?"

"I applied to the university at Madison."

"Ah, you'll not be so far away then. You can visit more. I always look forward to your stories, and now you can tell me your new ones!"

Dan nodded. "I'll come to see you. And yes, I'll tell you my new stories."

All through June, Pat begged Dan to come to Milwaukee. "Next week, for a day or two. We'll shoot baskets, explore the lakefront, maybe find a guy with a boat who'll give us a ride."

"I can't right now."

"You said we'd get together."

"We will." Dan didn't know what else to say. He could have gone the next week, but he didn't want to battle the Fernettan twins. Pat would urge him to return to Resurrection, and Jessica would lobby even harder for the university. She had already sent three letters promising Dan joy and happiness at Madison. As much as he wanted to see them, he wasn't ready for the hassle.

Besides, he still lay awake nights wondering if quitting was the right thing to do.

He wrote to Jessica once, without telling her he'd delivered his UW application to the registrar's office. Nor did he mention that he'd made an appointment with a priest at the major seminary.

Pat called again in mid-July. His dad had tickets to a Braves game.

Dan closed his catalog of Resurrection Major Seminary. "Yeah, I can come," he said. But he didn't say he'd ride the bus to Southport first. He'd keep his appointment at the seminary, then catch the North Shore train to Milwaukee and meet the Fernettans for the game that night.

The bus pulled into the Southport depot early enough for Dan to walk the mile and a half north to Bay View Park, where he spotted Kleissmann Hall's gray-and-black dome above the trees. His palms began to sweat. How much could he tell this Father Quince? Jake Arbuten had said most of the guys at the major went to Quince for confession when they'd done something embarrassing.

"He never judges," Jake said. "He says that's God's job."

Dan walked the familiar driveway from the park toward Kleissman. It was hard to believe he didn't belong here anymore. He stopped and looked around. No, he still belonged. They *all* belonged here, and always would, through their memories of praying and studying and living together.

Inside the old building, his sweaty hands stuck to the bannister as he climbed the central staircase to the third floor. At room 320 his soft knock echoed down the dark, empty hallway.

The door squeaked open. "Mr. Bates? I'm Henry Quince. Come in."

Father Quince was taller than Pat. He wore black jeans and a white T-shirt over a small pot belly. His black goatee was neatly trimmed but held more than a hint of gray below both ends of his thin lips.

There was hardly room to stand. Newspapers, magazines, books and loose papers covered the floor, the desk, the coffee table and all the chairs but one. That held a pizza box.

"Here," Quince said, "I'll clear a place." He tossed the pizza box toward the back wall where a hi-fi played classical piano, then he and Dan sat across the small room from each other.

Quince lit a pipe and Dan nodded at the hi-fi. "I remember 'em playing that record in the seminary library. It's pretty."

"Franz Liszt," the priest said after a few puffs. "Great pianist. Had lots of mistresses, too. I always envied the guy."

Dan's face grew hot. Damn, he was blushing again. Having a mistress was a mortal sin!

But maybe Quince meant Lizst's piano playing.

"Where'd you say you were from?" Quince's pipe smoke smelled sweet, different from a cigarette's bitter stink.

"Willow Run."

"Ah, yes, Sacred Heart. Popeye Straud's place."

Popeye? "You know Father Straud?"

"You probably never heard him called that, but it fit. Worst free-throw shooter this seminary ever saw. Stood at the line with his eyes bugging out at the basket. Guess he finally escaped his nickname hiding in the wilds of the Madison diocese." Quince took another puff. "Well, you said you have a decision to make."

Dan pulled a deep breath. "I left the seminary."

"Oh! You've already made it."

"But I'm not sure it's the right one."

"Mmm. That's tougher." Quince leaned back in his worn recliner and stared at the ceiling. The chair creaked as he pulled himself forward. "Tell me, why did you come to Resurrection in the first place?"

"To become a priest."

"Yes, but *why?*"

"Lots of reasons, I guess."

"Tell me some."

"To save souls, to help people get closer to God." Dan paused. "Guess those are kinda the same."

"Okay."

"To save my own soul, too. That sounds selfish, but it's probably my main reason. To do the best thing I could do with my life. To—"

"What about respect, getting looked up to by your relatives, friends and neighbors?"

"Well, yeah, that too."

"And a job with a steady income—low pay, but no layoffs—and the security of having a place to put your head after a long day?"

"I guess, but those sound so ... so—"

"Worldly." Quince smiled.

"Yeah, worldly." So why was he grinning? Those were terrible reasons to become a priest. Dan waited for Quince to congratulate him on his decision to quit.

"Those are *human* reasons. They're part of us. We're human."

"But," Dan said, "aren't we supposed to do everything for the glory of God?"

"Of course. But do we? God knows I don't. The better you understand ... no, the better you *accept* that we never become superhuman, the stronger you'll be as a priest. That is, if you decide to become one. Tell me more reasons, religious and human. Worldly, if you prefer."

More? It had been years since Dan listed them. "I can talk to people. I'd be a good counselor, give good sermons."

"Good."

"This isn't such a good one, but I'd like to coach my parish school's basketball and baseball teams."

"Somebody has to. Better someone who wants to."

Outside Quince's window, the maples lining the seminary drive led Dan's eyes toward Bay View Park and Lake Michigan. A white yacht sped south just inside the breakwater. His mind flashed to the last time he, Pat and Jessica explored the beach, but he shook his head and came back to Quince.

"Some priests say Mass too fast. I wouldn't." Dan paused. "Sorry, that's kinda disrespectful. They're good priests, it's just—"

"It's a fact. Facts don't disrespect anyone. Go on."

"I'd be kind in confession to people scared of getting bawled out for their sins."

Quince nodded.

"Visiting the sick, telling them God loves them, comforting people who've had someone die. Living—this one might sound a little strange—living close to the church so I could visit the Blessed Sacrament during the day. I like the ... the peacefulness, I guess. At the minor, that kept me going lots of times when I was upset about something."

"Good." Quince tapped his pipe in the ashtray. "Any others?"

Dan shook his head. "Being a priest's all I ever wanted to do, at least since second grade."

"Okay." Quince pulled himself from the recliner. He stepped to the window, put his hands on his hips, bent forward, then back. "Oooh. Whatever you do, exercise every day. And eat right. I didn't, and now I've got this pot and my back gets stiff." He bent forward again, briefly, then smiled. "Okay, now the other side: Why did you quit?"

"It's kind of embarrassing."

"A girl? You aren't the first."

"No. Well, yeah, there's one I like but it's not 'cause of her.... Father Pite told me to."

"Pite? Why?"

"That's what's embarrassing."

"So be embarrassed. It won't kill you."

Dan stared at the lake. Did his face look as red as it felt?

Quince waited.

"Father Pite said I couldn't come to the major because I haven't overcome my habit of … of self abuse."

"*Masturbation?*" Quince thundered.

Dan winced. Anyone in the hall would have heard.

"Hell," the priest said, "who has?"

"*What?*"

Quince laughed. "Lots of guys never stop, especially if they started as kids."

"But I've never heard—"

"Of course you haven't. And you won't. Who's going to admit it outside the confessional?" Quince relit his pipe. "So Pite said you had to quit because of *that?*"

"Yes, Father."

"*Idiot,*" Quince shouted. Dan jumped, and Quince laughed. "Not you. *Pite.*" He lowered himself onto a corner of his old desk where four large books replaced part of one leg. "Thanks be to God for the lake, and to the rector for assigning me a room where I can see it. I'd go bonkers on the other side. At moments like this I can gaze out, take in the timelessness of God's creation and forget the stupidity that surrounds us."

He set his pipe in an ashtray and shuffled to the window. "Ah, well, I should be kinder. We believe what we're taught, unless we take the time and make the effort to see if it makes sense."

"But," Dan said, "it *is* a mortal sin."

"Is it? Let's let God decide that, okay? Personally, I doubt it. Is every act—especially after it becomes a habit—a deliberate turning away from God? *That's* what mortal sin is, and I don't think masturbation qualifies."

"But—"

"Anyway, that's why you quit, huh?"

"Yes, Father." Would his cheeks ever cool down?

"Well, you asked my opinion, so I'll tell you: Pite's wrong. Someone masturbating in a seminary or a convent can still have a religious vocation. It's nonsense to think otherwise."

In a *convent*? *Girls* did that?

"Eventually, of course, you'll take the vow of celibacy. Then, some say, masturbation becomes an even greater sin. Well, I still say let God decide. It doesn't hurt anyone, and—"

"I fight it, Father, but I fail so often."

Quince turned. "Do you still want to be a priest?"

"Yes."

"Then go home, pray, and think it over. Don't let Pite decide for you. Do what *you* feel is best. If you want to be a priest, I think you should come back."

Dan arrived at Fernettans' in midafternoon. He and Pat had time before dinner and the Braves game to shoot baskets on the driveway.

Between shots, Dan said, "Thought you should know: I'm coming back to the seminary."

"That's great!" Pat said. "I've been praying so hard … that's wonderful!" He swished a free throw. "Have you told Jess?"

Dan held the ball and wiped sweat from his face. "I thought maybe you could after I leave."

Pat shook his head. "She thinks you're going to Wisconsin with her."

Bike brakes squealed along the front sidewalk. "Hey!" Jessica shouted before she jumped off. "Get your letter from Madison yet?"

"No, but my application's in."

"Great!" She flew into the house yelling she'd be right back.

Pat glared at him.

"Well, I did apply," Dan said.

"You have to tell her."

"I will, I will." Dan klunked a ten-foot shot off the front of the rim.

"Today."

"All right. As soon as she comes back." He did not want to do this.

Jessica let the screen door slam behind her. "Beat you both at HORSE."

"You two play," Pat said. "It's getting hot. I'm going inside."

"Chicken." Jessica warmed up with a half-dozen shots, said she was ready, and tossed Dan the ball. "Guys first."

"Unh-uh. Girls." He flipped it back.

Jessica dribbled. "You'll be sorry." She swished a fifteen-foot set shot.

Dan airballed his. *Get hold of yourself.*

"H," she said. "One shot, and you already have H. I'll move closer, give you a chance." She swished one from ten feet.

Dan's ball hit the backboard, the side of the rim, then the driveway. *Shit!*

Jessica held the ball. "H-O. You all right?"

"Let's go out back. You win … this time." He tried to smile. He led her to a small arbor under a towering elm and dropped into one of the lawn chairs. He watched her ease into the next one. Across the lawn, inside an open window, Mrs. Fernettan was cutting something for dinner.

Dan wasn't hungry. "I'm not going to Wisconsin, Jess."

Her head snapped toward him. "They turned you down? How—"

"I changed my mind."

"Don't joke around."

"I'm going back to Resurrection." There, he said it.

Jessica stared for a second. "You're kidding. You think this is funny after all these years and—"

"I'm sorry. I know I told you—"

"It's a bad joke. Stop it."

"I made a mistake. I still want to be a priest. I belong at the seminary."

"Bull*shit*," she said.

"Watch your language," her mother said from the window.

"BullSHIT!" Jessica yelled.

Mrs. Fernettan shouted something about not talking that way in their back yard.

Jessica stood. "I'll talk any way I want to imbeciles. Danny, you stupid, lame-brained idiot! You were that close to sanity, *that* close, and now you're blowing it. Oh God, I could cry 'cause you're so goddamned sure you're doing the right thing and you're not. Damn it! You're *not*!"

She started toward the house, then turned. "I should've known you wouldn't quit. You're just like Pat. Jeez, you guys. You'll be stuck at the major and I won't see you—*either* of you—all year. You get to come home three whole times, you know that? Guess they're scared us nasty old sinners'll contaminate you precious little lilies."

She stopped at the door. "Know what? I'm sure as hell going to try. Nothing else has worked."

The summer dragged, but September 1962 finally arrived. In the afternoon shadow of the seminary dome, Dan pulled a tan suitcase from the Pontiac's trunk. A new suitcase for a new era in his life: Resurrection Major Seminary.

The ordination class of 1969 was entering the major a year early because the minor had gotten too crowded with boys who wanted to become priests. Here, in their second year of college—sixth class, some called it—they'd wear cassocks and Roman collars and follow the same rules and schedules as the philosophy and theology students.

Dan had packed all the clothes he needed except for a zimarra: a black, medieval topcoat with a cape over the shoulders. He had to buy that here. The joke was, no place else would stock the ugly things.

He visited the chapel, and admired again the stained-glass windows. For six decades guys like him had come here to gather strength on their paths to the priesthood.

"Well, Lord, I came back. Thank you for bringing me this far. There have been times when I've been unworthy to be here, and I'm sorry for that. There are times I feel very, very weak, and sometimes I wonder if you truly mean for me to be here."

He stared at the ceiling and studied how the arches met at the top. "It's been years since I first felt your call to the priesthood. Now I'm here at your major seminary. But I still miss Willow Run and my parents, you know. Sometimes I'm afraid I won't make it through the long periods between visits. At the minor we went home every month, and I don't understand why we can't here. My parents pay my tuition and board. Why can't I see them more often? The rule book claims it's your will. It feels like some sort of punishment. But for me, or for them? Or do you think my parents are a danger to my vocation?"

Stop. God'll think you're whiny.

"I shouldn't complain, Lord. I do thank you for letting me come here. And thank you for Pat, my best friend. Thank you, too, for Darrin, my new roommate. Help us get along, and help me master the knowledge I need to serve you."

He studied the flickering of the sanctuary lamp, and Jessica's face seemed to appear as it had across the red candle at her prom. "Please let me stay friends with Jessica even if I do become a priest. She's a good person, and her joy and laughter have helped me a lot when I've felt depressed. Maybe I can help her discover you again."

Dan got up to leave, but turned back toward the tabernacle. "Do you think, Lord, that the new Vatican Council might do away with the celibacy rule before I take that vow?"

Darrin Greene was Dan's new roommate. He'd transferred to Resurrection the previous year from a seminary in Illinois. Greene smiled a lot and got along with all the guys except those who couldn't stand constant smiley faces.

"Hey, Bates, that side of the room okay with you?"

"Sure. It's fine. I don't care which—"

Jessica's voice came from down the hall. "Pat, I'll be right back. Hi, Go-Go … Meer, how are you?" Then she was standing in Dan's doorway, one hand on the frame below the open transom. "Danny, can I see you a minute?"

"Sure." He nodded toward Darrin. "This is Darrin Greene, my roommate. Darrin, Jessica Fernettan, Pat's sister."

"Hi! Saw you last year, when you came to pick up Pat."

She nodded, then Dan led her to the central staircase. They sat on the top step.

"I hoped I wouldn't see you here," she said.

"I can't talk too long. We're not supposed to be out here."

She touched his hand. "When will I see you next?"

"Christmas. I'll come to Madison over the holidays."

"That's too long. I'll come see you before that. Know what I'm going to do?" She didn't wait for his answer. "The major seminarians go for a walk to the lake every morning after breakfast, did you know that? Well, some day I'm going to be sitting in the park waiting. I'll jump out from behind a tree and hug you till you get so embarrassed you'll have to leave this place to escape the teasing."

She stood. "Well, that's all, for now anyway. I hope you have a good year, I guess, but I mean good by my definition, and that's a lot different from how the priests define it. And I'll write—"

"No, *don't!*" Danny grabbed her arm. "I don't know how they handle the mail here. The rector's really conservative. Maybe he reads it, or the guys who sort it do. Let me find out how it works, then I'll write to you first."

Jessica's eyes were wide. "Listen to yourself! The rector reads your mail? What country are you living in? What *century* are you in? I'll wait one week. I have your address and I know your room: four forty-one."

That night at his desk, Dan opened his copy of the rules. The major seminary's book was a lot thicker than the minor's. He'd considered showing it to Jessica as a joke, but it would have set her off again.

"Rules create discipline," the major seminary rector, Monsignor Nicholas Troden, wrote in the preface, "and discipline develops a strong priestly character. The success of his priesthood depends much on the student's attitude toward these rules.

"It is a sin to deny the moral obligation to obey them, as rules are seldom broken except through laziness, vanity, anger, or self-indulgence, vices which are at least venial sins." At *least*? Is Troden saying they could be mortal? They never claimed that at the minor.

"A seminarian, in preparing himself for the Holy Priesthood, must understand a higher purpose for these rules. They do not bind his liberty, but help him grow in his love for God." Jessica would be screaming *Bullshit!* by now.

He scanned other rules: "A seminarian may not leave the campus without permission. The penalty is expulsion. And even if you have permission to leave, you may not go to theaters, taverns, *et cetera*, or attend athletic contests." *They'll expel you if you go to a Braves game? I didn't know County Stadium was such a den of iniquity!*

"You may not have visitors without permission. Visitors may come to the seminary on the scheduled visiting Sunday, if there is one. The rector will decide." *If there is one? And when will it be? How the hell can anyone make plans? And why only once a year? It's like I told you: They're scared us sinners will contaminate you.*

Here was the part he was looking for. "The Seminary administration may inspect all mail, incoming and outgoing. You may not mail letters or packages when you are away from the campus and, on any mail you send, you must write your name and the seminary return address." Damn. How could he get a letter to Jessica? Maybe address it to "Jess." Troden might not realize Jess was a girl. But at Liz Waters Hall? Dan hoped the street address was enough.

"You may not visit each other's rooms. Visiting means going past a room's threshold. The seminarian whose room is visited is as responsible as the one visiting. You must personally answer any knock at your door, and may never invite anyone into your room." *I can see keeping* me *out, but the guys you live with?*

"You must stay silent inside the seminary buildings. The *magnum silentium*—the Great Silence—is in effect from the bell for night prayers until after Mass the next morning." *God forbid that you guys express an idea!*

"You must also remain silent between classes and while waiting for a class to begin. The five minute period between classes is not considered a recreation period." *Give you wild animals five minutes of "recreation" and who knows what might happen.*

"In the major seminary, you must wear your cassock outside your room, except for sports and work on the seminary grounds. You must always wear black trousers and black shoes and socks under your cassock." *Do you always wear something under that black dress, even on hot days? C'mon, who'd know?*

"In cold weather, you must wear the zimarra, the official cold-weather coat for major seminarians. On milder days you may wear a black jacket. Headwear is restricted to a biretta or a black hat." *Oh, you guys'll look so handsome! Actually, Pat showed me his zimarra. Ug-LEE!*

"During your vacations, you must remain above the moral level of the layman, exhibiting interior and exterior holiness to provide an edifying example to the laity and to uphold the honor of the Church." *C'mon, Danny, provide some good example. I'm a laity. I mean, at Holy Ghost they kept telling us we should act like proper young laities. That's what they meant, isn't it?*

"When you are away from the seminary during vacations, you must dress as a student for the priesthood. You must avoid unapproved theater performances and all dances, as well as the company of any person who may be a danger to your vocation."

Meaning me?

Yeah, Jess. Meaning you.

Are you going to avoid me like the rule says?

No.

"As a seminarian, you may not drive a taxicab or work in hotels, restaurants, theaters, dance halls, or at beaches, nor on behalf of political issues or candidates." *Some political issues are moral issues, Danny. They affect people's lives. Is the seminary saying you can't take a stand for justice, like supporting the voting rights of Negroes in the South?*

"When you return to the seminary after each summer vacation, you must provide a written report of your activities. *Ah, like show and tell in grade school, Danny. Will you say you saw me?*

Yes. I'll tell them everything.

Great! They'll kick your butt out of there. Then you can come to the U!

One month later, in October 1962, the Church's cardinals and bishops met in Rome to begin the Second Vatican Council. In chapel before night prayers, Monsignor Troden urged the seminarians to pray for the council's success. He didn't define *success*, but a council implied change, and Dan wondered if that scared Troden. It was clear from the rule book that the rector felt he already knew what God expected of his seminarians.

But maybe the council would change the celibacy rule! Yeah, abolishing celibacy would be a success. But Troden would have a bird.

After dinner several days later, the entire seminary was ordered to the gym. From a television on the stage, President John Kennedy informed them that Cuba had installed Russian missiles aimed at the United States. More missiles were on the way, the president said, and our navy was going to intercept the Russian ships and not allow them into Cuba.

No one said a word. Dan had never seen the guys so quiet. Were they thinking the same thing he was? *This could start a nuclear war.* Were his parents watching? If war broke out, he might never see them again. The seminary was near industrial cities along Lake Michigan, so he was in greater danger from the missiles than his parents were in little Willow Run. He hoped that, if he died, they'd know how much he loved them.

And Jessica. Her letters, which so far had made it past the censors, told how tough her nursing courses were, and about the joys and pains of the profession she wanted. He loved her too.

No, he couldn't. He was a seminarian, and she was still an atheist. But they were friends.

Dan headed for Quince's room for confession. He found a crowd surrounding the priest.

"This country's been lucky," Quince was saying. "People think war only happens 'over there,' except for Pearl Harbor. That was a shock, and tonight's another one: An attack could occur here, and we're scared."

More seminarians arrived, and Quince edged down the hall to create more room. "Maybe now people will realize what's important: life itself, and our relationships with God and with our families and friends. Maybe we'll stop thinking so much about our things.... Well, probably not." He ducked into his room and, one by one, the young men entered and confessed their sins.

Dan waited until last. "Father, I'm worried about my parents, like the other guys, but I'm worried about Jessie too. That's kinda weird for a seminarian, huh?"

Quince lit his pipe. "Of course you're worried. You love her."

"Father, we're just friends."

"Bates, I told you. Feelings don't disappear when you retreat inside these hallowed walls."

Dan slumped. "But they shouldn't be this bad. I'm aching to go to her, and to hold her and tell her everything will be all right."

Quince spoke softly. "At times like this you always will."

Dan waited for him to laugh, to say it was a joke, but Quince was quiet.

"Always?"

Quince nodded.

Dan looked toward the door. "Then I'm really not sure I can do this."

Chapter 16

The Cuban Missile Crisis faded and, with Quince as his confessor, so did Dan's doubts. He discovered a physical and spiritual security in the routine of life at Resurrection, and putting on his cassock and Roman collar each morning reminded him of the holy priesthood he was training for.

He saw Jessica three times that year: on visiting day in October, for an afternoon during Christmas break, and for a couple of hours at Easter. She said nothing about his leaving the seminary. Pat thought she hoped the major seminary's tougher rules would convice them to quit.

In her letters, Jessica discussed her classes and how she loved Madison.

In his, Dan said he was content. "The rules aren't so bad. We have to study a lot, so it doesn't matter that we have to stay in our rooms. True, on weekends I feel cooped up, but mostly I'm happy here, and Pat says he is too."

During the summer of '63, after sixth class, Dan worked both shifts during the pea and corn packs at the Willow Run cannery, but managed a couple of visits to Mrs. Reuter.

"You look happy now," she said. "That priest place agrees with you."

Dan laughed. "I'm happier, that's true. But I wouldn't say the place agrees with me, especially about the rules. They're kinda stupid."

"Tell me one."

"I'll tell you two. Getting to come home only three times a year, and no talking at night. The *magnum silentium*"—Dan drew out the words—"is Latin for the 'great silence.' But it's not so great when you have something to say."

"What do you do then, ignore the rule?"

"That, or write notes. Keep the silence, but still communicate. Pretty dumb, huh?"

Mrs. Reuter laughed. "Pretty smart, I think. You will do all right."

September came quickly, and Dan returned to Resurrection as a first-year philosophy student. Six years down, six to go. Halfway there.

Through four years of high school and two of college, Dan had looked forward to studying philosophy, to learning logical arguments for the existence of God that would free his mind from the doubts that nagged him.

And help him convert nonbelievers—like Jessica.

In compliance with the Church's Canon Law, Resurrection Seminary's college major was philosophy, taught "according to the order, doctrine and principles of Saint Thomas Aquinas." To earn their degrees, the seminarians had to master Thomism, Aquinas's thirteenth-century teachings.

Dan had looked forward to reading the great philosophers of the past and discussing how their ideas advanced or impeded civilization, but his professors concentrated only on Thomism. Even Quince. As liberal as he seemed in confession, Quince in class followed the text. He seemed unwilling to develop further Aquinas's seven-hundred-year-old theories.

"Of all the philosophers the world has known, we get to study *one*?" Dan complained to Pat during a walk to the lake in the first week of October.

"It's early. Once we're grounded in Thomism, they'll let us see how other philosophers compare."

"I hope so," Dan said.

On November 2, in their annual All Souls Day procession, the seminarians rustled through leaves covering the trails in the woods. The soft sound and sharp scent made Wisconsin tolerable in late fall, when trees were bare, skies cloudy, and the air raw.

That afternoon in class, a stout, balding priest stood behind Quince's desk.

"I'm Father Albert Herkimer. I'll be taking over Father Quince's classes, effective today."

Dan dropped his pen. Taking over? Why? For how long? Where was Quince? Who would he go to for confession?

Herkimer picked up the text. "I understand you're in the middle of chapter five. For review, we'll start that chapter over." He offered no explanation for why he was there. Instead, he started lecturing from the textbook. Its author, a Canadian priest named Henri Grenier, outlined what he believed Aquinas thought.

Pete Parensky interrupted once to ask Herkimer to clarify a passage, but the priest glanced up and said, "We'll get to that eventually."

Perhaps he saw Pete roll his eyes because Herkimer put down the book and took off his glasses. "Please have patience. All change is difficult, especially sudden change like this. I cannot tell you why Father Quince is no longer here. I received this assignment yesterday. Have you ever taken an exam you haven't studied for? That's how I feel today. Let's give ourselves time to adjust to each other, okay?"

All right, but where the hell was Quince?

That night, Pete handed Dan his mail, a letter from home and another envelope with a card from Jessica. This one showed the UW's Memorial Library and the State Historical Society, with the fountain on the mall between them.

"Remember here? The water froze the other day, so they shut it off and put an ugly metal cap over it. Now at Christmas I won't be able to splash you. But wait till spring. (I can't!)"

Dan studied the card. He could have been a student there. Funny how Jess, despite her threats, was no longer urging him to quit. Maybe she'd given up.

No, that wasn't likely.

That night Dan woke with an erection. He reached for his rosary. Then he recited his favorite 1953 Milwaukee Braves lineup: Billy Bruton in center field, Johnny Logan at shortstop, Eddie Mathews at third base … He drifted toward sleep, and he was walking off the pitcher's mound at County Stadium, but the hard white baseball in his hand had evolved into a soft pink breast. What was that girl doing in the dugout and where did the guys go and who switched the players' bench for a king-size bed? He slipped into the fantasies and the feelings that came with them.

A few hours later Dan woke again. Damn, he had to see Quince. Then—Oh God, that's right: Quince was gone. Even if he knew where, Dan couldn't leave the campus.

During Mass, Dan's mind refused to follow the prayers in his missal. This was the *major*, but there he was, clad in cassock and Roman collar, looking like a priest but sitting back to let his classmates step past him on their way to communion. They had to wonder how long he'd continue this charade before he dragged himself back to Willow Run, where he could confess his sins as a layman, not as a seminarian halfway to a celibate priesthood.

"Lord, forgive me," he prayed when the words in his missal blurred. Of course, if he was truly sorry he'd confess as soon as he could to *any* priest, even one who might scold.

So, after breakfast, outside the refectory, Dan walked up behind behind Father Herkimer. "Excuse me, Father."

Herkimer jumped. "*What?*"

"Sorry, Father. I'm, ah, Dan Bates? In first philosophy? Your afternoon class?" *Jeez, quit sounding as if you're asking questions.* "Um, I'm wondering if you'd hear my confession."

"*Now?*" Herkimer studied his watch.

"Well, yes, I thought maybe—"

"Is this an *emergency* confession you wish to make?"

Dan's face grew hot. "Ah, yes, Father. I—"

"Very well. Come with me to the chapel. But hurry. I have a class to prepare for."

Dan shivered in the dark chapel as he confessed. Until last year he had called his sin self-abuse, but Quince had said, "Call it what it is: masturbation. It is not self *abuse*, it's self-pleasuring. If it weren't, you wouldn't do it."

"Have you had the misfortune to commit this sin before?" Herkimer asked.

"Yes, Father."

"How many times?"

How many times? "I'm not sure. Quite a few."

"What's quite a few?"

Why did he ask that? Couldn't a guy just confess what he'd done last night and go? Dan's mind worked the math: If he averaged once a day, say three hundred times a year in his six years since puberty, that would be—Oh God—eighteen hundred times. Maybe two thousand, figuring days he did it more than once. He couldn't tell Herkimer that.

"I get tempted every day, Father."

"You commit this sin every *day?*"

"Yes, Father. I mean no, Father. Not every day, a lot of days. *Some* days. I used to, I mean, but not lately, except this once." He *had* done better this year. Sweat soaked Dan's armpits, the smelly nervous sweat that telegraphed fear to mean dogs. He had confessed those old sins. God had forgiven him. Why make him dredge them up again?

"You realize, I'm sure, that you will need to remain celibate as a priest. This seems very difficult for you."

"Yes, Father."

"Depraved abuse of one's body is a mortal sin for *all* young men, but it certainly constitutes a much more grievous offense against Our Lord when it's perpetrated by someone like yourself who's been offered the seminary as a refuge in which to perfect himself for the holy priesthood. Your peers outside these holy walls are beset with many more temptations than you are. *Their* sins are mitigated to a degree by the situations in which they find themselves, the temptations they can't avoid, the way women dress these days and the movies and now television. How in heaven's name do you plan to keep yourself pure after ordination when you will become subject to the awful temptations of this shameless world?"

How could anyone answer that? "I don't know, Father."

"What are you proposing to do to overcome this habit?"

"I'll fight harder, Father. And I'll pray more, especially when I get impure thoughts."

"You've already tried that, have you not?"

"Yes, Father." *Quince, where the hell are you?* "I don't know what else to do, Father."

"You must *fight* the devil!" Herkimer's voice carried through the chapel. "*Punish* your body for its sins. Sleep on the floor. Eat *half* the food that is placed before you. Shower in cold water. When a corrupt impulse presents itself, fall to the floor and perform pushups until your arms lack the energy to do what your body desires. Are you willing to do these things?"

"Yes, Father." He'd promise anything to get out of there.

"All right, then. For your penance recite five private rosaries—the community ones don't count—in the next five days. *Absolvo te* …" Herkimer recited the absolution and Dan began his act of contrition.

"Now go in peace and sin no more," Herkimer said. "Remember, you must continually deny your body's urges. With God's help you can do this."

"Yes, Father. Thank you, Father." *At last.*

Dan's very first denial of his body's urges was to *walk* rather than run from the chapel into the gray November day, where the wind cut at the sweat on his face and turned his wet armpits cold. After the intense heat of the chapel, it felt great.

Almost every day there were rumors: The archbishop had relegated Quince to a tiny parish up north; Quince had been bounced from the priesthood and no one knew where he was; Quince had disappeared after telling Troden to go to hell; Quince had told the archbishop to go to hell but apologized and got sent to a monastery to learn humility.

One night, Dan stopped for a moment in the chapel. "Lord, I miss him. You know that. Wherever he is, please keep him safe. He's one of your good guys."

In class a week before Thanksgiving, Dan said to Herkimer, "Father, I don't understand this part. The text says all things naturally seek their own perfection. I can see that for human beings because we're able to think, but I was wondering: How do animals seek perfection when they have no concept of it? They appear to be seeking just to eat and to avoid being eaten. And rocks and trees and grains of sand just sort of *are*. They don't seem to be seeking anything."

"Excellent question, Mr. Bates." Herkimer looked over his students. "Any ideas?"

"If God created everything," Pete Parensky said, "wouldn't it already be perfect?"

"Well, God created us," Herkimer said. "We're far from perfect."

"Because of free will," Pat said.

"Yes. That's why we are still *seeking* perfection."

"But animals and objects don't have free will," Pete said. "Are they already perfect?"

"But," Dan said, "if a dog bites somebody, is he really perfect, or still seeking perfection? Without free will, I'd guess he must already be perfect by the fact that God created him the way he is: to bite."

Herkimer shook his head. "Mr. Bates, must you reduce our discussions to such absurdity? A vicious dog has nothing to do with this."

Dan threw out his hands. "But Father, if Aquinas is correct that everything—which would include that dog—naturally seeks its own perfection, the dog's act of biting becomes part of that search, doesn't it?" Behind him, someone laughed.

Herkimer frowned. "Anyone?"

"We can't apply our own definition of perfection to everything," Pat said. "The dog may indeed be perfect in God's eyes if his act of biting is an expression of true dogginess ... um, so to speak."

Dan grinned. "Dogginess?"

Herkimer ignored him. "Excellent point, Mr. Fernettan. Perhaps what Aquinas meant was that all things seek their own perfection by fully being what God intended them to be when he created them: stone, tree, dog, what have you."

He turned toward his desk. "At any rate, I believe you'll find most of your questions answered in our text. If you concentrate hard on that, I suspect you will discover that Aquinas's ideas fit together in a way that will, eventually, make sense. Please be patient, study diligently, and give it more time."

"I still don't get it," Dan told Pat after class. "I see your point about perfection, but I don't understand animals or inanimate objects *seeking* it by any definition."

"Me neither," Pat said, "but Herkimer likes class participation. It makes us sound like we know what's going on."

"Except dogginess," Dan said. "I don't think that helped."

On Saturday's walk to the lake, the seminarians squinted against the morning sky as they stood atop the bluff in Bay View Park. On the lake, ripples from a soft breeze separated the sun into millions of pieces. No one seemed willing to break the mood, and none of them spoke.

On the way back, Dan said to Pat, "I don't understand the stuff I read last night. Grenier says God's existence is self-evident, but not self-evident to us. The dictionary defines *self-evident* as requiring no proof or explanation, so what does he mean?" Dan watched a cement truck roll south on Shoreline Road. "Besides, the existence of God isn't self-evident to Jess, and she's pretty smart. How can I pass Herkimer's course if I can't figure out what Grenier's talking about?"

"Memorize it," Pat said. "I don't get half of it either, but Herkimer has to pass us if we know it. I don't think it matters if we understand it."

"But it's stupid," Dan said. "It's like we're trying to figure out the unfigureoutable. The best minds in the history of man have theorized about God, but we're still stuck with believing, based on faith alone, that there's a Creator who started all this."

"That's why faith is a mystery."

Dan shook his head. "Jessica gave up her faith. If we don't find a proof that God exists, how is she going to get it back?"

Pat stared toward the seminary dome. "Maybe theology will clear it up."

Dan tried to laugh. "We talked about this in high school. We were waiting for *philosophy* to clear it up, remember? Now we gotta wait till theology? Besides, why should people have to study theology to find proof there's a God? Grenier claims it's self-evident."

In his next letter to Jessica, Dan didn't mention his problems with philosophy. Why give her more ammunition? "Last weekend Pat and I worked with the tropical fish in the basement. Some of us breed bettas (Siamese Fighting Fish) and (appropriately for here) angel fish. We have a ten-inch ribbon fish too, very pretty and graceful, in a long, narrow tank. He—we assume it's a he because he lives here—glides from end to end as if he's looking for a way home to the Amazon, but he keeps running up against the walls of his tank. I wish I could release him so he'd be able to swim free."

Jessica wrote back a few days later. "Your ribbon fish reminds me of you guys. I wish I could set *you* free. Like your fish, you have no idea of what you're missing.

"Hey, did you hear the one about God's identity crisis? God comes back to earth as a little kid and enrolls in a Catholic grade school. One day the nun tests God's class with questions from the Baltimore Catechism. 'Who made me?' she reads. God's little classmates recite the answer, 'God made me.' At this point little God starts sobbing and frantically waves his hand. The nun asks him what's wrong. 'But, Sister,' God says, 'if I made *them*, then who made ME?'"

"She sent it to me too," Pat said the next morning at breakfast. "It's not funny."

"Yes it is," Dan said. "It's a good question too. I'll bet Quince would love it. Jeez, I wish he were here."

Pat swallowed a bite of his sweet roll. "If he had stayed, you might feel differently. In class he didn't seem any different from Herkimer. I think it's the course material, or maybe the text."

"Did you mean *course* with a *u* or an *a*?" Dan asked. "It's coarse, all right. I'll bet Troden ordered them to use that book."

Days later, President John F. Kennedy was shot in Dallas. That night after dinner, Dan sat with a few others in the chapel before the rest came in for night prayers. He tried to pray, but no words came. Kennedy was president one second, dead the next. That quick. If it happened to the president, it could happen to anyone.

God bless America. In God we trust. One nation, under God.
Where was God when the assassin took aim?

In explaining the proofs of God's existence, Henri Grenier wrote that things move in this world, and everything that moves is moved by something else, until you get to an unmoved mover that you call God.

Dan searched for Pat, and found him in the magazine section of the library. "Did you read this? It's not a proof, it's another leap of faith. I can hear Jessie:

How do you know you'll eventually get to an unmoved mover? If you insist everything has to have a mover, you can't conveniently create an exception to that rule just so you can say there's a God." Dan flipped the book shut. "And ditto for that so-called uncaused-cause proof. I can't tell Jessie this stuff."

"I know," Pat said. "I tried."

"You talked to her? About this?"

"Yeah. And I also told her about the proof that says people have varying degrees of goodness, so there must be a God who is perfectly good. She disagreed, of course. She said she's studied how people developed morals based on rules that helped their cultures survive, and that's why there are so many different ethical systems. Besides, she said, there can't be a perfect good because what's good for some people may be bad for others."

"She has a point," Dan said.

Pat nodded. "She always did, even in grade school. She said she reads philosophy now to keep ahead of us. But we *know* there's a God. There has to be a proof somewhere."

Dan pushed his chair away from the table. "If there is, don't you think they'd have taught it to us by now? All we've done is discover more contradictions." He rose and slid his chair under the table. "I'll deny it if you tell anyone, but there are times I really wonder about this stuff."

Pat spoke quietly. "Sometimes we have to accept things on faith."

"Accept *what* on faith? The first thing we're told? The second? The latest? Most people keep the religion their parents taught them. That's faith, I guess. But if we're willing to believe everything on faith, without proof or logic, we can end up believing in anything, even Santa Claus or unicorns. There's no proof, but with faith we could believe in 'em. And now you're saying that's what we should do about God."

"Come on, it has to make *some* sense. Faith doesn't mean believing in just anything."

"That's my point," Dan said. "We see the contradictions in other religions as a reason for not believing in them. But when we find them in our own, we say we believe on faith. Either there's something wrong about our beliefs, or we need answers to the contradictions. Otherwise faith becomes nothing but an intellectual cop-out."

Pat shook his head. "No. Faith is a virtue. With it we accept the mysteries about God that we may never understand."

Dan led Pat to the library door. "I can accept mysteries. But I keep wondering why people are so willing to accept contradictions as part of their faith in God.

Contradictions are flaws—imperfections—but God is supposed to be all-perfect. The two don't match."

On the Thursday before Christmas, Jessica arrived to pick up Pat for the holiday break. From the dorm, Dan spotted her leaning against the car, hardly responding to the seminarians who greeted her. Something was wrong.

He hurried down the steps and across the parking lot.

"Danny!" she said. She opened her arms. "Please don't duck away. I was hoping you were still here. It's been a horrid semester." She wiped her eyes and tried to laugh. "Great Christmas greeting, huh? I'm sorry. It's just …" She kissed his cheek so lightly he thought maybe she missed.

Before Dan could say anything, Pat rushed out the door and tossed his suitcase into the trunk. He and Dan shook hands and wished each other a Merry Christmas. Jessica waved, then ducked into the car. Dan waved back as she and Pat pulled away.

It happened so fast, Dan hardly saw her. Why hadn't he stopped them? They could have talked a minute. He touched his cheek. *A horrid semester*, she said. Nothing in her letters indicated anything was wrong, so maybe there was nothing to worry about. Still, she'd never called anything *horrid* before. He turned back toward the dorm.

Father Herkimer was standing next to the door, frowning. "You'd best stop playing with fire, Mr. Bates."

"She's a friend, Father. Nothing more."

"I would hope," Herkimer said.

At Sacred Heart Church's midnight Mass, Dan, in his seminary cassock and surplice, responded to the prayers of Father Straud. At the prayer for the dead, he thought of Quince and prayed for his soul, just in case. Later he prayed for Jessica, a fallen-away Catholic who wouldn't be attending midnight Mass, or any Mass.

"Lord, help me learn the proofs of your existence so I can get Jessie to see her error and return to your Church. And please, whatever her problems are at school, give her the strength she needs to become a good nurse."

It was short, but God would know how much he meant it.

On a cold morning in February, Dan served as acolyte in the seminary chapel at a solemn high Mass closing the forty-hours devotion. For an hour at a time, pairs of seminarians had knelt through the night before the Blessed Sacrament.

After breakfast, the seminary granted a rare "general town permission" until 9:15 that night. The North Shore Line had shut down the year before, so Dan and Pat rode a bus to Milwaukee, where they went to dinner and a movie with Mr. and Mrs. Fernettan.

Ten days later, after Mass on Shrove Tuesday, the seminarians were again set free. Pat waited for Dan outside the chapel. "My place again?"

"Thanks, not this time."

"You're not sticking around here all day, I hope."

"I have permission to go home too." Dan smiled.

Pat's jaw dropped. "You can't take off and go see her."

"I'll get to Madison by noon. The 5:30 bus'll get me back in plenty of time."

"Don't. There'll be an accident or a snow storm or the bus'll break down. Something. Troden'll find out."

"No he won't. The bus to Willow Run goes through Madison. How would he know the difference?"

"Look, we'll call Jessie from my place and tell her you can't make it. She'll understand."

"Pat, we're juniors in college."

"You don't make sense," Pat said. "Last week you told me the forty hours had re-inspired you toward the priesthood."

"It did. In chapel at two in the morning, I loved that hour of solitude. I felt closer to God than ever. Nothing else mattered."

Pat's voice had an edge. "*Nothing else mattered?* Jeez, you could fool me, and probably everyone here, visiting an atheist girl at her secular college."

Dan laughed, then regretted it. Pat was worried. But he wanted to find out what was so horrid in Jessie's life. Maybe he could help. Or maybe not, but he could talk to her, hold her, possibly kiss her. And yeah, he looked forward to that too, so maybe he *was* a bit nuts. And if *he* couldn't figure himself out, poor Pat didn't stand a chance.

Pat stopped at his door. "She wants you to quit, and you're sneaking away to see her."

"I'll be careful."

"You say that, but you keep putting your vocation in danger." Pat shut his door.

Dan spotted Jessica right away in the small crowd that met his bus. She gave him a quick hug and they held hands on the way to her car.

"I'm glad you came," she said. "Does Pat know?"

"He told me not to."

"Of course! What if I chained you up and didn't let you go back?"

"He'd say 'I told you so.'"

At the state capitol they joined a class of fourth graders and their chaperones on a tour. The kids giggled when Dan and Jessica lay down with them on the rotunda floor to stare up at the dome.

Later, far above the rotunda, Jessica and the kids leaned over an iron railing to watch the people below. "Look!" She tried to pull Dan to the railing.

"Don't." He pushed his back tight against the wall.

Her laugh echoed around the dome. "You're more scared of heights than Pat is! Don't you trust your God to save you?"

Dan headed for the stairs. "I don't want to *test* my God. I shouldn't even be here."

After the tour, they crossed the street into the Park Motor Inn for lunch at the Top O' the Park. On their way to the elevator, Dan glanced at the front desk. Would he have the guts to register himself and Jessie into a room? Two red-coated bellmen stood near the desk waiting for a call, and the young female desk clerk caught his eye and smiled.

Dan blushed. He guessed not.

They took a table with a view of the capitol. Jessica leaned across the gold tablecloth. "A lot of legislators and lobbyists come here for lunch. If you quit the seminary, you could study political science at the U. Think of the good you could do, passing laws that help all the people instead of only the rich."

"There are many ways to do good," he said.

They ordered hot turkey sandwiches and Cokes, then admired the white-granite dome of the capitol gleaming in the early afternoon sun. After their drinks arrived in fancy glasses, they clinked a toast.

"To friends getting through college," she said.

"To both of our colleges. But I've been worried about yours. You said it was horrid."

Her eyes dropped. "I shouldn't have said that and run off. I was okay after a couple days." She stared toward the capitol. "Some kids I took care of at the hospital died, three of 'em in four days, and I sort of crumpled—inside, I mean."

"Couldn't you talk to someone?"

"I told my supervisor I was quitting, that I couldn't do it anymore. She spent an hour with me and I felt better. But I'm still scared about the next time. Other times. I know there'll be some." She squeezed Dan's hand. "I still wish you were here."

He squeezed back. Sometimes he did too.

Pat was waiting for Dan at the chapel door. "Did you go?"
"Yeah. It worked out fine."
Pat rolled his eyes. "Are you sure you don't want to quit?"
"No. Right now I'm not sure of anything."

That summer, Dan visited Pat and Jessica early in August, one month before they'd start their last year of college. After an hour of one-on-one basketball between Dan and Pat on a ninety-two degree day, they headed to the beach with Jessica.

Her white two-piece suit seemed daring, even immodest, but Dan didn't want to seem a prude, so he kept quiet. They dove and splashed through the waves, and Jessica stayed close. He didn't push her away.

Later, citronella candles perfumed the Fernettans' back yard to keep away bugs. Mrs. Fernettan had spread a white cloth across their picnic table, and Mr. Fernettan grilled brats and hamburgers. After everyone ate, Dan, Pat, and Jessica discussed the year ahead.

"I'll still be working with kids," Jessica said. "It's hard, but the kids respond so beautifully. You guys ought to become doctors!"

"Sure," Pat said.

"Really. You want to help people. Doctors do that."

"You work with the bodies," Pat said. "We'll work with souls. People need both."

Jessica turned. "Danny? You could be a doctor."

He squinted. Her head was silhouetted against the sun. "Same thing Pat said."

She headed for the house. "Jeez, you guys. You have five years to go yet. You complain the rules treat you like kids, but you refuse to join the real world." She returned with a beer and stretched out on the lounge. Her light-blue shorts weren't tight, but they were shorter than any Dan had seen her in. He stared at her smooth skin for a couple of seconds, then followed the line of her legs from her calves past her knees and thighs to the V. He blushed and looked away, avoiding her eyes for fear she'd seen him. He shouldn't be so crude.

All right, he was attracted to her, liked her, possibly loved her. But he couldn't ignore the intense spirituality that had flowed into him during last winter's forty hours devotion. There was no way he could give that up.

The flesh—Jessica's especially—was tempting but temporary. Only the spirit was lasting. He'd concentrate on the spirit no matter how much it cost him.

Unfortunately, with each peek he took at Jessica, the price went up.

Chapter 17

▼

After breakfast on a cool September morning two weeks into their final year of college, Dan and Pat walked in silence down the front drive with a hundred other cassock-clad seminarians. At Shoreline Road they crossed into Bay View Park.

Under a walnut tree along the park's main path, a woman sat alone on a green bench. Beneath a red beret, dark glasses hid her eyes, and her red-and-white windbreaker looked too thin to block the chilly breeze off the lake.

Dan spoke first. "Pat, it's Jessie."

She rose and stepped toward them. "Hi, guys."

Pat put out a hand as if to keep her away. "We can't talk. We're on retreat."

Jessica stopped. "I forgot." She glanced at the seminarians detouring off the path to avoid them. "I'm sorry. I just needed to see you guys, even for a minute."

"We can't talk," Pat said again.

Jessica turned to Dan. "Just a quick hug? Please?"

Pat pulled Dan's arm. "We can't!"

"We're on retreat," Dan said. *God, what a terrible way to say no.*

She dropped her head. "I had a bad night. Sorry."

Dan caught a glimpse of puffy, red eyes. He reached toward her, but she stumbled past him toward a gray Chevy parked along the road.

He started after her, but the guys were watching, and he stopped. Jessica's car dashed into traffic just ahead of a dump truck whose driver pulled long and loud on his horn. The Chevy raced ahead and disappeared behind the elms lining Shoreline Road.

Dan edged closer to Pat. "She was crying."

"She knows we can't talk."

"We should have asked what's wrong.'

"We're on retreat." Pat's voice was tight.

But the greatest of these is charity. Paul wrote that in his epistles. "Bullshit," Dan said. "Jessie's more important than a stupid retreat. We owe her an apology. A big one."

The annual visiting day was set by Monsignor Troden for a couple of weeks later on the first Sunday in October. Dan talked with his parents under an oak tree near Kleissmann's southeast wing. He kept an eye on Pat and Mr. and Mrs. Fernettan across the lawn.

Dan's mother was telling about friends in Willow Run who asked about him. "They all agree: Just one visiting day is ridiculous. We'll hardly see you this year."

"But *Troden* doesn't agree," Dan said, "and he makes the rules." Oh, shit, Pat was shaking his head at something his mother said. About Jess? He wished he could hear.

She hadn't written since the morning in the park. He'd sent her a note. "I was insensitive and stupid. I'm sorry." It was all he could think of to say.

His dad asked something. Basketball? Yes, he and Pat still played, mostly for exercise. The Fernettans were laughing. Great! Whatever was wrong, they could still laugh.

Dan led his parents down the drive into Bay View Park. At the green bench he could still see Jessica in tears, running to her car. Pat and his parents were waiting to cross Shoreline Road. They were laughing again. Jessica must be all right.

At dinner, Dan took a seat next to Pat. "Did your parents say anything about Jess?"

"A little kid she was taking care of died. After she left the park, she drove home and stayed overnight. That was good, because we weren't able to help her."

"We *refused* to help her."

"We *couldn't*," Pat said. "It was against the rules."

"The rules aren't that important."

"They have a purpose. You're ignoring that."

"But they're not sacred. We shouldn't ignore *people* because of 'em."

Pat adjusted his napkin. "If this weren't about Jessie you wouldn't say that."

"Bull. They say they're training us to be 'other Christs.' Comforting someone is a lot more Christlike than obeying a stupid rule about silence."

Pat turned to face him. "Have you considered the *reason* for the rule? The *purpose* of our silence? You're acting as if they created that rule for no other reason than to frustrate you."

"I'm saying there are more important things than silence."

"Silence helps us think, something we're supposed to do on retreat. Silence opens us to new ideas, to inspiration. I don't know about you, but I could use some of that right now. When you insist on gabbing, for whatever reason, it's distracting. To *all* of us. And some of us may not agree that your reasons are all that noble."

Dan turned his attention to the baked chicken. "That's tough. I still think it was a sin, our not doing anything for her. It was a lack of charity. And without that, what good is all that inspiration we're supposed to get from our silence?"

That night Dan started a letter. "Since that day I saw you in the park and did nothing to help you, I've decided I was wrong to follow the rule. I should have known you wouldn't come here without a good reason, and when I realized you were upset I should have given you that hug. I'm sorry, Jess. I failed to do what any concerned person, much less a real Christian, would do. I hope I never again let a rule stop me from helping someone.

"But your job sounds terrible. Are you sure that's what you want to do?"

A week later he read Jessica's answer. "Yes, sometimes it's terrible, but other times it's more wonderful than anything I can think of doing. When kids get better and go home, the looks on their faces and on their parents' faces are unforgettable. Or when one is scared and can't get to sleep and I sit and hold his hand and read him a story or rub his back till he drifts off, I know this is what I want to do.

"And you, having to obey stupid rules that stop you from helping people who need you, I ask the same question: Your job sounds terrible. Are you sure that's what you want to do?"

That night, Pat appeared with his philosophy text at Dan's door. "I was reading the chapter on sex. Have you seen it?"

Dan nodded.

"I couldn't believe it," Pat said. "Listen: 'Those who have engaged in sexual intercourse are *defiled*.' Defiled! That includes married people, like our parents, people who have received the sacrament of matrimony! What happened to sex being a gift from God?" He didn't look up. "Then it says, 'Only virginity preserves the integrity of the flesh.'" He lowered the book. "You know I don't question Church doctrine, but this is ridiculous."

Dan had read it, but Pat's reaction surprised him. "Did you read the rest?"

"I'm not sure I want to."

Dan took the book and turned several pages. "Here: 'Lust is an inordinate desire for venereal pleasure. If the abuse committed in the matter of lust totally impedes the begetting of children, in as much as a physical impediment is placed in the way of procreation by the wasting of the semen, there is a sin is against nature.' Birth control, in other words. Damn, I wish Quince were here. I have some questions for him."

"Me too," Pat said. "But I'm not going to ask Herkimer."

After Pat left, Dan opened his copy of the text. There were "four species" of this sin against nature, it said, including "uncleanness or effeminacy, which is the procuring of pollution without carnal intercourse for the sake of venereal pleasure (solitary sin)."

Pat was right. It was ridiculous. But it was, apparently, the Church's official position on sex. So how could Quince teach from this book and insist masturbation wasn't a sin? "Lust," it said, "is of its nature a mortal sin. Therefore all venereal pleasure willingly taken outside the state of matrimony constitutes a mortal sin."

The text contradicted everything Quince told him. So who was he supposed to believe, this book with its twisted view of sex, or the kind confessor who mysteriously vanished from the school?

A few days later, Dan slapped the latest *Catholic Herald Citizen* onto a library table.

Meer Mohrical was sitting next to him. "Something wrong?"

"The pope says he *could* relax the celibacy rule, but he won't. Because, he says, 'the Church has taken this sacrifice on herself freely, generously, and heroically.' What a crock."

A theology student whose name Dan didn't remember pushed back his chair. "You knew when you came here what you were in for, Bates."

"We thought we did. But at thirteen? Bull. The pope claims he speaks for us. Did he send you a questionaire? I didn't get one."

The theologian's face tightened. "Just because you have your little girlfriend in Madison, you think—"

"You jackass. That has nothing to do with—"

"You're too weak to be a priest," the older student said. "You'd do away with centuries of tradition just to avoid the sacrifices the rest of us are willing to make."

Dan's face was burning. "You haven't noticed those traditions the Council has already dropped? Wake up in chapel: The altar faces us now. *And* we recite the Mass in English. But *you'll* probably request a dispensation to revert to Latin so you can stay stuck in the past."

The theologian's face reddened. "Good thing you won't be ordained for a while. You need to grow up before they foist you off on some unfortunate parish."

Meer edged Dan toward the door. "Let's take a walk."

"I'm not done. Did you hear—"

"It's not worth fighting about. C'mon. Walk. It'll cool you down."

Late one afternoon during Christmas break, Dan met Jessica in a small cafeteria after her last class. They clinked glasses in a silent toast.

"Remember," she said, "when we were seniors in high school? How we felt so old? Now we're seniors in college. And we've been in college already as long as we were in high school."

"Time seemed to drag then," he said. "Not any more."

She nodded. "I'm looking for a job. At a hospital here in Madison."

Jessica sounded so grown up. Dan tried to smile. She was looking for work while he attended a school that enforced bedtimes on men in their twenties. "Pat and I have four years left at Resurrection. Next year we start theology." He tried to laugh. "In grade school, I thought the seminary would teach nothing but Latin and theology and how to say Mass and act like a priest. After all, what else would we need to know?"

Jessica sipped her drink, then put aside the glass. "You're going to do it, aren't you. You're going to walk around in your black dress for four more years, and then you won't even get to pick your job. They'll tell you where to go ... and what to do."

"You skipped the good parts: feeling close to God and helping other people feel close to him, too. It doesn't matter much where we wind up."

"I don't believe in a god."

"I wish I knew how to help you understand."

Jessica watched his face. "I still don't see enough good in your life to make up for all the bad." She slid from the booth. "Oh, hell, it's a waste of time arguing with you. Let's walk along the lake."

They kept slipping on the packed snow, and they each took off a glove so they could hold hands. The shifting ice cracked and made them jump, and they huddled against a tree and watched lights go on in houses across the lake.

"It's pretty," he said.

She nodded against his coat. "Sometimes I wish Mendota was big … like Lake Michigan. I miss the water and the sky meeting at the horizon." She squeezed him. "I always thought someday you'd join me here, but the other day I realized we never will go to school together."

"I know."

"A couple years ago I thought you were coming. I cried after you said you weren't. You told me you applied here, but …" Her voice trailed off, then recovered. "You didn't come here, but I'll always wish you had. And I think someday you'll wish it, too."

Three months later, Dan opened a letter from Jessica.

March 21, 1965.

Dear Danny,

Just a quick note to tell you I'm riding a bus to Alabama tonight with a bunch of students (and, you'll be glad to know, a Catholic chaplain from St. Paul's student chapel). If they're letting you read the newspapers these days, you know why. Negroes are peacefully demonstrating for their right to vote and whites are killing people because of it. Several thousand of us are going to march on the 25th with Martin Luther King from Selma to the state capitol at Montgomery.

"I needed to tell someone, but not my parents because they'd worry. And not Pat because he'd worry too and tell them. I'm telling you so someone will know where I went. BUT DON'T TELL PAT. I'll write again as soon as I get back. Wish me luck.

Love, Jessica.

Dan read the letter three times. She didn't want Pat or their parents to worry, but she didn't care if he did. Or maybe she thought he wouldn't. The envelope was postmarked Madison, two days earlier. Jessica was probably in Alabama by now. He slipped inside the chapel's rear door and knelt in the last pew.

He'd read about attacks on the freedom riders four years earlier, and he'd seen photos of unarmed marchers running from cops who sicced snarling dogs on them and from firemen who blasted them against brick walls with water from high-powered hoses. Now Jessica was there. Dan's knees went weak. He sat back against the edge of the pew.

"Protect her, Lord. She doesn't believe in you, but please protect her. Maybe she'll change her mind and know it was you. Even if she doesn't, you have to give her credit for this, for putting herself in danger so people can have better lives. Please let her be all right. *Please.*"

But his fear still wouldn't let him stand, so he sat back against the seat.

The sanctuary lamp glowed red in the darkness, a light proclaiming Christ's presence. But Dan shivered with a sense of isolation he had never felt before. He couldn't talk to Pat, because Jessica said not to. He couldn't talk to the other guys, because they might tell Pat. And he couldn't talk to a priest because Quince was gone and the others would ask why he was so concerned about a girl. Now he couldn't even talk to God, because God seemed to have abandoned the chapel.

A few days later, the *Catholic Herald Citizen* reported that the pope told his special commission on birth control "not to lose sight of the urgency" of the issue they were studying.

There were rumors at the seminary that the majority of the commission wanted to change the Church's teaching. Well, it wouldn't be long now. The pope had told them to hurry.

The letter Dan was waiting for came the first day of April.

"I saw terrible things," Jessica wrote, "but I'm okay. I'm back where it's safe, but those poor people have to *live* down there in the middle of all that hate. Of course it's up here too. People are so cruel! With stuff like that happening, I wonder why it matters if we graduate. Can we talk sometime? Hope so, soon. Love, Jess."

She sounded depressed. But she was safe.

At dinner that night, Pat's face turned red. "*Alabama?* And you didn't tell me?"

Dan concentrated on cutting his chicken. "She didn't want you to worry."

"So my sister could be anywhere, in any kind of danger, but I won't know because I might worry. Was she aware of how many people they've killed down there?"

"Yes," Dan said.

Pat didn't talk to him the rest of the night.

At the end of May, Dan tossed his black graduation robe over his head. "All straight?" he asked Darrin Greene.

"Perfect." Darrin held out his arms to let the wide sleeves hang. "You know, we might be able to fly in these things."

At 2:30, the Resurrection Seminary college graduation class of 1965 marched into the gym. Dan spotted his parents, then the Fernettans. Jessica flashed a smile and blew a kiss.

Dan blushed. He took his turn on the stage, shook Monsignor Troden's hand and tucked his diploma under his arm. But when he saw his parents, he pulled the diploma out and waved it at them. They looked so proud, and he was happy for them.

After he'd visited Jessica at the university, the seminary hadn't seemed like a college. For three years Troden and his rules treated them like recalcitrant children instead of college men. Troden told them when to get up and when to go to bed, when to talk and when to keep still, what to wear and what to eat, what to read and what to study.

Philosophy, their major field, had taught them only what ancient churchmen wrote. They were not supposed to read other thinkers, nor were they encouraged to develop ideas of their own.

Jessica had gone to a real college: a place to discover new ideas, to make choices and to learn from your mistakes, to talk to people who didn't agree with you, to meet different races and religions and cultures.

He was twenty-one. A legal adult. Could he tolerate four more years of what he'd endured for eight as a teen? Many of his classmates were giving up. This was their last day at Resurrection Seminary.

As Pat predicted, Jessica had intensified her campaign to get them to leave. In weekly letters she reminded Dan of his taste of freedom when he visited Madison.

"For you, those days were fantastic because they were rare. For most of us, days like that are normal. We're *meant* to live free, Danny. We're not supposed to be cooped up in a place where you need permission to sneeze."

She was right. But to become a priest he had to accept the crap that went with it. He'd keep his eye on his goal and visualize the satisfying life he looked forward to as a priest. Somehow he'd handle his last four years at Resurrection.

At the reception after the ceremony, Dan stood with his parents and the Fernettans. Monsignor Troden stood nearby watching the clock.

"Wow," Jessica said loud enough for the rector to hear, "you guys get a whole hour to mingle with us people from the outside world. Isn't that dangerous?"

Troden glared at her.

"Shut up, Jess," Pat whispered.

She got louder: "Aren't you guys free to express your opinions? Where I went to school we could say what we thought."

Troden headed their way. Pat rolled his eyes. Dan stepped next to Jessica. He had no idea what Troden would say or do, but she deserved to have someone with her.

The rector wore a forced smile above his red monsignor's cassock. His eyes glanced toward Dan, then stabbed at Jessica. "Are you disappointed about something, young lady?"

"Yes, sir, I am. Are you the boss?"

"I'm Monsignor Troden, the rector, yes."

"I'm Jessica Fernettan. My brother graduated today."

"Ah, yes. I'm pleased to meet you, I'm sure."

"You may not be so sure when I tell you what I'm upset about."

Troden stopped grinning. "And that is?"

"It stinks how you give us exactly one hour to celebrate with my brother and his friends. I came on a bus from Madison, and Danny's parents drove here from Willow Run. That's even farther. But you won't let us see these guys longer than an hour."

Troden stared at Dan. "How long did you *wish* to see them, Miss Fernettan?"

"It's not just the time, it's having to stay *here*. You've kept them cooped up all these years and today they graduated from *college*—they're twenty-one-year-old college *graduates*, for Pete's sake—but you won't even let them go out to a restaurant with their families and friends."

The gym fell silent. Dan's knees were shaking. Troden, he had to admit, scared the shit out of him.

The rector's voice carried through the room like a roll of thunder. "Miss Fernettan, I have been entrusted by God through the archbishop with training these men for the holy priesthood. They are not men of this world, and we hold them to a very high standard. It is necessary as part of their preparation to engage in a regular schedule of community prayer. If you would acquaint yourself with our daily schedule, you'd see we gather for such prayers in the chapel at five-ten."

He looked again at his watch. "The time is growing late, so unfortunately we were unable to provide more than an hour for this celebration."

"Then you should have started sooner," Jessica said, but her voice didn't thunder the way Troden's did. "You might have handed out diplomas at noon. That would have given us the morning to get here and"—she studied her watch—"three-and-a-half hours to visit."

No one else said a word.

"I also disagree with you, sir, about the hour growing late. You may be ready to roll up the seminary sidewalks, but in the real world the evening has just begun. You're treating your college graduates like kindergartners. *High-school* graduates celebrate more than this. And, as I'm sure you know since *you* aren't stuck here, the best restaurants don't open till five. I'll bet if you let these guys go out to eat with their families, they'll promise to say their dinner prayers!"

A few chuckles turned to laughter. Troden's face reddened.

"The rule is set, Miss Fernettan. It's for the best. Our goal is not graduation from school, but graduation into the fraternity of priests. That will come for these men in four years." He cleared his throat. "I don't expect you to fully understand, but at five-ten these seminarians, our future priests, will be in chapel. I'm sure they will include you in their intentions during prayer, so that you may accept their situation. God bless you for your concern."

The crowd parted for Troden as he hurried out the door.

Then a woman across the room yelled, "Good going, honey! We feel the same way!"

Others shouted, "Yeah, way to go!"

"Well," Jessica yelled back, "it won't do any good to tell *me*. You gotta get off your butts and tell *him*."

The room grew silent, and Dan grinned. It was one thing for this mouthy girl to confront Troden; it was another for her to scold *them*. People curled into circles of conversation. Jessica Fernettan's diatribe at the rector seemed forgotten.

Dan leaned close. "Nice, Jess." He wished he could pull her into his arms and kiss her.

But Jessica still frowned. "I don't mean just them, I mean you guys, too. You gotta stand up for yourselves and not let him get away with that bullshit."

She was right, but they hadn't and they wouldn't. Better to play it safe. Get to their goal. Only four more years to the priesthood.

He could handle four.

Three days later, the Archbishop of Milwaukee accepted Troden's resignation and appointed Father Salvatore Terry, longtime rector at the minor, the new rector at Resurrection Major Seminary.

"I'm happy and so is Pat," Dan wrote to Jessica. "But a lot of guys left. They're going to miss the changes that I think, that I'm *sure,* are coming. Terry's strict but you can talk to him. I mean *we* can, but you could, too. He wouldn't get mad if you questioned him. He'd explain his point, and if you still disagreed he'd say he was sorry but he hadn't changed his mind. Though sometimes he does. A few guys think the way Troden talked to you sealed his fate, but I suspect this was in the works for some time. Sorry, Jess, I don't think it was you.

"I'll see you next week at *your* graduation. We'll celebrate yours longer than we did Pat's and mine."

"I'm so glad you're coming," she wrote back. "I want a big hug. I'm excited, but nervous, too! University Hospital has hired me for its pediatric ward—exactly what I want to do! Oh, Danny, this is such a great time. Thank you for all your help. But I'm sad, too, that you've decided to go back. I hope for yours and Pat's sakes that this new rector makes the changes you want. The only change I want, though, is you leaving there. Forever. But you already know that, so I'll close. Hey, be BAD. (You've been good long enough.) Love, Jessica."

CHAPTER 18

▼

The seminarians found the notice taped to their doors: "September 7, 1965. Rector's Conference. Gym. 7:30 PM." It didn't say attendance was mandatory. At Resurrection, it didn't have to.

Everyone was seated by 7:30 when Father Salvatore Terry strode to a lectern at the center of the stage.

"So, gentlemen, here we are. I should add 'again' for many of you because we were together during your years at the minor. So, in case you've been out of the country, and for the record, in case we're supposed to keep one, the archbishop has appointed me your new rector here at Resurrection Major Seminary."

Several students yelled "Yeah!" and started clapping, but Terry's face didn't change.

"Gentlemen, let us see how you feel at the *end* of the year. We have a task before us that is unprecedented in our lifetimes, perhaps in Church history. The Second Vatican Council will soon complete its work, and among its directives are new guidelines for the training of priests."

Terry took the microphone from its holder and paced the edge of the stage, flipping the cord aside before turning back the other way. "So. We must find ways to challenge you with more responsibility, they say, to better prepare you for entering a rapidly changing world." He swiped at a fly determined to land on his forehead.

"That means we on the faculty must change rapidly also. Some of you have asked for, even demanded, such change." His eyes ran back and forth across his audience, and he smiled. "You may have heard the saying, 'Beware of what you ask for. You might get it.' Whether these are the changes you've been seeking remains to be seen."

Several seminarians started to fidget. *Change* was a word seldom spoken there.

Terry pulled at the left sleeve of his cassock and ran a finger around the inside of his watch band. "So. We will change. And we will pray that the Holy Spirit has guided the Council's collective wisdom so the changes it has directed will result in your becoming holier and more effective priests."

Everyone stayed silent except for a few coughs.

"So," Terry continued, "here is what we've decided so far. You may want to buy yourself a new winter coat, because you are no longer required to wear a zimarra."

Silence, then a roar. Seminarians laughed and shook hands. Someone in back yelled, "But what will we do with 'em?"

Terry smiled again. "Whatever you wish, but please don't wear them. Speaking of which, the wearing of cassocks is no longer required for trips to the joh … to the lavatories."

More cheers.

"So. Those of you in the habit of wearing nothing beneath them will need to make some adjustments."

Terry pulled a sheet of paper from his cassock pocket. "In the new daily schedule, we will begin classes immediately after breakfast, then attend holy Mass at eleven o'clock, after which we'll break for lunch. We'll recite evening prayers at seven-thirty, then you'll be responsible for your own study time and rest periods. We will, however, continue silence after nine-thirty."

Groans.

"But you may now talk inside Kleissmann Hall. And you may visit each other's rooms. Your first item of daily business, morning prayers, will begin at seven o'clock instead of five-fifty."

Wild cheers.

"So. We have deleted rising from your schedule. *You* decide when to get up. Just be in chapel by seven, wearing at least a cassock and a Roman collar." Terry paused and turned over his paper. "Perhaps most importantly, I wish to announce that the faculty and I will add you to the seminary's decision-making process. You will elect, from each of your classes, two members for a new student council."

Cheers.

Terry flailed at the air. The fly was back. "Of course, those of us appointed to lead this institution will still make the final decisions, but we want—"

Groans.

"BUT," Terry shouted, "we want your ideas. However, you are still obligated to obey the rules we set forth."

The groans grew louder.

Father Terry pounded the lectern with his fist. "*Hey!* Let's get something straight. The faculty and I will make our decisions as fairly as we can. We will follow the guidelines issued by the Vatican Council. But understand, those guidelines are not complete. We will experiment, and sometimes we may stumble, but I hope we can count on your assistance to continue our march toward the goal we share: getting you men to the holy priesthood."

He replaced the microphone and grabbed the lectern. "So. Let me assure you, advice from your student council will be very important to us. When we make changes, we will inform you of our reasons for those changes. You may not always like them, but I hope you will understand why we made them."

Silence.

Terry relaxed his grip, folded his list and eased it back into his pocket. "So. That's how we'll start our new year, except I have one more announcement. We have a new faculty member. Actually, a former member who has returned to our philosophy department: Father Henry Quince."

Dan jerked forward in his seat as the wild applause began. Quince? But ... but it was too late. He'd finished philosophy.

He sat back. Well, Quince could still be his confessor again. Dan joined in the applause.

The next morning, at the solemn high Mass to begin the school year, Father Terry chanted the entrance prayer: "O God, you have instructed the hearts of the faithful by the light of Your Holy Spirit. Grant that through the same Holy Spirit we may always be truly wise and rejoice in his consolation."

At Terry's right stood Quince, at his left Herkimer, both robed in white dalmatics that matched Terry's flowing chasuble. A dozen candles flickered on the altar, and a cloud of incense rose to the ceiling of the sanctuary and out over the chapel. The scent of beeswax and incense, the four-part harmony of the choir, and the dignity of the liturgy reminded Dan that this was a celebration of the priesthood, a preview of the glory of his first solemn Mass. For the rest of his life he'd savor these hours of communion with God, and as a priest he'd bring these feelings to others. At times like this he had no doubt about why he was there, about what he must do.

He thanked God for bringing him to this place.

That evening, in his fourth-floor room overlooking the woods, Dan organized the binder he'd bought for the semester's classes.

The Vatican Council was still in session, so the Church fathers could still modify the law on priestly celibacy. How could they not see the sense of letting priests marry? Ministers in other faiths married, and the Catholic Church hadn't demanded its priests stay celibate until the twelfth century. Even then, it took several hundred years before the rule was obeyed. Priests had been celibate for less than half of the Church's history.

Still, the year was off to a great start. He and Pat were in their ninth year, studying theology, starting the final third of their training. Terry was the rector, Quince was back, and Jessica had called the night before Dan left Willow Run to tell him how happy she was at her job in University Hospital's pediatric ward.

"Thank you, Lord," he prayed as he closed the binder. "Everything's falling into place."

He wrote to Jessica: "First day of classes today. Pat and I are so glad to finally be studying theology. Also, we have new rules this year. Actually, fewer *old* rules. We can visit each other's rooms, get up later and take more responsibility for our lives. And we're going to be assigned fieldwork in parishes. We haven't done that before, and I don't think I'm the only one who's nervous.

"We get only four days each for Thanksgiving and Christmas, *but* we get three *weeks* for semester break in January, from the 9th to the 30th. I'll get to Madison then."

Jessica's reply came a week later.

I'm really glad for you and Pat. He doesn't write much, so thanks for letting me know how he's doing. My job here is great. Sad too, of course, with kids being sick, but I'm happy I can help them feel better. Sometimes all I can do is stay with them a while so they don't feel so lonely when their parents can't be here. Be grateful for good health, Danny. Not everyone has it, and I feel depressed sometimes when I come home. But in the morning I'm all right again, at least till one of the kids dies.

Last week it was Jerry. His mom told me I'd made his being in the hospital easier, but after he died I was totally unprofessional and really embarrassed myself. I couldn't stop crying. I need to pull myself together or they won't keep me here. Those poor parents were comforting *me* when it was my job to help *them*.

But tell me, why are you so ecstatic over a few dropped rules? Jeez, you guys. You've been repressed so long you've gone giddy over how they've loosened (not removed) your chains. Look around: You're still stuck behind the same walls that have suffocated you all these years.

No, I won't suggest you quit now. I'll wait. Somewhere, somehow, something will make you doubt again, and when that happens, I'll *pounce*! (I hope my writing that doesn't get you into trouble. Or do the new rules let girls pounce on you?)

Love,

Jessica.

A month later, at dinner in the refectory, Dan ignored his chicken drumstick as he read a *Milwaukee Journal* article to the men at his table. "The headline says 'Pope Paul VI affirms celibacy.' He says: 'Public debate is not opportune on this subject which is so important and which demands such profound prudence. Furthermore it is our intention not only to maintain this ancient, sacred and providential law with all the force of which we are capable, but also to reinforce its observance, calling on priests of the Latin Church to recognize anew the causes and reasons why today, especially today, this law must be considered most suitable.'

The group had stopped eating, and Dan heard a few murmurs. "Then it says—get this—he ordered the bishops and cardinals at the Council to stop discussing celibacy, but—oh, this really helps—he said they can still write to him. Hell, we can *all* write to him. A lot of good it'll do if he's so paranoid he won't let the council fathers even discuss it."

"Don't be too hard on him," Pat said.

"I'll bet Paul wishes John never thought of this council. It's a thorn in his side. He almost had to listen to some good reasons for doing away with celibacy!"

Pat put down his fork. "There are reasons in favor of it, too."

"And the fathers would have mentioned 'em," Dan said. "So what's Paul afraid of?"

"Maybe he's just sure of where he stands."

Dan glared. "Yeah, he's 'sure' as in, 'Don't confuse me with facts, my mind is made up.' Well, the Holy Spirit is supposed to operate through the voices of the council, but Paul apparently doesn't trust that process. If I were the Holy Spirit, I'd be pissed."

Pat sat back. "I warned you not to get your hopes up."

Dan crumpled the paper and shot for the wastebasket. He missed, picked up the ball of paper, stood over the basket and dropped it in. "In other words, Paul is saying, 'Shut up and forget it, fellas. We're not sharing you with anyone, especially women.'"

"Sometimes," Pat said softly, "I don't understand why you stay."

"Because, contrary to what you and our dear pope believe, a married priest can work as effectively as a married Protestant minister or a married Jewish rabbi."

"That's not true. A celibate priest doesn't have the distractions a married man has. You ignored the last paragraph." Pat reached into the wastebasket and smoothed the paper. "Here: 'Through celibacy priests are able to consecrate all their love completely to Christ and to dedicate themselves exclusively and generously to service of the Church and to souls.'"

Dan pushed away his plate. "Well, loneliness can be a distraction, too. Did you see where Rome has ten thousand letters from priests asking for dispensation from their vows? Maybe that's why some bishops wanted to speak on celibacy."

"Well, there's nothing to debate now," Pat said. "Not anymore. Sometimes I wish it were different too, but the pope has spoken."

Dan leaned forward. "Then why did he invite the bishops and cardinals to write to him? Oh, I get it. He finds out who the dissidents are, then makes sure they're not promoted. Shrewd move."

Pat slapped his napkin on the table. "Why don't you quit if you're that upset?"

"This is important," Dan said. "Ten thousand requests for dispensation! How are we going to replace those guys?"

Pat stood. "God will send replacements. Or maybe he won't. Maybe the rest of us will have to work harder." He shook his head. "You sound as if you're the only one making a sacrifice here. Hey, guess what: I like girls too. So do the other guys. We feel the same temptations you do, but we manage. Quietly."

In December, the Vatican Council closed. Mandatory celibacy was still in effect.

Dan prayed, "Is that your rule, Lord? If so, I'll follow it, willingly. But if it's a hang-up of some old men in Rome who've walled themselves off from reality, I'm going to have trouble."

During semester break in January, Dan drove to Jessica's apartment. She lived in an old yellow house two blocks south of the UW campus.

She peeked around the door. "You're late. Do the new rules let you come late?"

"The new rules don't let me come at all."

"Then they aren't new."

He stepped in. "You're thinner. Are you working too hard?"

"And you're fatter. Are you sitting around too much? Escape into the real world and slim down. How's Pat?"

"He studies all the time. He'd quit basketball if I didn't drag him to the gym."

"Should I be worried?"

"I don't know. When the rules relaxed, Pat got stricter. He yelled at me when I wanted more things to change. One night he suggested I leave."

"That's good advice. You should follow it."

They walked four blocks along icy sidewalks to Paisan's. Dan ordered a large peperoni with mushrooms, then stared at Jessica across the table. She had finished school and was drawing a paycheck, working at a job she loved. He, on the other hand, was still in training, years from the work he wanted to do.

She stared back. "Doubts?"

"No. Sorry." It wasn't a lie, not at that minute. Sometimes though, questions about God and about his vocation kept him awake at night. But why tell her and get her hopes up?

She looked away. "Then maybe I shouldn't see you. Your certainty depresses me."

"On the other hand," he said, "we finished 'Introduction to Theology' last week and I still haven't found a proof that there's a God. I'm looking for one, you know, so I can show it to you and hear you say, 'How could I have missed that? Of *course* there's a God!' Maybe next semester."

"That's not likely."

The pizza arrived and they pulled slices onto their plates.

"I'm sorry," Jessica said. "Sometimes I like making fun of you. But really, there is no god, so you're never going to find the proof you're looking for. I know how you believe, and how Pat believes, and sometimes I think, 'Well, maybe,' but then I look at the kids in my ward and there's no god I could believe in, much less love, who'd let stuff like that happen to children."

She waved her fork. "I mean, *Danny*, there are kids with burns all over and kids with cancer and kids we can't figure out what's wrong. One bleeds from his rectum and he wakes up every damned morning with his sheets shiny red and sticky with blood and they keep doing tests and his blue eyes have a fear in them so deep I can't describe it. We wash him up and hang more blood to drain into him and we take away his bloody sheets and put fresh ones on and all he says in that little voice you can hardly hear is, 'Thank you, Beverly. Thank you, Jessica.'"

She wiped her eyes with a napkin, then flung it to the table. "Would *you* put a kid through that if you were an all-powerful god?"

He couldn't look at her. "How can you do that job *not* believing in God? I mean, priests run into bad situations too, but at least we know God will reward people for their pain." Jessica didn't respond. Dan lifted a fresh slice of pizza, then dropped it back on the serving plate. "I'm not hungry anymore."

"Me neither," she said.

They crossed the library mall and shuffled along slippery sidewalks past the Memorial Union to the lake, where the ice shifted and creaked and groaned against the gray rocks lining the shore.

"It's spooky," she said. He took her hand.

At a huge oak near the stairway to Liz Waters, Jessica pulled Dan closer. "Stay with me tonight."

"You know I can't."

But he held her, and Jessica rested her head against his shoulder. Most times he loved holding her, though sometimes he became aroused. But tonight he wanted to cry. His despair was for her, for her kids, and for himself, too, because he couldn't spend the night with her. And he couldn't find the words to help her.

"Father," Dan said back at Resurrection, "I need to go to confession." He lowered his eyes. It still embarrassed him to ask, even with Quince.

"Well! Come on in, Danny boy."

Dan's eyes snapped to the priest. Quince looked the same, though it was hard to tell standing in the dim hallway with the table lamp shining behind Quince's head. But something was different.

Inside the room, Dan smelled beer, and Quince had trouble focusing his red eyes.

"Danny, my boy," the priest said again. "C'mon in. C'mon in."

Dan already was in.

"Have a seat," Quince said, waving a hand toward a chair covered with two weeks' worth of *Milwaukee Journals*. "Been gradin' papers. Not yours, a'course. Diff'rent class. Ha! Not near as good as yours was, Danny. Yours was a good one. Whatta we got, three years before you guys move out? God, I'll miss you."

Dan stared at Quince. He should leave.

"Oh!" Quince turned from his desk. "What was it you wanted?"

"Confession."

Quince leaned forward, blinked two, three times. "Ach, you've noticed my problem. Shocked, huh. Shocked to see your ol' friend drunk."

"No," Dan lied. "No, I—"

"You're shocked. C'n tell it by your eyes, by your mouth." Quince turned back to his desk. "Never seen a priest in this condition, huh?"

Dan shook his head.

Quince eased himself into the chair behind his desk. "Well, get over it, Danny boy. If you become one of us you'll see it plenty, in lots more guys than me."

"I …," Dan started, then stopped. He had no idea what to say.

"C'mon, c'mon, sit down." Quince waved toward the chair stacked with papers. "Push 'em onto the floor. I'll toss 'em out tomorrow."

Dan lifted the papers in three bundles off the chair and stacked them against the wall.

"Good," Quince said. "I drink, okay? A lotta beer, a lotta times. Not many know, an' I'm sorry you found out. But that's what happens when you pop in on people without 'em knowin' you're coming. You see 'em as they are. No time to pretty up."

They stared toward the windows, away from each other. It was Dan's turn to talk, but he still couldn't think of anything to say. Would his confession be valid if Quince was drunk? Would Quince get upset if he left?

"Ha. Ironic, isn't it? Here you come tonight, all unholy, asking God's forgiveness, and you find your priest like this, done in by his failings like you been done in by yours. But, Danny boy, you forget, if you ever really knew, all of us humans stay subject to our own weakness. Maybe I told you that already."

"But I didn't know you—"

"Of course you didn't." Quince pulled himself from his chair. "People don't tell other people their failings. Jesus, man, I'm a priest! You think I'm gonna tell everyone I drink?"

He braced his hands on both sides of the window. "I drink and you masturbate, and we both want to shrivel up and duck under the couch when someone says those words. Lousy drunks, people say, too damned weak to leave the booze in its bottle. But hey, masturbating cuts stress, right? So does drinking. Bad as you feel later, that's how good you feel letting your hootch of the day flow down your throat and smooth over all your troubles. For a few minutes you forget you're a priest who's supposed to be goddamned perfect. You forget everyone's watching, waiting for you to reflect God's image at 'em. Shit. *Me* reflecting God. Shit."

He shuffled back to his desk. "Get over it, Danny boy. We all have something, every one of us, some secret weakness we hope never hurts anyone 'cept ourselves. Hey! Don't look at me all hurt or angry or ... condescending. We're human. Priesthood doesn't change that. Think I'da been knocked out of here if I didn't drink? Nah. Not even Troden would've done that. It wasn't my liberalness, it was the beer.... Shit, the beer."

Dan stared at his favorite priest.

Quince turned away. "Danny, don't tell anyone you saw me like this, *please.*"

"I won't."

"Oh man, you picked a godawful time to come." He ran his hand through his hair. "Why *did* you come?"

"Confession."

"Oh. Yeah." Quince reached for a purple stole, kissed it, and slipped it over his head. "How many times?"

Dan leaned forward. "Three, Father. I couldn't stop."

"I know. Me, neither. Just kept pouring 'em down. Well, for your penance, spend ten minutes in chapel, thinkin' about people like us. Living with our weaknesses, different ones, tryin' to do God's work despite 'em. Consider how God lets us fail like this, maybe to humble ourselves, to become kinder priests. You'll find out some day, Danny boy: It's pretty hard to bawl a guy out in confession for *his* sins when we gotta go back to our rooms and face our own."

In the middle of May, Jessica sent a card, wrapped in a letter as usual. "This is University Hospital, where I work," she wrote on the card.

Dan unfolded the letter.

> The other day, we were discussing God during a break. Donna said, "What do you suppose God did before he created the universe?" None of us had ever thought of it, how there would have been nothing for God to do for all eternity before creation. Even with three persons in the trinity, they would have had nothing to discuss, no news, nobody to gossip about because, being God, they were perfect and already knew everything about each other and nothing was happening because nothing existed.
>
> That's when I figured it out. You can tell this to your theology class: The beginning of the world according to Jessica Fernettan. The three persons of the trinity got bored one day, so they created a huge ball they could play catch with. It was their first attempt at creation, and they made the

ball of extremely dense matter, so it was very hard and their hands got sore after only a few catches. They hadn't created baseball gloves yet. (Maybe, being spirits like Donna said, they really didn't have hands or need gloves, but I can't figure out another way to get the idea across.)

Anyway, between their sore hands and the fact that all they could do was toss this ball between them, they got bored again and put the ball aside. After a while, maybe a few eons or so, God decided the ball was cluttering up his space. He exploded it, blew it to smithereens, so pieces scattered all over creation (so to speak).

And this is what we call the Big Bang.

Love,

Jessica

Dan smiled. He slipped Jessica's card and letter into his desk. Had she sent her theory to Pat?

Most likely.

Chapter 19

In September 1966, one week before Dan returned to Resurrection for his second year of theology, he and Jessica shared a sandwich on the Memorial Union's flagstone terrace. Dan shifted their chairs so they could look out at the lake. Several swimmers were diving off a nearby pier, taking advantage of the late-summer heat.

"Last Sunday," Jessica said, "one of the pediatricians invited our wing to his place. It's west of here, out toward Cross Plains, way up on one of those bluffs along highway 14. We took our swimsuits 'cause he has a pool. You should see it! Tall thick bushes all around, nobody else within a mile. We all agreed it was perfect for skinny dipping."

Dan's face grew hot. Had she swum naked with her friends? He didn't want to know. Especially if she had.

Jessica was staring at him. "Oh, for Pete's sake. Anything about bodies, you blush."

"Not like I used to."

"Ha."

He looked away. "Shit."

"*What?*"

Dan shook his head. "It just came out. Sorry."

She laughed. "I *love* talking to you when you cuss. I remember one day you and Pat swearing up a storm playing basketball. You both jammed fingers or something. It was great!"

"We thought we were alone. We don't talk that way around girls."

She slapped his hand. "*Girls?*"

"Well, yeah, you know, guys should treat girls with respect."

Jessica stopped smiling. "Gotta protect our virgin ears, huh?"

Again he looked away.

"Damn it, you don't have to protect us *girls*. You should have been in our physiology classes, seen what nurses see. Bodies, Danny. And all their parts. They all have names, and I've seen the parts and I know the names. Touched 'em too."

He blushed more.

A swimmer surfaced near the pier.

"Who do you think bathes people who can't do it themselves?" she asked. "Who pulls bedpans from under the patients' rear ends? Who wipes 'em clean?" She bent close. "It ain't the doctors, dearie."

Dan knew she was a nurse, and he knew what nurses did, but somehow he'd never imagined her doing the work.

"There are no *girl* nurses," she said. "Just women, like you guys are men. So stop blushing."

He folded his sandwich wrapper. There weren't words—at least none he knew—to explain why his gut still tightened when he talked about this stuff. Especially with a girl. No, with a woman.

Out on the lake, a sailboat heeled. Dan thought it was going over, but it righted itself, changed course and raced on. It looked so easy.

But that was a skinny little boat. He was a grown man, twenty-two already. Change would be difficult because he knew so little about life outside the seminary walls. And, he had to admit, most of what he did know came from Jessica.

One November evening, word spread through the refectory that Pope Paul VI had announced he was postponing his decision on birth control.

After dinner, Dan and Pat strolled along the trail into the woods. At a tiny creek, they watched the water trickling over the stones.

"I remember Paul ordering his commission to hurry," Dan said. "He told them the issue was important. Well, they hurried. And now he says their report isn't definitive."

Pat tossed pebbles into the stream. "The members don't agree on whether the Pill's moral. And Paul didn't get their report until summer."

"Four months ago. Is he a slow reader or what?"

"Come on," Pat said, "it's a tough decision. Imagine being the pope with the whole world waiting for you to announce it."

Dan straightened. "It's not tough, it's ridiculous. Only Catholics claim birth control's a sin. It's time we get into step with the rest of the world."

"The Church doesn't decide based on what others believe," Pat said. "It determines what God wants, then teaches it."

"Like we have a monopoly on knowing God's will. Hey, other religions aren't evil. They're trying to obey God, too."

"Well," Pat said, "the pope hasn't announced a decision yet. My guess is, he's planning a change but wants to get the wording right." He grinned. "So he can satisfy the conservatives."

At the start of Thanksgiving break, Dan and Jessica sat in a booth at Paisan's. After Dan slipped the last slice of pizza onto his plate, Jessica said, "Know what? I want to keep coming here ... with you ... even if you do become a priest. It'll become our own tradition."

"Will you bring your husband and kids?"

Silence. Then, "I was thinking of the two of us. Sharing a pizza over beer. Talking. Like now."

"Oh." Did priests go to dinner—alone—with women?

She folded her napkin, laid it next to her plate. "My friends say I'm nuts to like a guy who's going to be a priest, that you're choosing the Church the same way a man chooses a woman and—"

"The Church isn't a woman. It's all of God's people. God's called me to serve them, women and men. How can I refuse?"

"I don't believe in a god. You know that. But suppose your God *didn't* call you, would you want to become a priest anyway?"

Dan sipped his beer and slid his glass around the wet spot it left on the table. "I don't know. Most days I'm not aware of *wanting* to be a priest, I just *plan* to be one."

"And sometimes you doubt there's a god."

Dan sat back against the booth. "Sometimes." Again he made circles with his glass. "Yeah, there are times I wonder. If there isn't a God, becoming a priest makes no sense. I'd have given up a normal life for nothing." Another sip. "I try to ignore those doubts."

Jessica leaned toward him. "I have other friends who ignore their doubts. They never give their faith a thought. They're comfortable, they say. Is that what you're going to do, stay comfortable, not think about what you believe and its contradictions?"

Dan set down the glass. "Hey, I study theology. I think about this stuff all the time. I won't be comfortable, as you put it, until I find a proof of God's existence that will convince even you. And then, you know what? I'm going to write it up in a book. And I'll dedicate it to you, 'cause your leaving the Church is what's driving me to find that proof."

Jessica sat back and stared at him. Then she stood and took her purse from the table. "Well, I suppose we should go."

Dan slid from the booth. That was it? *I suppose we should go?* He had braced himself for an argument, but there was none coming. At least not tonight.

Four days later, Dan knocked at Quince's door.

Quince made a face. "I said not to come back until you've commited a real sin."

"This is different."

The priest waved him in. "We'll see."

They sat in Quince's mismatched but comfortable set of chairs. "Okay, start."

Dan stared out the window. "I kissed a girl too long."

Quince rolled his eyes. "Really. How do you know?"

"I liked it."

"I'd hope."

Dan blushed. "I read a column by a priest. He said there are two kinds of kisses, one where you're saying 'I like you' and another that says 'I like your body and I like kissing you.'"

Quince laughed. "Nobody but a celibate would categorize kisses that way. I told you last time, and the time before that, not everything having to do with bodies offends God. It offends the pope and a lot of priests, maybe, but not God."

"But that goes against—"

"The teaching of the Church. No. It goes against a conservative *part* of the Church. Unfortunately, those are the guys in power. And, of course, they claim to be the conduit through which the Holy Spirit speaks. But that's bull. Lots of Catholics, maybe a majority, use birth control. Some theologians—*Catholic* theologians—insist those people are acting responsibly in their God-given role of parenthood. But the official Church claims they're sinning. Which side speaks for the Holy Spirit?"

"The theologians, I hope."

Quince put his head back and let the chair cradle him. "The Church's prohibition against sexual pleasure is an attempt to control people. Through guilt. To me, *that's* a sin. I told you, stop confessing sex sins. God doesn't care. Racial hatred. Worker exploitation. *Those* are sins. They hurt people and they offend

God. The other stuff? Bah. It's idiocy and it's cruel, condemning young people for masturbating or kissing, and married couples for using the Pill."

Dan leaned forward. "But nobody agrees with you. They say what I did was a sin."

Quince smiled. "Nobody in the damned conservative hierarchy agrees with me. Have you forgotten those theologians?" He studied Dan's face. "You're really hung up on this, aren't you? All right, follow *them* if you want. Feel the guilt for the rest of your life. But I hope someday you decide to think things out for yourself. You do that now to a degree, but you stop halfway. You read *Keys of the Kingdom*. How far would Francis Chisholm have gone if he had obeyed every dictate of the Church?" He slumped back into his chair. "Okay, I'll give you absolution. I hope and pray that will settle your conscience."

When he finished, Quince pointed toward the door. "Now get out of here. And, one more time, stop thinking everything you do is a sin."

In the middle of May, Jessica sent another postcard. "I love this shot of Lake Mendota and Picnic Point in the spring. The greens are so fresh, and summer's ahead!"

In a letter wrapped around the card, she added, "This summer, when you're away from that place, look at the circular thinking and the lack of logic in religion. Count how many statements hedge with 'maybe' and 'perhaps.' People *believe* it but they don't *know* it. I'm flattered that you would do a book for me, but you're never going to find the proof you need to write it. And the thought of you spending your life searching for something that doesn't exist drives me nuts. And so does this wall that separates what we both believe. Damn it, Danny, why can't you see it?"

On the last day of classes, Dan sat alone in the chapel, reviewing the school year, trying to find peace despite his doubts and the rumble of car engines outside. He pulled a laminated card from his missal and reviewed the words of Henri Lacordaire, a French priest:

To live in the midst of the world, with no desire for its pleasures;
To be a member of every family, yet belonging to none;
To share all sufferings, to penetrate all secrets, to heal all wounds;
To go daily from men to God, to offer Him their homage and petitions;
To return from God to men, to bring them His pardon and His hope;
To have a heart of iron for chastity and a heart of fire for charity;
To teach and to pardon, console and bless, and to be blessed forever.

O God, what a life is this, and it is yours, O priest of Jesus Christ!

The prayer set an ideal that, after ten years at Resurrection, Dan still fell short of. But he would keep trying. Quince assured him that was all God expected. He'd be back in September. Two years to go.

Jessica called on a hot Sunday afternoon in July. "Can you come see me today? Please?"

When Dan picked her up, she was eager to leave her apartment. But she said little.

"Where do you want to go?" he asked.

"Anywhere."

"Picnic Point?"

"Fine."

At the tip of the peninsula they sat in the grass watching sailboats skim the bay between them and the university campus. A speedboat broke the quiet, then went away. The late afternoon sun threw golden light across the capitol dome and the rest of the Madison skyline.

Jessica pulled closer. "I wish we could sit here forever."

"You'd get bored."

"I *want* to be bored."

Dan waited for more. When she stayed quiet, he said, "They say talking helps."

Her eyes were on the grass. "They say a lot of bullshit too."

He waited.

"Another little kid," she finally said in a voice he could hardly hear. "Not even four years old, a boy ... a brain tumor. Headaches, seizures, the whole fucking bit. So the doctors decide to operate after they tell his parents there's no choice but to cut it out and hope."

Jessica took a deep breath and let it out slowly. "I was there when they took Joey from his room, the parents trying not to cry—not to *scream*, probably—telling him he'd be fine and the operation would make him all better. He was drugged, but you could see the panic in his eyes—in all their eyes. I walked with them as they wheeled him down the hall to the operating room. Danny, he didn't even take up a third of the gurney! His parents kept telling him they'd be there when he woke up and everything would be all right and soon he'd go home and play with his daddy again."

She started crying, and he held her. She turned her face against his chest, then pulled away and rolled face down in the grass, beating her fists against the ground. He went to his knees and rubbed his hand up and down her back, saying nothing, letting her pound the earth until she went limp, sobbing. He kept rubbing her back with his left hand, and wiped his own tears with his right.

Finally she was quiet except for spasms that shook her every few minutes. "I can't do it anymore. I have to find something else."

His hand caressed her back.

"Something without kids. I love them, but when there isn't anything I can do …" She took another deep breath. "You can guess what happened. During surgery. Three years old. I was with his parents when Doctor Robinson told them."

Dan's left foot was asleep, so he changed the position of his legs, but he kept rubbing Jessica's back. "You were there for them."

"Damn it, Danny, he *died*."

"Yes. But you were there. They weren't alone. That's important."

On the drive to her apartment, Jessica sat with her head on his shoulder. At the curb, her eyes asked him not to leave, and he followed her inside.

She lifted her feet onto her green-velvet couch, lay against its back and pulled him down to her. "Just for a while …"

He eased an arm under her head and wrapped the other around her back. Her blouse had pulled out of her jeans, and he jumped when his hand touched her skin. He rubbed higher on her back, over the blouse, but ached to stroke the smoothness one more time and he brought his hand lower and trailed two fingers along the strip of bare skin between her jeans and the blouse.

"Mmm-hmm," she said against his chest.

He shouldn't do this. He moved his hand back outside her clothes.

"It's okay," she said. She pulled him tighter against her and he was getting hard and he knew she felt it and it was wonderful and shameful and loving and sinful all at the same time. She said again, "It's okay," and she moved against him *there* so he had no doubt that's what she meant and his head drifted into a dizziness that left him thinking he'd never get off that couch again.

This was a sin, the Church said. He didn't care. He slipped his hand under her blouse so it was gliding flat across her bare back, moving up to her bra strap and past it.

She tugged at his shirt and slipped her hand across his back too and he'd never felt that from a girl and he stopped his own hand to concentrate on hers. She lifted her mouth and he kissed it, soft and long, and didn't stop when something warm and wet pushed through his lips and his own tongue slid against hers and he recalled Darrin Greene telling about the banned book he found unlocked in the seminary library. The book described French kissing, and it sounded so repulsive that day, but this day it brought a lovely warmth that Dan didn't want to end, even if it was a sin.

And it didn't end. But he didn't do more either because he had no idea what else he should do or what she wanted him to do, and for that night he decided this was enough, to lie together kissing, caressing, holding. He remembered his daydream on the bus after the prom, when he imagined the last dance went on and on and on. Tonight *this* went on and on, and it was better than that dance.

But it must be late. He pulled away.

"Danny?" Jessica breathed against his chest. "Danny? Keep holding me."

"What time is it?"

"Who cares?"

"It's late. I gotta go."

She pulled him against her. "Don't go."

He eased his arm from under her, tried to read his watch in the dark. "Where's the light?"

"Don't go," she said again.

"I have to!" It was almost midnight. They'd been on her couch in each other's arms, hands under each other's shirts, all those hours, squeezing tight all the way down to their ankles. It had to be a mortal sin no matter what Quince said.

Jessica stretched. "I'm hungry. Would you like a sandwich?"

"I have to go." It would be almost one by the time he got home. His parents would be worried.

She stood, her hair twisted every which way and her blouse hanging out of her jeans. She saw him watching and started laughing. "You don't look any better."

It was the first time that day he heard her laugh.

She tiptoed over and tossed her arms around his neck and drew him down till their noses touched. "You did it again. You made me better. But what will I do when there's another Joey and you're not here?" She sat down as though she might cry, but got up right away and headed for the kitchen. "I'll make sandwiches."

Dan ran his hands across the soft cloth of the couch and stared through the window at the corner streetlight. Jessica said he had helped her. But there would come a time when he couldn't do this, when he would have to ignore her calls.

Was tonight a sign from God that he should quit the seminary? Jessica's service—her *ministry*, it seemed—to children and their families suddenly appeared more important than his own.

Two years. He had only two years left to figure out what God wanted him to do.

Chapter 20

▼

"Those who wish to call themselves Catholic take upon themselves the obligation to obey our Holy Father, the pope," Father Otis T. Rinehardt told his third-year theology, matrimonial-law class. "As long as he does not declare artificial birth control to be moral under God's natural law, Catholics may not employ that means to limit their families."

Dan stopped looking out the second-floor window at the fall colors taking hold in the woods, glanced at Pat in the seat behind him, and turned to Rinehardt. He raised his hand but didn't wait to be called on. "But what happens when the pope changes his mind someday? I mean, after people follow his orders and wind up with more kids than they can afford?"

Rinehart stared for several seconds. "The parents you speak of will surely love those children with all their hearts. If they have left themselves open to God's will, he will provide."

"Not according to the poverty statistics."

Pat kicked Dan's chair.

Rinehardt peered over the glasses he kept low on his nose. The seminarians called him "Oter" because he scribbled his intials—OTR—on their papers when he corrected them. "What are you getting at, Mr. Bates?"

"I'm getting at kids who live with rats. Who go to school hungry. Right here, in our own country, and it's worse in others. God doesn't seem to get involved."

Rinehardt set down his notepad. "Your point, Mr. Bates?"

Pat kicked again, harder.

Dan pulled his chair forward, out of Pat's reach. "God isn't much help economically. If parents don't provide for their kids, no one does. My point is that the pope needs to take a good look at the realities of modern life before he decides about birth control. And he needs to decide quick."

Rinehardt pushed up his glasses. "I'm sure the Holy Father would appreciate your perspective on this, but I suspect he is quite aware of the realities of modern life, as you call them." He glanced around the room. "Does anyone care to comment on Mr. Bates's views?"

No one moved.

Rinehardt picked up his notepad. "Let's continue now on today's subje—"

"I have a question about that too," Dan said.

Kick. Pat's legs must have gotten longer.

Dan jabbed the air with his pen. "The pope insists birth control is a mortal sin, and that means people will go to hell if they practice birth control, right?"

"Once again: your point, Mr. Bates?"

"Well, we say people are obligated to form a correct conscience in line with the Church's teaching. What happens to those who've formed their consciences in that manner when the pope finally decrees that birth control does *not* violate the natural law? Will they be required then to *change* their consciences? And those who've died in the meantime: Will the people condemned to hell for using birth control get paroled into heaven?"

Oter's face turned red. "You know the answer to that, Mr. Bates. Those people made free-will decisions to act against God's will by disobeying the teachings of his Church while they were alive. And, I might add, you'd be more accurate saying *if*, not *when*, the pope changes his mind."

Dan leaned forward over his desk and tapped the clicker of his pen against the old wood. "But God doesn't change, does he? It will be the Church, whose teachings people are supposed to follow in forming their consciences, who will have been wrong. Could it be that God isn't really sending people who use birth control to hell, because it isn't against *his* law, just the Church's?"

Rinehardt walked toward him. "God will provide the answers in due time, Mr. Bates. That is why, I'm sure, our Holy Father is weighing his decision so carefully."

That night after dinner, Dan and Pat shuffled through red, gold and green leaves blanketing the path through the woods.

"I couldn't believe it," Pat said. "You kept digging your hole deeper and deeper. I kicked your chair three times. What was I supposed to do, break it over your head to shut you up?"

"You guys should ask more questions," Dan said. "Make Oter talk sense. He never did say what happens when people's consciences tell them the pope is wrong."

"But we can't ... *shit!*" Pat tripped over a tree root hidden under the leaves. Dan caught his arm until Pat regained his balance. "Jeez, you'd think we've walked through here enough to know the hazards. Thanks. Anyway, what I was going to say was, we can't have everyone deciding for themselves what's right or wrong."

"Why not?" Dan said. "Theologians decide for themselves. So do many lay people. The Church teaches that God judges us on our individual consciences. And that makes sense, doesn't it? Everyone knows their own situation and how their actions affect them and other people."

Pat shook his head. "You're getting into subjective morality. Don't pull that with Oter; he'll blow. Some acts, like murder, are intrinsically wrong."

"But the fifth commandment doesn't say 'murder.' It says 'Thou shalt not *kill*.' But the Church allows killing in war and as punishment for certain crimes, though Christ said to turn the other cheek and do good to those who hurt us."

"We have the right to defend ourselves," Pat said.

"Christ disagreed. *Do good to those who hurt you*," Dan repeated. "Who decides which of his teachings we're to follow and which ones we can ignore? And if the Church can justify some kinds of killing, why can't it justify some kinds of sexual expression, like making out and premarital sex and birth control? The sixth commandment forbids only adultery."

"The Church interprets the will of God," Pat said. "It's—"

"No," Dan said, "the *pope* interprets it. Remember, the Church is made up of its people. And some of them, even priests and bishops and cardinals, have different opinions on a lot of things, including birth control."

Pat smoothed some pebbles with his foot at the edge of the trail. "But they don't have the teaching authority that Christ gave the pope."

"Even when the pope teaches the opposite of what Christ said?"

Pat looked back toward Kleissmann. "Look, even when I agree with you—and I do more often than you think—I'm not going to admit it in class. I want to survive my last two years, get ordained, become a priest. You never know what they might hold against us. They could postpone—even cancel—our ordinations. So be careful, okay?"

Dan quit asking questions in class, and he and his classmates kept themselves busy with their studies and field placements. They did what the parish pastors told them to do, from teaching catechism in the grade schools to setting up tables for meetings of the Holy Name and Christian Mothers Societies. Dan loved it. Why did he have to wait two more years to do this?

Thanksgiving passed, then Christmas, and the seminarians celebrated the start of 1968 when the Green Bay Packers trounced the Oakland Raiders in the NFL Championship Game. But a week later, North Vietnam started its Tet offensive. Dan and Pat whispered in the library about Train. He'd written months earlier saying he was headed for 'Nam.

Dan handed Pat the front section of the *Milwaukee Journal.* "How can people care about football when their relatives and friends are fighting a war?"

"It helps take their minds off it."

"Maybe we need more minds *on* it so we can find a way to end it." He put down the sports page. "You realize … if *we* had quit, we might be over there."

"Mm-hmm."

"I'm glad I don't have to go," Dan said. "But I feel kinda guilty about it, too."

Pat folded the paper. "I think a lot of us do."

In early March, Dan counted the weeks: three before the archbishop of Milwaukee would accept his vow of celibacy and ordain him a subdeacon, the first of the Church's three major orders—subdeacon, deacon, then priest.

As a subdeacon, he would be called the Reverend Mister Bates. He'd looked forward to this for ten years. But now the doubts were back.

He stopped by Quince's room. "I haven't changed much," he said. "I still—"

Quince waved a hand in front of his face. "Yeah, yeah, yeah, you're quite the sinner."

"Pite wanted me to quit."

"I told you: Pite's an idiot."

"You said you were going to be kinder."

"*You* be kinder. Do it to atone for all those sins you're committing."

"You really think I should go ahead?"

"Only if you want to."

"I want to."

"Then go."

Just before eleven the night of Friday, March 29, Dan lay on his bed thinking about the next day's ceremony. The weather had flip-flopped again, from temperatures in the tens and twenties early in the week, when the seminarians froze on their walks to the lake, to record highs in the seventies. The low that night would be in the mid-fifties, and Saturday would be warm, too. They would roast in their ordination vestments.

Celibacy. The big vow. He'd made his decision, of course, long ago. He'd had lapses but, through confession—now called the sacrament of reconciliation—those failures had been forgiven. Thank God Quince had been there for him.

If a God had anything to do with it. Dan had shared his doubts with Pat, who recommended several books. Doubts were normal, the books said. Ignore them and they would go away. Dan ignored them, but they kept coming back.

That was normal too, Pat insisted.

Dan heard a soft tapping on his door. Odd at that time of night.

Monsignor Terry was standing in the hall. Oh, jeez. They had canceled his ordination. Pat had warned him to stop lipping off at Oter. But he had! He hadn't even asked questions. No, maybe one of his parents was sick. That would be worse. If—

"So, Mister Bates, I'm sorry to interrupt you at this hour, but you have a phone call. An emergency, I'm afraid. You will have to come downstairs to my office to receive it." Terry hurried down the dim hallway.

Dan followed. Oh God. His parents.

"It's a woman," Terry said on the stairs.

Oh shit, his dad. Sick? Or an accident? "Is it my mom?" As if Terry could tell.

"I don't think so. She sounds ... *young.*"

Jessica? Please, no.

Terry paused at a landing. "At first, I suspected a prank. We get those, you know, so I hung up. But she called back. So. I told her I'd take you a message, but she insisted she had to speak to you personally. Then she demanded I not hang up again as she was calling long distance."

Jessica. It had to be. Dan followed the rector into his office. In a corner opposite the desk, three red vigil lights flickered before a shrine of the Sacred Heart. Terry stood, arms folded, near the door.

Damn it, he'd told her not to call him there, no matter how upset she got when a child died. "Hello?"

"Danny?"

"Jess?" He said it softly. Maybe Terry wouldn't hear.

"I'm sorry, I had to talk to you. I got a letter from Pat today. He said you're taking your celibacy vows March 30. Is that true?"

"Yes, but—"

"That's tomorrow."

"Yes, tomorrow, but—"

"Don't do it, Danny."

"Huh?"

"Talk to me first."

Dan caught Terry's quizzical look. "I'm sorry. I don't know what to say."

"Say you won't do it."

"I can't."

"Is someone there?"

"Yes."

"Oh."

"I have to go," he said.

"*Wait*!" Her voice held the same desperation it had last summer after Joey died. "Don't take that vow. Please. I know you can't talk now, but I love you. I've tried to ignore it. I've gone out with other guys like Pat said, but I keep thinking about you and the times we've been together. And I think you love me too. Please wait … wait till after we talk one more time."

Dan was having trouble breathing. Was he holding his breath? "I have to go," he said again, so softly that she might not have heard him.

"Danny, wait! Talk to me first. Not on the phone, at the lake, in that park across the street."

"I can't—"

"I'm in Milwaukee. I'll be there by midnight."

Terry was walking toward him.

"I can't," he said again, but she had hung up.

"Trouble, Mr. Bates?"

"A friend. He has a problem."

"Oh? It sounded like a woman."

"Oh … yeah, it was. Calling about this friend—she's a friend too … *his* friend, I mean. She's trying to decide what to do. Wanted my advice, but I couldn't think of anything."

A lie. Sorry.

Terry fiddled with a glass paperweight on his desk. "That's unfortunate. So." He looked up. "Perhaps she will think of something, Mr. Bates. We'll say a prayer and hopefully things will go all right. I'll let you out."

Dan edged toward the door. "Yes. Thank you. Umm, I wonder if I could ask a special privilege, Father. I know this is out of the ordinary, but I'm really worried about her … about our friend. I'm going to have trouble getting to sleep. Could I perhaps take a walk through the woods and pray for—"

"Oh, no, no, no, Mr. Bates. I think not. However, if you wish, you may visit the chapel and pray as long as you like there."

On the way back to his room, Dan stopped at Pat's door. He tapped three fast, three slow, and three fast: SOS in Morse code, the signal they had agreed on if either of them needed to talk. They had never used it.

Pat peered out. "What is it?"

"Jessie called."

"Here? Oh, for Pete's sake."

"She wants to meet at the lake. At midnight."

"With us?"

"With me."

Pat stared into the dark hallway. "If you get caught, your butt is fried. You know that, don't you. They'll *never* let you take orders. Think about it: That's exactly what she wants. She's probably setting you up. I'll bet she even warned them to watch you."

"C'mon, Pat, it's Jessie. I can't let her sit there alone all night."

"Look, even if you get out without anyone seeing you—and that's a big *if*—the doors are locked. You can't get back in."

"I, um, thought maybe you'd open one when I come back."

"No."

"It's your sister."

"No."

Dan glanced down the dark hall. "Then I'll wait till seven when the doors open."

Pat rested his head against the door. "If you go, she's got you."

"I have to talk to her. I owe her that."

"*Not tonight, you don't!*" Pat yelled, and Dan jumped.

Meer Mohrical walked by on his way to the bathroom. "Jeez, Pat, keep it down, okay?"

Pat lowered his voice. "Do you have any idea how simple your life would be if you hadn't met her? Forget tonight. She'll cuss you out, maybe hate you for a while, but she's done that to both of us. Take your vows. Jess will get on with her life. That's what you want, isn't it?"

Of course it was, wasn't it? "I think so."

"Shit, you think so."

"I'm not changing my mind—about the priesthood, I mean. But if I don't talk to her, whenever I go to that park I'll see her there, waiting all night for a friend who never showed up."

Pat rubbed his forehead back and forth against the edge of the door. "You're going to blow it. The whole thing. She's my sister. I love her. But she's wrong to ask you to do this."

Dan turned toward his room. "I'll see you in the morning."

"Wait!" Pat caught Dan's shoulder. "Don't make it worse, whatever you do. Decide before you go what you want to say, say it, then send her home. Don't argue with her. I don't know what you'll do the rest of the night, take a walk and say some rosaries or something, but I'll come down first thing in the morning, before anybody else gets there. We'll walk back together so no one'll know you were gone."

Dan stopped at his room to grab his coat, then sneaked down the stairs. The creaks and groans of the old wood echoed like gunfire. He prayed he wouldn't run into a priest. Would that work—asking God for help to disobey a rule?

He made his way though the basement of the northeast wing, pushed open the door and ran for the closest tree. Behind him, the door locked. He darted from tree to tree along the front drive, ducking behind one when a car turned off Shoreline Road and Oter drove by in his black Impala.

Jessica's Valiant sat on the far side of Shoreline Road, a few feet from the park sign under a streetlight. In its dim light, Dan could see the rust eating away at her car. What was he going to say? He should go back, but he was locked out. He ran across the road, opened the passenger door and climbed in.

Jessica reached for his hand. "I had what I wanted to say all figured out when I called. Now I can't think of it."

"There's no rush. I can't get back in till morning."

"Pat'll let you in, won't he?"

"He could get expelled."

"Couldn't *you?*"

"Yes."

Silence. Atop the black water several miles out, the lights of a freighter drifted south. Too bad he wasn't on it.

She slid across the seat and put her head against his chest.

Dan gently fingered her hair. Damn. He'd mishandled their friendship from the start, at least from prom night when he kissed her. Instead of acting like a seminarian, he'd let her think there was a chance he'd quit.

"Kiss me, Danny."

He was going to say no, he really was, but when she turned toward him her face was so close. For a moment their lips barely brushed, then they pressed harder and he brought his fingers to her cheek. She opened her lips and worked her tongue gently against his teeth.

He pulled away.

"Your vow isn't till tomorrow."

"It's still a sin."

"I don't believe in sins. Besides, when people love each other it shouldn't be a sin."

"But—"

"Sins are evil. They hurt people. Even the god I *used* to believe in wouldn't send somebody to hell for making love when he's got his hands full with this stupid war. If your God gave us bodies, he must have expected us to enjoy them."

"He did. In marriage."

"Okay, let's get married."

"Jess ..."

A northbound car zipped past with its horn blaring.

"Assholes," she said. Again, she lay her head on his chest. "All these years I denied tomorrow would ever come. I had forever to talk you out of it. A thousand times I dreamed you'd quit. Now tomorrow you're supposed to take that vow to never marry, never make love. How can you do that?"

He didn't say anything. How could he explain it?

Her voice sharpened. "I told you before, you and Pat need to get out of there. Out of that prison you've hidden yourselves in."

"It's not like you think, Jess."

"Oh, bullshit! Let me out of here!" She flung open her door and ran toward the lake.

Dan was out his door almost as fast. "Wait! It's too dark. Don't run!"

She raced across the park lawn, slid down the bluff and fell into the brittle brown grass near the bottom. She rolled toward the beach and stopped face up.

He hurried down to her. "Are you all right?"

She propped herself up on an elbow. "I'm fine. But jeez, you guys are so wrong. What you believe about sex makes you miserable when you should be happy. Look at us! Friends all these years. What we did in my room last summer seemed natural and right because I loved you and trusted you and knew you wouldn't do anything to hurt me. But you say it was a sin. It *couldn't* be."

He didn't answer. It hadn't seemed a sin to him either.

She took his hand and climbed a few feet up the bluff. They sat with their arms around each other and watched the white tops of waves curling out of the black lake. The waves rolled across the stones along the beach and brought night smells of water and weeds and fish. A few stars created a ceiling above them, and to their right the Southport lighthouse flashed its beacon toward the lake.

"This is all I wanted," she said, "to be with you a little while."

He nodded into her hair, then leaned back against the cold, dead grass of the bluff and pulled her down next to him. They kissed soft and long, then hard.

She pulled away. "Can you go a lifetime without that?"

"I don't know."

"They want your answer tomorrow."

"I know."

She laid her head on his chest. "I hope you tell 'em *no*."

"There are lots of guys out there. You'll find somebody."

"Be serious," she said.

He caressed her hair. "I am." How could he not be? This was the last time he'd be with her like this, and he had no idea how he'd handle his jealousy toward the guy who got her. "I'll be happy for you, and Pat and I will visit you and your family and—" Dan's voice cracked and he reached for her and pulled her against him and buried his face in her hair.

Jessica broke away. "Wait here." She clambered up the bluff and disappeared. Minutes later she was back, smoothing three brown woolen blankets over the grass. "From my winter emergency kit. They're chilly now but they'll feel warm after we wrap up in 'em."

They lay against the bluff with their feet propped on a mound of sand at the edge of the beach. They kissed, sliding fingertips down each other's cheeks and necks, then across his chest and her breasts.

Dan tried to etch every touch into his mind. This was, the Church insisted, a mockery of the marriage Jessica would enter someday and a betrayal of the vow he'd take later that morning. But he kept kissing her, running his hands over her and straining against the full length of her. Churchmen had ranted against this for centuries, but tonight it didn't matter. All that mattered was getting as close to her as he could. Loving her like this couldn't be a sin. She was wrong that there was no God, but God was too busy to worry about people holding each other on a Lake Michigan beach.

God is love. The Church taught that. It meant their love for each other was a reflection of God's love for them. *Watch it. You're close to blasphemy.* No. He wasn't mocking anything or hurting anyone or defying God. He and Jessica were here to celebrate the love they had for each other, to hold each other one last time.

Dan trailed his hand from her forehead across her cheek to her chin and neck and down to her breasts, caressing them through her blouse until she said to unbutton it. He'd never done that. Maybe if he hadn't spent all his teen years in a seminary he'd know what to do.

She rolled across him. "Unhook my bra."

"I don't know how," he said, his face as hot as the first time he heard her say *breasts*. Was he embarrassed at the thought, or at having to admit he didn't know what to do?

She sat up and reached back for a half second, then lay down and put his hand on her left breast, smooth and soft and cool from the night air. He ran his fingertips over it, tracing its shape and exploring its nipple. His philosophy and theology texts warned that this would fill him with lust; instead he was filled with wonder at her softness compared to the bronze nude he felt one day in a Chicago park after he made sure no one was watching.

Her hand found his penis and made it harder. She didn't need help unbuckling his belt and unzipping his trousers and sliding them and his briefs over his hips so she could grasp him.

"Oh God, Jess." But he shouldn't mention God and he was sorry for that but he wasn't sorry for this and he couldn't stop now because his whole body wanted to push as tight as it could into her and then he felt his release into her hand and he arched and pushed and buried himself against her, shaking as he came. "Oh, Jess."

She kept stroking him, gently now, and he stayed hard. She sat over him, then slipped down onto him. It was so easy. How could something this wonderful be a sin? Jessica rose and fell, rose and fell, and maybe this could go on forever.

She moved faster and moaned and shook and cried out. He was hurting her, but maybe not because she kept moving on him and everything started again from deep inside and he tried to push her away but it was too late and he came inside her.

"I tried to pull out. Oh God, if you get pregnant … oh jeez, I didn't even think—"

Jessica put a fingertip to his lips. "Shhhh. Don't worry, I'm a nurse. I know what to do. It's okay." She kissed him. "It's okay."

He let himself relax. There'd be no unexplainable baby from this night, but the Church would never accept him as a priest if they found out birth control had kept him free to become one.

Jessica rolled to his side and flipped the blankets to cover them both. They cuddled and dozed, then watched the eastern sky turn pink over the lake with the light of a new day.

"Danny, how could this be a sin?"

He squeezed her. "I don't know, but the Church says ... oh, you know what it says. I don't believe it's a sin either, but we'd better get dressed. Joggers'll be coming through any minute."

By the time they heard footsteps on the paths above them, Dan and Jessica had fastened each other's clothes, straightened their hair with a comb from her purse, and started a breakfast of candy bars, potato chips, and Coke that he found in the back seat of her car.

She giggled. "More stuff from my emergency kit."

"You'll have to restock it," he said.

They shaded their eyes from a giant orange sun that reflected off the waves and created early morning shadows in the bushes and trees along the bluff.

"I'll always remember this," she said.

He kissed the back of her neck. "Me, too." Even if he didn't believe it.

They lay in each other's arms against the bluff and watched the park come alive with runners and walkers taking advantage of the warm, early spring air.

Jessica stroked his cheek. "Leave the seminary, so we can be together all the time like this."

Dan had never wanted so much to say yes. And how could he say no after they made love?

To go daily from men to God, to offer Him their homage and petitions; To return from God to men, to bring them His pardon and His hope.

God had called him to be a priest. That hadn't changed. He searched for words that would spare her, then realized his silence was torturing her more than his answer could.

"I can't." He watched the rhythm of the water. "If there was a way I could, God knows I would. But I truly believe he wants me to be a priest."

She rolled out of the blankets onto her back and stared at the sky.

Dan shivered, not from the air. He should have listened to Pat.

Jessica picked herself up, grabbed the blankets and folded them one by one. Without a word she tucked them under her arm, scurried up the bluff and ran to her car. Dan chased her, but slowed to a walk halfway through the park when she opened her door and bent to get in. Then she straightened and glared across the lawn at him.

He deserved it. He had done this all wrong. "I'm so sorry," he said, too softly for her to hear.

She ducked into the car and started the engine.

"Wait! I'm sorry!" He shouted this time. He sprinted toward the car, but she churned gravel onto the grass and sped north.

She was gone.

Dan retreated down the bluff to the beach. He slipped into his jacket and sat next to the bushes where he and Jessica had cuddled in the blankets. They'd made love, just once, and what happened here last night would never happen again. He rolled onto his stomach and stared at the dead grass. He had hurt her so badly. His Jessica. Oh, God, how he had hurt her. He should never have come here.

Chapter 21

"Danny!" Pat was making his way down the bluff. "Are you all right? Jeez, I saw Jessie take off like a bat out of hell. I was afraid you went with her."

"I probably should have."

Pat stopped just short of the sand. "She drove off like a maniac. What the hell did you say to her?"

"That I still want to be a priest."

"She'd have known that anyway if you had stayed in." Pat stepped closer. "Your eyes are red. I should have brought dark glasses."

"I didn't get any sleep." Dan zipped his jacket to the top. "I need to see Quince."

"*Quince?*" Pat turned away, then back, frowning. "Quince? … Oh, for God's sake, you didn't. You couldn't have, not with Jessie. Not last night. *Damn* it! No wonder she …" Pat shoved Dan's shoulder. "How could you? With Jessie! Damn you!" He walked across the sand toward the lake, turned, came back. "You're supposed to vow celibacy tomorrow. *Today!* How the hell can—"

"Pat, listen. It's not … it's not like they told us. It's beautiful, two people, the closest they can be together." Dan studied Pat's face. "I wish I could make you understand."

"I'd like to understand *you*. Shit." Again he turned away. "All right, find Quince. Go to confession. You can't be ordained in sin. Shit." Pat pointed. "You shouldn't be ordained at all."

"I'm not in a state of sin. At least not for that."

"Then you're in a state of denial. Jeez, how could you be so stupid! You're right: You have to see Quince. And I have to find Jess to see if she's all right." He started toward the bluff. "Damn you anyway!"

"Father, I think I need to go to confession," Dan said from the hall outside Quince's room.

Quince grinned. "You *think*?" He pulled open his door.

"I'm not sure where to start."

"Try the usual. Sit down."

Dan lifted the newspapers from the recliner and sat, leaning forward. "Bless me, Father, for I have sinned. My last confession was … let's see, to you the other day. Saturday."

"Yes."

"I'll start with a small one. I disobeyed the rule. I left the building last night."

"And?"

"And I"—how should he put this—"well, Jessie and I made love … all the way."

Quince blinked. "Okaaay." His voice had an edge to it, and he drew the word out so it sounded like a question.

"But it doesn't feel like we sinned, Father. I know what the Church says, but—"

"It doesn't *feel* like a sin?"

"No. I mean, it seemed like something we were *supposed* to do … this one time at least."

Quince just sat there. Finally, "So what about your priesthood?"

Dan leaned forward. "Oh, I still want to be a priest, yes." Quince was frowning. "I guess that sounds pretty strange … I mean, after last night and everything, but I do. I really do."

"Your love for Jessica—your *making* love—complicates that."

"I know. But what am I going to do? I'm supposed to take orders in a few hours, make my vow of celibacy. I know I can't if I'm in sin, and the Church says I am, but I don't feel like it, at least not from that—not from making love."

Quince shuffled to the window. He reached toward his desk for a pipe and stuck it between his teeth without lighting it. "Aside from what you feel, what do you *believe*? Do you really believe you're free of sin?"

"About the love-making part, yes, but—"

"As you know, some theologians insist we can't sin without the intention of sinning, without willfully turning our backs on God. Did you do that?"

"No."

Quince faced him. "Well, only you know what you had in mind, and I'm not going to judge you. God will, though, so you really need to examine your conscience. Carefully. Be sure you're being honest with yourself. More importantly, with Him." He sat down and wiped his forehead. "Sorry if I'm less than coherent, but this is a bit different from what we usually talk about. If your desire to be with Jessica—whether or not you make love again—is going to interfere with your life as a priest, I think you should give it up." He walked again to the window. "It's too bad this comes the morning you're supposed to take your vow. It leaves you very little time to decide, and I can't help you with it. No one can. But I'll grant you absolution for your sins, whatever they may be, and—"

"I upset her a lot when I told her I still want to be a priest."

"I suppose you did, and that's unfortunate, but—"

"That was a sin, Father. In my eyes, that *is* my sin—the biggest I've ever committed. I didn't turn against God exactly, but I really hurt *her*, and what we do unto others we do unto Him."

Quince had raised a hand. "Still, that's not a mort—"

"You've always said you'll respect my conscience, Father. And now it says I sinned. I let Jessie think I'd leave this place someday. Oh, I kept telling her I wouldn't, but I liked being with her, and I saw her whenever I could. That kept giving her hope. It's like I tricked her, you know? And that, I believe, is a mortal sin. 'Cause Jess got really hurt."

Quince stared out his front window. "All right. As I said, I'll grant you absolution for your sins, whatever they may be. But you're going to have to pray, Dan. Pray really hard. You have only a couple of hours. Which path are you going to take, the one you've followed all these years toward the priesthood, or the one you traveled last night with Jessica? If you decide to switch, it's no sin to leave, even now. But keep in mind: Solitary sex is one thing; it hurts no one and can be kept a secret. Sex with a woman is another matter; it's filled with the possibility of scandal and a ruined priesthood."

Dan nodded.

"For your penance, isolate yourself. Pray and meditate, by yourself, from now until the ceremony. You need to decide right now what you're going to do with your life. God bless you, and I've never meant that more than I do this morning."

Dan spent the next two hours in his room, kneeling on the bare floor at the side of his bed.

Last night was like a dream. But the sand in his shoes was real.

Can you go a lifetime without this?

After last night, how could he say yes? But he had to. He'd been at Resurrection for eleven years preparing to become a priest. He couldn't give up now.

He checked his watch, stood, slipped into his cassock and pulled a white surplice over his head. He lifted his biretta from its holder and walked alone to the chapel door, where he edged into the procession line with his classmates. Pat was staring at him, and Dan nodded, but Pat didn't respond.

Inside, the archbishop of Milwaukee accepted the seminarians' vows of celibacy and laid his hands on the heads of the new subdeacons.

Dan became the Reverend Mister Daniel John Bates II.

A couple of months later, Resurrection closed for the summer. Dan returned to Willow Run for a few days before the bishop of Madison would ordain him a deacon, the final step before the priesthood.

He dialed Jessica's number. She hadn't written and Pat refused to talk. Dan had no idea what he'd say to her, but he had to make sure she was all right.

An operator said the number he dialed was disconnected.

Changed?

No. Disconnected.

Was there another listing for Jessica Fernettan?

Not in the 608 area code.

Dan borrowed his dad's car and drove to Jessica's apartment. A young woman he had never seen before told him the apartment became available in April and she moved in May 1. She didn't know the previous tenant.

Dan raced back to Willow Run. After his parents went to bed, he sat at their desk and called Pat. "I hope I'm not calling too late, but I'm trying to find Jessie."

"She moved."

"I know. Where'd she go?"

"I can't tell you."

Dan stood and braced his back against the wall. "You mean she disappeared?"

"I mean she moved."

"Didn't she tell you where?"

"Yes ... but she said not to tell you."

Dan let himself slide down the wall. She wouldn't have—couldn't have—said that. But Pat wouldn't lie. Dan closed his eyes.

Pat spoke softly. "Look, I told her you two need to talk, but she told me to shut up, that if I said one more word about you she'd move again and not tell me where she went. So I shut up."

"Jeez, she must hate me."

Neither said anything for several seconds.

"Pat, I'd like to see you. I could drive down or take the bu—"

"No. My parents would rather not see you."

"Your par ... you mean they know about—"

"I guess."

"Jess must've told 'em."

"Well, *I* didn't."

"Maybe we could meet downtown."

Another pause. "I don't think so."

Dan forced himself to keep breathing. "Are you mad at me too?"

"What are you, a total idiot? Of course I'm mad at you. And at Jess. But mostly I'm mad at me. I should have stopped that asinine relationship of yours before it ever started. If I hadn't taken you home with me ... look, I'm sorry to put you off, but I don't feel like getting together."

"If you change your mind will you call me?"

"I have no idea what you're looking for. Worse, I'm not sure you do either."

"Pat, I'll try to—"

"I don't know what to say anymore. I have to go. Bye."

Dan listened to the dial tone for several seconds. He knelt next to the desk and slid the phone across the top to its corner, then rolled onto the floor and curled up with his back to the wall.

Oh God, he shouldn't have gone to the park that night.

A few days later, Dan and his Madison-area classmates knelt before the altar in St. Raphael's Cathedral where Bishop Rufus J. Elmendorf ordained them deacons of the Catholic Church. They were one year short of the priesthood.

"I can certainly use you," Father Straud said on Dan's first day assigned to Sacred Heart in Willow Run. "You're from here, so I get you first, *Reverend* Bates. How does that sound?"

"Great."

"There's plenty to do. But looking to the future, I'd like you to preach the homilies at some Masses this summer, maybe starting the Second Sunday after Pentecost, June 16. Pick a good topic. It's a chance to enlighten the people of your home parish as to what you've learned these past eleven years."

At Mass on June 16, Dan grasped the lectern. "Let us recall the words of this morning's lesson, John's first letter, chapter three." He forced his eyes across the congregation but didn't focus. That way, he wouldn't recognize anyone. The fewer distractions, the better. "'Now how can divine love abide in a man who has enough of this world's livelihood and yet closes his heart to his brother when he observes him in need?'"

There was a slight murmur from the congregation. "Loving God and loving each other is the foundation of the new testament," Dan continued. "There are many ways to show this love: through donations to the poor, visits to the sick, compassion for the troubled.

"Within charity, however, there is also a need for justice. As John said, if we have enough, we must share. But not only as individuals. Corporations have that same responsibility. They are required by law to pay a minimum wage, but they are required by morality, by God's law of love, to pay a *living* wage so their workers and their families will not suffer need and have to depend on charity for the basics of life."

After Mass, Dan greeted the people outside the church.

"We can't wait till next year when you say your first Mass," one said.

"We wish you could be assigned here after you're ordained," another said.

Finally, Luke Logan, owner of a machine shop on the west side, stopped after the others left. "Interesting sermon, Daniel, but I doubt John had employers in mind when he wrote that piece. Our company pays based on what people produce, and we have a right to a fair profit."

"Fair, yes," Dan said. "My point—"

"I got your point, Daniel, but I'm a bottom-line guy. The bottom line's gotta be there."

"Of course it does, Mr. Logan … um, Luke. But, you know, we do have things in common. I'm a bottom-line guy, too. And the real bottom line is: We're all going to die sooner or later. How we're judged—the *eternal* bottom line—will be based on how we've treated other people, not on the deposits we put into our banks."

Logan's face turned red. He stared at Dan, turned and walked to his car.

The next day, Father Straud called Dan into his office. "Um, Daniel, Father Korris in New Glarus needs some help. Probably will take you the rest of the summer, so we'll have to skip those other homilies. I must tell you, I got a bit of feedback yesterday. Several in the congregation felt you sounded awfully liberal.

Truth is, I'm sorry to say, I was disappointed. I had expected more religious content than social activism."

Dan knew his face was red. "So I ticked off Luke Logan and now you're getting rid of me? I thought you'd back me, Father. If we priests don't apply the principles of faith to daily life, who will?"

Straud's face turned red too. "Interpretations of those principles vary greatly, Daniel. I believe it will be helpful for you to labor a little longer in the Lord's vineyard, as it were, and gain some experience before deciding how we can best apply our faith to other people's problems."

No one answered the phone at Pat's, so Dan couldn't tell him how he got banished from his home parish after preaching his first homily. The worst part was telling his parents, but his dad supported him.

"That Father Straud sways whichever way the wind is blowing. It doesn't even have to be a wind: A breeze will do. Money did this, Danny. Logan is big money. Hell, he mostly built the school himself. Now Straud'll do whatever Logan wants. You were right what you said in your sermon, and I'm proud of you. You're better away from Straud. Don't be sorry."

Dan wasn't. Parts of God's message weren't popular, but people needed to hear them.

On his way to New Glarus, Dan stopped to see Agnes Reuter. After he told her what happened, she laughed.

"Oh, I'll bet Logan was pissed, Daniel." She glanced away. "Or shouldn't I say *pissed*? Anyway, he hates to be criticized. Did you know I worked for him?"

Dan shook his head.

"Several years ago. For about two months. That was all I could take of Luke Logan. Ha! We called him "Loot" because he wanted all the money for himself. He paid us as little as possible, of course." She laughed again. "Some of us called him "Loot" to his face. With his hearing problem, he couldn't tell the difference: Luke or Loot. But he heard you say what you said. Ooh, I wish I had been there … well, almost."

"I should have invited you."

"No. I wouldn't want to turn you down, and I would have. I don't believe the things you do. But I love it when you come by."

"I'm not sure when I'll be back in Willow Run," he said, "but I'll stop when I am."

Father Alexander Korris didn't let Dan preach either, but had him assist at Mass, visit the sick, and take communion to shut-ins. The poverty some people lived in shocked him. One family of eight was crowded into four rooms on the second floor of a gray-sided house, and the kids vied for his attention.

"Father, look at what I drew today."

"Father, I can draw too! Look at mine!"

"Father, look at our baby sister. Sunday we're getting her baptized. Are you going to pour the water on her head?"

Other children were worse off. Their parents—often single, usually exhausted—sat around the house expecting the older ones—seven or eight years old—to feed and clean the younger ones. Sometimes Dan pretended to have a cold so he could hold a handkerchief between his nose and the foul apartment air.

He marveled at sick people who bravely accepted their pain, and learned how eager most people were to talk. Often he had no idea what to say, but his visits seemed to comfort them. It was, of course, his connection to the Church that provided the comfort, and that was as it should be. *Lord, make me an instrument of your peace.*

He loved this work even more than he had dreamed.

But many nights, when everything was still, he lay awake. Was Jessica all right? Where was she? Had she forgiven him?

And Pat. Pat still hadn't called back.

Chapter 22

▼

Near the end of July, Dan was working on Sunday's bulletin in the parish office when he heard Father Korris bring in the day's mail. There was a long delay, then the pastor stomped up the stairs to the office door.

"Well, it's out," Korris said. "That encyclical we've been waiting for." He handed Dan a large envelope. "Read it at your own risk."

Dan scanned the first page. Pope Paul VI had titled his letter *Humanae Vitae*: "Of Human Life." In it, he insisted that every marriage act had to remain open to the transmission of life. The Church, under this pope, at least, would not end its condemnation of birth control.

Korris paced the floor near his desk, whacking flies with a plastic swatter. "It's bullshit," he said. "Utter bullshit. Paul's driving thousands from the Church. Maybe millions." *Swat.* "He could have changed it. It's so damned obvious God's will is open to debate on this. Hell, the majority of Paul's own commission said it's not a sin."

"Yes," Dan said, "so how could he—"

"Control. Paul wants control. Well, damn it, he can't have it. He's going to lose people with this, even priests and bishops."

Dan stared. Korris's face was red, and veins stuck out around both temples. Dan had seldom seen a priest that angry. "You?" he asked softly.

Swat. "Not yet. But, boy, it's hard to represent a pope who covers his cruelty under the cloak of God's law."

Dan studied the last page of the letter. "I don't know if it's cruelty. Ignorance perhaps—"

"No. Paul has the information, probably more than we do. But he wants power." *Swat.* "Damn. He's forcing gut-wrenching conflict on good Catholics who need to control the size of their families. We can't expect 'em to stay celibate like us."

Us? "Um, no ... that's true. We can't." His night with Jessica flooded Dan's mind. He was blushing. To hide it, he leaned over the desk for ... what? Something. *Anything.* Ah, a pen. He straightened, tapped the encyclical with its tip, and said, "So, does this mean they're going to make us teach birth control's a sin?"

Korris held the swatter behind him. "Rome will insist on it. But millions of Catholics ignore the ban now, and so do a lot of priests." He picked up the encyclical. "Does Paul really think women will stop using the Pill because of *this*? Or because we scold 'em from the pulpit?" His fingers tapped the top page. "I'm sorry for you young guys. Things looked great with John's Council making changes and letting laymen have a say in their Church. But now Rome's pulling back."

Dan searched for hope. "But a lot of bishops wanted Paul to drop the ban."

"And he'll tell 'em: Obey or go." Korris lowered his head. "Straud's gonna love this, he's so goddamned conservative. We were classmates, did you know that? Ha! When I heard he wanted to get rid of you, I figured you must have something going, so I grabbed you."

Dan glanced up, and Korris laughed.

"Yeah, Bates, we priests play our little games too. Guess that's part of your education this summer, eh?"

That night, in his room down the hall from the office, Dan reread the encyclical. Good thing it hadn't come out before he and Jess made love. No, what was he thinking? He didn't agree with what the pope said, and she didn't care. It wouldn't have mattered.

He wanted to talk to Pat, but would Pat talk to him? It was almost ten; he should be in. Dan dialed a few numbers, then stopped. Pat hadn't called. He must still be angry. But what was the worst that could happen? He might yell. Or hang up. It would hurt, but not as bad as the silence. Dan dialed again.

"Fernettan's. This is Pat."

"Hi. This is Dan."

"Oh." A pause. "I suppose you saw it."

"The encyclical? Yes. I ... well, I kinda thought maybe we could talk about it."

"There isn't much to say. It's stupid."

"I know." Dan paused, unsure of what to say. "It's great to hear your voice again." *Ask him!* "I wonder … Well, I still wish we could get together."

Pat didn't say anything for several seconds. "I don't know."

But he hadn't hung up! "We'll be back at Resurrection in a couple of months. We should talk before then, don't you think?"

"I don't know. Let me think about it."

"Sure." *Ask him about Jessica! No. Too soon.* "Um, how about I call you next week?"

"No," Pat said. "I'll call you."

"Okay." *But would he?*

Another pause, then, "Danny?"

"Yeah?"

"I talked to her yesterday. She's fine."

"I was wondering. Thanks."

Pat called the next day. "Okay, you're right. We'll be together at the sem anyway. Might as well talk. Do you want to come here, or shall I drive there?"

Thank God! It was over. Or it would be, after they got together. "I could use a city fix," Dan said. "How about the art museum?"

"Monday?"

"At eleven. I'll buy lunch."

"We'll eat along the lakefront," Pat said.

Dan worked to keep his voice calm. "Can't wait. See you there." Whatever Pat ate, whatever it cost, he'd be glad to buy.

In September, after dinner on their first night back at Resurrection, Dan, Pat, Meer and Darrin sat around their refectory table discussing the new seminary catalog that came out that day.

"'We have revised our course of study,'" Darrin read, "'to conform with the Decree on Priestly Formation of the Second Vatican Council and in recognition of the enlarged scope of the Church's mission in this world.'" He paused and read silently for a few seconds. "Okay, then it says they're going to emphasize, and I quote, 'a mix of academic studies with supervised field work in several areas of ministry.'"

"A mix?" Meer said. "What kind of mix?"

"I haven't gotten that far," Darrin said. "But get this: They're also setting up a graduate program for, and I'm quoting again, 'a master's degree in theology, a ThM,' unquote. And it's starting—get this—with the 1969-1970 school year."

"*Next* year," Meer said. "After we're gone. What does that say about the training they're giving *us*?"

Dan put his hands behind his head. "Well, we could go back to first theology. Start over. Then they'd have to give *us* master's degrees."

Pat laughed. "They'd spit."

"Say what you mean," Meer said. "They'd *shit!*"

"Forget it," Darrin said. "Let's get ordained and work the council's changes into our parishes."

Meer sat back and crossed his legs. "Question is, with the stuff they're letting lay people do, what's left for us? Have you thought about it? I mean, I can't keep books like a business school graduate, and I sure can't counsel as good as a shrink."

"Don't put us down," Pat said. "We have a lot to offer. Our commitment to people, for one thing. The Church is stressing pastoral ministry these days, and—"

"'Stressing' is right," Meer said. "But not the way you mean."

Pat laughed. "You can take it both ways, I guess. But listen: We're going to be the best they have at bringing God into people's lives. And that's what we're here for, isn't it? That's our commitment. Really, what's more important than that?"

Dan leaned forward. "Problem is, the council also stressed the individual conscience, and you can take that both ways too. How do we minister, so to speak, when people disagree with us, or when we disagree with each other, which priests already do? Our parishioners are going to wonder whose side God is on."

"It's already happening," Meer said, "people picking and choosing what they're willing to believe."

Darren grinned. "The ol' cafeteria approach to religion."

"Most of the changes are good," Dan said. "But people need time to adjust. I think most of 'em like the priest facing them, reciting the Mass together in English. And hey, you heard it here first: Someday seminarians won't study Latin."

"You're nuts," Meer said.

Darren laughed. "Not in *our* lifetime."

Pat shook his head. "Latin is still the language of the Church. It has been for a thousand years. That hasn't changed."

"But," Dan said, "the emphasis now is on communication. Latin's dead. Or will be. Soon."

Pat folded his hands on the table. "Even dead, it's a beautiful language. The Church will keep it alive." He looked at Dan. "At least in her priests, if not in the liturgy."

"But why?" Meer asked. "No one understands it."

"True," Darrin said. "Remember when Rome ordered us to study philosophy and theology in Latin? They—"

"Now *there* was a great idea," Meer said. "They scared the crap out of everybody, then dropped it."

"They had to," Darrin said. "No one knew it."

"Not well enough to learn philosophy," Dan said. "Remember, the Church adopted Latin back when it was the people's language. Tradition is all that's keeping it alive."

Pat shook his head. "We'll see."

On New Year's morning, Dan answered the phone.

"Happy 1969!" Pat said.

"Yeah," Dan said. "The year we've been waiting for. It's finally here."

"Do you realize how different things will be a year from now? But, hey, mostly I called to ask you to pray for a special intention—something really important."

Dan's gut clutched. "It's Jessie, isn't it? What—"

"Jessie's fine, don't worry. But this is a long-term project, so don't stop praying, okay?"

"It would be a lot easier if I knew what for."

"I know," Pat said. "But all I can say is that it's really important. To both of us. Okay?"

"If you say so. But I wish … well, what did you do for Christmas?"

"I was the deacon at midnight Mass. I gave the homily."

"That's great," Dan said. "Straud never let me close to the lectern."

Pat laughed. "You'll get another chance. *This year*, somewhere. But hey, on a happier note, did you see the news? That picture the astronauts took of Earth rising over the moon?"

"Yeah, kind of like a God's-eye view."

"I was thinking," Pat said. "People in power should have to study that image before they can decide things that affect other people. I mean, we'd better learn to get along. We're all in this together."

"Actually," Dan said, "we're all *on* it together—that little bitty ball out there in deep space."

Pat laughed. "Out *here* in deep space, I suppose we should say. It's so different, seeing our planet from out there, that we can't even figure out how to talk about it. You know what? They should bring out a poster of it. Nail one to the office wall of every president, prime minister, and dictator in the world."

"And the pope," Dan said.
"And the pope. Good idea. Anyway, don't forget to pray like I asked."
"Yeah. What for again?"
"Nice try. Just say 'Pat's special intention.' I'll tell you more when I can."
"It's about her, isn't it? It—"
Pat spoke softly. "When I can, okay?"

Something special. That could be anything. But it was Jess. It had to be, even if Pat wouldn't say. *Because* Pat wouldn't say. But what about her? Getting married? Pregnant? *A baby?* Dan counted. Damn, it was nine months since they made love. Could … no, Jessie said she had taken care of that. She was a nurse. Good thing. He wouldn't have known what to do. His friends in Willow Run had talked about rubbers, how you could buy them at the drug store. Dan thought of old Mr. Tillis in the pharmacy, of the high school girls helping in front. Even with the fancy name—prophylactic—he couldn't imagine asking for one.

Something special. It had to be special for Pat to ask him. And yes, the way Pat said it, it had to be Jessie. But what? Thinking of coming back to the Church? Pat was excited, it was in his voice. That could be it. Yeah, Pat would ask him to pray for Jessie's return to faith.

And for that, he would pray very hard.

On Holy Saturday in early April, on a walk through the seminary woods, Pat bent to examine green shoots peeking through the carpet of brown leaves. "They're brave. It's still cold."

A lone robin hopped ahead of them, then flew off.

"Jessica sent me a letter about robins once," Dan started, then decided not to tell Pat how she asked why robins died during a cold snap after Christ claimed God protected the birds. "This week," he said instead, "I was reading Christ's passion and resurrection in the gospels. Ever notice how the stories don't match?"

"Match? How?"

"In the details. They're all different."

"They were meant to be," Pat said, "or we wouldn't have four. But they all tell us Jesus died and rose again. That's what matters."

"I don't know," Dan said. "Remember Oter telling us the limitations of the biblical authors? Well, God doesn't have limitations. He could have inspired the writers to report his life accurately. If the Bible is his word, and if we're going to quote it to prove our points about faith and morals, shouldn't the facts be straight?"

"A lot of those stories are metaphors. The details aren't important."

"I disagree. The resurrection is the key to Christianity. What happened that first Easter is vital to our faith, but the gospels contradict each other. When the women went to the tomb, was the stone rolled back before they got there, or after? Did they find angels or men, one or two of them, sitting or standing, inside or outside? This is all pretty basic stuff. Did the women tell people what they saw or not? Did Jesus appear first in Jerusalem or in Galilee? The gospels claim all of these. They can't all be true."

"The resurrection is true," Pat said.

"But how can we convince others? If one historian said Lincoln gave his Gettysburg address at the train depot, another claimed he spoke at the battlefield, and a third insisted it was at the White House, wouldn't you wonder if Lincoln actually made that speech?"

"Not if the basic story was there. The speech itself is the important thing."

At the creek, they turned back toward the seminary. "Well, the more I study it," Dan said, "the more I wonder. About the Bible, I mean. In John, um … thirteen, I think, Simon Peter asks, 'Lord, where are you going?' Then, three chapters later, John says Jesus scolded the disciples because none of them had asked where he was going. Who had the short memory, John or Jesus?"

"You're hung up on minutiae," Pat said. "You have to concentrate on the basic message: the mystery of Jesus coming to Earth, dying for us and rising again, giving us his commandment to love one another."

Dan decided to shut up. Pat might think he doubted too much to be ordained. But he kept finding contradictions. It worried him.

"If you ask for anything in my name," Jesus said, "I will do it." "Everything you ask and pray for, believe that you have it already, and it will be yours." "Ask and it will be given to you," he said. "For the one who asks always receives."

It wasn't true. Jesus's words were clear, but the profs always qualified them.

"Only if what we are asking for is consistent with God's will," Herkimer said. But Jesus didn't say that, and if he meant it what was his point? There was no sense in asking God to do what he planned to do anyway.

"Only if we are not selfish in what we ask for," Oter said. Well, you might call people selfish for requesting their own good health, but parents praying for their children? Jessica had told stories about parents sobbing in the hospital chapel while their children had surgery.

For the one who asks always receives. When their child survives, parents say, "Thank God," as though he were responsible for the cure but not for the illness.

Or, if their child dies, they say, "God's will be done," admitting that God wanted their child to die.

For the one who asks always receives. Jesus didn't include a qualifier.

In class and during meals, Dan watched his classmates search for the intellectual certainty they'd been taught the Church brings to daily life. But, between their arrival at Resurrection in 1957 and their planned ordination in 1969, the second Vatican Council had changed Church life forever. There was little certainty now.

In the fifties, pastors—the shepherds—ruled their parishes. The parishioners—the flock—carried out the pastors' wishes. Then, in the sixties, bishops ordered pastors to set up parish councils to share decision making. Some parishes, Dan heard, hired administrators who told their priests what to do.

He and his classmates would have to carve out their ministries with the role of priests less defined. They would offer Mass and the sacraments, but then what? No one knew.

Dan had seen some of the changes during his summer in New Glarus. Father Korris and the parish council had argued about issues, though without the personal attacks Dan heard about in other parishes. But sometimes the council voted against Korris on issues he felt strongly about. They had him order conservative textbooks for the parish school. It was an example of a pastor not calling the parish shots anymore.

And once the new priests left Resurrection, they would no longer have the support they provided each other for twelve years. They would start new lives in parish rectories, subject not to the rules of the seminary, but to those of the pastors they were assigned to.

The night before their ordination, Dan and his classmates laughed and talked and drank in Monsignor Terry's living room. Dan stood in the corner near Terry's desk, watching a few of the guys bouncing their knees. Was it eagerness to start new lives, or anxiety about what they were getting into? For twelve years, Resurrection Seminary protected them from the world; tomorrow it would toss them into it. They'd step out for the first time carrying Christ's message to the people of their new parishes.

It seemed more than a bit arrogant.

Darrin waved from across the room, got Dan's attention, and pointed to an empty chair. Dan shook his head. He preferred to stand and watch his classmates' faces on this last night they'd be together as seminarians. By this time tomorrow they'd be priests; then, after a week's vacation, they'd move to their first assignments under pastors they might not know and might not like. Where would the bishop send him? To an Alexander Korris, who welcomed change? Or to a Popeye Straud, as rigid and controlling in his parish as Troden had been at the seminary?

Near midnight, Pat, beer in hand, squeezed past Meer Mohrical and leaned across Terry's desk. "Danny, it's a long drive home. You won't get any sleep tonight."

"It's our last night," Dan said. He raised his glass. "Coke. I'll be fine."

Pat lifted his beer in salute, and Dan watched him return to his chair. Pat would be a good priest. But what about him? Would his parishioners like his homilies? Allow him to share their joy at weddings and baptisms, their sorrow at funerals? Would they trust him in the confessional?

A few weeks earlier he had received his chalice: a shiny gold cup with a tall stem and a wide base. An obsidian ring circled the center of the stem and a pewter Chi-Rho was mounted on the base. He designed it and his parents paid for it: their ordination present. He loved it, and them.

But they didn't know, for all the studying he'd done, that he still had doubts. Maybe the other guys had them too, but could theirs be as bad as his?

Still, someone somewhere must have done the unthinkable: quit the night before ordination. How did that poor guy tell his classmates, his professors, his parents?

Dan forced the thoughts aside. Too weird. Only he would think about someone quitting this close to ordination. At the edge of the desk, his hand grazed Terry's phone. He'd talked to Jessie on that phone. *That night.* Tomorrow, she'd be in Milwaukee for Pat's ordination, also Sunday at his first solemn Mass. If he quit, he could see her.

You left? Finally! But why did you wait till the last minute?

Theirs would be Pat's first wedding: the uniting in holy matrimony of Daniel John Bates II and Jessica Marie Fernettan. Dan saw himself and Jessica facing each other at the altar with Pat announcing, "You may now kiss the bride."

Dan tried to shake the scene from his head. Pat was right: He'd better head home. He swallowed the rest of his Coke, then made his way around the room, shaking hands with each classmate. He approached Pat last.

"Can you believe this?" Pat asked.

"Twelve years," Dan said. "And it ends tonight."

Pat smiled, just a little. "I used to complain to God that tomorrow would never come."

Dan tried to smile, but gave up. "Well, it's here, for better or for worse. Jeez, that makes it sound like a wedding, doesn't it."

"Well," Pat said, "in a way we'll be married to the Church. But, hey, stop talking. Go!"

Dan touched Pat's arm. "See you next week." Then he turned and walked out the door.

The next day in Madison, Dan and eight other deacons followed three acolytes into St. Raphael's Cathedral. Behind them marched the priests and bishops presiding at the ordination. A block away, the white dome of the state capitol gleamed against a deep blue sky. Just days ago, it seemed, Dan and Jessica had joined fourth graders lying flat on the rotunda floor.

The boys leading the procession slowed to let their eyes adjust to the cathedral's dim light. The organist pounded out a grand welcome as the group walked slowly toward the altar. It was decorated with spring flowers and dozens of candles, each adding its scent of beeswax to the incense rising from the gold censer at an acolyte's side.

Dan smiled at his parents standing to the right of the aisle. How time had passed, and how the world and the Church had changed, since they first drove him to the seminary in 1957.

The day he met Jessica.

He checked his watch. Pat was marching at this moment into St. John's Cathedral in Milwaukee. Dear Pat, so sure of himself and his vocation. Jessica would be there. Had she returned to the Church? Or did she still think Pat was tossing away his life? Did she ask him one last time not to go through with it?

A blast from the pipe organ brought Dan back to St. Raphael's. His class was, he'd read, one of the first to be ordained in a new ceremony adopted by the Consilium for the Implementation of the Constitution on the Sacred Liturgy. The changes highlighted the transfer of priestly power through the bishop placing his hands on the heads of those to be ordained.

It was during the Litany of the Saints that Dan knew he was in trouble. After the party in Terry's room, he'd driven home to Willow Run and slept only three hours. Now, as he and the other ordinands lay prostrate on the sanctuary floor, Dan fought to keep his eyes open. He stared at the carpet and identified the colors of individual threads—two shades of gray, three of green, three of blue, one each of orange and red and yellow—while the celebrant and the choir exchanged phrases of the interminable litany.

"Saint Peter … Pray for us. Saint Paul … Pray for us. Saint Andrew … Pray for us. Saint James …"

Dan's eyes closed. Saint James. James. He'd seen a western, on television or at the movies, when was that? Years ago, no matter. About the James gang led by Frank and Jesse. Jesse James. Jessie Fernettan. Where was she? In Milwaukee. No, here she was in Madison, riding through the cathredral's front door on Jesse James's horse. Clip clop, clip clop, clip clop, down the center aisle. No, Jess, you can't bring that horse into the sanctuary. No, don't dismount. You can't come in here either. No girls allowed. Get back on the horse, Jess. Please … stay away. You—both of you—have to get out of here. No, no, no, you can't lie down here with me, I'm being ordained. Look up there. See the bishop? C'mon, Jess, get up! Jeez, don't you ever listen?

The celebrant and the choir finished the names of the saints, but the litany continued, praying now that God would deliver the congregation from various evils.

"From the snares of the devil … Deliver us, O Lord. From anger, and hatred, and all ill-will … Deliver us, O Lord. From the spirit of fornication …"

"Did you hear that, Jess? Fornication—that's what we did at the lake. I love your lying here beside me, but you really must leave. Someone's going to notice."

The litany continued in the celebrant's deep voice: "That you would confirm and preserve us in your holy service …," and the choir's harmony: "We pray you to hear us."

"That you would lift up our minds to heavenly desires …"

"Listen to that, Jess. *Heavenly* desires. My desires for you have not been heavenly. They—"

Dan woke to the rustling of vestments as the bishop and his helpers made their way to the altar. Oh God, what had he missed? Moving only his eyes, he stretched his gaze as far as he could. The other guys were still on the floor too. Thank God. The celebrant and the choir had finished the litany and the ceremony would move along faster. He'd stay awake now. But the dream had been so vivid that he glanced around for a sign of Jessica.

Or of a horse.

Dan called Pat that night. "Well, we're priests. Congratulations to us, I guess."

"We're in the big money now," Pat said. "Twenty-four hundred dollars a year. Our cars will rust away before we finish the payments. But we do get room and board."

"Talking about rusty cars, is Jessie there?"

"She's out with a girl friend. She's fine, but there's no change in what you want to know."

"I'm glad she was there for your big day."

"Days," Pat said. "Today and tomorrow. Remember how we promised we'd assist at each other's first Masses? We never dreamed we'd celebrate them the same day."

"Say hi to her."

"I will."

"I'd like to come over."

"Don't. She hasn't changed her mind.... I asked."

Dan's evening at home might have been just another seminary break except for relatives, friends and neighbors dropping by "to see the new Father Dan" and to scoop noodle casseroles onto paper plates. Dan gauged the time: Leave Willow Run at seven, get to Milwaukee by nine, visit with Jessica for a few minutes, get back by eleven.

He wore a forest-green, short-sleeved shirt until their neighbor Mrs. Millin wanted to pose next to him for a picture but complained to his mother that "Father Dan doesn't look the priest."

He changed into a black shirt and slipped on a new Roman collar. Mrs. Millin smiled. Eight o'clock; he could be home by midnight.

Several Sacred Heart classmates dropped by, led by Eddie Schmertz. Some had married girls he knew, and several showed pictures of their kids. Most left early, but Eddie stayed.

In a corner of the kitchen Dan asked him if he'd seen Kathy Sherman.

"No, she married Coop and they moved somewhere west, like Dubuque. Too bad, too. She was a neat girl."

"Yes, she was," Dan said. Nine o'clock; he couldn't make it back before one.

His visitors trickled out, wishing him—"Father Dan"—the best and hoping they'd get to hear one of his sermons someday.

"Come and say Mass for us," Mrs. Wuenchel said.

"Tomorrow," Dan said. "I'm celebrating my first solemn Mass here tomorrow."

Ten o'clock; he wouldn't make it to Milwaukee that night.

Chapter 23

Dan kicked off his covers and rolled to the other side of the bed. His first night as a priest, and he couldn't stop old movies of Jessica playing in his mind. Kissing in the car after her prom. Lying naked in her blankets on the beach. Watching her car disappear behind the trees along Shoreline Road.

He hadn't seen her since, but she was in Milwaukee. So close. So *damned* close. Pat said she was all right, but how could he be sure?

God help him. He would make one hell of a priest if he couldn't block thoughts of a woman on the night of his ordination. He rolled back across the bed and pulled the blankets over him.

Dan had groaned when the sunlight flooded his room. He recalled checking his clock around midnight, two, three-thirty and four-fifty-five. By nine-thirty, however, he was up, dressed, and standing in the Sacred Heart rectory, where his head still felt wrapped in gauze as he vested for his first solemn Mass with Fathers Popeye Straud and Al Korris. Against his better judgment, Dan had followed tradition by picking his pastor for his deacon. But he placated himself by choosing Korris for subdeacon. At his first Mass he'd be flanked by both ends of the philosophical spectrum.

Dan draped the amice across his shoulders, tossed the alb over his head, then pulled in his gut before tying the cincture around his waist. Ah, vanity.

He reached for Sacred Heart's finest set of vestments, heavy eggshell-white cloth trimmed in red and gold. He slipped the maniple onto his left arm; draped the stole around his neck and crossed it over his chest; and finally put on the chasuble, the large cloak decorated on the front and back, but open at the sides.

By this time, he knew, parishioners, relatives and friends were climbing the worn stone steps of the old church. They had supported him for twelve years with their thoughts and prayers. And, of course, with money. He should want more than anything to say this Mass for them. Instead, he was woozy after a lousy night's sleep.

Pat would be vesting now too. Pat, the consummate seminarian. The pious one. He would feel like a new priest *should* feel, enjoying the pageantry of his first Mass. With his parents. And his sister.

Stop it, Dan told himself. For Christ's sake, you're vested for Mass. He smiled. It was, literally, for Christ's sake. He had not taken the Lord's name in vain.

But where was the feeling of triumph? Today was IT, what he had studied for—sacrificed for—for the past twelve years. He should be ecstatic: He had made it! Instead, he wished he were in Milwaukee, acting as Pat's deacon. He should have put his own Mass off for a week so they could have been together. So he could have seen Jessica.

He gripped the dressing table. "Please, God," he prayed silently, "don't let my reasons include her. I've promised myself to you. Jessica is gone. I chose you, Lord. Clear my mind, this day and every day, so I can serve forever as your priest."

Popeye was talking. "… You're going to remember this moment all the days of your life, the Mass, the people, the whole bit." He put out his hand. "Congratulations, Daniel. A great day!"

Al Korris, too, shook his hand. Korris was a great priest, a compassionate man who would never rise to power. Damned conservative hierarchy.

Popeye again, to Dan, with genuine respect in his voice: "It's time, Father." Dan had to give Straud this: Despite their differences, the man seemed to accept him as a brother priest.

The procession—acolytes and priests—made its way from the rectory to the church's front door, where they stepped into the entryway and marched solemnly down the center aisle. Dan had been baptized here, received his first communion, been confirmed, and graduated from eighth grade. Now, in this church he had grown up in, he would celebrate his first solemn Mass.

From their pews the people watched, smiling and nodding. Dan smiled and nodded back. Then he saw her, five pews from the front on the right side, third person from the aisle, her light-brown hair in a ponytail the way he liked. Jessica turned to face him.

It was a woman he didn't know.

Get your mind on the Mass.

A nod to smiling Mrs. Ripenska. Daily communicant. Saw her every day when he was home on vacation. Dan glanced around. The place was packed. Hands reached from the pews to touch his sleeve. To honor him. No, to honor his priesthood. He kept forgetting: He was now a priest. So many times he had thought this day would never come. But it had, suddenly.

"Hi, Dan!" A child's voice. Joe and Millie Krenzel's five year old from across the street, grinning and waving. Joe tried to shush him and hold him back, but Dan waved the boy to the edge of the pew where he grasped the tiny hand.

"Anthony, it's so good to see you." *Let the children come to me*, Jesus said.

Dan was into it now, the people, the pageantry, the Mass. The choir's voices rose to a crescendo and shivers of joy ran up his back. The three priests stepped to the altar and Father Daniel John Bates II began the prayers of the Mass.

He couldn't take his eyes off the faces that reflected their pride in him, the boy who had walked among them in their little town. Now here he was, a priest, and some of them believed it put him so near to God that people like them could, just by standing next to him, come closer to heaven. The hymns, with the flowers and candles and incense, combined with the people to shake away his fatigue. Surely it was God who brought them here today to provide that extra push he needed into the priesthood. In the offertory prayer he remembered them back to God.

"Receive, O holy Father, almighty and eternal God, this spotless host which I, your unworthy servant, offer to you, my living and true God, for my own countless sins, offenses, and negligences; and for all present here, as well as for all faithful Christians both living and dead, that it may profit me and them as a means of reaching salvation in the eternal life. Amen."

And again during the prayer for the living: "Remember all of us gathered here before you. You know how firmly we believe in you and dedicate ourselves to you. We offer you this sacrifice of praise for ourselves and all who are dear to us."

The distractions had left.

Then the consecration of the bread into the body of Christ: Dan picked up the flat, round wafer off the gold paten and held it between him and the congregation. "The day before he suffered, he took bread, and looking up to heaven, to you, his almighty Father, he gave you thanks and praise. He broke the bread, gave it to his disciples and said: Take this and eat it, all of you; this is my body." And when Dan raised the consecrated host above his head for all to see, he flushed with a pride he could never admit to anyone.

When the Mass was over he gazed out at the people, spread his hands toward them and said, "The Lord be with you."

"And with your spirit," they said.

He raised his right arm and made the sign of the cross: "May almighty God bless you, the Father, and the Son, and the Holy Spirit."

They crossed themselves. "Amen."

He paused. It was too bad this moment had to end. He had much to be grateful for. "The Mass is ended. Go in peace."

"Thanks be to God."

The organist and choir struck up a very loud *To Christ the King*, and Dan followed the procession out, thrilling to his favorite hymn. He returned smiles and handshakes along the way, recognizing faces he'd spotted the day before at the post office and others he hadn't seen since some Christmas years ago when he served midnight Mass and held the paten under their chins for holy communion.

Outside, they came one by one in the reception line, smiling faces of all ages, greeting the other priests and Dan's parents, stopping in front of the new Father Dan to congratulate him and ask his blessing. The old people remembered when he was little and played Mass in his basement. His Sacred Heart classmates recalled the candy wafers he placed on their tongues.

"But the sermons!" Dan said. "Don't you remember my sermons?"

It got a laugh.

He winced as old people called him Father. He'd never get used to that, especially from couples he had always called Mr. and Mrs. when he met them after church or walked by as they tended their gardens.

Then he saw Jessica, seven back in line. There was no mistake this time, though she looked a little heavier and her hair was cut short. Distance and dark glasses hid her eyes. His gut cramped as a woman in front of him said, "Isn't that right, Father?"

"Oh, yes. I'd say so, yes." He hoped it was the correct response.

And then the next pair, a lady with a girl about ten, telling Father Dan she had watched him walking to Sacred Heart School when he was her daughter's age and it was wonderful having him return home this way.

Jessica was closer. They locked eyes and he flushed. Everyone must have noticed.

Next, an old man of few words, thank God, just "Congratulations, Father," followed by a family of four whose dad wished Father Dan could remain there long enough to "instruct these two" so they'd grow up shining examples of the Catholic faith like Father Dan himself. Then three more, a shy couple and an old woman whose reedy voice Dan couldn't understand.

Jessica shook hands with his parents, stood for a second in front of him, then threw her arms around him and pulled close as he wrapped his arms around her. Her lips brushed his cheek and she whispered, "I'm happy for you, Danny. Be a great priest."

She slipped from his grasp and headed up the sidewalk, replaced by a young couple who thought it was so great how Father Dan had brought this great honor to Sacred Heart, which was one of the greatest parishes they'd ever belonged to and certainly deserved this great honor.

"Jess!" Dan called. "You'll be at the dinner?"

She didn't turn around, just shook her head and walked faster.

And the woman next in line hugged him though he didn't want her to, didn't want anyone to, so he could feel as long as possible the press of Jessica's body against his. The woman said "Congratulations, Father," as Jessica disappeared behind a house on Second Street.

"Excuse me," he mumbled, "I'll be right back." He broke from the woman and ran down the block Jessica had walked down and turned at the corner she had turned at and saw her driving away in a yellow '69 Dodge Dart.

He yelled, waved and yelled again, but the car rolled on. Above the bumper was a Minnesota license plate.

"Jessie!" Dan shouted. A woman walking her baby in a silver stroller stared at him. He had forgotten: He was still vested for Mass.

The brake lights came on, and Dan lurched forward, but they went off again and the car turned onto Morrison Street, the fastest route to I-94 and Milwaukee. He walked back to the church wondering what to say. The people in line stared with glum faces at the new priest, the pride of their parish, as he returned from chasing a woman he had just hugged. Dan kept his eyes down, avoiding those of his parents and the two priests and the people in line.

"Sorry to keep you waiting," he told them.

No one said it was okay. Tonight, he was sure, Willow Run would attempt to guess who the woman was that the new Father Dan had chased. And they'd talk of his nerve, coming back to the reception line as if nothing had happened. Dan greeted a family of four he had seen once at Mass, then the Grunewalds, a friendly old couple who farmed north of town.

And then Kathy Sherman ... Kathy Cooper now. She was laughing. "Who was *that*?"

"The Grunewalds."

"Not them, the girl."

"Oh. An old friend. How are you, Kath?"

"It was the Popcorn Girl, wasn't it. Damn, I never thought. And there I was, right behind her! So ... the flame still flickers. Do *I* get a hug like that?"

Dan reddened and put his arms around her.

After they broke, she said, "Not quite like hers, but pretty good. Hey, congrats. Keep in touch, okay? You oughta come to our reunions. You missed the one in sixty-six."

He nodded.

"Come to our next one. Ten years in seventy-one. We'll have you do the blessing. Actually, we could have used you last time. The place damned near poisoned us. Food blessed by a priest can't poison people, can it?"

Dan offered no guarantees.

Agnes Reuter came three people later. "Ah, Daniel. *Father* Daniel now. Nice ring to it."

He had invited her, but didn't expect her to come: Willow Run's nonbelieving recluse in a crowd of believers. "Mrs. Reuter, it's so good of you to stop by. *Daniel* is still fine."

"Only if you will call me Agnes, all right? For a small time there, Daniel, when you took off down the street, I thought I got in line too late." She grinned. "Did you catch her?"

"No."

"Too bad." Agnes glanced back at the line of people murmuring and shuffling their feet. "Daniel, you must pay no attention to the looks these ... these people give you. They will never understand. But you will make a good priest. I've known that since you were coming by my house for cookies and the other children told me you were going to that school."

"Thank you," he said.

Her face turned grim, and she brushed the tips of three fingers down Dan's left cheek. He felt them tremble. "Daniel, perhaps I shouldn't ... well, I saw how you looked at that girl and hugged her so tight. Oh, Daniel, I hope very much that I am wrong, but I ... I am so afraid that you have made a terrible mistake."

Chapter 24

Three days after their first solemn Masses, Dan and Pat stood atop a limestone bluff at Cave Point in Wisconsin's Door County. The early-morning sun reflected off the Lake Michigan waves, and every few seconds water the color of turquoise swelled and dashed itself with a loud whoomp against the hollowed-out rock beneath them.

They had driven north together to spend their week's vacation before reporting to their first assignments as priests. Along the way, they had passed several orchards. Dan recalled picking cherries with the Fernettans—a decade ago. He leaned against an oak and studied the movement of the water. "Jessie's in Minnesota," he said.

Pat fiddled with his camera, then squinted into the viewfinder toward several trees growing out of fissures in the rocks. "How can anyone doubt there's a God when they see the beauty he created?" He took two steps back and pointed toward Dan. "Stay where you are but turn a little to your right. Yeah, like that." He clicked the shutter, stepped to his left and clicked again. "How'd you find out?"

"I saw her license plate after she came through my reception line." Dan didn't mention his chase.

Pat pointed to Dan's left. "I'd like a silhouette of you against those waves washing over the rocks in the background." *Click.* "I wondered where she went ... okay, now go over there, out of the way. I want one with nobody in it." *Click.* "She came late for the dinner. Told me she'd stopped to visit a friend and lost track of the time." *Click.*

Dan wrapped his arm around the trunk of a birch and peered over the edge at the water roiling below. He still hated heights. "We're priests now. You can tell me where she is."

Pat shook his head.

"C'mon," Dan said. "I've checked every Minnesota phone book in the library."

Pat opened the back of his camera, pulled out the exposed film and inserted a fresh roll. "She isn't listed. Let's head over this way. I want some shots along these bluffs. Believe me, the minute she changes her mind, I'll let you know. But don't ask anymore, okay?"

Dan watched the water. "No promises."

The following Sunday evening, Father Nicholas Grume stabbed a slice of medium-rare roast beef, pushed it into his right cheek and chewed. His eyes seemed focused on a cobalt-blue votive candle flickering before a statue of the Virgin Mary in his rectory's dining room. The Bishop of Madison had appointed Grume pastor of St. Bartholomew's parish at Bellamy nineteen years ago.

"You're his thirteenth assistant," Bishop Elmendorf had told Dan the day he assigned him to St. Bart's. "I have every confidence that you and Nick can work together profitably in the Lord's vineyard."

Dan didn't share the bishop's optimism. He'd gotten the word on Grume from guys ordained ahead of him. Jake Arbuten even called to sympathize.

Grume swallowed, then waved his fork in a circle over the lace-covered table. "Just so you are aware, Father Bates, here at St. Bart's we do not accept excuses for the use of artificial birth control. Any excuses, from anyone." He stabbed another slice of beef. "Not to cut you short on your first day, but scuttlebutt among the pastors is that you guys fresh out of Resurrection seem a bit wishy-washy on the matter. Holy Mother Church says birth control is a sin, and that is what we preach here. No sense confusing people."

"Okay," Dan said. *Okay?* C'mon, he was a *priest* now, a minister of the Church. He and Pat had discussed this for years: Do what they had to do at the seminary to get ordained, then follow their own consciences when they reached the priesthood. Father Francis Chisholm in *Keys of the Kingdom* had done that. Besides, they had kowtowed enough at the seminary to last a lifetime. As priests, they would demand the same consideration they were expected to give.

Grume stopped the fork halfway to his mouth. "Hm. Last guy I had here gave me an argument, something about the primacy of the individual conscience. I asked him, right here at this table, 'If every Tom, Dick, and Harriet made up their own minds about right and wrong, what would be the role of Holy Mother Church?'"

Dan smiled. A rhetorical question, no doubt, but he would pretend not to notice. "Well, probably to teach them about God, say Mass and administer the sacraments. Those were Christ's instructions."

Grume put the fork on his plate. "Do we have a problem here?"

"I hope not," Dan said. "I thought you were trying to find out what I knew."

Grume picked up his fork again and waved it around. "In the confessional we are obligated to procure a firm purpose of amendment, that is, the penitent's promise before God to discontinue birth control in the future, before we administer absolution and permit her to return to the sacraments."

Dan sipped his wine. "As we must do with any sin. But what if their consciences tell them birth control is a gift from God, like other medical miracles, that enables them to regulate their lives in his service?"

Grume leaned across the table. "No one's conscience does that. If it does, that conscience is *wrong*."

"But if it's their conscience, that's what they must follow."

"No! That's what they must *change*!"

Dan shook his head. "Still, until they do, they must follow it. Because that's what they will answer to God for: their conscience, right or wrong."

"That's religious anarchy! No! When Rome speaks, Catholics must listen."

Dan's face was getting hot, and he worked to keep his voice level. "According to the Vatican Council, the Church consists of its people. Think about that. Because if it's true, Rome should listen when *they* speak."

Grume gripped the table. "What has that seminary come to? I studied there, and we never thought … Fooey! Enough of this. If I ever hear that you've absolved a girl on the Pill without making her get off, I'll call the bishop and your butt'll be out of here the next morning. Understand?"

Without making her get off? Dan held back a laugh. Grume didn't know the slang. "The people in the pews, the ones filling our collection baskets, are more the Church than the two of us are, and you and I, even as we argue, are more the Church than the pope in Rome. If you don't believe that, read the documents of Vatican II. You might learn something."

Dan stopped too late. His last crack was uncalled for, and he knew it.

Grume turned red. "I'm your pastor! You can't talk to me like that!"

"I shouldn't have to," Dan said. "You should know this stuff." *Damn it!* His first night at St. Bart's and he had dug himself a hole he had no idea how to get out of.

Grume's face was still red, but he lowered his voice. "Look, we can compromise. I don't care what you think. I'm concerned with what you do. As long as you're assigned to my parish, you'll act on the teachings of Mother Church. You must understand: From my long experience as a pastor, disagreement about doctrine does nothing but confuse the faithful. We do them a grave disservice if we allow that to happen."

Dan stirred peas into his mashed potatoes and gravy, creating an impromptu casserole. "I'll do my best."

Grume watched him. "Good." Then he laid his fork at the side of his plate, got up, and abandoned the rest of his roast.

On a hot afternoon the following Saturday, Dan dripped sweat during his walk from the rectory porch to the church sacristy. The rectory was a fifty-year-old, two-story, white clapboard house with black trim. The church next door was close to ninety, a beautiful old German building constructed of the same yellow, cream-city brick as the seminary's Kleissman Hall.

Inside the church, Dan pulled aside the heavy maroon curtain and ducked into the center stall of the confessional. He forced himself to inhale the stale air. Where was his seat pad? Grume had sent it to the cleaners, promising it would be back by Saturday. Either the cleaners were late or Grume was still mad.

Within fifteen minutes Dan was shifting from side to side on his oak chair. His butt was already sore. Guys ordained ahead of him had warned that hearing confessions was a pain in the ass, but he hadn't suspected they meant it literally. Next time he'd bring a pillow.

Another penitent. He slid open the panel.

"Father, we got three kids." The voice was young, female, tired. "We've only been married four-and-a-half years, and now I been putting him off ... my husband, I mean, and he's getting frustrated 'cause I promised when we were dating that after we got married we could ... you know, all we wanted. But the doctor says rhythm won't work for us. We did it like he told us but it's failed twice already. We need to be able to, you know, make love without my getting pregnant every year."

Dan waited. He had hoped he wouldn't get one of these for a while.

"Father, I'm only twenty-six. We'll end up with fifteen kids at this rate. Is that what God wants? I'm not from this parish, but I can't go back to my own about this. My pastor says only God can decide how many kids we have. Well, God's given us three, and I love 'em all, but it's getting really hard and we can't afford any more. We run out of money every week and we don't have any more room in the apartment. Everything's gotten so expensive and the kids aren't even in school yet!"

Dan shifted again and wiped his face. His cotton handkerchief was already soaked. He should have brought a towel. "Do you truly believe three is all the children God wants you to have?"

"Yes, at least for now. We—"

"How about your husband? How does he feel?"

"He already quit going to church 'cause of this. Says it's none of Father's business."

"I'm sorry," Dan said. Could he agree with her husband and still represent the Church? He stalled. "What does your own conscience tell you?"

"I know we're supposed to trust God to provide, but he sure isn't doing so good. Not for us anyway. We never go out. I cooked macaroni and cheese three times last week, and now we aren't supposed to, um, you know, make love any more either?" She started crying.

"What would you like to do?" Dan was aware he was stalling.

"They say the Pill lets you ... you know, do it without worrying. I want to keep Bob happy, but I want to stay Catholic too. I know the pope says we can't use it, and that's what our pastor keeps harping on every Sunday like it's the only sin people commit these days." She paused, and Dan heard her take a deep breath. "I've started using the Pill, Father. I'm using 'em and we made love three times this week. Those are my sins."

Dan shifted. "Do you believe they really are sins?"

"The pope says so. Our pastor says so."

"But do *you* say so?"

She didn't answer right away. "When we made love last time, Father, I felt ... free, like never before. I didn't feel like it was wrong. It seemed ... well, like I said, free. I didn't have to worry. Except afterwards. Then I worried it must have been a sin. Because of the Pill, I mean."

Dan shook his head. Poor woman, she couldn't win. "Well, let's look at it this way. The Church teaches, although not as publicly as it should, that each of us must form his or her own conscience. Of course, the Church expects us to form them in line with its teachings, but our ultimate responsibility is to God. What do we honestly believe he wants us to do? We actually must decide ourselves what is moral or sinful for us."

"That's not what my pastor says, Father."

"Mine, either," Dan said, "but I'm afraid our pastors are wrong." Could he say *full of shit* in the confessional? No, but it was tempting. "If you honestly believe that the pope is wrong about birth control, and a lot of people do, including many priests, bishops and theologians, you should ignore what your pastor preaches and follow your own conscience. On the other hand, if your conscience tells you the pope is correct, you must follow his teaching."

The woman's voice rose to a higher pitch. "But how can I know I'm not being selfish, or kidding myself? My pastor told me I was, um … rationalizing. To excuse my sins, he said."

"Your pastor said that?"

"Yes, Father."

"Then your pastor's an idiot."

"*What?*"

Damn. He'd stepped over the line again. "What I mean is, your pastor is wrong to accuse you of sin. Only you and God know if you've acted according to your conscience. Of course, this is not something to decide lightly. We need to examine the effects our actions have on ourselves and on the people around us. That, I believe, is how God wants us to decide. Remember, he said to treat other people the way we would treat him."

"My kids deserve a good life, Father. So does my husband. And me, too." Her voice was calmer. "I know people who are happy with their umpteen kids, but I couldn't handle that. And Bob and I deserve to … you know, be together. I mean, we are married, and the priest told us during instructions that sex … um, you know, that making love is our reward from God for raising a family. Isn't that why we weren't supposed to do it before we got married? Now they're telling us we can't do it *after* we're married either."

Dan wiped his face again. The thin handkerchief was dripping, and it merely smoothed the beads of sweat across his face. "Yes, it would seem that's what they're saying."

"It's not fair, Father."

"No. It's not."

"I don't think God would do that to people."

He shifted. "I don't either."

She paused again as though she wasn't sure she'd heard him correctly. "But how can we be right and the pope be wrong?"

"The Church hates to admit it, but popes have been wrong before. Many times."

"But maybe my pastor's right. Maybe I'm trying to justify making my life easier."

Dan rested his head against the confessional wall and closed his eyes. Poor woman. Three kids in four years, and she feels guilty for trying to keep her life from unraveling. "You and your husband will sacrifice a great deal, raising even three kids. Does God expect more? Only you can decide that."

"But, father, *how?*"

"In the context of your own, your husband's, and your children's lives. Maybe you can't decide it today. Maybe the best we can do for now is to grant you forgiveness for whatever sins you've committed and give you time to study and pray about this. Perhaps—"

"*Study*, father?"

"I mean you might read things that various theologians, even those from other religions, have written about birth control. We Catholics aren't the only ones trying to follow God's law. Remember, God gave us brains. I think he expects us to use them, not to let a pope or a priest or anyone else decide for us what is right or wrong. Only we ourselves know the problems we face in our lives."

She seemed to have run out of questions, and Dan gave her absolution. He hoped she would return the next Saturday, but she didn't come back then, nor the following week.

Had he said the right things? He would probably never know.

There were others. Same problem, different stories: No children until settled in careers. Spread out the kids' ages. Find a bigger house for the two they already have. Caring for a sick parent and can't handle a baby now.

They would have to decide for themselves, he told them, even the ones he thought were selfish. He suggested guidelines, but it wasn't his decision.

"Damned right it's our decision," Nicholas Grume told Dan and three priest guests from Milwaukee at dinner in the rectory a few weeks later. "Who's to decide if we aren't?"

"The people," Dan said. He sipped white wine from a crystal glass, rejecting the temptation to drain it in one gulp and run. "People must form their consciences—"

"According to the teachings of Mother Church!" Grume said. He looked toward the other priests.

"That is true," the tall one said. "No matter what we individually think, the pope has now spoken on this."

Dan eyed the wine bottle. His glass was empty. "But even respected theologians dispute what the pope said in *Humanae Vitae*." He tried to sound reasonable. No sense setting Grume off again.

"Only in theory," the heavyset priest said. "In practice, people must—"

"Follow their consciences like the rest of us," Dan said, too quickly.

"No!" Grume started to stand, but sat back down. "And don't interrupt our guests. Theologians' discussions are for internal consideration. As I've told you, we can't be confusing the faithful by bickering among ourselves."

"They're already confused," Dan said. "Your 'bickering' between priests and bishops is showing up in newspapers and magazines across the country."

The third priest shook his head. "Yes. It's a scandal. So unfortunate. They really must stop arguing in public. They do so much damage to the Church that way. I fear God's wrath will be upon them."

"His wrath should be upon the pope," Dan said. "He went against the majority of his own commission. Did he think the Holy Spirit skipped their meetings?"

"Enough!" Grume yelled. "We'll discuss this tomorrow at breakfast, Father Bates. I suggest you conform your thinking to the Church's official position by then. Because if you don't, by God, you're going to be out of here."

Dan stood. "Leave God out of this. You couldn't care less what God wants as long as you keep your control over people. Remember, we're supposed to—"

"Get out!" Grume said.

"Jesus said we're supposed to love one another." Dan moved toward the door. "But this power play by the pope and some of you priests will go down in history as one of the Church's greatest sins against its own people." He nodded toward the third priest. "That's the scandal!"

From the front window of his bedroom, Dan watched Grume's guests walk to their car. Man-oh-man, what was he going to do now? He stepped over the magazines scattered across his floor and pulled a suitcase from his closet.

May as well start packing.

Chapter 25

Dan put aside the newspaper and leaned back in his chair. Tomorrow would mark his fourth month in Bellamy after Elmendorf turned down Grume's request to transfer him. It shocked both of them, probably the first time they felt the same emotion about anything.

He liked the people and the town, a quiet little place southwest of Madison. And maybe he'd be staying a while. He worked at not riling Grume, and the pastor seemed to mellow.

The phone rang. It was Pat.

"I'll be in Madison next Monday."

"Great," Dan said. "I'll meet you for lunch."

"No, it's business this time. Remember Jim Groppi?"

"That priest who drives everyone nuts?"

"He's leading a march to the capitol to protest the welfare cuts. I decided to join them when they get there."

"I should too," Dan said. "But I've never done anything like that."

"Me neither, but I decided it's time. The stupid legislature voted to give a family of four $208 a month. For *everything*: food, rent, clothes, utilities, school supplies ... everything."

"That's less than we make."

"I don't know how far that stretches in Bellamy, but here in the city kids were already going hungry."

"Maybe the legislators don't know that."

"They know. Lots of us wrote letters, even called them, all the stuff they say good citizens should do. But there's an ugliness in Madison that's ... well, beyond reason. One senator said charity is a job for churches and civic groups, not for the state. Just a total abdication of responsibility. So I'll be there Monday, though my pastor's afraid I'll get arrested."

"What are you planning to do?"

"I'm kidding. It'll be peaceful. Come along. The more clergy we get, the louder we tell them those cuts are immoral."

The next morning at breakfast, Dan told Grume he needed Monday off.

Grume stirred sugar into his coffee. "But you have off on Thursday."

"I'll trade. A group of us are going to meet at the capitol because the legislature cut back on welfare payments."

"It's that fool Groppi, isn't it? I read about him and his demonstrating." Grume waved his spoon. "The lawmakers are doing their job, God bless 'em, balancing the budget and getting people to shoulder their own responsibilities."

"They're balancing their budget by stomping on the poor. I told my friend I'd be there."

"Well, I need you here. Besides, I can't have you making a fool of yourself and causing a scandal. What will our parishioners say?"

"It's not a scandal to help the poor. It's a scandal *not* to."

"The best way to help is let people pull themselves up by their bootstraps."

"Christ never mentioned bootstraps. Besides, people on welfare can't afford shoes, much less boots. That's why I need to go."

Grume slammed down his spoon. "Oh, all right, go. Get thrown in jail. At least you'll be out of my hair, no thanks to Elmendorf, who insists I make a regular priest out of you."

In Madison on Monday, Dan found Pat at the edge of a crowd milling around on the capitol steps. "What are they going to do?"

"March around, I guess, then sit in the assembly chamber when the legislators meet this afternoon. I thought maybe we could catch some assemblymen on their way in and try to get through to them that an affluent society has an obligation to its poor."

They joined the noisy crowd as it pushed its way into the capitol, then stopped near the rotunda stairs when the leaders ignored the guards' requests to leave and broke through a locked door into the assembly chamber. Angry shouts echoed off the marble walls.

Dan had to yell for Pat to hear. "This isn't going to help!"

Pat shouted back, "Writing letters hasn't helped either."

A tall, thin man rushed past them.

"He's an assemyman," Pat said. "C'mon."

Dan and Pat followed the man as he approached Groppi in the chamber. They caught only parts of what he said, but he was telling the priest that his group was hurting its cause, that he and other assemblymen would try to cancel the cuts. But to do that the assembly would have to meet, so would Groppi please have his group clear the chamber?

Dan waited for Groppi to give the order.

Instead, two members of the group grabbed the assemblyman's arms and hustled him from the room. Others knocked over chairs and climbed onto desks and kicked off lamps, papers and books.

"What the hell are they doing?" Dan said. "And Groppi's letting 'em do it."

Pat's face turned red. "It's like he *wants* to get arrested. Well, I don't. Let's get out of here."

They pushed their way through the crowd and finally squeezed outside, where they discovered National Guardsmen marching up the wide sidewalk toward them. Dan and Pat hurried over to two police officers.

"What are they going to do?" Pat asked.

The shorter of the two eyed them. "They're getting the punks out of our capitol."

"If they use force," Pat said, "it's going to be bad."

The taller policeman cocked his head. "With all due respect, Fathers, your people are in there trashing the place."

Pat tugged at Dan's sleeve. "Let's go. There's nothing we can do."

"I guess not." Dan watched the Guard marching into the building. "I'm glad we came back out. But it makes me mad, you know? Laws are just what the people in power decide they should be. There's nothing particularly moral about 'em, and these cuts are definitely *immoral.*"

"But it was supposed to have been a peaceful demonstration," Pat said.

"I know. But poor people don't have any power to pass laws. And when their so-called representatives ignore them, like they did your letters, some are going to react like this."

"But damn it," Pat said, "we're priests. There has to be something we can do."

Dan waved a hand toward the capitol. "Groppi's got his plan, the crowd is worked up, and the Guard has its orders. Think anything we can say will make a difference?"

Pat started down the walk. "No, I guess not. And that scares me."

On Wednesday afternoons, Dan visited hospitals and nursing homes. At Hilltop Home in Bellamy, nurse Ann Howley told him a new resident wanted the priest to stop by.

"She has an odd name, Father. She'll expect you to make a joke about it."

Dan knocked, then pushed past the half-open door. "Penny Nichol?"

"Over here." A tiny woman sat in a gray-vinyl chair next to a window overlooking a garden of wilted flowers done in by an early frost. A faded silk robe of red, pink, and yellow blossoms enveloped her skinny body. Fine strands of white hair stuck out every which way from her small head.

"I'm Father Bates. The nurse said you wanted to see me." Probably a confession, or maybe she wanted to talk about going home to God.

"Gonna do a joke about my name?"

"Huh? Oh … well, I didn't plan to."

"Everyone else does."

"Mmm. I try to be different."

"I wasn't sure you'd come. I'm an atheist."

"Ann didn't tell me, but I'd have come anyway."

"Born an atheist as Penelope Johnson. I married Nichol. He was Catholic. Died nine years ago. Doubt he's in heaven, though, and not just 'cause there ain't one."

Dan paused. "Is this some kind of a joke? Send the priest to the resident atheist?"

"Unh-uh, no joke. I asked for you. Lillian next door says you're nice to talk to, and I figured one more stop wouldn't kill you. Might even broaden your mind."

Dan grinned. "I already have an atheist friend. Two, in fact."

Penny seemed to be studying the flowers. "Really. *Two*. Well, does that fill your quota, or can you take on one more?"

"I suppose it won't hurt, but I don't want my bosses getting suspicious."

She looked up. "You sure you're a priest? You don't talk like one."

"Okay, how's this: Bless you, my daughter."

"That's real good. You pass. How often do you come here?"

"Every Wednesday."

"Great. I'll cancel my appointments." She opened her right hand. "Look here." A shiny dime lay flat in her shriveled palm. "It's mine, right?"

Dan stepped back. "I guess so. Sure."

She grinned. "Now you can tell your friends you saw a Penny Nichol dime."

He took a step toward her and shook his head. "Not *my* friends. If I told 'em a joke that bad, they'd draw and quarter me."

Pat called that night. "Believe it or not, they didn't arrest anybody Monday. But Groppi sure screwed up."

"True," Dan said. "But this bunch of legislators are such assholes. They hurt people, then get all bent out of shape when their victims don't act nice. They're idiots."

Pat spoke quietly. "I've been wondering if we did the right thing … going there, I mean."

"I have no sympathy for 'em," Dan said. "The assembly, I mean. Maybe some of Groppi's guys wanted to trash the place from the start, but I think most marchers were trying to get across how bad the cuts are."

"Did you read where the governor was going to ask them to rescind the cuts? But he never got to speak. I keep thinking we should have helped that guy—his name was Mittness, the paper said—the assemblyman who tried to talk sense to Groppi."

"Maybe," Dan said. "But I'm not sure we'd have changed anything. This legislature has it in for the poor. They aren't going to listen to anyone who disagrees with 'em."

"Not all of them."

"Most. Look at the vote. Oh, some are all right, I suppose, like that one guy, but the majority? Hopeless. Groppi's guys hurt themselves in the short run, but I wonder if some of those bastards at the capitol won't think twice before pulling this crap again."

Two weeks later, Dan and Pat met at the lakefront in Milwaukee. They tried to get together each month, and their frustrating day at the capitol didn't count.

"Something embarrassing happened the other day," Pat said. "I was counseling a woman—a widow. She was depressed. As she was leaving, she put her arms around me and asked for a hug. I didn't know what to do."

"You hugged her, I hope."

"Yeah, but jeez, it was uncomfortable. She's pretty … and nice."

Dan watched a couple holding hands as they walked along the path. "She's probably also very alone, scared out of her wits. We all need hugs, some times more than others."

"Jessie said that too. And, before you ask, she's fine. The way she put it was, 'For Pete's sake, hug the girl.'"

"So she and I agree on something. Do you believe us?"

"Problem is, she's coming to see me again next week—the widow, not Jess—and I'm actually looking forward to it." Pat lowered his voice. "I even hope she'll want another hug."

"Good! Hug her again."

"Come on, you know how fast things can go from one stage to another."

"So stick to stage one. Just hug."

"What if I get turned on?"

"Ignore it. Besides, you'll be too nervous. I know. Jeez, I *hate* what the seminary did to us. We're afraid to hug frightened widows, for Pete's sake. Tell you what, give her two hugs—one for me."

A few days later, Dan poked his head around the nursing home door. "Afternoon, Penny."

"Hi, whatever-you-want-me-to-call-you. Forgot to ask last time."

"*Dan* works."

"You don't insist on *Father*?"

"I won't live to be old enough to have been your father."

"Ha-ha. Good one. Whatcha going to talk to me about today?"

"God, of course. That's my job."

"Oh, alleluia."

"You said you were *born* an atheist?"

"Aren't we all? Oh, I got baptized, Grandma Wilkowski's doing, but that was it. 'Cept for times I'd visit her. Those Sundays she marched me off to church."

"What did you think about God?"

"Didn't. Never felt the need."

"And when you die?"

"Ha! Like I'm going soon and you're worried about my soul? Hey, we die. We're gone. We disappear. Ta-ta. That's it."

Dan pulled up a chair. "Doesn't that philosophy take a lot of the joy out of living?"

"My friends ask that. Nope, it adds to it. Gives me freedom to think, to decide what I want to do. See, unlike you, I don't have to worry about some High Scorekeeper watching over my shoulder so he can decide where to ship me in the afterlife."

"You've never been sorry not to believe in God?"

"Of course I have. When my mother was dying, I wanted to do something for her. Believers can pray, feel they're helping in some way, right? Nonbelievers can't. One day Mom said, 'You know, Penelope, if there *is* a heaven, we can look forward to meeting there someday.' I thought that would be neat. I actually hoped for it. I said, 'Yeah, Ma, do you think maybe …?' And then my mother and I stared at each other and we started laughing out loud, and at the same time we both said, 'Naaahhh.' But then I was kind of sad too, you know?"

"Yes," Dan said, "I think I know."

Chapter 26

By three-thirty on a warm fall afternoon, the St. Bart's kids had already stampeded from the school. Inside the front door, Dan balanced a box of books in his arms and nudged his right hip against the panic bar. Sister Xaviera had said he could borrow a few titles from the school library. They had such great books for kids these days, with color photos and lively graphics, so different from the drab, black-and-white volumes he had studied at Sacred Heart.

"Make sure you bring 'em back first thing Monday morning, Father," Sister Xaviera had told him. "You have some of the kids' favorites in there."

"Yes, Sister." *Yes, Sister?* Was he a parish priest or a grade schooler?

His arms ached by the time he lugged the books across the street in front of the nuns' convent. He needed to start working out. He recalled Quince's warning about a pot belly and a bad back. Maybe he'd start a basketball league that winter.

The white, two-story convent reflected the late-afternoon sun. Half its space stood empty because the Franciscans had sent only four nuns this year. Parishes across the country had the same problem: It cost a lot more money to hire lay teachers.

From near the church a half block away, a child screamed, "Leave me alone!" Near the back wall, between two overgrown bridal wreaths, five boys surrounded a smaller one.

Dan set the box of books on the convent lawn and ran toward them. The largest boy pulled the small one from the wall, then flung him back against it where he crumpled to the ground and covered his head. The big kid kicked him in the thigh and yelled, "Next time I tell you to do something, you'll do it, right?"

The boy sobbed and nodded.

Another kick. "Say it!"

The small boy ran a sleeve across his face. "Right."

One boy spotted Dan, said "Oh-oh," and took off. Three others followed. The bully stayed and stood over his victim.

"What are you doing?" Dan asked.

"Nothing, Father."

"Who's that?" Dan nodded toward the boy on the ground.

"Friend of mine."

"You have a strange way of treating your friends."

"Just a friendly argument, ain't that so, Lester?" He nudged Lester's thigh with his foot.

"Mm," the boy said. He crouched deeper into the dirt and leaned hard against the red bricks as though a secret door might open and let him escape.

The bigger boy smiled. "See, Father?"

"A friendly argument," Dan said, and the bully nodded. He'd missed the sarcasm. So had Lester, whose eyes pleaded for the priest not to leave. "Okay, he's Lester, but who are you?"

"Bobby Weishaus."

"What's your argument about, Bobby?"

The boy shrugged. "One of those things between friends. Right, Lester?"

Lester nodded, eyes toward the dirt.

"See?" Bobby said. "Everything's fine."

"I don't think so." Dan worked to keep his voice level. "Something's bothering me, Bobby. It's ... well, what you're having with Lester isn't an argument because you're not discussing different opinions. And it's not a fight because the only one hitting someone is you. What's really going on?"

"I told you. Nothing."

"Nothing?"

"Mm-hmm. Jus' stuff between us kids."

Dan's face burned. Fifteen years earlier, on his way home from Sacred Heart School, he had sat trapped against a neighbor's house with Reedy Mindlesohn kicking him. Two women waggled by in high heels and Dan pleaded with his eyes for help the way Lester did now. But the women walked on, shaking their heads.

"Kids these days," one said.

Up to that moment, Dan had never cursed anyone because the nuns said it was a sin. But he cursed those women, and he wasn't going to give Lester a reason to curse him.

"Take a look around, Bobby. Where are you?"

"Huh? Um ... back of church, I guess."

"Right. You're assaulting Lester on church property. I work for the church, you know. Part of my job is to make sure kids feel safe here."

"Okay, Father, we'll go someplace else. C'mon, Lester." Bobby tugged at Lester's arm. Lester pulled it away and twisted toward the wall.

"Lester-r-r-r," Bobby said. "Remember what we talked about?"

Lester sobbed and rose to his knees.

Dan stepped forward. "No, Lester's not going with you, Bobby. You're a bully. Has anyone ever told you that?"

Bobby looked up.

"I've seen you in school," Dan said. "What grade are you in?"

"Eighth."

"Sister Xaviera's class. By now, then, you've heard it's wrong to beat up other kids."

Bobby shrugged and turned away.

"Look at Lester," Dan said. "Can't you see how miserable he feels? Little kids should be able to depend on strong boys like you for protection. Wouldn't it make you feel better knowing they looked up to you like that?"

Bobby shrugged again, then kicked a small stone toward Lester and grinned when the small boy cringed.

This kid wasn't getting the message. Bobby would start in again on Lester as soon as Dan was out of sight—hell, he wasn't even waiting for that—and Lester would be too scared to tell anyone.

"Okay, Bobby, you don't care what I think, but listen. If you bother Lester again, I'll bother you. Got that? Whatever you do to him, I'll do to you."

Bobby's eyes widened. "You can't do that. You're a *priest*!"

"Doesn't matter. You're bigger than Lester and I'm bigger than you. I don't really want to do anything bad to you, and I won't, as long as you leave the little kids alone. Do we have a deal?"

"Priests can't hit kids. No grown-up can. I'll sue! I'll tell my dad and he'll call the cops. He knows the chief! You'll go to jail!"

"Go ahead. Tell him. Tell everyone you want. But make sure you tell them this: Father Bates will not let big kids hurt little ones. I'm going to watch you, Bobby, 'cause you're a coward. If being a bully is so much fun, I'll have some fun, too. We'll have ourselves a 'friendly little argument' like you said you were having with Lester."

"Stay away from me," Bobby yelled. Then he ran.

Dan watched him go. Damn. He had said too much.

And too little, Danny. Bobby is a troubled child. You need to offer him the same compassion you gave Lester.

Why did he keep imagining Jessica's voice when he hadn't seen her in years? Well, this time he didn't agree with her. Lester needed protection. That came first.

I don't disagree, Danny. But the best protection you can offer Lester is to help Bobby get over the cause of his bullying, and how can you do that now that you've scared him away?

Dan became aware that Lester was standing next to the church wall. "You okay, Lester? I'll walk you home."

The boy patted the dust from his pants, then he and the priest walked past the church, shooshing through yellow leaves covering the sidewalk.

"I'm sorry you're gonna get in trouble 'cause of me, Father." The victim blaming himself.

"It wasn't because of you, Lester. It was because of Bobby. And because of me. Bullies bothered me when I was your age, and I swore I'd stop 'em when I grew up. It's not your fault."

"If I did pushups and learned how to fight, I'll bet he'd leave me alone." Lester looked up at Dan. "He's going to tell his dad on you."

"We'll see. But I want you to let me know if Bobby or anyone else bothers you again, okay?"

"That's tattling, Father."

"Yes it is, but tattling isn't bad. Bullies like Bobby tell kids it's terrible so they can pick on them and get away with it. They're cowards, so they make up rules like 'no tattling.' Well, *my* rule says 'no bullying.' It's a better rule, don't you think? Besides, Bobby said he was going to tell his dad about me, didn't he?"

"Yeah," Lester said. "And he will, too."

"Well, isn't that tattling? Bobby isn't even following his own rule."

Lester laughed, a sweet sound that made Dan glad he'd run Bobby off. They stopped in front of a small clapboard house with a screened front porch.

"Here it is, Father. Thank you."

"You're welcome, Lester. See you Monday in school."

"Father, do you think you could call me *Les*?"

"Sure, Les."

The boy stepped onto the porch, waved, and went inside.

Dan listened to the leaves as he shuffled back to the rectory. He was going to be in trouble again.

Grume met Dan at the door. "You had a phone call."

Bobby had worked fast. Dan blushed. "Father, I—"

"Sister Xaviera," Grume said. "She's hot. Something about your leaving a box of books on the convent lawn."

Dan ate little that night, his stomach flip-flopping each time the phone rang. When the call finally came, the old pastor grew quiet.

"He did?" Grume said. "Of course you can come over."

The two priests met Adolph Weishaus at the door. He was a short, wiry man with lonely strands of hair combed across his almost-bald scalp. At twelve, Bobby was bigger than his dad.

"How could you talk that way to my son?" Adolph shouted from the steps. "Threatening an eighth-grade boy! What kind of a priest are you?"

Grume pulled him into the entryway and pushed the door shut. "Come in come in come in. Come into the parlor, Mr. Weishaus. Yes! We can discuss this in the parlor."

"There's nothing to discuss! This … this so-called man of God threatened to beat up my Bobby. A priest in my own parish. After all I've done. I can't believe it."

Dan kept his voice calm. "What did Bobby tell you I said?"

Grume touched Dan's sleeve. "A minute, Father Bates. Let me handle this." He cleared his throat. "What did your son tell you Father Bates said, Mr. Weishaus?"

"That the priest—not you, Father Grume, the young one, *him*—said he'd beat him up." Adolph turned to Dan. "Threatening a child. Shame on you!"

Dan blushed. "Did Bobby tell you the rest of the story—about what he was doing before I talked to him?"

"What does that matter? He's only a boy!"

"He was beating up a little boy, Mr. Weishaus. Your son is a bully."

"A bully? What do you—"

"Father," Grume said, "perhaps you should—"

"Not mention the part Bobby left out? Why wouldn't you want to hear that? Because it complicates things? Do you have a better idea about how to protect little kids from a bully?"

Grume patted Dan on the arm. "In my experience, it's usually better to let children work out their own problems. Perhaps your youth and—"

"My youth, hell! Bobby attends St. Bart's, but teaching him Christian principles hasn't stopped him. And my talking to him didn't work, so I tried fear. Maybe I—"

"You threatened him!" Adolph said.

"I'll talk to him at school Monday, apologize for scaring him, and try again to persuade him to use his size and strength to protect little kids, not hurt them. But we have to do something, and if Bobby refuses to change we need to set up some consequences. That's what I was trying to do, because he apparently hasn't had to face any"—Dan stared at Adolph, then at Grume—"from his parents or anyone else."

Adolph's face became redder, and his eyes were huge. "Now you're insulting me and my wife! Father Grume, are you going to let him get away with this?"

"I will certainly talk to Father Bates, Mr. Weishaus. I think he already sees—"

"*Talk* to him?" Adolph was shaking. "You get rid of him, or I'm going to the bishop!"

Grume stepped back and rubbed his hands together. "Mr. Weishaus, there's really no need. I'm sure we can work out something to the satisfaction of all concerned."

"Work *him* out," Adolph said. "I'll give you two days." He threw open the front door and tromped down the sidewalk.

Grume stepped behind his desk and drew back the chair. "Have a seat."

Dan folded his arms. "I'll stand."

Grume leaned over the desk. "What the hell were you thinking?"

"I was thinking," Dan said, "to protect Lester. What do you *think* I was thinking?"

"You blew it all out of proportion."

"How would you know? You weren't there."

"You can't threaten children and then insult their parents. That man is one of the biggest donors in this parish."

"So we have to let his kid beat up little ones? For Pete's sake, I don't want to beat up Bobby. But when I saw him snarling over Les in the dirt I couldn't think of a damn thing that would work better with that little sadist. I still can't. Can you? Resurrection doesn't have classes in child psychology, you know."

Grume held the edge of his desk. "That's why it's best to let children settle things themselves."

Dan stepped toward him. "If someone broke in here tonight, what would you do?"

Grume stood straight. "Huh? I'd call the police, of course. What's that got to do with this?"

"C'mon. You wouldn't stand up to the thief like a big boy?" Dan paused. "You have no idea what I'm getting at, do you? Why should you get police protection when you force little kids to go it alone against bullies twice their size?"

Grume cleared his throat. "They have to learn to handle themselves sooner or later."

"But only while they're kids. Once they grow up big and brave like you, they get to call the cops."

"That's enough."

"No, it's not. Bullying is child abuse. We can't turn our backs on it. Bobbie Weishaus should be arrested for assault. What if Les's dad came here demanding you protect his kid?"

"I'd tell him to teach his son self defense."

"I'll bet you would. But if Bobby attacked *you*, you'd call the cops."

"That's it! I've had it! No more!" Grume pointed to the door. "Get packing! I'm calling Elmendorf first thing in the morning. This time, by God, he's gonna transfer your ass out of here."

Dan stopped at the door. "I can only hope."

On Monday morning, Dan went to the school. At recess, he drew Les aside and told him about his transfer.

"It's 'cause you got me away from Bobby, ain't it."

Dan nodded. He wasn't going to lie.

"It ain't fair. They should kick Bobby out of here, not you."

"I shouldn't have threatened to beat Bobby up."

"You didn't! At least not if he left me alone." Les started crying. "Everybody worries about Bobby, but they don't care if he beats *me* up, do they?"

"I've warned Sister Xaviera and Father Grume about him, Les. If you have problems, I want you to tell one of them, all right?"

"Are you sure they'll help me?"

Of course he wasn't sure. He could see Grume telling Les to grow up and be a man, then forcing him back onto the playground to face Bobby again.

And Grume wouldn't lose his job over it.

Dan checked his watch. He was due to teach Les's class after recess. "Go to the bathroom and wash your face, Les. Take your time. When you feel better, come into the classroom. I'll tell Sister Henrietta you're doing something for me and you'll be along in a little while. Okay?"

Les nodded and ran. He came into the classroom about ten minutes into Dan's lesson.

Dan's anger toward Grume and his fear for Les left him rambling, forgetting half of what he wanted to say. The bell for lunch ended his embarrassment. The kids filed out, and Dan was saying goodbye to Sister Henrietta when he noticed Les sitting at his desk.

"He said he feels sick, Father."

"Sick with fear, probably. He's being bullied by Bobby Weishaus. And Grume doesn't give a damn."

Sister Henrietta's face turned red.

He had offended her. "I'm sorry, Sister, but—"

She shook her head, waved him off. "That Father Grume gets me so mad sometimes."

"Well," Dan said, "that's partly … no, that's mostly, why I've been transferred."

"I see," she said. She stood with him and watched Les. "I suspected something was wrong." She walked slowly toward the boy. "Les, Father Bates just told me about Bobby. I didn't know about it, and I'm sorry. But if you have any more problems with him, or any problems like that with other children, I want you to tell me, okay?"

Les turned red, but nodded.

"I mean it, Les," the nun said. "I'm not going to let Bobby or other kids hurt you, understand? There are things that we—Sister Xaviera and I—can do to help, and I promise we'll do them. All right?"

The boy nodded again.

Sister Henrietta walked back to Dan. "That promise goes to you too, Father. I don't want you to leave here thinking we're going to ignore something like that." She smiled. "You must understand, Father: Sister Xaviera and I *do* give a damn."

For the first time in his life, Dan wanted to kiss a nun. "Thank you, Sister. You don't know how much I appreciate that."

They shook hands.

Despite his comment to Grume, Dan didn't want to leave. Bellamy was his first assignment, and he'd gotten to know the people and their problems.

The morning before he moved, he visited Hilltop Home for the last time.

"A new priest will come to see you," he told Charlotte Esterman.

Lillian James cried. "It won't be the same, Father. We'll miss your jokes."

"The next guy might tell better ones," he told Irv Tatnell. "Then you'll wish I had left sooner."

With all of them, there was a little talk, a laugh, then tears, their hands clutching his, knowing they would not see him again.

It's cruel how they ship you guys around. Cruel to you, of course, but even more cruel to those who love you.

Yeah, Jessica would say that.

Penny Nichol was sitting in her gray chair, staring out on a gray day. There was nothing in the garden except a row of potted mums lining the stone path. "I heard," she said. "Damn it all."

"Another priest will come."

"I don't want another priest. I want you. You don't try to push your God down anyone's throat. I mean, Lillian's nice, but she thinks she has to convert me before one of us dies."

"I've never had much luck with that."

"You make people feel good. That's more important."

"Tell me something, Penny. Without God, you're alone. Aren't you scared?"

She pushed her chair away from the window and turned to face him. "We're *all* alone, Dan. 'Cept for each other, of course, 'cause there's no one up there. Sometimes I think people fail each other because of their attraction to spirits. And I mean ghosts, not booze, though I suppose they both apply."

She said it with little emotion, the way he remembered Sergeant Friday speaking in *Dragnet*: *Just the facts, ma'am.* But Dan wondered: Who had the facts: he with his faith, or she without one?

"Just 'cause our brains work a smidgen better than other animals'," Penny went on, "doesn't make us special. I keep wondering if there's a second or two before we die when we realize this is all there is."

"Or," Dan said, "that we're headed somewhere for all eternity."

Penny laughed. "To oblivion's my guess, the same place we were before we got born. That doesn't scare me. But a long, painful dying does, with all the misery that goes with it. I've always been amazed at how we're willing to put animals out of their misery but we refuse to do it for ourselves. No, we'd rather force people in agony to drag out their end. But, still, once we're dead, we're dead. Count on it, Dan."

Dan stepped close and touched her cheek. "Bless you, Penny."

She squeezed his hand. "You take good care of yourself, Dan. No one else is going to."

On the drive home Dan thought of Penny. She was nearing the end of her life but gave no sign of believing in God. For years he had assumed Jessica would eventually come back to the Church, though maybe not until she faced her own death. But now, after talking with Penny, he wondered.

Oblivion's my guess. Once we're dead, we're dead. Count on it, Dan.

He prayed for Pat's special intention and for Jessica to regain her faith—maybe the same thing—as well as for himself, to gain a stronger faith than he felt that day.

CHAPTER 27

▼

"Thought I'd better give you my new number," Dan told Pat by phone a few weeks later. "Elmendorf's assigned me to St. Jerome's in Madison, a little west of the U. Lots of students. He says it's temporary, that he'll move me after I get counseling and stop embarrassing him."

"Be careful," Pat said. "Don't get suspended."

"I'll try. But sometimes they get me so mad."

"That's why they want you in counseling. Meantime, pick some battles you can win. Convince Elemdorf you're on his side. Right now he's not sure. You're scaring him."

Dan found the office of Bert Covington, ACSW, on the ninth floor of a building on Madison's capitol square. In the waiting room, a laminated sign leaned against a green vase: "Please have a seat. Bert will be with you shortly."

He opened a *Wisconsin Tales and Trails* magazine to a photo of the Cana Island lighthouse in Door County. Pat's pictures were as good. He should send some in.

The inner door opened. A tall, goateed man Dan's age stuck out his hand. "Dan Bates? Bert Covington. Come in."

Dan glanced around the office. Photographs of rivers, ornate buildings, and trains shared wall space with certificates of Bert's credentials.

"Nice pictures," Dan said. "Did you take 'em?"

Bert ran a hand through wavy black hair. "Mm-hmm. Helps take my mind off stuff I have trouble forgetting." He eased into a black leather chair across a low wooden table from Dan, who sat in the chair's twin. Bert opened a manila folder and studied a sheet of paper inside. "Let's get business out of the way first. I'm to bill the diocese for our sessions, correct?"

"Yes, but if they want you to report what I say, I'll pay it myself."

"No, they've agreed our discussions are confidential."

Dan studied Bert's certificates. "Are you a psychologist?"

"Social worker. ACSW stands for Academy of Certified Social Workers. That's the national association's way of saying I'm qualified to do this."

Dan leaned back. "I'm not sure where to start."

"Why don't you tell me why you're here."

"I get mad."

Bert laughed. "How does that differ from the rest of us?"

"I'm a priest. I embarrass the diocese."

Bert set the folder aside. "So maybe the diocese needs counseling." He grinned. "But you're here and they're not, so tell me how it's a problem for you. Getting mad, I mean."

"The bishop pulled me from my parish because I threatened a bully. I did it to keep him—the bully, not the bishop—from beating up little kids."

"And it cost you your job."

"Yeah," Dan said. "But I don't think Elmendorf—the bishop—understood that the bully just wouldn't quit. I suppose I overreacted, but it's like the bishop and my pastor—ex-pastor now—don't give a damn about the little kids, just the bully and his dad. I'm worried about the little ones."

Bert was silent for a few seconds. "So, if I'm hearing you right, they want you to figure out a way to act on your commitment to people without getting yourself in trouble."

"That's about it," Dan said.

Bert smiled. "I think we can do that."

On the Saturday before Christmas, Dan settled into the confessional in St. Jerome's church. The line of penitents stretched to the balcony stairs near the back door. Hearing hundreds of confessions—many from people who came only at this time of the year—was the worst part of the holiday. Footsteps from the first in line echoed off the terrazzo floor. Dan slid open the left panel.

"Bless me, Father, for I have sinned." Feminine voice, young, but older than most students he'd heard here. "Father, I'm a stewardess flying out tonight. I'm afraid I might be in mortal sin."

"All right. Go on."

"I made love with my boyfriend last night."

"All right."

"And we used a condom."

"Okay." At least they were responsible enough to avoid a pregnancy.

"But I don't feel sorry for it, Father."

"I see," Dan said. "How long have you known this man?"

"Since he moved here two years ago. We love each other, Father. We've tried to stay pure, but last night we started kissing and after a while he started touching—"

"Why do you think you're not sorry?" *Damn, he hated details. Celibacy was tough enough without listening to a play-by-play of others' escapades.*

"It just didn't seem wrong, Father."

The words he'd said after his night with Jessica. And Quince hadn't doubted him. But Dan said—and he had no idea why—"The Church, of course, insists any sexual expression outside of marriage is a sin."

"Yes. And I've always believed that. Till last night. It was … um, nice, Father. I mean, if you've ever … ah, I mean … oh." She coughed. "What I mean is, it didn't seem like a sin, Father."

"What would a sin seem like?" *Jeez, stupid question.* Quince never asked *him* that. Why was he being tougher on this woman than Quince was on him?

"Well, like if he forced me to do things I didn't want to do. Or maybe if we did it without protection and took a chance on my getting pregnant. Those would be sins."

"But the Church also condemns artificial birth control."

"Yes, well … I know that, Father, but I've never agreed with it. None of my friends do, either. I'm sorry, but it makes no sense at all."

"So your conscience is clear on that?"

"Yes, Father."

"I'm not sure, then, what you're asking forgiveness for."

"The sex, Father. I don't feel as sure about that, though I don't see how the Church can call making love a sin."

Dan didn't either. "Well, as a priest I can't tell you it's all right. But I can advise you to consult your own conscience. That's what you must obey. What does it tell you?"

"Like I said, Father, I thought it was a sin before, but now I don't think so."

"All right." He had decided the same thing after he and Jessica made love. But, as a representative of the Church, he wasn't supposed to tell that to anyone. How would Quince handle this? Dan spoke softly. "Each of us must listen to our own conscience. You seem to have considered the seriousness of your actions and come to a conclusion that satisfies yours. I'll grant you absolution for any sins you have committed and for which you are sincerely sorry. For your penance say five Our Fathers and five Hail Marys."

He hoped he'd said the right things.

"Your anger comes from you, not from them," Bert Covington told Dan during their session between Christmas and the start of the new year.

Dan stared at the skinny branch of a birch tree stuck into a heavy vase on Bert's desk. Three red and two green balls and a few strands of tinsel hung from the twigs sticking out on the sides. Bert had a weird sense of humor about the season. "But my bosses say such stupid stuff. That's what makes me mad."

Bert leaned forward. "No, *that* doesn't make you mad. If you're going to feel less angry and get into less trouble, you'd better accept the fact that you're the one making yourself mad *about* the things they say. Your friend Pat—are his bosses smarter?"

"No."

"Does he get as angry as you do?"

"No. Pat's more laid back."

"So *he's* different, and that's what makes him react differently to the same stupid stuff?"

"Yeah. Pat just gets kind of annoyed."

"Really. But, if what your bosses say causes *you* to feel angry, why doesn't it also cause *Pat* to feel angry?"

"I told you, he's more laid back."

"So, if you were more laid back like Pat, you wouldn't get so mad?"

"I guess."

"And why do you suppose Pat is more laid back than you?"

Dan shrugged. "He's probaby more philosophical about things."

"Meaning?"

"He seems to think what they say isn't so terrible."

Bert grinned. "Just stupid and bad."

"I guess you could put it that way."

"Pat gets annoyed and doesn't like what they say, but he doesn't go off the deep end like you do."

"Right."

"Okay. If *you* thought what they said was only bad, not terrible, do you think you might be less angry, maybe only annoyed like Pat?"

Dan smiled. "Probably, but I'm not sure that's possible."

"To you, everyone had better make sense."

"Well, yeah, I—"

"You not only *want* them to make sense, you *demand* they make sense, right? Or *boom!*"

Dan blushed. "I guess that's true."

"But your demanding that people make sense doesn't make sense either."

"Sure it does. They have a lot of power over a lot of people. They're supposed to make sense."

"You sound as if there's a rule for it. But the universe has no law requiring people with power to act sensibly. Or even morally, for that matter. Yet you act as though there is such a law. You demand they follow it, and you get angry when they don't."

"And Pat accepts it? That's the difference?"

Bert leaned back. "Part of it. Look at how your attitude differs from Pat's—you demand, while he only *prefers* that people do the right thing—and notice how your feelings fit your attitude. Am I right in saying Pat *wants* Church leaders to act more sensibly, but doesn't *demand* it like you do?"

"I guess."

"And he avoids the trouble you keep getting into."

"Yeah."

"Is it possible Pat's way of looking at life—his philosophy, as you say—makes more sense than yours?"

Dan jerked forward. "Hey! Whose side are you on?"

"Yours. I know this isn't easy to hear. But listen, in some cases, our feelings are caused by a chemical imbalance. Medication's the only way to fix that. In your case, I'm convinced it's your cognitive processes—that's jargon for your thinking and attitude about things—that are causing your anger."

"But if my bosses didn't hurt people, I wouldn't get so mad."

"True, but you can't change or control them, only yourself. And only you can decide if you want to. Showing anger and forcing a confrontation may be strategies you'll still decide to use. Some people do that effectively. But even then, you can *feel* less angry while you *act* however you want. You can feel calmer and decide more rationally what actions might work toward your goal. So far, you've acted only out of anger—you've exploded, so to speak—and you've not only felt miserable from the adrenaline in your system, you've made bad decisions and lost your battles. And your job."

Bert came around his desk. "So, your anger gives you at least two problems for the price of one. The first problem—them being stupid, even cruel—is bad enough. But you can't control that. So the question becomes, do you add those second and third problems, emotional misery and possible punishment, to your first one?" He clicked off the recorder and ejected the tape. "Review today's session and think about it. We covered a lot today. Write down your questions. We'll talk more next time."

During the summer of 1970, Dan anticipated another year at St. Jerome's. He liked living near the UW campus, though he avoided places where he and Jessica had spent time—especially Observatory Hill and Paisan's.

Over the winter, Bert Covington had helped him look differently at the Church and its hierarchy. He still got annoyed, but became less angry, less often, and for briefer periods than before.

Bishop Elmendorf apparently noticed the change. In August, he assigned Dan to St. George's Church in Avon Park, a city of six thousand in southern Wisconsin.

There, on a hot summer evening ten months later, Dan was washing his car when pastor F. Chandler Redding called him into the office.

"Letter from the bishop," the pastor said. "The anniversary of *Humanae Vitae* is coming up, and Rufus wants our homilies to remind the faithful that the pope's encyclical remains in effect."

Dan folded his arms. "I can't do that. I'm convinced birth control doesn't violate any of God's laws. It's immoral to tell people something's a sin when it's not."

Redding set a glass paperweight on top of some papers. He didn't look up. "Well, the pope has decreed that it is a sin. Our bishop wants us to remind people of that."

"The pope is wrong about this."

Redding stood. "I know some of you young guys consider yourselves higher authorities than the pope, but we all must listen to him as a source of unity in the Church."

"God will judge my conscience, not the pope."

"But you are a priest. And you vowed obedience to the authority of Rome." Redding examined the paperweight and set it back down. "Look, I'm sorry, but if you won't speak on your assigned topic next Sunday, I'll have to call Rufus and request your transfer."

Dan stepped toward the desk. "C'mon, Chan, I've been here almost a year. I've done good work. You told me yourself old people and the sick look forward to my visits. The kids in school pay attention to my talks, and I hear more than my share of confessions. I—"

"And heaven knows what you tell them in there." Redding put his hands on the desk. "If you're advising 'em the Pill is morally acceptable, God have mercy on your soul. Hardly anyone confesses that to me anymore. Is that what you're doing—telling people it's okay—so they all come to you?"

Dan shook his head. "Most Catholics disagree with the pope. They're not going to confess it to *anyone* if they don't think it's a sin." He headed for the door, then stopped. "I've enjoyed my work here. But I have to be honest with people ... and with myself. Do what you have to do."

Pat slammed down his fork. "Your pastor has asked the bishop to pull you from the ministry, and you sit here over dinner and ask me about Jessie. Damn it, Jessie's fine. You're the one with problems."

Dan didn't look up. "Does she have a boyfriend? Is she married? Any kids?"

"She's fine. That's all she wants me to tell you."

"If she weren't, would you still say she was?"

"Yes. No. Hell, how do I know? She's fine. If she weren't, I'd ... anyway, she's fine."

Dan stared at his friend. "You haven't exactly convinced me."

"Yeah?" Pat sat back. "You haven't exactly convinced *me* you want to stay a priest! You still don't keep your mouth shut. Didn't that Bert guy get through to you?"

"I still say the truth."

"Your 'truth' feeds them ammunition. Ammunition enough to fire you. Stop confronting them. They hate that. Shut up and nod your head so they think you're agreeing with them. *Then* do what you want. Nine times out of ten they won't even notice."

"But if we're right, why keep quiet?"

Pat rolled his eyes. "Oh, man, I thought you were better. Play Bert's tapes again, will you? You're killing your career. Think of the things you love: saying Mass, visiting the sick, teaching the kids. Think, damn it!"

"I do."

"Really? You could fool me. Keep on the way you are, and they won't let you do *anything*. We don't have a union, you know. If they want you out, you're out. You've read the papers. Rome's booted priests, even bishops, who've challenged them on birth control."

"So how do you do it? You don't agree with them."

Pat leaned forward. "Ignore the crap. Ignore the pope, the bishop, the pastor when they don't make sense. Focus on your people." He paused. "That's not a perfect answer, of course. Maybe someday they'll come after me too. But that's the beauty of celibacy."

Dan laughed. "*Beauty?*"

"Yes. If they dump us, we can beg, borrow or steal if we need something to eat. We can sleep in our cars if we have nowhere else to go. We have no wives or kids to worry about. I base my priesthood on what I believe, but I keep my mouth shut, and it's working."

Dan shut his mouth, and his problems with Father Redding and the chancery stopped.

"I hate it when you're right," he told Pat.

He focused on the Mass and on his Sunday homilies, on teaching the kids in school, on visiting the sick and administering the sacraments. Baptism was best. Its simple ceremony welcomed new members into the Church, and there were smiles on the faces of the parents, godparents, and family. He loved watching the babies' expressions with their budding personalities: quiet and curious, cooing and content, squirming and crying. Of course, they all squirmed when he poured the water across their foreheads, but some screamed and others glanced around with a look of "What's going on?" And the little brothers and sisters frowned at the babies' discomfort, looking at their parents and at Dan, the accusation in their eyes: "You should stop that. The baby doesn't like it."

Matrimony left him with mixed feelings. He still had trouble talking to women—women, hell; anyone!—about sex. Of course, every couple he instructed asked about birth control. He told them about *Humanae Vitae*; then, to be fair to them and to his own conscience, he said many people thought the pope was wrong. He encouraged them to read, discuss, and form their own opinions. There was always a chance, of course, that one of them would tell Redding what he was saying. But Redding never said a word.

The weddings themselves were fun, but as Dan witnessed the exchange of vows and the smiles of the bride and groom, he knew half the marriages wouldn't last. Perhaps the receptions held a clue. Some became crude drunken parties that obliterated the dignity and beauty of the sacrament he had just witnessed.

In his visits to hospitals and nursing homes, he continued to be amazed at how people accepted death. Not all, of course. Some fought to the end. With the dying, Dan recited the prescribed prayer: "Free your servant from sickness, restore him his health, raise him up by your right hand, strengthen him by your power, protect him by your might and give him back to your holy Church, with all that is needed for his welfare."

But he often came away from the visits disturbed at how helpless he was. *Ask and you shall receive.* Christ's words. Still, no matter how fervently Dan asked, God's power never showed up to strengthen these poor people. They always got weaker and died. His old doubts crept back, but each day he tried to bury them in the joy of his work in Avon Park.

Five years later, in the spring of 1975, Dan and Pat climbed the granite bluff on the east side of Devil's Lake. Below them, two yellow-and-green locomotives pulled a Chicago and NorthWestern freight train along shiny tracks at the edge of the water. The engine's horns echoed off the bluffs that circled the lake.

"Made a visit to an old couple yesterday," Dan said. He sat down on a rock along the trail. "Husband and wife for almost sixty years, old and sick. Kids scattered coast to coast. Enough money for food, but not for the drugs they need. They're gonna have to sell their house. Not their house, their *home*. And I couldn't think of a damned thing to do except refer 'em to the county."

"You were there for them," Pat said. "Somebody cared; they weren't alone."

Dan pulled his canteen and took one gulp of water. "I was there ten, fifteen minutes. They *are* alone."

Pat drank too. "But your presence reminded them that God doesn't abandon them. They can call you any time."

"With the same result. Or lack of one. Hell, I didn't think of God once while I was there, just how terrible I'd feel in their shoes."

"Even so, as a priest you reminded them of God, that they're never alone."

Dan strapped the canteen to his shoulder. "Think so? Or is God just an invention of man, a hedge against the ultimate loneliness? He's certainly no help at finding food or medicine."

Pat capped his bottle and pushed it deep into his pack. "Enough. Let's hit the trail and think about how high we want to climb. We should have met in Milwaukee and gone to a Brewers game. It's our day off but here we are talking about work." He laughed. "We're supposed to be refreshing our minds and bodies for the battles ahead."

Dan took the lead and talked over his shoulder. "Are you always as happy as you seem?"

"Of course not," Pat said. "The priesthood hasn't come close to what I thought it would be before the Council. Remember when priests ran their parishes?"

"Yeah, but I like having people tell us what they think. It's a lot healthier for the Church, even if it's not as comfortable for us."

Pat laughed. "That reminds me: At our last parish council meeting a woman demanded I sit in school all day to spy on what those liberal nuns and lay teachers were telling her children."

"What did you say?"

"I told her it was the liberals who won her the right to tell me that, that her friends the conservatives would have quoted Paul's letter demanding that women keep quiet in church."

"Good one. She say anything?"

"She made a face. I told her if we had a conservative parish, I'd call the shots myself and tell her and everyone else how to think and what to do."

Dan pulled himself onto a ledge and crawled to one side to make room for Pat. "Funny how fast people forget."

Pat pulled two granola bars from his backpack and handed one to Dan. "At any rate, I'm doing work that I mostly love, within the bounds of my pastor and the parish, of course. Sometimes I feel so good about making someone happy, or at least less miserable, that I doubt I've gained any eternal merit."

"No emotional pain, no spiritual gain?"

Pat laughed. "Something like that."

"Maybe the seminary should have taught us social work. People call about problems that have nothing to do with what we trained for. Praying doesn't get the job done. I finally set up a file of agencies: welfare, counseling, private charities, employment, even the cops. I make a lot of calls. It keeps me from feeling helpless."

Sometimes, especially during weekday Masses, Dan thought he must be invisible. The old people kept their heads down and mouthed their prayers with loud whispers. But on Sunday mornings, he became the center of attention as he sang the high Mass and presented his homily.

One crisp fall day, Dan preached one of his favorite sermons. "No matter if we work as bankers or doctors or diggers or depend on welfare, no matter if we keep house or teach or clean buildings or run corporations, no matter if we make decisions in a penthouse suite or pick peas off the dirt, we are human and therefore equal in God's eyes. So why do we look at each other differently?"

Dan's words reminded him of Paul's letter to the Galatians: "All baptized in Christ, you have all clothed yourselves in Christ, and there are no more distinctions between Jew and Greek, slave and free, male and female, but all of you are one in Christ Jesus."

No more distinctions between male and female. Someone should read that verse to the pope. How could he refuse to ordain women?

Sunday mornings went fast, but the afternoons dragged. Dan had to stay in the rectory because somebody might call. No one would, of course, but someone *might*. Hey, if he was on call, shouldn't he *get* a call? By the end of the Packer game—with no one to cheer with, who cared what the team did—Dan almost wished someone was dying so he'd have to drive out to see them. He clicked off the TV. There was no sound in the rectory. Maybe if he opened a window he'd hear birds. Or a car or a motorcycle or a truck. Leaves in the trees. Anything. He lifted the phone, listened to the dial tone. He opened the refrigerator long enough for its condenser to kick in.

He dialed for the time. A young woman's voice told him it was three twenty in the afternoon. "Thank you," he said when the recording stopped. "That's very nice of you. Could I interest you in a candlelight dinner tonight, just the two of us, in one of Avon Park's finest restaurants?"

He listened to the buzz. "Ah, you're speechless at my offer. Perhaps you don't get them often. I don't either, I'm sorry to say. But listen, there's a play called *A Man for All Seasons*—have you seen it? Perhaps we could go someday. It's about St. Thomas More, a man beheaded by Henry the Eighth in the sixteenth century for refusing to sign a paper. Anyway, at his trial More pointed out that, by law, his silence actually indicated consent. So, thank you for your silent consent to my offer. I'll pick you up at six."

He set down the receiver. Damn it, where was Jessie? If he knew, he'd call her. He wouldn't even care if she hung up. He'd get to hear her say hello.

Many of those interminable Sunday afternoons brought back doubts. Did his priesthood mean something beyond helping a few people feel happy for a couple of minutes? Or had he—and they—been taken in by a myth about a God who supposedly looked over them?

The priests ate well at St. George's. Dan's belt was already out two notches since he first got assigned. He was reading the *Avon Post* over breakfast when Chan Redding came in from Mass and slipped two slices of bread into the toaster.

"I need you to cover the Holy Name Society meeting tonight."

"Okay." Dan flipped open his pocket calendar. "Oh, wait. I'm sorry, I promised Mrs. Kwadinski I'd drop by for Bible study. Her last heart attack pretty much confined her to home."

Redding watched the toaster. "Put Mrs. K on hold. I need you here."

"She's not well, you know. Her husband died last year."

The toast popped up and Redding flung the slices onto the counter and shook the heat from his fingers. "She oughta sell that big house and move in with somebody. Anyway, the Holy Name guys are looking forward to your leading the prayer, telling a few jokes, joining their card games. Makes an impression, one of us attending. If we're generous to them, we can expect they'll be generous to us."

Dan shook the sports page open.

Redding twisted the cover off the jam. "So you'll be there, right?"

Dan set the paper on the table. "Mrs. Kwadinski needs me a lot more than the Holy Namers do. Those guys can enjoy each other's company without me, but if I don't show up at Mrs. K's she has no one to talk to. The guys'll get along fine, probably get in a few jokes I'd inhibit 'em from telling."

Redding glared. "I'm entitled to your obedience. I'm your pastor."

Dan tried to smile. "True. But remember, you're the pastor of *all* the people in this parish, and Mrs. K is entitled to some pastoral concern too. If she gave a few grand a year—was generous, as you call it—you'd be pushing me over to her place every other day. But she can't afford a penny, so you want me to waste my time at a stupid card party."

"It's not a waste," Redding said. "It—"

Dan put up a hand. "Tell you what. I'll round up a few Holy Name guys and take 'em with me. The Bible study'll do them good, and afterwards we can play cards and tell jokes with Mrs. K. She'll be delighted."

"So you're going to disobey me. The bishop will be interested in this. We have, I recall, been down this path before."

The letter from Bishop Elmendorf arrived a week later.

Dear Father Bates,

I have full realization that you have labored diligently at the problems we've documented in your dealings with other people, but you seem not to have been fully successful. I must inform you, in all fairness, that I will not be able in good conscience to offer you a pastorate in the future until such time as you discontinue your contentiousness against every institution with which you come into contact. Please adjust your behavior in line with the requests of your pastor, Father Redding.

With best wishes,

Rufus

Dan read the letter several times. He wouldn't respond, of course. Pat would kill him if he did. But he couldn't help thinking of what he'd like to say: Dear Rufus, to keep myself in good conscience I must continue my contentiousness against every institution whose policies and practices cause people pain. And that includes our own. With best wishes, Dan.

Chapter 28

A cold, late-April rain pelted Dan's face during his sprint from the rectory's back porch to the priest's sacristy. Inside Avon Park's old sandstone church, he used a handkerchief to dry his face. On a morning like this, only the regulars would attend the Mass, maybe a dozen men and women, all of them old.

He stepped into the sanctuary. The sweet scent of lilies permeated the church. In the days after Easter, the altar society had placed small bouquets of early spring flowers—crocuses, daffodils and tulips—between the lilies, then tied red, white and blue ribbons imprinted "God bless America" onto the vases.

Would people ever accept God as Lord over all, and not tie religion to patriotism? Oh well, it was 1976, the nation's bicentennial. Even the railroads had painted some of their locomotives into patriotic colors.

The USA was 200 years old. He was 32—was that still young?—and next month he'd celebrate his seventh anniversary as a priest. *Celebrate?* He was still on notice from the bishop that he wouldn't get his own parish until he stopped acting "contentious."

That was why Dan had taken a certain satisfaction in Elmendorf's having to appoint him interim pastor at St. George's after Chan Redding's stroke in February. There was, the bishop had made clear, no one else available. The number of priests had continued to slide, making some people—including priests—question the wisdom of the Church's refusal to ordain married men and women.

He returned to the sacristy and lifted his chalice from the cabinet. Caroline Schmidt would come, as she had each day since Halloween when her ten-year-old Kristy, riding her bike just a block from their house, got hit from behind by a drunk driver.

"Where was God when Kristy needed him?" Everett Schmidt asked that night through his tears. "Where was her guardian angel, or has the new Church dropped them, too?" Poor Everett hadn't been back to church since the funeral.

There were no answers for parents who lost their children. Jessica had warned him of that. Children, it seemed, died often, and his seminary training and short experience as a priest gave him little to say. "We can't always understand God's will, but we must pray to accept it. Somehow, in a way we don't know, all that happens is part of his divine plan."

Killing kids is part of God's plan? What kind of a God is that?

He hadn't seen Jessica since his first Mass, but in his mind he still heard her questions and comments. Of course, if it were his child, he'd ask that, too. An all-powerful God could cure kids if he wanted, and a good God would want to.

He had to stop thinking about it. Priests shouldn't be angry at God.

Dan cut across the sanctuary and his faint shadow moved along the wall opposite the red lamp. The altar boys' sacristy was still dark. He'd wait a couple of minutes, then light two candles for the low Mass. He glanced at the censer in the corner and inhaled its mix of incense and charcoal from yesterday's high Mass. Long-handled candle lighters hung against the wall, and a row of cabinets held black cassocks and white surplices in assorted schoolboy sizes.

When his watch read six-twenty Dan grabbed a candle lighter, let out an inch and a half of wick and bent it. He hadn't lit candles since high school. He glanced around the room. Where did they keep the matches?

The sacristy door burst open and Wigs Hartley, a sixth grader who combed his thick blond hair five different ways each day, stomped in. "Mornin', Father! Man, it's wet out there. And *cold!*"

"Mornin', Wigs. Yeah, a great day to stay in bed. I really appreciate your showing up. Who else is scheduled?"

"Terry McCarty, I think. But he missed school yesterday. Must be sick."

"Up to going it alone?"

"Oh, sure. Done it lotsa times." Wigs buttoned his cassock and tossed a surplice over his head. "I'll do the candles if you want."

Dan handed him the lighter. "One on each side."

Wigs nodded. He strode to the censer cabinet and pulled a box of wood matches from the back of the top shelf.

"So *that's* where you keep 'em."

Wigs lit the wick. "Us servers hide 'em, Father. That way you can't get along without us."

"We can't anyway, of course, but don't tell the others I know it. I don't want you guys getting big heads."

Wigs grinned, then marched into the sanctuary holding the lighter with two hands like a pole vaulter on his approach. He reminded Dan of someone from a long time ago. A classmate he served Mass with at Sacred Heart? He didn't know.

During the Mass, the dozen parishioners prayed along in a low murmer, but when Dan began the Nicene Creed they stood to proclaim their faith.

"I believe in one God, the Father almighty, maker of heaven and earth, and of all things visible and invisible," they recited with him. Their faces expressed an absolute certainty in what they were saying. "And I believe in one Lord, Jesus Christ, the only-begotten Son of God."

No, I don't.

Dan glanced around. Had he said that out loud or, he hoped, merely thought it? Wigs didn't look up, so it must have been a thought. But what a time to think it. People couldn't read his mind, thank God.

If there is a God.

Then Wigs did look up, and Dan realized he'd stopped reciting. He rejoined the congregation, "And on the third day he rose again, according to the scriptures."

But the scriptures contradict themselves. Jessie's thought. Ignore it.

"And I believe in the Holy Spirit, the Lord and Giver of life, who proceeds from the Father and the Son."

No. There's no one out there.

Finally, the Creed was ending. "I confess one baptism for the forgiveness of sins. And I await the resurrection of the dead, and the life of the world to come."

No, I don't. Not anymore.

"Amen." Dan gripped the altar and closed his eyes. This time it wasn't Jess. These thoughts were his. He should race back to the rectory and go back to bed until his brain cleared. No, he had to finish the Mass for these people who had come to church this awful morning. He went on, praying as devoutly as he could, but wondering to whom.

If he ignored his sudden disbelief, it would disappear—eventually. But it wasn't all that sudden, was it? He'd had these doubts before, had spotted unexplainable contradictions in the scriptures and in Church doctrine. But today the doubts seemed much more intense.

He recited the offertory hymn, then raised to eye level the paten holding the flat, round wafer of unleavened bread. "Receive, O holy Father, almighty and eternal God, this spotless host which I, your unworthy servant, offer to you, my living and true God, for my own countless sins, offenses, and negligences; and for all present here."

The words left him as cold as the air outside. He was speaking to that air as if someone beyond this world might be persuaded to take away their troubles. After all, they'd pulled themselves from their warm beds on a miserable morning to appear at this shrine, to mouth the sacred words fervently enough, they hoped, to satisfy whomever—whatever—was out there listening.

Dan poured wine and water into his chalice and held it up as he had the bread. "We offer to you, O Lord, the chalice of salvation, humbly begging your mercy that it may arise before your divine majesty as a pleasing fragrance for our salvation and for that of the whole world. Amen."

He looked past the chalice at his people kneeling spellbound at the gold cup he raised before them, a cup of wine.

The doubts were taking him over, as they must have Jessica years ago at the U. But he couldn't give this up—this ceremony, this sacrifice he offered daily as a source of strength for these people … and for himself.

He prayed on, reciting the prayer of the preface loud enough for the people to hear, loud enough to drown out the ideas bubbling inside his head. He led them into the "Sanctus" he had loved so much in the Latin Mass, but in English now: "Holy, holy, holy, Lord God of hosts. Heaven and earth are filled with your glory. Hosanna in the highest. Blessed is he who comes in the name of the Lord. Hosanna in the highest."

How could he turn away from this? How could he dismiss its meaning? Surely there was a God, and surely there were as many ways to pray as there were human beings, but the Mass had come down through the centuries from learned and holy men, doing this, as Jesus ordered, in his memory.

Time for the consecration. If he no longer believed, did he keep his powers? Could he still change the bread into Christ's body, the wine into his blood? Again Dan searched the faces of his people. He knew their troubles, knew why they came here. Despite their problems, their eyes—their *hopes*—were focused on him, their priest, and on the bread and wine he was to transform into the body and blood of the Christ who someday would relieve their physical and emotional suffering. He would complete the Mass for them, do it despite not believing. And, if he was wrong, if there was a God watching, he would commit his greatest sacrilege.

Dan lifted the wafer into his hands. He and his classmates had trained for twelve years before being ordained to do this. He prayed aloud so the people could hear, "The day before he suffered he took bread, and looking up to heaven, to you, his almighty Father, he gave you thanks and praise. He broke the bread, gave it to his disciples and said: Take this and eat it, all of you; this is my body." Dan had said these words for seven years and always felt Christ enter the bread as he said them.

But not today.

He held the bread high for the people to see, then lowered it and placed it on the paten. He reached for the chalice. "When supper was ended, he took the cup. Again he gave you thanks and praise, gave the cup to his disciples and said: Take this and drink from it, all of you; this is the cup of my blood, the blood of the new and everlasting covenant—the mystery of faith. This blood is to be shed for you and for all men so that sins may be forgiven. Whenever you do this, you will do it in memory of me." He raised the chalice. His body felt numb and the chalice started to slip, so he lowered it quickly, then gripped the altar to steady himself.

After Mass, the people shuffled out, their voices protesting the damp cold.

In the sacristy, Dan turned to Wigs. "Thank you. Great job on a lousy morning."

"You're welcome, Father. I'll put out the candles."

Dan locked his chalice in the cabinet. He'd been a Wigs only a few years ago, eager to serve Mass for the priests. But today … well, maybe he'd come down with a flu, a fever affecting his brain. He would eat breakfast and take a nap before hospital visitations, and tonight he'd skip recording this episode in his journal. Tomorrow he'd laugh at how the human brain could flip-flop in a minute what a guy had believed for a lifetime. Thank God he was a priest, able to see these thoughts for what they were. How did lay people handle them? Is this what happened to Agnes Reuter? To Jessica?

He hung his vestments in the closet. The doubts would disappear; they had before. He walked to a prie-dieu near the altar and gently lowered himself to the cushion. Mass—even an early Mass on a cold morning—had never drained him like this. He stared at the tabernacle, then at the red-glass candle that signified the divine presence. "Lord, make me an instrument of your peace."

The doubts always left when he prayed. God always came back to him.

But not now. He took a deep breath. Perhaps they didn't leave because they were no longer doubts. His questions had started when he was eight, when he saw the smoking ruins of St. Mary's. Why would a God destroy his own house with lightning? Why would he let people suffer so terribly from disease, from wars and natural disasters?

Over the years Dan had found answers that satisfied him, at least for a while. He had accepted his dilemmas as divine mysteries, evidence that man's mind can't begin to understand God's will. He accepted the idea that everything that happens is—in some unfathomable way—part of God's design.

Everything. Even a priest suffering doubts about God.

But today the old answers didn't work. Why did God torment people—*him*—with mysteries? Why didn't he demonstrate his existence and declare what he wants? An infinite number of self-styled prophets proclaimed *they* knew, but they contradicted each other, then persecuted, even killed, those who disagreed.

Not all of them can be right. Are any?

In the server's sacristy Wigs waved, flicked the light off and pulled the door shut. Dan walked to the altar and adjusted the white tabernacle curtain. He pressed his hands to the altar, felt tremors through his body. He *must* be sick. But Doctor Vanh wouldn't be in for a couple of hours.

No. How could he explain that the shakes started after he discovered he no longer believed in God?

His eyes scanned the church. He was alone, and he went behind the altar to switch off the lights. Despite the clouds, the sky had gotten brighter, and hints of red, blue, green, and yellow filtered through the stained-glass windows onto the pews and walls of the old church. He lowered himself again onto the prie-dieu and bent forward to rest his face in his hands. He stared again at the flame inside the red glass. If the divine presence didn't exist, where had his comfort and strength come from all these years?

He laughed aloud, then glanced through the church to be sure no one heard. "Okay, Lord, administering one of your little tests, are you? A bit tougher than the others. No, a lot tougher. Let's get it over with, then hurry up and tell me I passed."

The doubts had started during Mass with the creed. Dan recited it again, word by word, sentence by sentence. No, he didn't believe in one God, nor in one true Church. No God; no Church. This morning he believed nothing, and he couldn't believe *that*, either. A priest doesn't toss away the foundation of his life in one morning.

Despite the chill, sweat trickled down his forehead. One drop missed his eyebrows and worked its way across the bridge of his nose. He reached for it, too late. It ran into his left eye and stung. He dabbed it with his handkerchief, still damp from before Mass. It seemed so long ago. He blinked several times to clear the pain.

Maybe he could blink his doubts away too.

He stared at the tabernacle as if it held a message, a note pinned to its veil. Perhaps, "Yes, Daniel, I am here. Believe in me. Ignore the doubts; don't let them undermine your faith."

But no message appeared. "Lord, don't do this," he prayed. "If faith is a gift, don't take it from me. I'll pray harder. I'll stay more attentive when I offer Mass. I'll visit more sick people. I'll prepare better before teaching the kids. *Anything*. But to stay in your ministry, I must have faith."

More sweat, strange on a cold day. He was sick. The doubts had to be coming from that, eased along by his many weaknesses. From vacillating about Jessica in his seminary years. From the impure fantasies that still plagued him. From the solitary abuse of his priest's body. From the sacrilege of wondering at communion how it would feel to French kiss those pretty pink tongues on which he placed the Eucharist.

Through twelve years in the seminary he had looked forward to ordination and the priest he would become: prayerful and pious, full of wisdom and zeal, an example of Christlike goodness to the people entrusted to his care. But he'd fallen so short. God had many reasons to punish him.

If there were a God. No, there *had* to be. If not, the guilt that drove him so many times to confession would become laughable except for the embarrassment it had brought, for he would have offended no one. And, if there were no God, he'd have rejected Jessica for nothing.

Daniel, I am so afraid that you have made a terrible mistake.

No. Mrs. Reuter was wrong. There had to be a reason for the life he'd chosen, a reason for the sacrifices of millions of people through centuries of belief. There had to be a God, even if the seminary's endless philosophy and theology classes had failed to prove it. There *had* to be, because if there weren't—

Dan stopped the thought. "Lord, if you don't exist—"

He cut himself off and again started to shake, this time from laughter. Who was he talking to? *Lord, if you don't exist.* Good God, he was going nuts.

He had to talk to someone—someone real—but to whom? The seminary trained him to dispel others' doubts, and he had, countless times when people came to him in agony over their disbelief. He argued the best he could to bring them back to faith. Sometimes he failed; he never saw those people again. But when he succeeded, when they appeared again at Mass, his whole body celebrated because he'd done what he'd been ordained to do: He had saved souls for Christ.

Who now would save him? *Save?* What was he thinking? With no God, there is no salvation. No heaven, no hell. He didn't *need* saving.

He pushed himself up from the kneeler. The scuffing of his black shoes on the hardwood floor echoed off the stone walls until he reached the carpet, then the church again went silent. He closed his eyes and took a deep breath. Hot beeswax from the candles. The smell took him back to second grade and his first communion when he and his classmates—boys in sport coats and girls in white dresses—carried foot-long candles down the aisle of Sacred Heart Church. After that morning, he had looked forward to the great feasts of the church when dozens of candles perfumed the church. Beeswax, he believed, was the fragrance of God.

The rain had stopped but the wind slammed the sacristy door shut behind him. He tucked his head against the cold for the thirty steps to the rectory's back porch. In the kitchen he opened the refrigerator. Oof! A stink from a spoiled leftover. What did he push toward the back last week to eat the next day? Oh, yeah, a haddock fillet from Frankie's downtown. He'd forgotten it, regretted wasting it. He pulled out a half-full gallon of skim milk, took a swig from the bottle, peeled a banana, and ate slowly in front of the overgrown plants hanging inside the dining room's bay window. He stared at the stone wall of the church. Did anyone live there?

He returned the milk bottle to its shelf, passed the dining room table with yesterday's *Capital Times* and that morning's *Wisconsin State Journal*, and opened the door to the office, still more Chan Redding's than his. He settled into the high-backed swivel chair and closed his eyes. Through high school, college, and theology, he had trained for the priesthood. It was the only life he knew. If he left, he'd be cutting himself off from the Church. For all its faults, it was still the system that sustained him, emotionally and economically.

"Ask the bishop for a short leave," Pat told Dan over beers in Milwaukee that night. "Make a retreat. There's a good place north of Chicago. I have the number. They helped me a lot."

"Helped *you?*"

"Last year. Gentle men there. They brought me back."

Back? Back from where? Dan stared.

"I'm sorry," Pat said. "I couldn't call you. It's great you trust me. I just couldn't."

"I didn't come to tell you. I was feeling so goddamned lonely that I just wanted to see you."

"I drove to one of those lookalike Chicago suburbs," Pat said, "where I went to confession to a priest who wouldn't know me from the cardinal. I wore street clothes and stood in line with all the other penitents worrying about what the priest would say."

Pat laughed. "I startled him, poor guy. 'Bless me, Father. I'm a priest too, and I'm in trouble.' That's how I started. I was shivering and my armpits were soaked. Know what he said when I finally told him I doubted God? 'Oh, *that*.' Like he heard it every day. At the end he said he thought at first I'd gotten a girl pregnant or burned down my church for the insurance. Anyway, he told me about this monastery. He'd gone there, too."

"Him too?" Dan said. "Why the hell do they keep this stuff secret? Here we are, struggling alone, feeling weird, afraid to talk to anyone. Jeez!"

"We discussed that at the retreat. Some of us felt we weren't living up to people's expectations. Or our own."

"Okay," Dan said, "a retreat's fine, but what do I do tomorrow and all the next days till I get there?"

"*Act* as if you believe. Do things the way you've always done them. Then, when this finally blows over, no one will suspect a thing. The day my faith came back, I walked to a small stream running through the property. I sat on a ledge above a rapids and listened to the water tumbling over the rocks, and I wondered how I could have doubted that God created such a beautiful place."

Dan concentrated on performing his duties as usual the next morning at Mass and during his visits to a dozen people at Avon Park Memorial Hospital. He'd seen these patients before, and he said the same things, but he feared they might notice a change. Mrs. Dorret gave him a strange look when he told her he'd pray for her, but skipped promising he'd be back. He didn't want to lie.

That night, he pulled a heavy cardboard box from the back of his closet and poured through seminary papers and diplomas and pulled out a maroon letter R. He opened his 1961 yearbook to Jessica's autograph.

Call me anytime.

She hadn't meant it. No, be fair. She meant it then, but how could she foresee what would happen? Things change. People change. *He* was changing.

Dan spent two days at the retreat house, talking mostly with an old priest. The man surprised him with his knowledge of the world, and Dan told him so.

"Ha," the old priest said, "you think we stay so sheltered in the monastery, eh? Tell you something: We are human, too, and we watch what goes on. You city guys cannot come here to, as you say, 'get away from it all,' and shock us.

Unh-uh. We know our fellow man the way God created us, with all our holiness and sinfulness and weakness. We are one, all of us."

Both mornings Dan pulled himself from bed before the alarm and walked the dirt path to the creek. He sat atop a flat rock—maybe the ledge where Pat rediscovered God—and listened to the water swirling around boulders and splashing through crevices until it cleared the rapids and flowed smoothly into the woods.

"Reflect on the qualities of the water, where it comes from, what it means to life, where it goes," the old priest said. "*That* you'll have a hard time doing in the city."

Pat had reveled in the beauty. But, if God created that, he created the ugly places too. The water came from upstream and went downstream. A map would show where from and where to. If the universe had to be set in motion by a God who's greater than his creation, it followed that God would need a creator too. If God didn't, the universe didn't either.

"Go home and continue to think," the old priest said. "And *pray*. God is very patient with us, especially when he tests us like this."

"You keep saying God is testing me. Is he that insecure?"

The old priest looked pained. "I don't know. All I know is that he does. Often. *Too* often, in my opinion. But God doesn't ask my opinion."

From Chicago, Dan drove I-94 to Milwaukee. If Pat stopped being his friend, he would lose everything. He had to find out, and he decided to get it over with.

When Pat answered the door, Dan shook his head.

"Shit," Pat said. He stepped back to let Dan in, then went to the kitchen.

He brought out two Millers. "I bought these for the celebration, but I guess we'll drink them anyway."

"Funny," Dan said on their way to Pat's living room, "I feel like celebrating. Except for not knowing what I'm going to do and for wondering how you and my other friends and relatives will take this, I'm beginning to feel at peace."

"You can't. When I doubted, I was miserable! I didn't find peace until I found, or refound, God."

Dan eased into a recliner and set his beer on an end table. "This isn't doubt anymore. I'm certain. Certain, at least, of what I don't believe. Now I have to figure out what I *do* believe."

Pat shook his head. "Not that quick. It can't be."

"It wasn't quick. I did a year of thinking in the past week."

"You're giving up too fast. It's only a test. It'll pass."

"I'll ask you what I asked the old priest in Illinois. Is your God—"

Pat waved like he was erasing a blackboard. "*Our* God."

"Is God so insecure that he has to test his subjects to be sure of their fidelity, or whatever it is he wants of them?"

"Of course not."

"But you say he's testing me. If I called every day demanding you drop what you're doing and spend time with me, you'd figure I was insecure, wouldn't you?"

"That's different," Pat said.

"How?"

"It just is. We don't know each other's minds, but God does. He knows what we're thinking. We can't lie to him."

"I'm not lying, I just don't believe it anymore. And I don't know how to say this, but I feel so free now."

Pat stared at him. "Free?"

"Free to figure out what's true. To look at everything and decide for myself. But I'm scared too," Dan said. "Not of God or his hell, because I think there's no such thing. I'm scared of people, of their reaction. You, for example. Can we still be friends?"

Pat stretched his legs. "We'll work that out. But don't make things so final. I thought I'd never believe again, either, but faith is a gift, and God will give it back to you."

Dan finished his beer. "I don't think so. While I watched the water flowing down the creek, I saw faith as a suspension of our demand for evidence. We believe in gods despite no proof for them."

"True, there is no definite proof—at least none we've discovered so far—but there are indicators that make it likely God exists. We have to trust from the evidence we have that he's really there."

Dan stood. "I'll look at it. But let's not argue today. I'm afraid you're going to get upset, even if I don't ask you or anyone else to follow me."

Pat held the door. "Of course I'm upset. After what we've been through all these years, I can't believe you're leaving the priesthood ... and the Church."

"I am sorry," Dan said. "I want to stay friends. The possibility of losing that scares the hell out of me. But strangely enough, the retreat put me at peace with leaving, and on the drive up here I wondered: Are people going to be upset because I'm giving up *my* faith, or because I'm giving up *theirs*?"

Dan forced his way through the motions of his priesthood for two days, saying Mass ("This is my body; this is my blood"), teaching the kids in school ("Jesus loves all of us, no matter what we look like, how much money we have, or where we live") and visiting the sick ("God is aware of your suffering; offer it to him").

On the third day, he called Pat. "I can't do it. I hate frauds, and I keep saying things I no longer believe. These people need a priest, not a Hollywood actor."

"Have you prayed?"

"There's no one to pray to."

"There *is*. Pray and you'll see. God will answer you."

"Pat. There's no one there."

Silence. Then, "Danny, why did you call me?"

"I don't know what to do."

"But you won't do what I suggest."

"I can't. Not anymore."

Pat took a deep breath. "Well, if you're going to leave you have to tell the bishop so he can replace you. And you have to tell your parishioners. Unless you're willing to stick it out and give yourself more time."

"I can't.... Pat, we've made a mistake!"

"No. There *is* a God, whether you believe in him or not. He's been there all along, he's there now, and he'll be there when you decide to come back to him. But for now, if you've made up your mind, I agree. You need to get out of there."

"But I have nowhere to go!" Dan blushed. He wanted the words back. They sounded so desperate. Pat would remind him that he should have thought of that before he turned his back on God.

"You can come here," Pat said. "We have a room. You can sort things out and we can talk, and I'll pray for you whether you like it or not. And if you tell me not to, even once, I'll kick your atheist ass out, understood?"

"Understood." A train horn sounded twice from the Milwaukee Road yard four blocks away, low-pitched blatts from one of the railroad's orange-and-black locomotives. "Pat? Thank you. I owe you. I know you disagree with me and probably wish I hadn't called you, but I appreciate this. I'm packing. I'll be there sometime tomorrow."

"Come when you can. If no one answers, wait on the porch. It's enclosed and there are books to read. Spiritual reading, good for your soul."

"Pat ... did Jessie ever come back to the Church?"

"No."

"Do you still pray for her?"

"Yes."

The train's engineer whistled for the McKee Street crossing—two longs, a short, another long—and Dan heard a parade of steel wheels clacking over joints between old rails. If he hurried he could swing into an empty boxcar and roll out of town to Chicago and from there catch another train and not give a damn to where. When the train stopped, he'd stop. He stepped to the front door and pulled it open.

It was a long train: The caboose hadn't cleared McKee yet and the engines were whistling for County T west of the city limits. God, he wished he were on it, stretched out on a sheet of cardboard, nibbling chips and sipping beer with his back against a boxcar wall, watching Wisconsin fields and forests whiz by the open door in a blur of late-spring greens and yellows.

He caught the irony of mentioning a God he no longer believed in. He needed a new vocabulary.

The rattle of the train faded, and Dan eased the door shut. The train had left without him. He was still at the rectory, and he had work to do.

Chapter 29

▼

"Dear Bishop Elmendorf," Dan wrote in his best script, "I regret to tell you that I must immediately discontinue my duties as a priest."

No. Despite his anxiety, he didn't regret it. He dropped the paper into the basket next to his desk, then started again. "Dear Bishop Elmendorf, I hereby resign as a priest. I am sorry for the inconvenience this will cause you, the Diocese of Madison, and the parishioners of St. George's in Avon Park."

He did regret the inconvenience. He scanned the letter. It was enough. "Sincerely, Rev. Daniel J. Bates II."

Habits die hard. Again he rewrote the letter, this time leaving out the "Rev." He stamped the envelope, then decided to drop the letter at the chancery in Madison on his way to Milwaukee.

He picked up another sheet of paper. "Dear parishioners," he started. But they weren't his parishioners anymore. He started over. "Dear people of St. George's parish, I have greatly enjoyed serving you as a priest, and hope I have given you as much inspiration and joy as I have received from you. I wish to thank you and inform you that I must leave St. George's now. I realize this is sudden, and I am sorry for the inconvenience it will cause. I have informed the bishop about this, and he will arrange as soon as possible for you to have the services of another priest.

"I wish all of you the best. Love one another. It's ancient, but still excellent, advice."

At the trailer rental Dan asked the attendant to mount the hitch to his bumper.

"Nothin' to it," the man said. "A kid can do it."

"I don't have a kid."

The man stared at him. "Sir, I'm all alone here. Another customer could come in any second. I'd have to stop and wait on him."

"That'll still be faster than me growing a kid to do it," Dan said. If he'd been able to take a shop class at the seminary the way Eddie and his friends had at Willow Run, he might not be so incompetent with tools.

The attendant mounted the trailer with no interruptions. He didn't say "You're welcome" when Dan thanked him.

At the rectory, it took him several tries to back the trailer up to the porch steps. By then, five neighbor kids were watching from the sidewalk, giggling. He lugged his easy chair and two dozen boxes of books, clothes, vestments, and his chalice down the steps, then into the trailer where he pushed them tight against the sides. Maybe Pat could use his priest things.

Finally, he went inside to phone the president of the parish council, attorney Leo Toombs, at his office.

"I'm sorry, Mr. Toombs is in conference, Father. Can I take a message?"

"Um … yes. Leo's president of our … of St. George's parish council."

"Yes, Father."

"Please tell him I'm leaving the parish today and I'll lock the rectory and put my keys on the kitchen counter next to the sink. He has a key to get in."

"Okay, Father. When shall I tell him you'll be back?"

"Well, um, that's the point. I won't be back. I'm leaving … for good."

Silence. Then, "Just a moment, Father."

Seconds later, Leo's voice. "What the hell, Father Bates, you're *leaving*? The bishop never announced it, did he? Or did I miss it? It's been a goddamned zoo … sorry, Father, a real zoo around here."

"No, this is very sudden and it's not the bishop's fault. I'm, ah, resigning from the priesthood."

"*What*? C'mon, Father, you're shittin' me, right? I mean, pardon the French, but you gotta be joking."

"No, I just called to—"

"But, Father, you didn't give notice. I mean, what are we gonna to do for a priest?"

"I'll inform the bishop about it when I get to Madison this afternoon. He'll send one."

"Elmendorf's gonna be pissed, Father. I know him. Besides, priests can't quit at the drop of a hat, can they? I mean, shouldn't you stay at least through Sunday? There must be *something* in your contract that says you can't quit like this."

"I do wish you and St. George's the best, Leo, but I have to—"

"You have to meet with me first, don't you? I mean, with the council?"

"I'm sorry, that's not possible. I—"

"But, Father, you gotta! You can't just—"

"I'm sorry, Leo, I have to go." They were about to battle, and neither would win. Better to seem crass and cut it off. "I do wish you the best, Leo. Thank you for all your help. And again, I'm sorry. But I really have to go."

"Wait! You're going to talk to the bishop?"

"This afternoon."

Leo took a deep breath. "Well, I sure don't understand this, Father, but good luck, I guess."

"Thank you. Take care of yourself, Leo."

Dan drove downtown, almost clipping a stop sign at the corner when he forgot to swing wide enough for the trailer to clear.

The young woman at the bank, Jeanette, had waited on him before. "*All* of it, Father? Checking *and* savings?"

"Yes," Dan said. "I'm moving. You can give me large bills."

Jeanette counted the money. "Where are you going, Father?"

Dan paused. Why keep it a secret? "Milwaukee."

"I've been there. It's pretty by the lake."

"Yes, it is." He pushed the money into his wallet and turned to go.

"Father," she said, "I'm not a Catholic, but I know people will be sad to see you go."

He tried to smile. "Thank you, Jeanette. I appreciate that." Leaving Avon Park suddenly became a lot harder.

Dan kept watching the trailer in his mirror. His car seemed to have grown a tail. He stopped at a gas station in Evansville and plunked change into a Coke machine. Caffeine should help keep him awake. Twenty miles yet to Madison.

By now Leo would have contacted the rest of the council. Elmendorf too. None of them would understand, but then Dan hardly understood it himself.

Most people would insist he was wrong. If he were, would an angry God condemn him to hell, or would a merciful God credit him for intellectual honesty, even laugh at his mistake? But every time he considered it, he became more certain. He'd found no way to prove there is a god. There was the universe, Earth, nature, and people. We really didn't know where we came from or why we were here, but creating gods was not the answer. And how many people seriously considered the question? Most stayed in the faith they were born into.

Dan checked the trailer. A station wagon was following, close. Stupid tailgater. He tapped the brake pedal to flash his lights, and the wagon eased back, then zipped past him. Idiot. He recalled Papa Hambone on Madison radio during visits home from the seminary: *Drive as if every other guy on the road is a nut. You'll be surprised how often you're right.*

At the chancery in downtown Madison, Bishop Elmendorf had left word with the receptionist that he wanted to see Dan.

The bishop met him at his office door. "Leo Toombs called."

"I stopped by to give you this letter," Dan said, then followed the bishop to his wide, wooden desk. "I'm sorry to drop this so suddenly in your lap, but I've decided to leave the priesthood."

"So Leo said. But if you wish to resign," Elmendorf said, "there are procedures. If you need more time, perhaps another retreat—"

"I appreciate that, but the one I made convinced me I'm on the right track."

The bishop paced behind his desk. "You must understand, you have obligations to St. George's, to your fellow priests, to me, to God—"

"I'm sorry, but that's why I'm leaving. I don't believe in a god anymore."

Elmendorf dropped into his high-backed chair and pulled a pen from its holder. "I can permit you a sabbatical, time to think things over, however long you need. This is so sudden. It would be best not to burn your bridges."

Dan pushed his letter across the desk. "I know, but—"

"We've had our problems, of course, but you've been an excellent priest, conscientious and popular with your parishioners, if not with your pastors." Elmendorf started writing. "Hold onto your letter for the time being. After a period of reflection, if you rediscover your faith, you won't have left—not officially—and we can pick up again with the least amount of trouble for us all."

"That's kind of you, but … well, I know this seems sudden, but I have thought about it for a long time. In the last week it's all come together, inconvenient as it is in many ways."

The bishop sat back. "It's a woman, isn't it? It's always a woman, but we make other excuses."

Dan laughed. "I'm sorry. I know it's not funny, but I've heard that so often it's become a cliché. No, this is a matter of faith … lack of faith, actually." He began feeling sorry for the bishop. "I do want to thank you for your help the past seven years. And for your offers today." He turned to go.

Elmendorf hurried around the desk and beat Dan to the door. "Father Bates, we will pray for you. We wish you the best in whatever life you decide to lead. Other than that, there's nothing we'll be able to do for you. But please keep your mind open to the grace of God. Perhaps someday you'll find your way back to him. And to us." He extended his hand.

Dan shook it.

By the time Dan reached his parents' house in Willow Run, his hands were sweating. He'd tell them he resigned, that's all. No sense arguing about beliefs.

"But what are you going to do?" his mother cried. "All you've been is a priest."

"I'm smart, Mom. I'll find something."

"What will we tell people who ask why you're not a priest anymore?"

"Tell them I decided to do something different. People change jobs all the time. That's what I'm doing."

"Have you really thought this through?" his dad asked.

"I went on a retreat and talked to a wonderful old priest there. And I've talked with Pat." Dan smiled. "Pat's been terrific. He's argued with me, pleaded with me, and finally offered me a room at his place while I get settled. I'll give you the address."

His mother frowned. "Do you have to stay way over in Milwaukee?"

"Mom, I went to the seminary before I was fourteen. I'm almost thirty-three now. Milwaukee isn't as far as Southport." He hugged her. "Whatever you're cooking smells great. Am I invited?"

"Of course," she said, and Dan settled at the table with his parents. They spoke only of people and events in Willow Run. For a moment, Dan's anxiety about the next few days disappeared.

After dinner, he walked to Agnes Reuter's. She led him into the kitchen.

"No cookies today, Daniel, only tea."

"I'd love tea." She looked thin. He wondered how well she ate.

Back in the living room, Agnes eased herself onto the couch. Dan set the cups of tea on two end tables, and the steam spread a warm, sweet scent through the room.

She caught him staring. "I had surgery. Woman stuff. Don't worry, it's not catching."

Three tall, overflowing bookcases stood along walls decorated with a pattern of yellow fleurs-de-lis. Propped atop a marble mantel was an eight-by-ten, black-and-white portrait of a World War Two soldier.

Agnes followed Dan's eyes. "That was my Joseph. I still miss him."

"Yes. When I was little, people said he was very nice. I'm sorry I never met him."

He told her his plans.

"Ah, so I can't call you *Father* anymore."

"You never did."

"Ha! No, I guess not."

A black-and-white cat padded in from the dining room and stared.

"Spike," Agnes said, "don't be rude. Say hello to Daniel."

The cat meowed and made a smooth leap onto Dan's lap.

"Spike!" She started to get up, winced and sat back. "Sorry, Daniel. Spike, you weren't invited."

"Yes, he was," Dan said. "I patted my knee." He stroked Spike's neck and the cat nestled into his lap and started to purr.

"So, Daniel, are you happy?"

"Content, I guess. But I have more questions than ever about life and what it means."

Her hand shook as she set down her cup. "Nonbelievers will always have more questions, I think. We aren't so certain of things. That's why I prefer to call us skeptics. And that's why it's important to read, Daniel. In fact, I have books you might like to see, by people who have gone through the same thinking we have." She raised a hand. "I'll point. I'm not going to try to get up. Over there, middle shelf, that set of twelve green books."

Dan found them, *The Works of Robert Green Ingersoll*. "His name seems familiar. Oh, I remember, it's one that Jessie said I wouldn't find at the seminary. I looked in the library, but she was right. And then I forgot about him."

"Most people don't know of him," Agnes said, "and that's a shame. He was called the Great Agnostic, as well as the Great Orator. In his day—he died in 1899—people came from all over—and paid a dollar or more, a lot of money then—to hear him speak. Can you believe it, they would listen to men like him—orators—for hours! Just for fun! Today, nobody wants to sit still for even for a few minutes."

Dan opened one of the volumes. "This has 'Why I Am An Agnostic' in it."

"Yes, take that one. It's a good one to start with. But first pick a section, see if you might like it."

His eyes traveled over the pages. "Here he says, 'By some accident I read Volney'—I haven't heard of him either—'who shows that all religions are, and have been, established in the same way—that all had their Christs, their apostles, miracles and sacred books, and then asked how it is possible to decide which is the true one. A question that is still waiting for an answer.'"

"Yes," she said. "And there are other parts I think you will like."

"Here," Dan said: 'I know that life is good. I remember the sunshine and rain. Then I think of the earthquake and flood. I do not forget health and harvest, home and love—but what of pestilence and famine? I cannot harmonize all these contradictions—these blessings and agonies—with the existence of an infinitely good, wise and powerful God.'"

He turned a few pages. "Oh, and here at the end, I love this: 'When I became convinced that the Universe is natural—that all the ghosts and gods are myths, there entered into my brain, into my soul, into every drop of my blood, the sense, the feeling, the joy of freedom.'" Dan stepped toward Agnes. "That's the way I feel now—free. But I'd better quit reading, or I'll stand here the rest of the afternoon and ignore you." He raised the book. "Can I really take this?"

"Of course," she said. "For as long as you want. And the others are here when you're finished."

Dan put the book under his arm. "Thank you."

Agnes struggled to her feet. "Next time, Daniel, I'll have cookies for you to take, but now you need to find that young woman you chased on your big day."

"You remember that, huh? She's probably married by now, with two or three kids."

Agnes cocked her head. "Maybe, but you must find out, Daniel. Until you do, you will always wonder, and you will not be totally free."

Chapter 30

A few days after Dan moved into Pat's rectory on Milwaukee's north side, he started work at a downtown sporting goods store.

Pat had helped him get the job. "It's nothing you're used to, but you said you wanted something quick. I've known the owner since I bought my first baseball glove."

"It's fine," Dan said. And it was. His years as a priest helped him deal with people, and he enjoyed the physical work of stocking shelves and setting up equipment. He also had no problem with his work schedule: Retailers, like priests, worked weekends.

On a Friday evening three weeks later, he deposited his first paycheck. At the rectory, he opened the refrigerator to make a turkey sandwich. The door chimes rang, and the sound of Pat's footsteps was followed by muffled voices at the front door.

Pat ducked into the kitchen. "Hey, don't spoil dinner. I thought we'd go out, but first I have to talk to these people. Wait in my office; I'll use the living room. Give me ten minutes."

Dan slid the turkey and mayo back into the refrigerator. His stomach growled a complaint. Ten minutes? He hoped that's all it was.

He headed for the office. Odd. Other times it was the opposite: Pat talked with people in his office while Dan sprawled across the living room couch.

Pat's office had piles of paper covering every piece of furniture except for his burgundy easy chair, so Dan sat there. Outside a tall window next to the desk, two squirrels ran down the thick trunk of an oak tree and disappeared around the side of the house.

Along two walls, Pat's bookcases bulged with the latest theological works as well as familiar old volumes they'd studied at the seminary. End tables were weighted with newspapers and magazines, mostly religious. A mimeograph waited to spit out Sunday's bulletin.

Dan stood, stretched, and stepped around the desk. Even the visitor's chair held a delicately balanced column of paper. A mild sneeze, much less a touch, would topple it to the floor. No wonder Pat decided to meet in the living room.

He surveyed Pat's desk. He hadn't seen clutter like this since he visited Quince the day before ordination. How did Pat find anything? Most of this could be tossed and the space freed up—for new stuff, if nothing else.

Then he saw the letter.

Actually, it was the envelope he spotted, business-sized, addressed to Pat in Jessica's handwriting. Voices still came from the living room, but he didn't dare pull out the letter. He flipped open his datebook and copied the return address: 2939 Charlesworth Avenue; Minneapolis, Minnesota.

So Jessica's in Minneapolis. Or was. He studied the postmark. Six months ago. The letter might have announced a move.

The living-room door squeaked and footsteps, laughter and goodbyes echoed in the hall. Dan plopped into the easy chair five seconds before Pat burst into the room.

"Another wedding! This fall. Now, where shall we eat?"

"In Minneapolis," Dan said. "I want to eat in Minneapolis."

Pat glanced at the envelope. "I thought you might."

"Careless of you."

"Mm-hmmm." Pat showed no regret.

Dan studied his watch. "How long does it take?"

"Six or seven hours. That would mean midnight if you left now, not a good time to surprise a woman you haven't seen since ... when *did* you last see her?"

"After my first Mass." Dan replayed the scene in his head. The dark glasses. *Be a great priest, Danny.* Her lips brushing his left cheek. The chase. Agnes Reuter: *I am so afraid that you have made a terrible mistake.*

It was time to fix the mistake. His heart pounded. "I'll start at midnight, get there first thing in the morning."

"Don't," Pat said. "She works seven to three, but tomorrow she's off. She'll sleep in."

Dan headed for the door. "She'll be up by noon, won't she?"

"Noon? Yeah. That should work."

"You could call her. Let her know I'm coming."

"No. I don't even know you're going. You might get halfway there and chicken out. I will tell you this, though: She hasn't changed her mind about seeing you. About *not* seeing you, I mean. You're on your own."

At five the next morning, a Saturday, Dan raced west under the I-94 streetlights past Milwaukee County Stadium. Pat had agreed to call the store and tell them he was out of town until Monday on a family emergency.

"It's not really a lie," Pat said. "You two need to talk."

Northeast of Madison, Dan passed the exit for Willow Run. His stomach tightened. It was too early to stop at his parents' house anyway, and he didn't want to see them until he came back. What news would he have? He'd have seen Jessica. Maybe he'd be moving to Minneapolis. Maybe she'd be coming back to Wisconsin. Or perhaps she was already married.

Two hours later, at a truck stop near Tomah, Dan pulled off for gas and caffeine. He was halfway to Minneapolis and still hadn't decided what to say.

Hi, Jess, how are ya? *Ugh.*

Hi! Bet you thought you'd never see me again, huh? *Maybe she'd wish she hadn't.*

Jess! Good to see you again! *Maybe he should call her Jessica.*

Long time, no see. *Ugh again.*

Hi. *Yeah, maybe just hi. See how she reacts.*

But what if she scowls, or stares at him as if she's forgotten who he is? He had to say more than *hi*. But what?

An hour later, south of Eau Claire, he decided. "Hi, Jessie. How are you?" Simple and sweet. Well, not sweet, but to the point. Polite and warm, but not gushy.

The heavy traffic through St. Paul surprised him. He stayed in the right lane, letting cars and trucks roar by on his left. Then, after a thirty-five-mile-an-hour curve, he spotted a sign: *Exit Only.* Damn. He eased into the next lane and caught a couple blasts from an air horn. He'd cut off a semi. Dan's hands started to sweat. He floored the accelerator until he could see more than the truck's grill in his mirror, then hit the brakes to avoid rear-ending a plumber's van.

He was going to die on this godforsaken freeway before he ever got to see Jessie.

Half an hour later, Dan pulled to the curb across the street from Jessica's yellow, two-story house. He stared at the glassed-in porch. Maybe she wasn't home.

He took deep breaths to ease the pounding in his temples, and wiped wet palms across black trousers. He rested his head on the steering wheel. What was the matter with him? He was a thirty-two-year-old man, not some teenaged kid on his first date.

Jessica's house sat among older homes on a street lined with large oaks and maples. No people, no cars moved as far down the street as Dan could see. He checked his watch. Noon. Years ago he'd watched Gary Cooper and Grace Kelly in *High Noon*.

I will tell you this: She hasn't changed her mind about seeing you. About not *seeing you, I mean. You're on your own.*

It was High Noon on Charlesworth Street.

Dan shuffled along Jessica's sidewalk. He stumbled, but didn't fall, against a section of concrete lifted an inch or so by a root, then climbed Jessica's gray wooden steps to her porch door. His mind worked his first line: *Hi, Jessie. How are you?* No. He should be more formal. *Hello, Jessica.* After all, it had been almost seven years.

But *damn*, he should have worn something with color. His white shirt and black pants made him look like a priest. Or a Jehovah's Witness. At least he had skipped a tie.

He pushed the doorbell. The *ding-dong* sounded harsh, and without thinking he said "Shhh." He was wiping sweat from his forehead with the back of his left sleeve when Jessica stepped onto the porch and opened the door.

"Hi," he said.

Chapter 31

Jessica eased the door open a couple of feet, closed it halfway, stood there. Her hair was darker than Dan remembered, but still short, the way she wore it when he saw her after his first Mass, the day he chased her.

He tried to smile. "Hi, Jessie."

"Hi."

She kept staring. Wasn't she going to invite him in? "How are you?" he asked.

Still she stared. "I'm fine. What do you want?"

Want? He hadn't rehearsed that. "Um ... to see you. To talk."

She didn't move. "What about?"

What about. What about. "To see how you are. To tell you what's happened."

Nothing.

"Can I come in?"

Her eyes narrowed.

Pat was right. She *didn't* want to see him.

Dan's words came faster. "For a minute, okay? Then I'll go if you want."

She flipped the door open and headed back inside.

Dan stepped into the porch and took a quick survey. Clean and neat. But there, in the far corner: a bicycle, a basketball, and a baseball glove. Agnes Reuter had been wrong. Jess had kids. No wonder she didn't want him there. What if her husband came home? He followed her through the living room into her kitchen.

"I was making tea."

"Sounds great," he said before he realized she hadn't offered any.

She reached into the cupboard, stretched past a green cup that matched hers, and pulled out a blue one. "Milk? Sugar?"

"Straight."

She wrinkled her nose, poured hot water, dipped a tea bag, and set the blue cup on the table in front of him. "You can sit there."

"Thanks."

With her foot, Jessica edged a wooden chair from the other side of the table. Her face had filled out and her chin wasn't as sharp, but her skin was still smooth, still fair. He'd have recognized her on the street.

She took one sip. "All right, what happened?"

"Didn't Pat tell you?"

Her face tightened. "Tell me what?"

"I've been living with him."

Her left eyebrow twitched the way it had in high school. "You guys are gay?"

Dan laughed, regretted it. "Nonononono, not that. I left the priesthood … and the Church. Pat's letting me stay with him."

Her eyebrow arched higher.

He wished she'd say something. "I don't believe in a god anymore." Would he ever get used to saying that?

"Really." She stirred her tea. The clinking of the spoon against her cup echoed in the quiet room. *Really*? Was that all she was going to say?

She went back to the stove, poured more tea. Did she giggle, or was he hoping? She returned to the table. "You quit … *everything*?"

Dan nodded.

"And Pat's letting you stay with him?"

"Yeah, after telling me to pray, think, go slow. And he said he's going to pray for me like he still does for you."

She smiled. *Finally*. "That's what I love about my brother: He follows to a T what he believes, but he doesn't try to ram it down anybody else's throat."

Throat. Dan couldn't resist staring. He recalled kisses. On Observatory Hill. In Bay View Park. "Pat's still the best friend I have. I kinda dumped myself on him."

Jessica brushed strands of hair from her eyes. "If he didn't want you there, he wouldn't have let you move in. Pat's nice, but he's not soft." She stirred her tea, then looked straight at Dan. "C'mon. Is this true, or is it one of you guys' lousy jokes?"

"It's true," Dan said, maybe too fast. But she didn't react. He finished his tea and waved off more. "Pat said you didn't want to see me. And he wouldn't tell me where you were."

Again she stared. "Then how did you find me?"

"A little detective work." Should he tell her? No, maybe later.

"It *is* a surprise," she said.

Dan checked her hands. No rings, but what about the bike, ball and glove? "Are you still a nurse?"

"Mm-hmm. At Compassion Memorial Hospital. Still pediatrics. And no, I'm not married."

Had she watched his eyes, or was she still reading his mind?

She carried both cups to the sink. "Came close once, but decided unh-uh. Didn't want to lose my independence."

Came close? That meant a guy in her life, maybe intimately. Dan's gut cramped. The idea of her with another guy … he stopped the thought, set his eyes on a child's artwork taped to the front of her refrigerator. Well, she wouldn't be the first to have a child outside of marriage. He nodded toward the drawings. "The artist … yours?"

She looked away, then back. "A boy. Ours."

His heart jumped, but then he laughed, slapped his hand on the table, and shook his head. "Sorry, Jess. For a second I thought you meant *ours* ours. I forgot about the guy you almost married."

She turned to the sink, swished water and soap in the cups, held them under the faucet and set them upside down in the rinse rack. She spoke so softly Dan hardly made out the words. "No, Dick isn't Mike's dad."

Two men in her life? Again, Dan felt the clutch deep in his gut.

Jessica dried her hands and came back to the table. "You don't get it, do you, Danny? Mike is ours. *Ours.* Yours and mine."

Dan gripped the table with both hands. "But how could you … we … that one night was the only … you said—I remember you saying it on the beach—you were a nurse. You knew how to, you know, make sure. I mean how … didn't it work or what?"

She flicked something—a crumb?—off the tablecloth. "I lied."

"*Lied?*"

Jessica turned toward the window. "I wasn't on the Pill that night."

Dan couldn't speak. He recalled his panic, how she held him tighter when he tried to pull out, how she insisted it was okay, how she assured him she had taken care of everything.

Her voice became firmer, and she watched his eyes. "I wasn't on the Pill."

He pushed back his chair. "Well, why the hell not?"

Jessica turned toward the drawings on the refrigerator, then back. Her eyes were wet. "I *wanted* to get pregnant that night. Then I could tell you—or the seminary or the bishop or whoever I had to—that you couldn't become a priest, that you'd sinned … sinned in the worst possible way. It was my last chance to stop you."

Dan stared out the window at the trees in Jessica's back yard. The leaves hung motionless in the still air. She had seduced him, lied to him, had his baby and never told him. Pat had known, and *he* hadn't said anything either. His best friend! His son was already seven years old, and he hadn't known the boy existed because these "friends" had kept it a secret. Dan tried to keep his voice steady. "But you never told."

She studied her hands. "You wanted to be a priest. You kept telling me that, and you told me again after we made love. Damn it all, if three minutes after you make it with a girl you tell her you're going to go ahead that very day and vow celibacy forever, you've pretty well told her to buzz off, that you have bigger plans than *she'll* ever fit into."

Two tears fell from her cheeks to the tablecloth. Should he offer her a handkerchief?

"I didn't mean it that way," he said.

Her eyes flashed. "*I didn't mean it that way?* My brother said the same fucking thing! '*Danny didn't mean it that way.*' Damn it all, you guys don't know *shit* about some stuff, you know? You don't know *shit!*"

She kicked her chair aside and walked to the window. "I've told you before, and I've told Pat too, but I've never meant it like I do today: I *hate* that God-damned ball-squeezing school and what it did to you guys." She turned. "*You* guys? I hate what that stupid hell-hole did to us *all!*" Her knees bent and she slid down the wall, then squatted against it, crying.

Dan started toward her, reaching—

"NO! Stay away!" She ran into the living room and flopped face down on the couch, her back rising and falling as she sobbed.

He watched for a second, then retreated to the back of the kitchen and rested his head against the refrigerator decorated with his son's drawings. Damn, he shouldn't have come. What made him think this would work? He listened to her crying. He couldn't leave her alone like this. But *damn*. He shouldn't have come.

The phone rang. Jessica picked it up. "Yeah, lamebrain, he's here, like I should tell *you*? Thanks a lot for the warning. I *know* you knew he was coming, and it …

I might *run*? Run *where*? Pat, sometimes you are so full of shit. Where would I go, to Canada?" She forced a laugh. "I suppose I could live with Eskimos in an igloo without a phone. At least then I wouldn't get totally inane calls like this one. It took me two seconds to figure out how Danny found me ... You're right, Einstein, it's *not* going so well. Sorry to prick your idiotic do-gooder bubble. What the *hell* did you hope to accomplish? ... So he's *not* a priest anymore. Think that makes a rat's-ass difference after eight god-damned *years*?" She slammed down the phone and threw herself back on the couch.

It rang again. Jessica rolled onto the floor and grabbed the receiver. "What." She listened, then yelled, "Danny, my dear helpful brother wants to cook up more great ideas with you."

Dan reached for the phone at the far edge of the counter. "I'll take it out here."

"Go ahead, but I'll still hear you."

He didn't care. "For Chrissake, Pat, you knew I had a son and you never said a word. What the hell kind of a friend are you?"

Pat's voice shook. "I'm sorry. I did what she wanted.... Do you remember when I asked you, years ago, to pray for something special? It was for him. For Mike. That's when he was born."

"That doesn't come *close* to what you should have done."

Pat spoke softly. "I don't know what to say."

"*Good!*" Jessica had picked up the other phone. "I'm *glad* you don't know what to say. Maybe then you won't say *anything*, 'cause everything you've said so far has been a crock of shit. Maybe you should hang up and work your little pea-brain to death and come up with something that makes sense. *Jeez*, you guys." She slammed the phone down again.

"Are you still there, Danny?" Pat's voice shook so badly Dan didn't catch all the words.

"I'm here."

"I'm sorry. I really am."

"Yeah, I suppose. But, *Pat*, not to tell a guy he has a kid! How could you do that?"

"It's what she wanted. She had a right."

"What about *my* rights? That's my *son*!"

"Let her explain, okay? You might still think we were wrong, but let her tell you why. Maybe you'll understand. I'm as sorry about this as anything I've ever done, but I hope you work something out so you both can be happy. So all *three* of you can be happy. Mike figures into this, too, you know."

Dan couldn't think of anything to say.

"Call me later, will you?" Pat's voice was still shaky.

"We'll see."

Pat let out a breath. "Okay, we'll talk then. 'Bye."

Dan walked toward the living room. At the end of the hall, Jessica stood at the bathroom sink washing her face. He watched, but it seemed an intrusion, so he turned away and let himself fall into a black recliner. He closed his eyes and, pushing with his right foot, gently rocked.

"So now what?" Jessica stood in the doorway, combing her hair.

"So now I guess I should meet Mike."

"He'll be here in a few minutes. Probably with his friend Joey."

Dan's belly flipped. What do you say to a seven-year-old son you've never seen? How do you tell a boy you're his father when neither of you knew the other existed?

"I'll tell him the story," she said—was she reading his mind again?—"so today just be an old friend visiting, okay?"

He nodded. "Jess, why didn't you tell me?"

"*Tell* you? How? I changed my mind about tattling even before I knew I was pregnant, and by then you had taken your vow. If I had told them, they'd have dumped you."

Dan shook his head. "But—"

"They'd have *dumped* you, Danny. And once you were ordained ... well, how do you tell a priest he's a daddy without screwing up his life? Pat said you were a good priest. That was what you wanted. I didn't want to mess it up."

Dan blinked twice. "We'd have worked something out."

Her eyes flashed. "Worked something out? The only thing *out* would have been *you*, right on your celibate ass! What was there to work out? Priest plus kid equals scandal. No parish on whatever-god-you-believe-in's good earth will accept a priest with a kid."

"You never know. One might have—"

Her voice got louder. "Think so? Well, I asked around." Softer. "Yeah, I really did, 'cause I hoped different. But the answer was always the same: *No way!* So I kept my secret, and Pat did too—till now—and I moved here where nobody knew me. I made great friends and Mike and I have done fine."

Dan wiped his eyes so he could see. "Maybe we could've—"

"*No.* It was the right decision. Even if it hurts you now."

She made it sound so logical. But damn it, they had a son. She should have told him.

"Oh hell, Danny, I wanted to tell you so many times: right there in your reception line after your first Mass; every time Mike woke me in the middle of the night or threw temper tantrums. You don't know how many times ..." She spoke faster. "One day a couple of years ago I was so mad about something he did that I dialed right up to your last number before I hung up."

"You dialed—"

"I've always had your number. In case I changed my mind."

"I wish you had."

"No. When I left you at the beach that morning I was getting out of your way. That was my last shot, my last of many—prom, high school graduation when I thought sure you'd join me at Wisconsin, college graduation, finally the beach. I lost every damned time." She grabbed a tissue off the end table and wiped her nose. "You chose the priesthood. And after a while I honestly hoped you'd be happy in it."

She looked at her watch. "Mike will be here soon, and I have to change." She started toward the hallway, then pointed to a pile of photo albums on a bookcase in the corner. "You'll want to see those, how he grew over the years."

The albums were dated with a black marker. Dan pulled the bottom one, "1968-69," and lifted the cover. On the first page was a five by seven of Jessica at the oak tree in her parents' back yard. She was staring into the camera, holding her very large belly. She wasn't smiling, but she didn't look upset either. Below the photo was the date: 11/29/68. Exactly eight months after they'd made love on the beach at Bay View Park.

He stared at her belly. That was his baby inside her, and he'd known nothing about it. *He* should have been taking these pictures, not Pat or their parents. He recalled his first Mass, Agnes Reuter's trembling fingers against his cheek: *Oh, Daniel, I am so afraid that you have made a terrible mistake.* The image in the album blurred. He ran his fingers across his eyes and started turning pages.

Baby pictures came next, photographs of Mike and Jessica, of Mike and the Fernettans, of Mike and Pat. Pat, smiling, holding the baby. *His baby.* Dan slipped the album back onto the bookcase and opened the most recent one, "1976." Jessica had written "Mike's week at Pat's" across the top of the first page. There were pictures of Mike outside Pat's church; outside the rectory; *inside* the rectory, bouncing on the bed in the room Pat was letting Dan use. Dan had to sit down.

The back door burst open and two boys about eight years old ran in, spotted him, and stopped. "Who are you?" they said at the same time.

"I'm Dan, Jessica's friend."

"Uncle Pat's friend Dan?" The boy had a thin nose and a pointed chin, with blond hair above ears a little too big for his head.

Dan couldn't stop staring. "You must be Mike. You've heard of me?"

"Uncle Pat told me about you and him playing basketball. Is he coming today, too?"

"No, but he said to say hi."

The boy's smile faded. "If he'da come, you and Joey and him and me could've played. There's a hoop by our school." He looked around. "Where's Mom?"

"Right here." Jessica came around the corner, wiping her hands. "About time you guys showed up."

"We stopped at Peter's first," Mike said. "He showed us a new game he got."

"And he's bringing it to the sleepover," Joey said.

Jessica showed the smile Dan could never resist. "*Sleep*over? It sounds like you guys won't sleep at all! So, you've met Dan?"

"Uh-huh," Mike said, "but I thought I never would." He looked up. "Uncle Pat said you never get the same day off he does. But maybe someday you can and visit us when *he* does!"

"I'll try," Dan said.

Jessica shot him a look, then turned to the boys. "Okay, scoot. Dan and I have to talk before I run errands. Grab a snack and go pack!"

The boys pulled cookies from a ceramic jar and scurried up the stairs, but Mike popped back down a few steps and shouted, "Nice to meet you, Dan!"

"Go!" Jessica said.

Dan touched her arm. "He's very polite."

She moved away. "Some days." She wiped the edge of the sink with a yellow dishcloth. "This is going way too fast. I need time to get used to it."

"Eight years isn't fast."

"I'm talking about this afternoon."

Mike called from the stairs. "Mom, can I wear my blue shirt to church tomorrow?"

"Yes, *if* you change before you play ball."

"Church?" Dan said.

"He goes to Mass with Joey when he sleeps over."

"You let him do that?"

"When he wants to. Look, Mike knows I'm an atheist. And he knows his Uncle Pat and most other people believe in a god. I've told him why I don't, but I also tell him everyone has to decide those things for himself."

Dan shook his head. "But kids are so impressionable. He might—"

Jessica stepped toward him. "Don't you dare scold me about Mike. If he wants to go to church with a friend, he *can*, damn it! Besides, right now religion's the least of my worries. I have to figure out how to explain *you*."

"Have you told him anything ... about his dad, I mean?"

"I told him his dad and I were good friends, that we decided not to get married and he moved away before we knew I was pregnant."

"Not actually a lie."

Jessica draped the cloth over the faucet. "No, but that's not to say Mike won't consider it one." She glanced at the clock on the stove. "I have to take some things to a friend. Mike's going to Joey's, and I'll drop them off on the way."

"I can do that. Then you can head straight to your friend's and I'll get more time with Mike. Later we can have dinner."

"Not so fast."

"Breakfast?"

"I'm sleeping in. And slow down. I mean it."

"Pat's not expecting me till Sunday night. Eating together tomorrow and Sunday isn't fast. We have a lot to catch up on."

"Let this settle a bit. You just got here."

He tried to smile. "Lunch?"

"No. Maybe. Hell, I don't know. I need time, don't you understand? You show up and seem to think eight years will fall away like they never happened. Well, they happened. I lived 'em, and Mike lived 'em too. Now his Daddy shows up and I have no idea what to tell a little boy, but I have to tell him something, and soon."

"I could help."

"Yeah, by going away. Mike's going to be mad, mad at you for not being here all this time and mad at me for lying to him. Oh, yeah, he's going to be pissed—even at Pat, whom he adores—and I don't blame him. Your being here would only make it worse."

"When will you tell him?"

"Tomorrow, the next day, I don't know. As soon as I figure out what to say and convince myself I can handle what he's going to think about me. I've always played it straight with him, except for this, so he's going to lose trust in me, and I don't like that."

"I'm staying in town tonight, whether I see you tomorrow or not."

She shrugged. "Call after ten."

"I will."

"And don't be surprised if I tell you not to come. This is so ... so damned unexpected. I figured someday you might find me, but you'd be a priest, another uncle to Mike, like Pat. That's all I ever prepared for. Not this."

The boys hopped down the stairs, Mike with a sleeping bag. "We're ready if you are!"

Jessica walked toward him. "Dan's offered to give you guys a ride. That all right?"

"Sure!" Mike said.

Dan opened the door. "I'll call you tomorrow, Jess."

She nodded, pulled Mike to her and kissed him, then turned away. But not before Dan saw her tears.

Late the next morning Dan and Jessica sat across from each other in a cafe near her house.

"I love him," he said. "You've done great."

She shot him a look. "Visit a few more times. We're far from perfect."

The waitress brought their orders and set them, one at a time, on the table. "Will there be anything else?"

"No thanks." Dan leaned forward. "I want to do more than visit. We should get married."

The eyebrow shot up. "Danny, *jeez*. What the hell do you expect? You arrive one day and want to get married the next? Didn't being a priest teach you anything about reality?" She put down her fork. "Nurses don't get rich, but you've seen the house. We're doing all right. Why should I change?"

"The three of us together would be even better."

"I'm not sure about that."

"Mike's mine, too. We need to form a family."

"He doesn't even know you yet. And you don't know him."

"But I want to. And I will. Besides, I know you. I've never forgotten you. I still love you."

Jessica pounded the table. "*Stop it!*"

Customers and staff turned to see what was going on. Dan blushed. Jessica lowered her voice. "Sorry. But damn it, things change. You love the girl at the beach. That's not me anymore. I love being a nurse, and except for Mike, that's where I spend my time. What makes you think I need help?"

He pushed himself back in the booth. Maybe it was selfish to barge into their lives. Maybe she *didn't* need him. Maybe they'd never renew their old relationship or grow into a new one. But now that he'd met Mike, he wanted to be part of his son's life.

"I'm sorry," she was saying. "That didn't come out the way I wanted, but I'm scared." She reached for his hand and Dan closed his around hers. The soft skin he remembered from years ago had calloused. He stroked the back of her hand.

"Don't," she said, and pulled it away.

"That wasn't a come-on. I'm scared, too. Who do we have to hang onto besides each other?" He paused. "That didn't come out the way I wanted, either. You probably have lots of friends you can turn to. Right now I have only Pat … or maybe not, after that call."

"We were mean," she said. "But Pat's Pat. He'll take an apology. And yeah, my friends have been great."

"But there's no guy?" Dan hoped.

"I'm a mommy and a nurse, and I'm happy with that. At least I've *been* happy with it."

"And now I'm here. Does that make you *un*happy?"

"It makes me wonder. It complicates things. And I hate complications."

"We should get married."

"You keep saying that." She slid out of her seat. "I'm not sure it's a good idea."

"Jess, we have to think of Mike."

"You're going too fast. Back off."

They met again the next day for brunch at the coffee shop in the Templeton Hotel where Dan stayed the weekend.

"Well, I told Mike," Jessica said. "About us. He didn't seem upset, but I'm not sure it sunk in. There'll be questions, maybe accusations. Be ready."

"And us?"

"Damn your one-track mind. It's your third day here. Visit when you want. We'll see how it goes. Mike just met you and I'm not sure I know you anymore."

He set down his fork. "That's my fault."

Jessica folded her napkin. "It's nobody's fault. All those years you were at the seminary, Pat warned me about you. And I know he warned you about me too, but he didn't have any luck with either of us." She stood. "I need time to think this through. For Mike especially, but for me too."

Chapter 32

That afternoon, on his way back to Milwaukee, Dan stopped to see Agnes Reuter. She was looking better. "I'm returning your book," he said. "And I found Jessie."

"Oh, Daniel, that is wonderful. Come in. Tell me."

Spike peered around the dining-room doorway, waited until Dan got seated, then jumped into his lap.

"I'm still having trouble believing it."

"Yes," Agnes said, "After all this time, I'm sure you are."

"No, it's—well, I mean, I not only found *her*, I discovered she has a son—*we* have a son. My son. Mike. He's almost eight years old." Dan was blushing. "It's kind of hard to explain."

"You don't owe anyone an explanation, Daniel. But I will bet that was a shock!"

"But there's a problem too. I want to get married, but Jessie doesn't. She says it's too quick. But with a little boy, we should be a family!"

"I'm sure she was as surprised to see you as you were to find a son!"

"Well, yeah, I suppose she was."

"Give her time, Daniel. Give her a chance to think. See what happens." Agnes pulled herself to the edge of her chair. "Do you have time for tea?"

"Of course."

She led him into her kitchen. "Yes, tea, and we'll celebrate. You stopped being a priest, but now you're a different kind of father! We'll toast to your new life!"

"It does feel strange. But nice. And thank you again for the book. Can I take another one?"

"Of course."

"I want to tell you another part I really liked in that first one." Dan opened his datebook and flipped a few sheets. "Ingersoll said, 'Is there a God? I do not know. Is man immortal? I do not know. One thing I do know, and that is that neither hope nor fear, belief nor denial, can change the fact. It is as it is, and will be as it must be. We wait and hope.' I love his humility, his willingness to admit a lack of knowledge. And I guess I agree with him—I think I'm more an agnostic than an atheist, though I like your word skeptic too. And freethinker."

"You have lots more reading and thinking to do, Daniel. This—this freedom—is all new for you. Plus you now have a son! You will be busy, but please don't forget to come visit me."

Dan gave her a hug. "I promise, I won't forget."

An hour later, Dan told his parents about Jessica—and Mike.

"Seven years old?" his mother said. "But you were a priest then, Daniel ... no, that was *before*! How could that happen? Why didn't you tell us?"

His dad was staring at him.

Dan glanced around the familiar living room. It seemed strange, though, telling this story here. "I didn't know about him either, not till I found Jessie." Again, he was blushing. His dad was still standing at the front window, and hadn't said a word.

"Will the two of you be getting married then?" His mother's voice seemed full of hope.

"I want to. But Jess and I have a lot to talk about. She's been raising Mike by herself."

"I'm not surprised she didn't marry," Mrs. Bates said. "I've always felt she was waiting for you."

Mr. Bates turned. "What are you talking about? She never even told him about the boy. Apparently she didn't mind waiting forever." He pointed at Dan. "That boy is as much yours as he is hers. And he's our grandson, too. Don't let her keep us in the dark any longer."

"When will we get to meet him?" his mother asked.

"Soon. Well, after she explains it all to him. But you'll love him. He's a neat kid."

His father shook his head. "Even so, that girl had no business seducing a man about to become a priest. I can't say I care to see her again, though if you marry I suppose—"

"Dan ..." Mrs. Bates glared at her husband.

"Look," Dan said, "she didn't *seduce* me. You have to understand: *Her* parents are as angry at me as you are at her. But it's time all four of you realized your little darlings didn't grow up to be angels."

His father sat down. "You know, if you were still a priest this would be one hell of a scandal."

"That's why Jessie kept it quiet. She didn't want to hurt me."

"That was thoughtful of her," his mother said.

Mr. Bates nodded. "Yes, I'll give her that."

"Well, I always thought she was a good girl," Mrs. Bates said. "I still do, even if she made a mistake."

Dan leaned forward. "*She* didn't make the mistake, Mom, I did. And I don't mean getting her pregnant."

In Milwaukee, it was raining when Pat met Dan at the rectory door.

"I'm sorry …," they both started.

"Hurry up and come in," Pat said. "You're getting wet."

Dan went into the bathroom to towel off his head. "It feels strange being back. Everything's different. And I owe you an apology, though I still don't understand—"

"And I don't know how to explain it," Pat said, "except I really felt she was right."

"You didn't have to tell the *world*," Dan said, "but you could have told *me*."

"It would have complicated things."

"But they wouldn't be so complicated now."

Pat nodded. "That's true." He paused. "I really am sorry. It may have been a mistake—not telling you, I mean. I don't know anymore."

"Well," Dan said, "that part's over. Now Jess and I have to figure out what to do."

Early in June, Dan and Pat celebrated a warm evening with two cold beers on the rectory's screened porch. "I've decided I'll teach," Dan said. "English and Latin, in a high school. I've checked around. I can get a loan for a master's in education. UW-La Crosse has a two-year program, and there I'll be closer to Jessie and Mike."

"So I shouldn't get used to having you around," Pat said.

"I'm going to hate leaving," Dan said. "It's been nice, kind of like being together at the seminary."

Pat smiled. "At the seminary you'd have to join me at Mass."

Dan smiled back. "True. But I did say kind of."

For the rest of the summer, Dan worked at the sporting goods store. He had off on Tuesdays and Wednesdays and, by four o'clock Tuesday mornings, he was speeding west out of Milwaukee. By noon he was in Minneapolis, eating lunch with Jessica and Mike. Afterward, he and Mike played baseball in back of Mike's school.

On Wednesdays Mike went to Joey's, and Dan met Jessica in the hospital cafeteria.

"He's such a neat kid," Dan said late in July. "We get along really well. You've done a great job."

Jessica frowned. "Has he mentioned anything about being mad? At me, I mean, for not telling him you were his dad?"

"No. Does he seem angry to you?"

"Not angry, but more distant. All he said when I told him was 'Okay,' like every kid has to wait seven years to find out about his dad. It's got to be bothering him."

Dan leaned forward. "Has he ever told you he wishes we'd get married?"

Jessica's head shot up. "No."

"Well, he has me. Sometimes he talks about Joey having two parents. Then he says he wishes he did too."

Her eyes flashed. "Of course you haven't said anything to encourage that."

"*No!* For Pete's sake, Jess, I—"

"Of course not. He doesn't say one word to me about it, but he comes right out with it to you. That's bullshit, Danny. It won't work."

"Honest, I—"

"Forget it. I have to go to work." She disappeared through the door without looking back.

A week later, Jessica took a day off, and Dan drove her, Mike and Joey to a small beach along Lake Minnetonka west of Minneapolis. The boys ran ahead to the water while Dan and Jessica pulled towels, blankets, and a picnic basket from the trunk of his car. Jessica was wearing an orange cotton top over her swimsuit, and Dan wondered what kind she had on.

She set the basket on the ground. "I wouldn't have agreed to this if we hadn't already promised him before our conversation last week."

Dan took his eyes off her legs. "I keep telling you: I have *never* prompted Mike on what to say, to you or to me. He has a mind of his own, you know that. But damn it, he's right. We should get married. I'm not a priest anymore and he deserves two parents."

She raised the cover and peeked into the basket. "Good, I didn't forget the pickles." She pulled the handles together. "It's been eight years. People change."

"You wanted me to change. I'm sorry it took so long."

She threw a huge red-and-orange towel over her left shoulder. "Well, I've changed too, a lot more than you suspect. Have you ever considered that maybe, after all these years, I'm not in love with you anymore?" She started across the parking lot.

Dan leaned against the car. Had she really said that? He watched her walk away, then looked past her to Mike and Joey splashing in the shallow water. For Mike's sake, he would do the best he could today, then head home and decide what to do next.

His mind raced with arguments to change Jessica's mind. But if she didn't love him, what could he do? He locked the car and ran, catching up to her at the edge of the asphalt. He stopped but she continued onto the beach.

"Hey," he said, "aren't you going to take off your shoes?"

"I may—when I get to the water."

"But you always go barefoot on sand."

"When I'm with people I trust. Right now I don't feel that way about you."

Dan kept his shoes on too and followed her to the water. He hoped Mike and Joey wouldn't notice that he and Jessica were saying very little to each other.

Later, with his car parked at Jessica's curb, Dan hugged Mike goodbye a little tighter and a little longer than usual. He gave Jessica a quick glance before she turned away, then he got into the car, waved to Mike, and headed home.

During his drive back to Milwaukee, Dan kept asking himself how he could persuade Jessica to marry him. Mike deserved a dad. Jess deserved a husband. And, damn it, he deserved to be that dad and husband. But she kept putting him off, and now she'd accused him of prompting Mike to suggest a wedding, as if she didn't even trust him to tell the truth about their son.

Flashing red lights reflected off his mirror. Ambulance. Dan braked and pulled onto the shoulder, but the lights stayed behind him. Damn, it wasn't an ambulance.

"Sir, do you have any idea how fast you were going?" the tall trooper asked.

"No, I'm sorry, I wasn't paying attention. I had something on my—"

"Can I see your license, sir? I had you doing eighty-five."

"No way! I never drive that fast." Dan pulled the card from his wallet.

The trooper examined Dan's license. "You were passing everyone in sight, Mr. Bates, including me. I was doing sixty-five and you went *poof*. Too fast to let you off with a warning. I'll be right back."

Shit. Now this mess was costing him a ticket and who knows how much money. Okay, if Jess didn't want him, he'd stop wanting her, too. Maybe that's what she was waiting for. Then she could blame him for rejecting her again. Why else would she act like this?

"I wish you'd move here instead of to La Crosse. Then you could live with us," Mike said on Dan's next visit. They were lying under a tree next to Mike's school after Dan hit him some fly balls on a hot August afternoon.

Dan thumped the fat end of the bat against the ground. "I do too."

"So why don't you?"

Didn't Jessica explain any of this? "Well, for people to live together, they all have to want to. Your mom says she's not ready for that yet."

Mike's eyes got big. "Know what? Maybe she'd let you if you begged. She thinks about it all the time after you go back to Uncle Pat's."

"How do you know?"

"Sometimes I catch her sitting at the table—in the kitchen—staring out the window. Like the other day—last Saturday, when I came home from Joey's. I said, 'Thinking about Dan?' and she said 'Uh-huh.' And then I said, 'Do you wish he'd live here with us?' And she said, 'Is that something you'd like?' And I said 'Uh-huh' and she said, 'Well, we'll see.' So maybe if you told her it was a ten-wish she'd say yes."

"A ten-wish?"

"Yeah, you know, something you really, really want. A one means you don't care if you get it or not, and a ten means you'd do anything for it."

"Oh. Does that work?"

Mike shook his head as though he couldn't believe he had to explain this to an adult. "Of course it works. Like on Mom's days off, she'll ask how bad I want to go to a Twins game or something and maybe I'll say eight. But she might say nine or ten for the zoo, so hers is a bigger wish than mine and we do what she wants. But sometimes mine is bigger and we do what I want, see?"

"I think so. But why not say yours is a ten all the time so you always get to do what you want?"

Mike rolled his eyes. "'Cause you gotta tell the truth, that's why."

"Oh, yes, of course," Dan said. He blushed, and he put his arm around his son. "Believe me, kiddo, my wanting to stay with you is definitely a true ten-wish."

Ten-wish or no, Jessica didn't change her mind. At brunch the next day, she toyed with her salad. "Look, I need to be sure. Mike is, but he doesn't get to decide this."

"Well, I want you to know, *he* brought it up yesterday."

She nodded. "He asked me the other day too."

"And you said—according to him—'We'll see.'"

"I didn't want to give him a straight-out *no*."

"You keep telling *me* no."

"You're a big boy. Mike's not."

Dan slid out of the booth. "It's amazing how fast I lose my appetite when we talk. You're not going to change your mind, are you? I don't know which is more cruel, keeping Mike's hopes alive or killing mine for no reason."

She followed him out the door. "What do you mean, no reason? I have *scores* of reasons, but I don't have to list them for you. It's enough that I'm committed to Mike and to the kids at the hospital, and right now I don't want to make a commitment to you."

Mike was at Joey's, so Dan dropped Jessica at the curb. Neither said goodbye.

CHAPTER 33

▼

In late August, Dan swung shut the double doors of his U-Haul trailer, then turned to Pat. "I'm going to miss you. How can I thank you?"

"By being good to Mike. Jessie's done great with him and he's a terrific kid, but he needs you too. And—this'll be harder because I know you're still upset—be nice to Jessie too. She's still hurting, and I don't know any way to help her except be kind." He studied Dan's face. "Will you do that?"

"Of course. We are speaking again, sort of."

"Then you've thanked me," Pat said. "Except you have to come back and visit. Bring Mike and Jessie too. And study hard in school." He laughed. "I'm preaching."

"It's your last chance for a while, to me at least. But remember, La Crosse is halfway to Minneapolis. You can stop and see me too. I won't even complain if you preach."

A few months later, on Thanksgiving, Mike pushed himself from the table. "The turkey's good, Mom, but I'm full. Can I go over to Joey's?"

"It's Thanksgiving. I—"

"Joey's mom said it's all right."

"But don't you want dessert? Dan brought pumpkin pie and real whipped cream."

"Can I wait till later? Joey'd probably like some too. Can I invite him? Please?"

"I thought Joey has guests."

"I already know his grandma and grandpa."

"All right, but that jacket you wore yesterday isn't warm enough. Wear your green one."

"Aw, Mom, Joey calls it my Packer jacket. My blue one's warm enough."

Dan leaned toward Mike. "I think everyone should wear a Packer jacket."

Mike grinned and stuck out his tongue.

Jessica pointed at him. "The green one, or stay here."

He stomped out of the room. "Jeez, you'd think *you* were the one going outside." He ran up the stairs, and a minute later tore back down and headed for the door wearing blue.

"Hey!" Jessica yelled.

"*Mah*-om, it's over twenty. I checked the thermometer! I'll roast in the green one."

She paused, then waved her hand toward the door. Mike dashed out. She and Dan stared at each other.

"He's just like *you*!" they said at the same time. Jessica's laugh echoed through the room, and Dan ached again to stay there and hear it every day.

"It's been six months," he said. "We have fun when we're together—mostly. I don't smoke, drink, or do drugs. We agree there's no god, so I know you're not holding that against me. What is it?"

She stared into the candles at the center of the table. "I just …, well, before you showed up I was happy being Mike's mom and working with the kids at the hospital. I'm still happy with that. I don't think you realize how much I'm there. I usually stay beyond my shift. So many of the kids need attention."

"But getting married wouldn't have to change that. I understand your dedication over there." He pressed his fingers into the tablecloth. "But you know what? There are times I think you're still trying to punish me for choosing the priesthood over you."

"I probably should. Have you ever realized what a kick in the teeth that was? We made love, then you said, 'Gee, that was nice but now I'm going to be celibate. Ta-ta!'"

Dan closed his eyes. "That was cruel. I was stupid." He searched her face for any signs of change. "Since I found you, there have been times you seemed to forgive me, like that day you reached for my hand. And sometimes I still feel the way I did that night at the beach. I want to hold you, know we're finally together after all these years."

She looked away.

"Do you ever think back to your prom—you said you'd remember it forever—to our walks in Bay View Park, and that trip to Door County—"

"Of course," she said. "And if I thought we could bring them back I'd let you move in tonight. But we can't bring them back, and right now I'm not willing to risk what I have."

Mike burst in the front door, followed by Joey. "Hey, Dan, tell Joey why you have to go back to La Crosse tonight."

Dan wanted to say, "Because your mother won't let me stay here," but he played along with Mike's joke. "I have homework."

The boys giggled. "We don't," they both said. Mike added, "Yeah, just the kids do who didn't get all their work done Tuesday."

Dan leaned toward them and wrinkled his brow to look mean. "You guys are lucky *I'm* not your teacher. I'd give you so much homework you'd only have time to eat *part* of your dinner. The turkey and vegetables, yes, but *not* the pie and ice cream!"

Mike and Joey laughed and followed Jessica into the kitchen. "We're ready for dessert, Mom, but he shouldn't get any till he's finished his homework!"

Dan blocked the doorway. "Okay, but then *everyone* has to wait. And I'll take the pie and whipped cream home. Then, after I finish, I'll eat it all myself!"

The kids squealed and moved between Dan and Jessica. "Okay," Mike said, "you can have yours now too. But when you're a teacher I hope you don't come to *our* school. You're too strict!"

During the drive home, Dan grinned at his memories of the day. He had a lot to be thankful for, especially sharing laughs and taunts with the kids. But Jessica could enjoy that every day. It wasn't fair. He had already missed much of Mike's childhood, and weekly visits left him craving more.

Two days after school let out for the winter holidays, Dan and Mike boarded Amtrak's eastbound *Empire Builder* at the old Great Northern station in downtown Minneapolis. Seven hours later, Pat met them at the depot in Milwaukee.

"Uncle Pat! We ate breakfast in the dining car, right along the Mississippi," Mike said. "Sometimes another train went *whoosh!* right past our window. And then we went up in the dome—have you ever been in one of those, Uncle Pat? We could see all over and watch where our train was going down the tracks."

"You make me wish I could ride back with you," Pat said.

"You can! That guy over there will sell you a ticket."

Pat tousled Mike's hair. "Someday I will. I promise."

Dan decided to spend his 1977 spring break in Minneapolis. Late on the first afternoon, Jessica was cooking, and she shooed Dan and Mike out of the house, but they stopped long enough to grab two still-warm cookies off the counter.

"Out, or starve!" she shouted, and they ran out the door coughing on the crumbs they inhaled while laughing.

In back of Mike's school they shot baskets. After the sun dipped behind the building, Mike insisted on shooting a few more but, after he lost sight of the ball and it almost hit him in the face, Dan called a stop.

Jessica met them at the door twirling a dishcloth. "Where were you guys?"

Mike rolled his ball toward a corner of the porch. "Playing. You said 'Leave,' so we left."

"Yeah, but I didn't say take an overnight trip." She snapped the dishcloth at Mike. He jumped and the porch echoed with his laugh. It was so much like Jessica's that Dan ached to grab them both and squeeze tight and tell them he was going to stay with them forever.

But Jessica was already headed back to the kitchen.

That summer, Dan spent all his spare time in Minneapolis. Mike seemed to enjoy his company and kept saying he wished Dan lived there. Jessica indicated she liked having him around, too, but she continued to put him off when he suggested they marry.

In May 1978, the University of Wisconsin-La Crosse awarded Dan a master's degree in education, and that fall he began teaching English and Latin at Riversmeet High School on the north side of La Crosse. His life would have seemed perfect if he could have gone home every night to the woman he loved and their son. But Jessica and Mike were still in Minneapolis, three hours upriver.

In October, math teacher Gwen Tronning stopped by Dan's room. "Some of us are cooking out Saturday. You're invited if you don't have other plans."

"I did," he said, "but I can change 'em." He would drive up to Jessica's on Sunday.

After the cookout, Dan and Gwen walked through a park along the Mississippi.

"You're new at Riversmeet," she said. "Nobody knows much about you."

Dan smiled. "We're even. I don't know much about you either."

She gazed toward the water. "Some of us have tried to call you on weekends, but you never answer."

"I visit friends out of town."

"Oh." She looked away. "Not many people teach Latin. Where did you learn it?"

"In church."

"Which one? I haven't seen you at mine."

"I don't go anymore. I'm an agnostic."

"That's kind of like an atheist, isn't it?"

"Neither believes in a god, but an agnostic is less certain. More open to evidence, I think."

"They're both rare in this town."

"Any others at school?"

"You're the first one I know. You'll do fine if you're not obnoxious about it."

"Okay. But I don't want people trying to convert me back, either."

Gwen jumped in front of him and placed her palm on his forehead. "BELIEEEEEVE!" she yelled, then stomped around laughing on the grass beside the path. After she stopped, she said, "You should have seen your face."

Dan smiled. "I *told* you I don't know you. You could be a Jesus freak for all I know."

"I could be." She fell in beside him. "So, are you involved with someone?"

"I am, but she's not." Maybe that was more than he should say.

"Ex-wife?"

"We haven't gotten that far."

"I did." Gwen didn't say more, and Dan didn't pry.

"Riversmeet's been good to me, good *for* me," she said. "I hope it will be for you, too."

"I like it so far," he said. "And I enjoyed the party."

"Then come to more. We have them a lot."

In Milwaukee the weekend before Thanksgiving, Dan spotted Hans Kueng's new book, *Does God Exist?*, on Pat's coffee table.

"I know you like Kueng," Pat said, "if for no other reason than his writings keep pissing off the Vatican. Care to borrow it?"

"Sure. I suppose you'd like a report when I'm done."

"If you feel like doing one."

"Let me hear you conjugate *amo*," Dan told his Latin class two weeks later. "Miss Kettler, you first."

Tracy Kettler, a tall senior with long blond hair, stared at him. "Um, a-MO."

Dan waved his hand. "Wait. Put your gum back in its wrapper, please."

"But it's still fresh."

"That's unfortunate."

A muscular boy in the back row straightened in his seat. "It don't hurt to chew gum in class, Mr. Bates. It even helps some of us think, and a lot of our teachers say we need all the help we can get, ain't that so, Trace?"

The girl nodded.

Dan didn't recall Bruce Thomson saying anything in class before. "Mr. Thompson, you don't have me for English, do you?"

"Unh-uh. I got Mr. Honnard."

"Well, I suspect Mr. Honnard would be happier if you said *doesn't*, as in 'It *doesn't* hurt to chew gum in class.'"

Bruce grinned. "I knew you'd come to see it our way, Mr. Bates." There were giggles around the room.

Dan pointed at Bruce. "Cute. You got me." He turned back to Tracy. "Deposit the gum, please." She rolled her eyes and took the gum from her mouth. "Thank you. Now, conjugate *amo* for us. Here's a hint: The accent goes on the first syllable."

Tracy swallowed. "Um, a-MO, a-MAHS, a-MAHT."

"*First* syllable."

She screwed up her face. "C'mon, Mr. Bates, does it really make a difference?"

"Only getting it right versus getting it wrong."

Bruce Thomson leaned across his desk. "Mr. Bates, it hardly seems—"

"Mr. Thomson, please raise your hand if you have a question."

"Whoa, Mr. Bates. I thought we got done with that stuff last year. We're seniors now."

"In our class discussions you may cut in at will, but for recitation I want to call on you one at a time. How will I know if Miss Kettler knows the answer if someone else blurts it out? Miss Kettler, AH-moe. Take it from there."

Bruce Thomson raised his hand.

"A minute, Mr. Thomson. Miss Kettler?"

Tracy Kettler shifted her weight to one leg. "AH-mo, AH-mahs, AH-maht, Ah-MAH-mus?"

"Yes."

"Ah-MAH-mus," she repeated, "ah-MAHT-tis, AH-mahnt?"

"Excellent. But don't make it a question. Say it as if you know it. And now tell us what it means."

"I lo-o-o-o-ove," Bruce Thomson cut in, giving the word an infinite number of syllables. His classmates cracked up.

Dan did too. "I hope you do, Mr. Thomson. I hope we all do. What was it you wanted?"

"To ask if you're always going to be so strict, Mr. Bates. I mean, you're acting so fussy with accents and all that."

"Yes, Mr. Thomson, I'm always going to be so strict. It's the only way I know to teach Latin, or English for that matter, because that's how I learned. Yeah, I'm going to be very fussy. You might even end up calling me fuss-EE."

Gwen invited Dan to her apartment for a late dinner after the Riversmeet Raiders' first basketball game. Afterward, they nestled on the couch in the soft light of a dozen candles, and Gwen opened the drapes to a view of the Mississippi. A towboat was plowing its way upstream. Toward Minneapolis. Toward Jessica and Mike.

"It's going where I go on weekends," he said. "Minneapolis."

Gwen wrinkled her nose. "My ex lives in St. Paul. I never go there. So you'd like to get on that boat?"

"For the scenery, maybe. But it's too slow to go visit someone."

Dan and Gwen started dropping in on each other at school, asking questions, commenting on the administration, saying good morning and good night, just being around if the other was in a bad mood. Sometimes she patted his arm, and he punctuated his sentences with a squeeze of her arm or waist.

On her couch after another game, she curled up next to him. To Dan it seemed as natural to hold and kiss Gwen as it had Jessica. He had forgotten how good it felt to make out, but he didn't go beyond kissing.

It was she who moved his hand to her breast. "You're holding back."

"Sorry. I haven't done this a lot."

She sat up. "Oh. Are you gay? It's all right."

"No." Should he tell her? Why not? "I used to be a priest."

Gwen bolted to the window. "A *Catholic* priest? Oh my God."

"It's all right. I quit."

She shook her head. But doesn't the Church say, 'Once a priest, always a priest?'"

"What sense does that make? Nobody says, 'Once a teacher, always a teacher.' I told you I don't believe in a god. That didn't bother you."

"But you were a *priest*. I ... I think I'd better turn on the lights."

Chapter 34

In January 1979, a blizzard closed schools across the Midwest. Dan watched the snow whip against his dining-room windows while he lifted his portable typewriter from the floor to the table. Then he began his report.

> Dear Pat,
>
> I finished Kueng's book last night. I was disappointed. He cites the human longing for certainty as an indication of a god, but not as a proof, and he finally admits there are no proofs. That surprised me, not that there are none, but that he admits it and still decides to believe.
>
> Kueng claims our partial goodness demonstrates the existence of a perfect good which we call God. By that logic, however, we can claim that our partial *wickedness* shows the existence of a perfect *evil* which we call God.
>
> Then Kueng insists that if our lives are not to be meaningless we have to admit God exists. But that 'if' makes it only a wish, not a proof.
>
> He says most people must first believe in a god through faith before they can accept the intellectual evidence, and therefore believers shouldn't take pride in believing because they didn't figure it out themselves but were given their faith from God. If that's true, people should not condemn nonbelievers because their faith was withheld by God.
>
> It disappoints me that Kueng admits there are no proofs, but still insists the existence of a god is more likely than not. Since there are no proofs either

way, it makes more sense to me to stay neutral and open to further evidence.

Anyway, thanks for lending me the book and I look forward to seeing you soon.

Dan

In mid-May, Dan was editing his final Latin exam for the 1978-79 school year when Pat phoned.

"Remember the day I promised Mike a train ride? Well, Congress has ordered Amtrak to cut nine trains this fall and—"

"In the middle of a gas shortage?" Dan said.

"Another reason to call it the House of Reprehensibles. Anyway, one of those trains is the *North Coast Hiawatha* running from Chicago through here and La Crosse and Minneapolis out to Seattle. I want to ride it before it's gone, just out and back. Care to come along?"

"Of course. Have you invited Mike and Jessie?"

"She can't go, but Mike and his friend Joey can. I'll get tickets for the four of us. Oh, I warned Mike we'll be on the train five days in a row."

Dan laughed. "And he said 'Great,' didn't he?"

"Did he tell you already?"

"No. But I've ridden with him. The kid loves trains."

Shortly after nine o'clock on a Monday night in late June, two Amtrak locomotives eased an eleven-car train to a stop at Minneapolis-St. Paul's new Midway Station. Dan, Mike and Joey watched from the glass-walled waiting room filled with passengers waiting to board.

Ten-year-old Mike stood on tiptoes with his face pressed to the window. "Is there gonna be room for all these people on our train? Are you sure Uncle Pat is on it? It's really long. How are we gonna find him?"

The gates opened, and the crowd surged onto the concrete platform alongside the train. Attendants in red jackets directed passengers to coaches or sleeping cars. Pat was waving from the door of a dome coach near the center of the train, and Mike and Joey zigzagged through the crowd to reach him.

Minutes later, their *North Coast Hiawatha* curved across the stone-arch bridge near St. Anthony Falls, and Dan gazed out the dome windows at the lights of downtown Minneapolis. He stayed awake most of the night, and Pat and the boys did too. He watched Mike and Joey nudge each other and point out things in the little towns they rolled through.

The next afternoon, the train cut through Homestake Pass in the Rocky Mountains, then snaked between huge rocks onto a steel bridge hundreds of feet above I-90 near Butte, Montana.

Mike pointed. "Look at those trucks down there, Uncle Pat! It's like we're flying!"

The second night, Dan's sleep was broken by patches of rough track. Pat slept through them but the boys, sitting across the aisle, were again awake, whispering secrets in the dark.

Wednesday morning, they stepped from the train and checked their bags at Seattle's King Street Station, then walked to the waterfront for a ferry ride across Puget Sound. On the return trip, Pat took pictures of Mike and Joey at the railing with the Seattle skyline behind them.

Mike reached for the camera. "Let me take one of you, Uncle Pat."

Pat grabbed Dan and pulled him to where the boys had stood. "Watch the background," Pat said. "Don't make it look like the Space Needle's growing out of my head."

Mike giggled and stepped back and forth. "Right here it does, Uncle Pat!" He snapped the shutter, and he and Joey stomped around in circles, bent over laughing.

After the ferry docked, they walked along the waterfront, stopping for dinner at Ivar's Acres of Clams. The boys giggled at the motto on the placemats, "Keep clam," then headed for the bathroom.

Dan put down his menu. "Thanks for suggesting this. They're having a great time."

Pat took a few shots of the waterfront out the window, then put his camera away. "They're not a bit grouchy. I'm surprised because they haven't had much sleep."

The waiter approached with their appetizers, and Dan unfolded his napkin. "They'll fall asleep one of these nights. Even those two can't go forever."

"I've always wished we could get together more," Pat said, "just the two of us, but I'm glad we brought the kids." He stopped smiling. "But I wish Jessie had come too."

Dan sipped his ice water. "She'll wish it too after Mike and Joey tell her about it."

The boys returned, and Mike pulled Pat's shoulder. "Uncle Pat, you gotta come see the bathrooms."

Dan stared at his son. Mike had done it again, gone straight to Pat when he wanted to share something. On the train, on the ferry, and now here, it was as if he weren't there.

"Ah, sure," Pat was saying, "but let's wait until *after* we eat."

"Okay," Joey said, "but you guys are gonna laugh. The doors say *Buoys* and *Gulls*."

They laughed, all four of them, but Dan wished he had the father-son relationship he saw between Pat and Mike. At the same time, he regretted his feelings. Pat had brought them on this long-awaited trip and of course Mike wanted to share as much of it with his uncle as he could. Still, it could have, should have, been different.

That evening, they boarded the eastbound train, which paused the next day for servicing at the red-brick Billings, Montana, depot. From his seat in the dome, Dan watched Pat out on the platform shooting pictures of the dining car crew as they loaded supplies.

After the train pulled out, Pat said, "That's probably the last time I'll ever be through here on a train. Where are the boys?"

"Walking through the cars."

"They did that twice last night. It's the same train."

"It burns energy, and they like peeking into empty bedrooms in the sleeping cars. They asked why we couldn't ride in one. I told them how much it costs."

Pat grinned. "I got an idea. You and Jess should take a trip like this. Maybe in the fall. Ride the *Empire Builder* when it gets the new Superliner cars. Splurge a little. Get yourselves a bedroom in the sleeping car."

"Oh, yeah. Jess would be thrilled."

"I don't want to pry, but is she giving any sign you'll ever be more than friends?"

"No. And I think we're both getting comfortable the way it is. Well, comfortable isn't the right word, for me at least. I'm starting to accept it, but I keep hoping for more. I visit on weekends, spend time with Mike, then the three of us go out to eat. What I miss is the day-to-day stuff: Mike's school stories, his problems, hearing him laugh. And Jessie too."

Three green-and-black Burlington Northern locomotives raced by with a freight train. "I'm sorry it hasn't worked out," Pat said. "I'd have bet anything you and Jess would be together by now."

That night, as they rolled across the Dakota plains, Dan and Pat stared straight up through the dome windows at a sky full of stars. Across the aisle, Mike and Joey were curled up asleep.

"Our last night on the train," Pat said. "It's kind of sad."

Dan nodded. "But you'll get to ride a few hours yet after we get off."

"It'll be lonely without you guys."

Dan reached across the aisle to pull Mike's jacket over his shoulders. "I was thinking about this afternoon when I said I was starting to accept Jess's and my relationship. Sometimes that's true, but other times I'm bitter, with myself about choices I've made and with Jess for hers now. I drive up to the Cities wondering why I bother, then we start joking around and she lets out that laugh, and I know why. But if I try to hold her, she pulls away."

Pat wiped the glass on his telephoto lens. "I wish there were something I could do. She's making a mistake. I've told her that."

"One night last month we stopped by the hospital on our way to dinner 'cause she'd forgotten something. You should've seen the kids' eyes light up. We were already late but she kept saying, 'Wait, there's one more I want to say *hi* to.' We wound up visiting every kid on her ward. She told them I was her friend. One little boy—about seven, pale and skinny with some godawful disease I can't pronounce—wiggled his finger for me to come over to his bed after Jess went into the next room. He asked if I was really her friend, and said I was lucky 'cause Jessica was the nicest girl he'd ever met in his whole life and he wanted to marry her when he got better. He wondered if I'd mind."

Pat shook his head. "What did you tell him?"

"What *could* I say, 'Get in line?' The kid's dying and he was so goddamned serious about it. I put my hand on his shoulder and said, 'It's fine with me, 'cause you're right. She *is* the nicest girl you'll ever meet.' But, you know, that made me even more depressed. Sometimes, on the way home, I want to skip past La Crosse, just drive on down the Mississippi all the way to New Orleans. Get away, start over. And forget Jess. But then there's Mike."

By fall, Dan had settled into a routine. He taught at Riversmeet during the week and visited Jessica and Mike on weekends. He enjoyed their time together, but no longer asked Jessica to change her mind.

Sometimes, during the drive to the Cities, he recalled his first trip to Minneapolis and his certainty that Jessica would welcome him back into her life, that they'd live happily ever after. Now, three years later, he was as celibate as the Church could ever want its priests to be.

Pite, wherever you are, I hope you're happy.

In the spring of 1980, Dan agreed to coach third base for Teenie Taylor's Riversmeet Raiders. After a few games, it became apparent that Teenie knew baseball but demanded little discipline from his players.

After Dan suggested enforcing a few rules, Teenie said, "I know these kids, Bates, known 'em since they were in Little League. Keep 'em loose, that's my motto. Too many rules'll cramp their style."

It was Teenie's team, and Dan backed off. He enjoyed coaching, and the issues in baseball didn't compare to those during his time in the priesthood, when Church decrees like the birth control encyclical had livelong effects on people's lives. As a teacher, he ran a strict classroom and the kids seemed to respond. He had, he decided, a pretty good life despite the dissapointments.

During Christmas break, Dan stopped to see Agnes Reuter. "Brought your book back," he said when she answered the door. "It really helped me put my thoughts together, and I decided I was more an agnostic like Ingersoll than an atheist like Bertrand Russell."

"So you've been doing a lot of thinking, Daniel. That's good. What else have you discovered?"

"A new magazine just came out from a group of humanists, and they agree a lot with what I think too." Dan laughed. "Or me with them."

"I get *The Humanist*, and I was going to tell you about it. It's not new."

"No, this one's called *Free Inquiry*. This is the first issue, and it has an article called "A Secular Humanist Declaration." Most of it makes sense to me. It talks about free thought, in people being allowed to study and think and believe the way they want."

"Yes, that's important, even if many people prefer to let their leaders do their thinking for them."

"And I like this one, because it relates to my old religion's preoccupation with sin and telling people what's right or wrong: 'For secular humanists, ethical conduct is, or should be, judged by critical reason, and their goal is to develop autonomous and responsible individuals, capable of making their own choices in life, based upon an understanding of human behavior.' I didn't know it at the time, but that's what I was trying to do about birth control—teach people to make responsible choices instead of dictate to them."

"So you were already a humanist, Daniel. You needed only to become secular."

"I like what they say about the responsibility of schools, too. It's something to keep in mind as I choose the literature I assign the kids to read. 'We support moral education in the schools that is designed to develop an appreciation for moral virtues, intelligence, and the building of character.' And they add, 'Secular humanism is not so much a specific morality as it is a method for the explanation and discovery of rational moral principles.'"

Agnes nodded. "But many people don't believe that. They think secular humanists are out to undermine all of our country's moral values. Of course we are, if they mean the punishments they impose on other people's behavior that doesn't hurt anyone. You may have to be careful in your school, Daniel. If people find out you're a humanist, they may want you fired."

"I'll be careful. My values haven't changed. I just think they're based on what's best for people, not the commandments of a god I don't think exists. But as long as I teach and try to exemplify those basic values, I think things will be all right."

"But some people will not look deep enough to know that. The label itself will fire them up against you. Don't stick your neck out too far."

A year later, Tommy Herns, president of the Riversmeet High School graduating class of 1982, poked his head into Dan's room. "Mr. Bates, I have a favor to ask."

Dan waved him in.

"Mr. Bates, our class voted I should ask if you'd be willing to give our graduation speech."

Dan nodded. Of course he would, with more than a little sadness. He had tried to hide it, but the class of '82 was his favorite. He and these kids had entered Riversmeet together in the fall of '78. After four years, they were moving on, no longer kids. And he was older too, thirty-eight already. Damn. Round that off and he's forty. Maybe it was time *he* moved on.

For the kids, of course, in their haste to become adults, the years at Riversmeet had passed with agonizing slowness. But for him they'd come and gone like a runaway train hurtling out of control. He smiled at the redundancy in his cliché, but that's exactly how it felt.

When he first came to Riversmeet, he wrote in his journal daily to document his new life. By Easter, however, he was writing once a week or less. At the start of the next school year, he wasn't sure which desk drawer hid the book. Maybe if he had kept writing down things that happened, short reflections about teachers and students who came into his life, the years would have passed more slowly.

For four years he had taught other people's kids in La Crosse while his own son had grown into his teens in Minneapolis. He recalled Jessica at Mike's age, and their son was proving equal to his mother's independence. Mike was usually gone when Dan got there and, the few times he was home, said little more than "Hi, how's it goin'?"

"Well," Dan would like to have said, "it's going too goddamned fast, that's how." It was scary the way the years lumped together, one barely different from another. Time hadn't done that when he was younger, when it had been divided into school years and graduations and important birthdays in the rush to grow up. At Sacred Heart and Resurrection he had ached to reach adulthood, unaware that life would become a vast plain of time like the flat Dakota prairies he saw three years earlier from a dome coach on the *North Coast Hiawatha*.

"Speeches on nights like this are supposed to be idealistic," Dan told the graduates and their families and friends on a hot night in early June. The heavy air reminded him of the night he graduated, twenty-one years before, in a maroon gown similar to the ones these kids were wearing. To his favorite class, he spoke of his favorite classmate.

"I have a friend who's a great photographer, but his favorite picture wasn't taken by him. It's a shot called 'Earthrise as seen from lunar orbit,' snapped by an astronaut from the Apollo Eight spacecraft in December 1968. You were about four years old then, still ten years from entering Riversmeet, but you may have seen that picture on stamps your parents brought home from the post office. A craggy moonscape appears in the foreground and, right above it, our planet Earth rises as a small blue-and-white ball floating in the vast blackness of space."

Dan kept his notecards in front of him, but he didn't need them. He knew what he wanted to tell these kids. "All of us, with our different races and nationalities and religions, live together on that little ball. Wouldn't it be great to keep that image in our minds as we work to make life on Earth a bit better for ourselves, the people around us, and those who come after us?

"Many of you have already done that: You've tutored other students, entertained us in your plays and concerts, visited the sick, written for the school newspaper, wowed us with your athletic skills, and generally stayed out of trouble you might have been sorely tempted to get into."

He leaned across the podium and looked into the eyes of these young graduates he would miss so much. Tommy Herns, so serious. Billy Jerston, always grinning. Tina Kettler, Tracy's little sister, chewing gum. All of them, on their way out of Riversmeet. "Allow yourselves to feel proud about the good you've done here. Then go out into the world and do some more. Do what you can to make that little ball in that picture a more peaceful place to live."

Two years later, in the spring of 1984, Jessica said to Dan, "Mike's pitching Tuesday, his first start. Any chance you can come?"

Dan shook his head. "I have practice.... He's *starting*? He's only a sophomore."

"The coach says he's very good. Mike won't say it, but I know he'd love having you here to see him."

"I'll talk to Teenie."

On Monday after practice, Teenie Taylor drew circles in the dirt with a bat while he talked. "You gotta set priorities in life, Bates. You wanna coach for me, you gotta be here, watchin' *our* team."

"It's one day, Teenie. My kid. His first start." *Don't beg. Just go.*

Teenie shook his head. "Hey, he's that good, he oughta be livin' with *you* so he can pitch for *us*. Can't even justify sending you to scout 'em. Minnesota team … we ain't ever gonna play 'em anyhow."

Dan turned toward his car, then back to Teenie. "We do have to set priorities, don't we."

Teenie nodded.

"Well, I appreciate the reminder. Something like that, it can slip your mind, you know?"

Teenie nodded again.

"My kid's first start. Gee, I wonder what my priority should be." Dan unlocked his car. "See you Wednesday."

Mike pitched all seven innings and won, 5-1. Joey caught, and Dan saw Mike shake off Joey's sign only once. But Dan's joy at watching his son pitch was tempered by the thought that he wouldn't get to see the rest of Mike's games.

After the coach dismissed the team, Mike and Joey, still in their gray-and-green uniforms, met Dan and Jessica behind the bleachers.

Dan put his hand on Mike's shoulder. "Great game."

Mike smiled. "We scored early so it was pretty easy today."

"Ha," Joey said. "They're good. The way you were throwing, though, we could have shut 'em out."

"I just threw what you called."

"You stayed ahead of the hitters," Dan said, "got your first pitch over. Keep that up."

Jessica poked Dan's side. "You're coaching. Be a fan."

"You're right." He touched Mike's arm. "Great job. I gotta get up here to see you more, unless you guys want to come live with me and play for the Raiders. We could use you."

Jessica pounded Dan's shoulder. "You can't recruit high schoolers!" She turned to the boys. "You guys got plans or would you like to join us for pizza?"

"The team's going out to eat," Mike said. He turned to Dan. "Sorry."

"I enjoyed watching you pitch," Dan said. "You guys have fun."

Mike turned to Jessica. "Joey and I are going to run home and change. Then I'll call Uncle Pat, let him know we won. See you by nine, okay?"

The boys headed for the parking lot, but Mike ran back toward Dan. "Hey, thanks again for coming up."

A year later, during the 1985 spring break, Dan and Mike rode Amtrak's *Empire Builder* to Milwaukee to spend two days with Pat. Both mornings, Mike got up early to serve at Pat's Mass, then the three went out for breakfast. They talked baseball, which was fine with Dan because he didn't know what to say about Mike's going to Mass. He agreed with Jessica that Mike should decide for himself about religion, but feared Mike was getting too close to Catholicism.

At the Milwaukee station, Dan boarded the train for the trip home. From his window seat, he saw Mike still on the platform with Pat. Mike said something, and Pat shook his head. Then again, more forcefully. Finally, Pat put his hands on Mike's shoulders, leaned close and spoke. Pat looked serious. Mike shook his head.

The conductor called "All aboard" and Mike stepped into the coach. Dan returned Pat's wave, then watched him walk head down toward the parking lot. Mike sat down beside him and stared straight ahead, and Dan decided not to bother him. But in Minneapolis, he asked Jessica what was going on.

"Nothing I know of," she said. "They've always been close. I'm sure they talk about more than baseball."

"It looked like they were arguing. I've never seen them do that before."

Jessica threw up her hands. "Danny, they're people, and people argue. I doubt there's a problem. If there is, and Mike asks, we can try to help. If he doesn't, I'm sure they'll handle it."

One day after he watched the Riversmeet Class of 1985 graduate, Dan found Mike at home with Jessica. He invited them to a little pizza place he'd discovered in downtown St. Paul. The high wooden partitions, dim lighting, and soft music reminded him of Paisan's, where he and Jessica used to eat in Madison.

Dan hung their jackets next to the booth, sat down and grinned. "Why do you guys live so far north? It's *spring* in southern Wisconsin, for Pete's sake. You don't even need a jacket."

After the waiter brought their order, Dan watched his son. They hadn't shared many meals lately. "One more year till graduation, right?"

Mike nodded, his mouth already full of pepperoni and mushrooms. "Mmm-hm."

"Any plans yet ... after that, I mean?"

"College." Mike looked toward Jessica, who watched Dan.

"Picked one yet?"

Mike nodded.

Jessica looked away. "Let him eat, Danny."

"I just wondered. I haven't heard anything."

She twirled cheese around her fork.

Mike kept his head down while he stabbed at a piece of peperoni. "I'm going to Southport."

Dan smiled. "UW-Southport. Great! A friend of your Uncle Pat's and mine"—he turned to Jessica—"you remember Train, he went there. It was called Southport State then."

Jessica looked down.

"So," Dan said, "have you considered a major?"

Mike looked up. "Not UW. I'm going where you and Uncle Pat went: Resurrection Seminary."

CHAPTER 35

▼

Dan glared at Mike, turned to Jessica, then switched back to Mike. "Is this a joke?"

Mike stood, seized his jacket from the booth wall, and leaned toward Jessica. "Didn't I *tell* you he'd say that?" He ran toward the exit.

Jessica slumped against the back of her seat. "I found out last month. He wants to be like his Uncle Pat." Her eyes were on Dan. "He's *always* wanted to be like Pat, but I never expected this."

"Is this why he doesn't date?"

"He's gone out. And Pat says the seminary's different now. Guys can leave campus any time they want. They even take classes at the U. I don't think Pat's happy about that, though. Sometimes he's kind of conservative."

Dan tossed his napkin on the table. "Pat can go to hell."

"*What?*"

"He couldn't have kids of his own in that sex-repressed outfit we got caught up in, and I escaped, but he got even, didn't he? He got my kid to follow in his goddamned footsteps."

"You idiot, Pat didn't do this."

"Oh? I wasn't around for Mike's first eight years, so Pat got a running head start, didn't he. Well, it looks like it paid off. Mike's decided to follow him."

"I've never seen you so paranoid!"

"Have you watched him when Pat's around? Hell, Mike served Mass for him every day we were in Milwaukee. And I told you how they were talking next to the train. It reminded me of our trip to Seattle. All the way there and all the way back, Mike ate with Pat, sat with Pat, and when he spotted something interesting he tugged at Pat's sleeve. Now this. Shit."

"Calm down. He's going to be a priest, not a pimp."

"There's a difference?"

Jessica slid across the booth. "Damn it! I don't believe in a god any more than you do, but yeah, there's a difference, a *big* difference. Are you paying, or me?" Without waiting for Dan's answer, she pulled a twenty from her purse. "Drive me home and go get some sleep, enough that you can carry on a rational conversation about this. Then call me. *Maybe* we'll talk."

Neither said a word on the way to Jessica's. Dan let her out, then hurtled south toward La Crosse. His son, a priest. Shit. And there was nothing he could do about it.

Yes, there was. Pat could change Mike's mind. He'd drive to Milwaukee. Dan checked his watch. No, it was too late. But he'd call when he got home.

"We need to talk," Dan said when Pat answered.

"What's wrong?"

"Mike's wrong. He told me his college plans."

"Resurrection?"

"Of course Resurrection. That's where you told him to go, isn't it?"

"No," Pat said, "I—"

"You got exactly what you wanted, didn't you?"

"*No!*"

"We all know he wants to be like you."

"I told him *not* to go there. We've been arguing since the two of you came to Milwaukee. But he had already decided. I was trying to talk him out of it before he got on the train."

Dan lowered his voice. "Talk him *out* of it?"

"Yes."

"I … I thought … it seemed—"

"Mike *thinks* he wants to be like me. He doesn't see me inside. Maybe I've gotten too good at hiding my frustration. He sees the outer priesthood, and that he likes. Hell, even *you* liked it."

"Can't we stop him?"

"He'll be eighteen."

"Damn."

The next time Dan visited, Jessica set the table for two. Mike was at Joey's.

"Don't read anything into it," she said. "He made plans last week."
But a week later, Mike was gone again. And the week after that.
Dan poured a beer in Jessica's kitchen. "Notice a pattern here?"
She shrugged. "I think it's a coincidence, but if you want I'll talk to him."

The following week, Dan showed up early.
Mike met him at the door. "Oh, hi. Mom's in the kitchen."
Dan forced a smile. "How've you been? It's been a while."
"I've been pretty good."
"Playing ball this summer?"
"Pitching in one of the city leagues."
"Maybe I'll drive up some day to watch."
Mike edged toward the door. "That would be great. I was just leaving for Joey's. We're working on my curve."
Dan watched his son disappear around the corner, then stepped into the kitchen. "He's giving me the cold shoulder, Jess. Didn't invite me along, nothing."
"He's had a bad week. Lost a close game the other day on a wild pitch."
"Quit covering for him. He never said anything about winning or losing, just that he had to work on his curve. He's still pissed."
"He's afraid you think he's stupid for taking religion seriously."
"You're an atheist. Doesn't he worry *you* might think he's stupid?"
"I've told him all his life it doesn't make any difference to me. I still mean that."
"Well, tell him for me, too."
"*You* tell him! If I do it, he'll say the same thing you said: 'Quit covering for him.' He's like you in a lot of ways, Danny."

A year later, Dan drove alone across Wisconsin, headed for Southport and the seminary for his twenty-fifth high school reunion. The urge to turn around grew stronger the closer he got. This would be the first time he'd seen the guys since he left the priesthood ten years earlier. Pat was still his friend, but he'd said he wouldn't be there.
The seminarians had lived like brothers, packed into old dorms or cramped into small rooms, under rules that decreed what they must do, where, when, and how. Why was never asked. Anything sexual—even sensual—in thought, word or deed, was a sin. Transgressors stood in the emergency confession line before Mass.

Damn. What a way for a kid to start his day.

Dan and his classmates had shared a lifestyle that disappeared. Few, if any, would shed a tear about that.

Still, something drew him back. The camaraderie perhaps. Or the feeling he'd had all those years: that after ordination all things would be possible, that when he would finally get to take Christ's message into the world, everyone he met would be converted through his holy example and the persuasiveness of his preaching.

Dan blushed. He had actually believed that. Had the others too, or had he been that much more naive?

At the lake, he turned south on Shoreline Road, swung through the curve a block from the seminary and took his first look in years at the Resurrection dome.

The Resurrection Seminary High School class of 1961 gathered around picnic tables under the maple trees outside the old gym. Behind them the newly painted gray-and-yellow dome atop Kleissman Hall rose against puffy white clouds in a cerulean sky. Most of the guys were there, as well as a few professors, and they gave him a warm greeting.

"Guess what," he told them, his voice the one he'd used there years ago in confession, "my son is coming here this fall."

Expressions of disbelief, of sympathy. Quince, who'd heard that voice many times, laughed. He wore a purple paisley sportshirt, and Dan couldn't tell: Was he still a priest?

"There are worse things your boy could do," Quince said. "The seminary's come a long way from how it was when you were here."

"And he waited till after high school," Darrin Greene said. "He's not dropping off the face of the earth like we did at puberty."

But Meer Mohrical frowned. "We spent our teen years here. It killed our sexuality. Hell, I still get embarrassed at things they say on the sitcoms."

"We came too early," Steve Towan said. "It warped a lot of us, even those who didn't finish. The healthy ones were the guys who didn't give a shit, the ones we got mad at for disregarding the rules."

"But you have to let him come if he wants to," Meer said. "Four years ago, no. You can stop a fourteen year old. But eighteen? Unh-uh."

Darrin laughed. "He's gotta find out for himself. You can't tell a kid that age anything."

Pete Parentsky nodded. "Like Father Quince said, though, things are different now."

Father Quince. So he was still a priest.

"The guys come and go when they want now," Pete continued. "They go to movies and play music in their rooms. Some of 'em even date. Can you imagine us doing that?"

Steve crumpled a can and tossed it into a barrel. "Even *imagining* sex was a sin. Remember impure thoughts? Mortal sins, every one of 'em."

Meer put his arm around Dan. "Just think, Bates, your kid's not gonna go through all that. He already knows infinitely more about life than we did at his age, though that makes it a mystery why he wants to come here at all. But, hey, it's his choice."

Dan nodded. "He wants to be like his Uncle Pat."

Meer looked around. "Speaking of whom, where *is* Pat?"

"I called him," Pete said. "Claimed he was busy."

"He's *always* busy," Meer said. "Too damned busy. He used to join us for nights out—nights *in*, actually, 'cause we'd meet at someone's house for pizza and poker—but lately no one's seen him. He's working his ass off, and that's not good."

Pete frowned. "Actually, he's working more ass *on*. Pat's gained weight—a lot of it—over the past year. Bates, you're his friend. What's the story?"

"I don't know. Last time I called he sounded really beat."

"Call him again," Darrin said. "Tell him to get his butt down here. We want to see him."

Kleissman Hall still smelled of floor wax, pipe smoke, and beeswax candles. From the far end of a dark hall, the aroma of hot beef and chicken drew Dan toward the kitchen.

"Phone?" he asked a woman stirring a pot. She pointed toward the other side of the room, where he spotted a phone near one of the large windows. Outside, his classmates talked and laughed. He stopped to watch.

Darrin Greene had left the priesthood after twelve years and was in public relations for a Milwaukee company. Pete Parensky and Meer Mohrical were still priests and seemed to like it. Meer was teaching in a Catholic college. Dan wasn't sure what Steve Towan was doing. And where was Train? He hadn't sent back his reservation. No one had heard from him since he returned from Vietnam. Damn, he'd like to have seen him again.

They were alike in many ways. The world they had shared no longer existed, but the connections did. They accepted each other, no matter their weaknesses or failures. They all had them, some more serious and embarrassing than others. But no one brought them up. It was, Dan decided, Christianity at its best.

"Daydreaming? You aren't in my class, you know." Quince had come up behind him. "Followed you in, thought it might be easier to talk." He looked a bit stooped—from the bad back he'd complained about the day they met?—but his eyes were bright, and Dan was sure this was a man who could still surprise you.

"I'm glad you could come," Dan said. Except he had no idea how to tell Quince he was no longer a priest, no longer a believer.

"I was sad to hear you left us. A huge decision—tougher, I'm sure, than the one you made the first time I saw you."

"I struggled with it."

Together they watched the men on the seminary lawn as they might have twenty years earlier. "The day we met," Quince said, "you had already decided to leave the seminary but weren't sure it was the right decision. I hope you don't mind my asking, but I am curious: Have you ever had doubts about this one?"

"No. And I don't mind your asking."

"I predicted it, you know. Your leaving the priesthood, I mean. No, you couldn't know, I never told you. Ha! Actually, I predicted we'd both be gone by now. But I've stuck it out."

"Same question," Dan said. "Any doubts?"

"Sometimes. And a few regrets, as you can imagine. But mostly I'm glad I stayed, though I don't know if the archbishop shares that feeling. I keep to myself, make my own decisions. Every few years I re-read *Keys of the Kingdom*—the front cover's taped on now—to remind myself how Chisholm did it. I dissent quietly, and they let me fill in around town. I'm not ecstatic, but I'm content. I decided that's good enough."

Dan grinned. "If I'm wrong and you're right, your ecstasy will come later."

"True. We'll see, won't we. And sooner than we'd like."

Dan got Pat's answering machine. "I'm at the reunion. The guys say get your butt down here. That's a quote. We eat at six. Come see us for a short time at least."

After the reunion, Dan took a room at a Southport hotel. Early the next morning he drove to Milwaukee, where he caught Pat on his way to the rectory after Mass.

"Hey!"

Pat's smile seemed thin. "Hi. You alone, or did Jess come, too?"

"Just me."

"I considered coming last night."

"You should have."

"I've gotten fat. I'll look better for the next one."

"We didn't stand around admiring physiques."

"Just the same ..." Pat looked away.

"They're worried about you. For good reason."

"I'm fine."

"Like hell. You need to slow down, do some things you enjoy. When was the last time you grabbed your camera and went shooting?"

"I will, as soon as I get time."

"You need to *make* time, or you're gonna run out of it."

Pat opened the screen door and directed Dan in. "I suppose you'd like breakfast."

"Pretty lousy invitation."

"Take it or leave it. I live alone. I don't have to be polite this early in the morning."

"What's on the menu?"

"Cereal and bananas, milk included. Toast if the bread's not moldy."

"I'll skip the toast. How fresh is your milk?"

"Bought it yesterday."

They took their bowls of cereal to the dining room where Pat pushed aside a few weeks' worth of *Milwaukee Journals* and *Sentinels*. "Haven't eaten in here for a while."

"You eat in the kitchen, on the run, right? You gotta slow down."

"Can't." Pat stared past Dan to the lannon-stone wall of his church. "This place needs three priests. It has me." He set his bowl on the table and eased into one of the wooden chairs. "I know you don't believe I advised Mike not to go to the seminary, but I love the kid like he was mine. Why would I steer him into this?"

"He wants to be like you."

"I told you: He wants to be like he *thinks* I am. He has no idea how lonely this job gets."

They ate in silence for a while, then Pat tilted the cereal bowl to his lips and slurped the last of the milk. "One of the perks: I can do that living alone."

Dan threw his napkin, hit Pat's shoulder. "It's gross, and you have company." But it was great to hear Pat laugh.

Pat rested his chin on his clasped hands. "I've never told you how important your calls and visits have been. Even messages, like yesterday. Some days I feel like nobody gives a damn."

"Hey, the guys wanted to see you. They give more than a damn. But you have to, too."

Pat edged toward the window. "This is a good parish. I should be happy here." He turned. "Between us, okay?"

Dan waited.

"I need a *yes*," Pat said. "Between us?"

"All right."

"Not even Jessie."

Dan frowned. "Okay."

"The priest stuff's great, like you said when you quit. But I get sick of living alone with no one to tell how my day went, good, bad or indifferent. I always knew it would be tough not having someone to say 'I had a shitty day' to, but it's even worse not having anyone to share the *good* stuff with."

Dan nodded. "Yes, I—"

"Little things. A neat wedding or a baptism where the baby coos instead of cries, or a sudden thought that moves me closer to God. Or to ask advice, like what to tell Mrs. Jacobson in the nursing home who's mad at God for letting her get sick and taking her husband last year. She yells if I even mention God. So what do I say?"

"I don't know.... I really don't."

Pat paced the room. "When I first felt depressed, I convinced myself I was physically sick. I mean, priests can't be psychologically weak, right? That's what they told us, isn't it? If we accept God's grace, we'll stay strong. Suck it up for God and carry on. So that's what I did: I prayed for strength and waited for it to come. I'm still waiting."

Dan studied his friend's face. "So when did you last get out and have a good time?"

Pat shrugged.

"How about today?"

"To do what?"

"Anything. The zoo. The Mitchell Park conservatory. The lakefront. A whorehouse."

Pat laughed, and again it was great to hear. "I wouldn't know what to do at one."

"Me neither, but it doesn't matter. *They're* supposed to know."

"I'd be too nervous to enjoy it." Pat's smile faded. "Besides, I can't get away today. I have people to see."

"See 'em tomorrow."

Pat walked to his desk and flipped two pages in his appointment book. "I might fit them in tomorrow if I stay a few minutes less at each one."

"Put on something casual. Let's get out of here."

Pat started toward his room, then stopped. "Someone might call."

"Your answering machine works."

"But if we don't get back till late—"

"Have your tape refer 'em to another parish if they need someone. Hell, leave the chancery number. Let the archbishop find 'em a priest."

Pat laughed. "It's good that you quit. You've lost your concern for parishioners in need."

Dan grabbed Pat's arm and pulled him down the hall. "And you've lost yours for a *priest* in need. I don't know your parishioners, but the priest is a friend of mine."

They returned to Pat's rectory in time to see Johnny Carson say goodnight. They'd spent their day at the lake skipping stones into the waves, shooting pool—poorly—in a seedy downtown bar, eating lobster at a restaurant overlooking the harbor, and watching a night game won by the Brewers at County Stadium.

Dan popped a beer and sat down to read the *Milwaukee Journal*. He heard the tinny voices of Pat's phone messages.

Then Pat stomped into the room. "I *told* you I shouldn't go. I was due at the hospital to see Mrs. Sweeney, but I didn't go, and she died. A nice old lady. She needed me, but I wasn't here. I—"

"Damn it, Pat, you can't be here twenty-four hours a day, seven days a—"

"Yes, I can! I *told* 'em I would! 'Call me if you need me,' I said. Well, Mrs. Sweeney needed me and they called, but I was out having a good time." He went to the window and rested his forehead against the glass.

Dan stepped around the table and put a hand on Pat's shoulder.

Pat threw it off. *"Come on out and play, Pat, you need to get away.* So I was a little down. I wasn't as down as Mrs. Sweeney is, was I? She's *really* down. She's *dead!* And her priest was out shooting pool so he'd *fe-e-el* better."

"You had no way of know—"

"Go to bed, Danny."

"First let me—"

"No! *Go!*"

"He's better," Jessica told Dan at her house the following weekend. "I said I was coming to see him and he insisted he was busy."

"Of course."

"'Busy for who?' I asked. That confused him. 'I got things to do,' he said. 'Who for?' I asked again. 'For the parish,' he said. 'No,' I said, 'for *whom*? I want to know who's more important to spend your time with than your twin sister.' He hesitated, and I let him have it. 'You tell your parish-council president or your archbishop or your pope or your God or whoever you consider your boss to bug off, 'cause I'm coming tomorrow, and it's un-Christian to turn away visitors, especially family when they drive all day to see you.' He said okay."

Jessica pulled a bottle of water from the refrigerator. "He's awfully heavy, and his eyes don't twinkle anymore, did you notice? I took along an album of pictures from his ordination. He had that sparkle, remember? I pushed him in front of a mirror. 'Look,' I said, 'it's gone.' I shoved a picture in his face. 'This is when you loved people and wanted to serve them the best you could. Now you've run yourself down because you still love people but you think you have to serve them *beyond* the best you can. Your God may be all-powerful, but you're human, damn it. That means you've got all the limitations your God placed on people, and you're slapping him in the face if you try to outperform him!'"

Dan couldn't help grinning. "What did he say?"

"What *could* he say? He gave me that same sort of spiel—without God, of course—when I became a nurse and tried to work twenty-four hours a day 'cause patients I loved died while I was off-duty. I told him too, 'Even Jesus slept and went to parties; why can't you?' He looked a little sheepish. I do hope he starts taking care of himself."

A year later, in March 1987, Teenie Taylor retired. Dan took over as Riversmeet's baseball coach. The early-spring practices went well but, after the first exhibition game, star pitcher Jason Brell's dad stopped Dan behind the dugout.

"Jase says you benched him for wearing his jersey outside his pants."

"That, and for sassing me when I told him to tuck it in."

"Will he start our next game?"

"If he wears the team uniform. We tuck our shirts in."

"Well, you know, Jase is young. He likes that ragged look a lotta pros and college guys wear these days. Remember, Coach, you aren't preaching to people in church here. This is baseball. You got a bunch of healthy young men out for some fun."

"Fun as a team, Mr. Brell. Teams wear uniforms. The kids can dress ragged, as you call it, in their pickup games."

"C'mon, Coach, this isn't the sixties. Lighten up."

"I'm a teacher, Mr. Brell. As a coach, I teach discipline, individual effort and team pride. We may lose some games, but we won't look sloppy doing it."

Brell leaned in closer. "I'm warnin' you, Bates: You're going to lose these kids. They're good; they can take you all the way to the championship if you give 'em a chance. But they won't tolerate a bunch of petty rules."

The next day, French teacher Corinne Michaels pulled Dan aside on his way to a meeting in the principal's office. "Hey, Coach, can you tell me why basketball and football and wrestling have cheerleaders but baseball doesn't?"

"No. Never gave it a thought, actually."

"I coach the cheerleaders. Would you like some at your games?"

"Ah, no, thanks. I have enough problems right now with uniform issues. One of the dads appealed to Koenig to make me let his son wear his jersey outside his pants."

"Jason Brell." Corinne grinned. "I heard kids talking. Who says he can't?"

"Me. It's one of my 'petty' team rules."

"Teenie let the kids get away with a lot. They're used to it."

"Well, Teenie's gone. If Koenig wants somebody else, that's fine. I'm on my way to tell him that."

"Sounds exciting. Want me there? I'm a union steward."

"Jeez, I hope we don't need the union. It's just a stupid meeting."

"Weird things happen in stupid meetings."

"Okay, c'mon along if you want."

"Mr. Bates," principal Carlton Koenig said, "Mr. Brell agrees that teams need a certain level of uniformity in their, ah, uniforms, and that there must be a certain, ah, level of discipline in a team sport such as baseball. But he feels at the same time that you could allow the boys some discretion—some freedom, so to say—in the issue of *how* they wear their uniforms. Shirts outside the pants won't affect how the team performs, will it?"

"It lets 'em play looser," Brell said before Dan could answer. "You can't play good baseball all tight." He turned to Dan. "As a coach you probably know that."

"Probably. My players do have some discretion—some freedom, so to say. They can roll up their sleeves or take off the sweatshirts under their jerseys if they'd like. Would you suggest I let 'em wear their caps beak-backwards if they want to?"

Corinne laughed, and Brell glared. "Bates, for Pete's sake, stick to reality. A shirt hanging out has a certain macho look to it, like a kid's been playing hard. Nobody's going to turn his cap around and look like a damned fool."

"Glad to hear it. Hey, if the guys want to *look* like they've been playing hard, they should play hard. Slide into a base or dive at a ground ball. A little dirt on the unie looks macho as hell."

"Mr. Bates," the principal said, "Mr. Brell has pointed out that sports writers are, um, writing that our team has a chance to win the state championship this year. I'd like to—"

"But," Brell jumped in, "the team won't win if the top players don't like playing for you."

Dan got up. "They're good players, good kids. If they're dedicated, they can go a long way, even with their shirts tucked in." He looked at Koenig. "Is that it? I have an appointment."

The principal glanced from Dan to Brell, then nodded.

Brell looked from Koenig to Dan and back again. "Wait, we haven't settled anything."

Dan stopped at the door. "Mr. Koenig, am I still the coach?"

"Of course," Koenig said.

Dan turned to Brell. "Then the only thing we haven't settled is whether Jason's willing to wear the team uniform."

"You did good," Corinne said over a deep-dish pizza at a riverfront restaurant. "You didn't need me there at all. But aren't you missing your appointment?"

"We're in the middle of it. I was hungry. Besides, I couldn't stand it: a meeting with a high school principal over keeping a shirt tucked in."

Corinne chased a bite of pizza with beer from a glass mug. "It's the times."

"Tough. I've had it about how educators should adjust to the times."

"I didn't say you should change, just that's why you have the problem."

"It's not a problem I care about. I have more important things on my mind right now." He told Corinne about Mike's plans.

She toyed with the handle of her mug. "Have you done what his mother suggested, talk to him about it?"

"Most of the time when I visit, he's gone, and when he's been there it hasn't seemed like a good time to say anything."

"Why not write him a letter? That might work better than talking. You can write down exactly what you want to say without getting interrupted. And your son can read it without wondering what he should be saying back."

Dan had passed Corinne Michaels a thousand times in the halls, nodded to her in the teachers' lounge, asked directions one time to a colleague's room. He stared at the black curls around her ears, the full lips colored in a light flesh tone that let their shape demand attention. *Bee-stung*, that was the word magazines used to describe the lips of sultry actresses. But Corinne wasn't sultry. She was funny and wonderful to talk to. How had he overlooked her all these years?

"Um," he said, "do you have papers to correct tonight?"

"I have a test I need to grade in two days."

"Shoot."

She laughed. "That means *no*. I can correct 'em tomorrow night."

He wiped his hands on the napkin and reached for his wallet. "It's pretty along the river. Care to walk off some of this pizza?"

"Sure, but tell me first: Could you use another assistant coach?"

"Well, I haven't replaced myself yet. Are you recommending someone?"

Corinne folded her napkin and took a quick sip of water. "Yeah. Me."

CHAPTER 36

▼

Dan and Corinne had walked only two blocks beside the black, choppy waves of the Mississippi before the rain started.

"It won't last long," Dan said, and they strolled on. But the wind came up and whipped the rain into their faces.

"My house!" Corinne shouted, and they ran to their cars. Dan followed her to a story-and-a-half bungalow a few blocks from Riversmeet. Inside, he admired the photographs that covered her walls: views of France, group and action shots of her cheerleading squads, and scenes from school plays. She was the drama coach.

"When's your next one?" he asked.

"Fall. *Fiddler on the Roof* with the music department. It'll be great. Our kids have tremendous voices. You'll have to come."

"The story is sad. I'll probably cry."

"And men aren't supposed to, right? Gotta be macho. Well, I hate macho. It's so fake."

In the kitchen, Corinne popped open a can of cat food, and a calico appeared at her feet. "Puzzles, how can you eat this stuff? It stinks." She spooned the glistening mess into a saucer and set it on the floor. Puzzles dove in, and Corinne opened the refrigerator. "Wine? I have a Riesling. I like it cold."

"Sure," Dan said. "I don't like macho either, but where I went to school—at a Catholic seminary—we were *supposed* to be macho. I found out when I needed a transcipt that the priests rated us on our manliness. I guess I passed." He paused. How would she react? "I was a priest."

"I heard. What church do you go to now?"

"I quit when I left the priesthood." Might as well tell it all. "I don't believe in a god."

Corinne eased the cork from the bottle and poured the wine into two glasses. "So now you're an atheist?"

"More an agnostic. Or maybe both. Neither believes in a god."

"Then what's the difference?" She opened a box of crackers and sprinkled some on a plate.

"An agnostic says there's no way to tell whether or not there's a god, and an atheist just doesn't believe in one. There's a joke about the difference: An agnostic is an atheist with no guts."

Corinne laughed. "I heard it, but the punchline was balls."

"I was trying not to be crude. Besides, there are women agnostics."

"So you have no guts?"

"Some might say. On the other hand, I hate not being as certain of things as I used to be. But I want proof, and there's not much out there."

Dan picked up the plate of crackers and Corinne carried their glasses to the living room. He set the crackers on the coffee table in front of her maroon couch.

"I don't think the labels are important," he said. "I keep wondering, what *do* I believe? So far I believe in nature, in science, and in people. And I seem to agree a lot with people called secular humanists. At the seminary, they warned us about those guys."

"I'll bet," she said. "Well, I believe in God, but I doubt he's as interested in us as a lot of people claim. I suspect he shakes his head and laughs at us a lot."

"You may be right." Dan sipped his wine. "I like this cold, too. You know, I've found teaching is a bit like being a priest, except the kids ask more questions than most parishioners."

"Kids question everything," Corinne said, "and that's healthy, though I hate not knowing all the answers."

Dan laughed. "But that's healthy too. They find out we don't know everything, that there are things for them to discover and decide for themselves. When I was young, I couldn't wait to grow up and answer everyone's questions. I was so naive."

"Me too. The adults I knew as a kid acted as if they knew it all. I guess I didn't ask hard-enough questions."

"These days," Dan said, "people hardly ask at all. They seem to believe without wondering what they're believing in. They've gotten away from the curiosity people seemed to have around the turn of the century. Some called themselves 'freethinkers' then, a great word that's hardly used now. A friend lent me the writings—long speeches, actually—of one of the more famous ones, Robert Green Ingersoll. Ever hear of him?"

Corinne shook her head.

"He was an orator—they'd talk for hours at a time. And people listened—it was recreation then, unbelievable today, of course—and paid a lot of money to hear them. Most people didn't agree with Ingersoll's views on religion, but they still came to listen. 'The Great Agnostic,' they called him, but he also spoke on the sacredness of the family, in favor of women's suffrage, and against slavery. He was financially independent, and I love his idea that he spoke for people with religious doubts who had to keep quiet for fear of losing their jobs."

"He doesn't sound so terrible," Corinne said.

"No," Dan said. "He was attorney general of Illinois, and some Republican leaders asked him to run for governor while hiding the fact that he was agnostic. Ingersoll refused. He told them it's immoral to conceal information from the public. Of course, that's unbelieveable today, too. He's pretty much forgotten now."

"I haven't heard of him—till now, anyway—and I think I'm pretty well read."

"I read more about him in a humanist magazine—*Free Inquiry*. I was amazed at how closely his philosophy—and theirs—matches mine. Or maybe mine matches theirs. But I especially like their idea of working to make this life as good as it can be for everyone because it's the only life we're guaranteed to have."

"I like that too," Corinne said. "What I find interesting are people like politicians and corporate leaders who claim they're so Godfearing but then step all over other people to get rich and powerful. They never mention Christ's teaching to sell everything and give the money to the poor."

Dan smiled. "I wonder why."

"It's fun talking to you about this stuff. One of the kids who went to France last year mentioned in his report that Europeans don't seem as hung up on religion as Americans, and it got me thinking that I should be more up on this stuff."

"I'll bring some magazines next time. If humanists don't scare you. They do some people, though other names don't seem to frighten them as much—nonbeliever and skeptic, for example, labels for people who don't claim to know it all."

Dan put down his glass. "And speaking of knowing it all, exactly how much do you know about baseball?"

Corinne laughed. "Boy, there's a topic switch you don't hear every day.... Okay. I pitched Little League. A long time ago, of course. I'm a Brewers and a Cardinals fan, the Brewers 'cause they're in Wisconsin and the Cards because they're on the Mississippi, like we are. One team in each league."

"Who'd you root for in the '82 Series?"

"Both. It was great! I couldn't lose, and it went seven games. Anyway, first thing, the Raiders needs new caps. Teenie had no color sense. Yellow hats with maroon *R's*: Yuck! We should get maroon caps with black beaks and black *R's* outlined in gold."

"I'll defer to your fashion sense," Dan said. "What about the game?"

"Our guys can run. We should steal almost every time we get on base. Hit and run with our three, four, and five hitters. And don't hesitate to pull the pitchers; we're strong in relief. Except Brell; he gets better in the late innings. I can coach third; we'll run till the other teams prove they can throw us out." She grinned. "You were way too timid coaching third last year."

Dan hadn't expected a critique. "How so?"

"In your last game, you stopped Pecore at third when Dewey doubled to right. Their right fielder had made a terrible throw to second in the first inning. He'd never have gotten Pecore at the plate, but you held him and we didn't get that run. Then they tied us and won in extra innings. We needed that run. Run, run, and run some more, especially with these guys." Corinne smiled. "So, am I hired?"

Dan faked a frown. "After calling me timid? Don't you know anything about applying for a job? You can't criticize the interviewer. Oh, what the hell." He lifted his glass. "To my replacement as third-base coach. I can't wait to see Roger Brell's reaction."

He also couldn't wait to see Corinne Michaels' black curls peeking out from under a maroon-and-black baseball cap.

After school on March 21, Dan waited for the kids to clear out of Corinne's room. "That bright-green blouse is perfect!" he said when they were alone.

She grinned. "Perfect for what?"

"For celebrating the first day of spring. Let's go somewhere."

"Why don't you celebrate up north? … Hey, I know you go to Minneapolis to see that Jessica, but you keep asking me out. What gives?"

"I visit my son. Jessie and I are just friends."

"Bull. You love her. I can tell. Besides, I have two tests to correct."

"You have the weekend. And I'll help."

"Help? You don't know French." She stacked papers to carry home, and Dan slipped behind her and kissed the back of her neck. She ducked. "Idiot! The door's open."

He put his arms around her waist. "But it's spring! I feel young, and my thoughts have turned to love."

"You're over forty, and your thoughts have turned to lust. You love *her*."

"Would I be in La Crosse on a day like this if Jess and I were lovers? Besides, next fall Mike heads for the seminary and I'll hardly see him."

She pulled his hands away. "Then you won't drive up there every weekend?"

"I guess it depends on whether she and I stay friends."

Corinne piled several books at the side of her desk. "What did you do to her?"

Dan took a deep breath. "We made love one night, then I became a priest anyway."

"And you stuck her with a baby. Lovely."

"I didn't find out about Mike till after I left the priesthood."

"How old is he?"

"Seventeen."

She erased the chalkboard. "Almost grown up. It's time Jessica did too."

Dan straightened. "Hey, she's a good nurse. And she raised Mike by herself."

Corinne put the eraser in its tray and slapped chalk from her hands. "Thing is, she didn't have to. At some point, a grownup stops punishing people. Seventeen years? It's time she got over it." She stuffed the papers in her backpack. "So now you know what I think: You love her and you should truck your things up there and tell her to stop playing games 'cause you're moving in."

Dan cocked his head. "Sounds macho. I thought you hate that."

"Most of the time." She hoisted the pack to her shoulders. "But sometimes you have to act, you know? The old cliché: Do what you gotta do." She took his arm. "But do that tomorrow. Today, let's celebrate spring."

They drove north to Trempealeau, then into Perrot State Park, where they climbed the trail up Brady's Bluff.

At the summit they took in the panorama of the river, from south of the dam below Trempealeau to north of Winona, Minnesota. A Soo Line freight train rolled along the other side of the river, its horn echoing off the Minnesota bluffs. Inside the log shelter, Dan pulled Corinne onto the narrow bench. They kissed, then watched a white towboat pushing its string of rusty barges toward St. Paul.

"They move so slow," she said. "I'd go nuts working on a barge."

"I'd love it: seeing the river, taking in the sights all the way to who knows where and not worrying how fast I got there."

The Riversmeet High baseball team accepted Corinne as a coach, and Jason Brell probably had a lot to do with the lack of comment from his dad. The Raiders led the Great River League in stolen bases and took first place. *La Crosse Tribune* sportswriters predicted a run to the state tournament, but the Raiders lost in the sectional tournament one to nothing, despite Brell's great pitching.

After the game, Roger Brell walked over, nodded to Dan and hugged his son. It went against the redneck image Dan had formed of Brell at the early-spring meeting in Koenig's office.

Jason jogged toward the players' bus, leaving his dad and Dan to face each other.

"Well, Coach, we didn't quite make it."

"No. I'm really sorry for Jason and the seniors. We had a good chance." Dan waited for Brell's reminder of his prediction last spring.

"Jason says we wouldn't have gotten this far without you."

"We won a lot of our games with his arm. And he'd have won this one if we'd have scored. I hope I didn't put too much on him."

Brell shook his head. "He told his mom and me this was his favorite season ever."

"That's great to hear."

"Yeah, but now it's over and he's pretty down." Brell glanced toward the bus. "He'll snap back, though. Might as well tell you, I had a lotta doubts about your third-base … um, coachess, but Jase and his friends told me to clam up. She turned out good." He laughed. "Better watch out, Coach. Some of us might lobby Koenig to give Miss Michaels your job."

"It was Brell's idea of a joke," Dan told Corinne that night. But Brell was right: she was a great baseball coach.

Later, they watched the Minnesota Twins on TV. Dan drifted toward sleep sitting on Corinne's soft couch, and she laughed and shook him. They kissed, then she started some classical guitar music on the stereo and lit three candles on a bookcase.

"It's been a spring like I've never had before," she said, "exploring up and down the river, coaching baseball, talking, sitting together like this."

They kissed some more, and the scent of cranberry from the candles drifted through the room. Dan floated away from the excitement of a long day toward a dreamy peace. Corinne pulled him down and stretched out beside him. The only sound came from the stereo, and Dan fell asleep.

It was dark when he woke up. He kept his eyes closed. He had been here before, lying on a couch like this. Years ago, in Madison. This time, though, he wouldn't panic; his parents weren't expecting him home. Still, a guy staying overnight could damage a girl's reputation. He stroked her hair. Strange, he didn't recall it being curly, but he was still half asleep and it was difficult determining what was real and what was dream.

He gave her a gentle squeeze. "It's late, Jess. I have to go."

She slid off the couch and ran across the room to a chair near the bookcase where one candle still burned. It threw enough light for Dan to see Corinne's black curls.

Oh shit. Please, no. He'd only dreamed it, not said it. Please.

"Corinne." It was a whisper, barely audible over the happy strumming of the guitars.

She didn't move.

"Corinne."

He closed his eyes. If he fell back asleep maybe he could undo his mistake.

"Dan," she said, "you'd better go."

He was awake now. "Corinne, I'm sorry. I just—"

"You have to go to her. I've told you that before."

The last song on the stereo ended, and the room fell silent.

"I'm sorry," he said.

"You still love her." Corinne's voice was so soft Dan could hardly hear. "I knew it, but you kept denying it and I tried so hard to believe you." She started to cry.

Dan moved toward her, but she waved him away. He sat at the edge of the couch. "Are you sure you want me to go?"

"No," she said, louder now. "I'm not sure at all. I want yesterday back, I know that. But different. Change the game so we win. Change us together on the couch so it's the start of something."

He moved toward her again. "Corinne, I—"

Again she waved him away. "No. You'd better go. Please."

He edged toward the door, then stopped. "I'll see you Monday at school, all right?"

Her head stayed down. "All right."

He opened the front door. "I am sorry. Really."

Finally she looked up. "I know.... So am I."

Dan waited until noon, then crossed the bridge into Minnesota and raced north on 61.

"Give us a chance to make it work," he told Jessica. "I promise: If it doesn't, I'll leave."

She walked into the dining room as if to escape him. "It has to work for both of us, Danny. I don't think it will."

He followed, and stepped in front of her. "But we haven't tried! Nothing is certain in life. It's all chance, and we have to take a chance to let it—let us—work."

"Danny, I love your coming to see me. But I like it when you leave, too." Jessica shook her head. "I didn't mean that, not the way it sounded. I mean I like living alone. I'm my own boss, I can set my own hours. I'm able to stay with the kids at the hospital as long as I like—as a volunteer when my shift is over. Do you understand?"

"No," he said, but it was a lie. Sure, he understood—he even loved—her independence. And her work with sick kids was phenomenal. But at what cost?

"You're just like your brother," he told her.

She raised an eyebrow.

"Look at yourself! You live alone like Pat, and all you do is work. Pat's a priest, and you may as well be a nun. No vows, of course, but you tell me the difference."

She walked back into the living room and stared out at the street. "Pat does it for God. I do it for the kids. Some of them, their lives are going to be terribly short. Unlike Pat, I don't think there's a heaven for them to go to, so I want to help make those short little lives as fun and as interesting and as pain free as I can. Sometimes that takes more time than the hospital schedules me for."

"I'm not saying it's bad," Dan said, "but it leaves no time for anyone else." He almost said "me," but it sounded too much like self pity. Still, what did it matter? There was nothing here for him. He was, Corinne noted, over forty, and time kept racing by. His trips to Minneapolis had fallen into a rhythm where he no longer could distinguish one from another.

But Corinne was wrong, too. He couldn't go to Jessica. She had filled her life and had no room for him. And then he realized: His relationship with Jessica was exactly the one he had hoped for during his years in the seminary. He had gotten exactly what he wanted. Except now he wasn't a priest.

Dan left Minneapolis that evening. On the drive home he thought again of getting away—of heading downriver to New Orleans. He'd savor the drive, stopping at every overlook, historical marker, and little town along the way. By the time he reached the mouth of the Mississippi, he'd have left behind all ties to his old life. He'd start over where no one knew him, where no one would get freaked out by his priesthood or by his dreams of a woman who wouldn't have him.

Dan checked the light traffic behind him and slowed crossing the Mississippi on the I-90 bridge. He glanced at the water below. Someday he would follow this river south. Behind him, a semi rushed up. Dan pressed the accelerator, shook his head and laughed. What was he thinking? He couldn't run from himself. Jessica was a friend, a woman as devoted to sick children as her twin brother was to souls. His and Jessica's relationship wasn't what he wanted, but as a friendship it wasn't bad.

On Monday Dan's grip slipped as he pulled open the Riversmeet door. What was he going to say to Corinne? What would she say to him? He spotted her down the hall, outside her room, talking to students. He called her name, hoped she'd wait, broke into a run. How often had he yelled at kids to walk?

She waited.

"Hi," he said. "I … I just wanted to say hi."

"Hi." She cocked her head. "Did you go north?"

Dan nodded.

"And?"

He spread his arms. "I'm here."

Corinne frowned. "Your Jessica is an idiot. But you still love her, don't you?" She put a hand on his arm. "Just the same, if you feel like it, drop by after class."

"I will. Yes." He turned, then again, making a circle. "Corinne … thanks."

She tried to smile, but gave up. "Being friends isn't even close to what I hoped, probably the way things aren't what you wanted with her. But we have to deal with reality, don't we? That's what I keep telling the kids. I suppose I should take my own adv—"

The bell drowned out her last syllable. She squeezed his arm. "Talk to you later."

Dan nodded, and Corinne followed her students through the door.

Life kept a certain rhythm over the next few years. Dan taught, visited Jessica, coached baseball, and walked along the river discussing school and philosophy with Corinne. Mike was at Resurrection and loving it. Only the kids entering and graduating from Riversmeet broke time into sections.

In his literature classes, Dan found that each student experienced the same story in a different way. Every year, he assigned *To Kill a Mockingbird* because of the story's complexity and its effect on the kids' thinking.

On their first day, he tried to prepare them for the novel's variety of themes.

"It's not just a story of a brave lawyer defending an innocent man," Dan told them. "It's not just a story of racial prejudice, either, or of hypocrisy, of people letting their emotions, rather than their brains, rule their actions. It's a story about growing up, not just physically and intellectually, but emotionally. So, as you read this story, watch how the characters react to the things happening in their little town."

And then he assigned essays. He told the kids to write their thoughts as they read and to summarize, in at least three sentences each day, what they read and how they felt about it. He was prepared for the groans. He understood them. Studying this novel—which included a lot more than reading it—was hard work. But he expected most of his students, in the end, to find the work rewarding.

So he pushed them. He assigned pages to be read every night, and then they discussed those pages in class the next day. At the end, he had them write a longer essay about their reactions to the story. They could base it, if they wished, on their daily notes, which became for some a kind of reading diary.

Dan loved reading the essays:

"Atticus and Miss Maudie treated the little kids like they were adults already. That surprised me. At first I thought it was bad, but maybe it was good because I wish my parents and teachers treated me and my friends more like that."

"I hated how the adults were such hypocrites. Mr. B. said this was a story about growth, but the kids knew more about justice than those grown-ups. Why do kids turn into hypocrites when they grow up into adults?"

"Where I used to live there was a girl like Boo. Kind of crippled and different, I mean. And I wouldn't play with her. I wasn't really mean, mostly I just ignored her, but maybe that was meaner. After reading this book I thought I might have liked her if I had gotten to know her. Or I could have treated her nicer, anyway. Now I'm mad at myself because I moved away and it's too late to fix it. And I'm kind of sorry I read this book because I didn't feel this bad before."

She deserved a response, and Dan wrote on her essay: "But reading this taught you to look at people in a different way. It's true that you can't change what you've done in the past—none of us can, no matter how deeply we wish we could—but now you know you can treat people more compassionately in the future. So even if the book caused you pain from your memories, it also helped you decide to act more kindly toward others in the future. I think that's something you should feel proud of."

Dan recalled his conversations with Pat about the many ways in which people search for meaning in their lives. Literature was obviously one of those ways, and he was so glad he had decided to teach it.

Dan had seen Pat a lot less than he wanted, but an invitation he received in the mail one Monday in June 1991 gave him an idea.

That evening, he phoned Pat. "How about a free chicken dinner Friday night? My treat."

"What's the catch?"

"You have to meet me in Willow Run."

"Why?"

"For the free dinner! Look, the Willow Run class of '61 invited me and a friend, if I can find one, to its thirty-year reunion. I went with most of those kids—when we *were* kids—to Sacred Heart School, so I decided to go."

"Why would I go to a reunion where I won't know anyone?"

"You'll know me."

"Where I won't know *two* people?"

"For the dinner. And I'll throw in a tour of Willow Run."

"Sounds like a big night."

"Got better plans?"

"Yeah, I need to clean my betta tank. Did I tell you Jessie gave me a turquoise-blue betta? For serenity, she said. Only my sister would buy a Siamese *fighting* fish for serenity."

"Your fish'll survive. It's a carp. Its ancestors lived in mud puddles."

"But I won't be able to see its pretty colors if the water gets cloudy. I'll lose my serenity."

"Look, I paid for two dinners. I'll sit with you and include you in the conversation and buy you Coke or beer or wine or whatever it is you're drinking these days. You'll feel very serene."

"You'll buy me a grasshopper?"

"Anything."

"How can I resist? Drinks, dinner, and a tour of Willow Run. Wow."

"It's casual. No ties. Or Roman collars."

Pat laughed. "I can't wait."

In Willow Run, the smell of cooking peas from the cannery drifted over the town.

"If that's the vegetable with tonight's chicken, I'm heading for McDonald's," Pat said.

Dan turned off Main Street. "This town doesn't have one."

Pat sniffed. "I can get my day's serving of veggies by inhaling this air."

Dan cut the engine in front of his parents' house, and his mother met them at the door.

"Daniel! And Patrick! It's so good to see you again!" She stared at Pat in his open-necked, yellow-and-green striped shirt. "Did you leave the priesthood, too, Patrick?"

"No, Mrs. Bates, I'm still a priest."

"Good," she said. "I'm proud of you. Daniel's son is studying to be a priest. Oh, but you know that. He's your nephew!" She gave Pat a hug, then Dan. "I'm proud of you, too, for different reasons. Lots of 'em."

They headed for the screened porch, where Mrs. Bates fluffed a pillow at the back of a chair while Dan embraced his father.

"A lot of the kids," she said, "are—"

"They're not kids anymore," Mr. Bates said. "They're almost fifty!"

"Still kids to me. Anyway, your classmates, Daniel, some of 'em asked if you're coming tonight. Kathy Sherman said you'd better. She's teaching school here in Willow Run now, did you know that? Divorced, too. Never had kids, thank God. That guy she married, he never treated her right. I can't remember his name. Do you, Dan?"

Mr. Bates shook his head. "I'd try to forget it if I did."

Mrs. Bates went on. "He was mean to her. No reason for it. Kathy was always nice. Cooper, that was his name. He was a jerk." She looked toward Pat. "Daniel liked her when he was in high school. Some people thought he'd leave the seminary for her."

Pat grinned. "I can't wait to meet her. Some of the guys at the seminary thought Danny would leave for my sister."

"Yes. How is she?" Mrs. Bates asked.

"I saw her last week," Pat said. "She bought me a betta."

"Well, I'm not in favor of the lottery, but they say it helps with the property tax, so I don't say anything. You go ahead and bet all you want."

The Hillside Lounge on Willow Run's north side was hosting two reunions that night. The parking lot was nearly full, but Dan edged his maroon Volvo into a stall near the back door.

Kathy Cooper, wearing a tight red dress, met him and Pat inside. "You guys look way too old to be with the class of sixty-six, so you must be ours. Hi, Danny! I'm glad you came." She hugged Dan, then stared at Pat. "I hope you aren't a classmate. I have no clue."

"Kathy Cooper, my friend Pat Fernettan from Milwaukee." He'd let Pat handle the priest thing. Kathy, for all the abuse she'd taken from her husband, looked too young for either reunion.

"Hi, Pat." Kathy glanced at the door. "Is he the only one you brought, Danny?"

"Um, yeah, the two of us. That's all I paid for."

"Well, hell, the reason I wrote 'Dan Bates and friend' on your invitation was I figured I'd finally meet Popcorn."

"Pop … Oh, Jessica! It's been a long time since I've heard her called that. Well, Pat's her twin brother."

"Not the same, as if you didn't know." Kathy turned to Pat. "Nothin' against you, but I heard about your sister and Danny Bates for so many years that I told myself I'd rig it to meet her someday. That's why I volunteered for the invitations committee. Okay, live and learn. Five years from now I'll spell out who the friends are supposed to be. You can bring 'em both, Danny."

She stopped smiling. "Um, I should tell you: In the booklet I'm still Kathy Cooper, but this fall I'm taking back my maiden name."

Dan touched her arm. "Sorry it didn't work out, Kath."

"I'm a lot better off." She glanced toward the entrance. "Hey, I have to go greet people. Save a spot for me at your table, okay?"

Eddie Schmertz was master of ceremonies. After dinner he told stories from the class's high school days. Kathy did her best to explain them to Dan and Pat. Then Eddie turned toward their table. "Hey, there's Danny Bates with Kathy Sherman. Danny and I were buddies, but he abandoned us after eighth grade for that seminary in Southport. I remember his visit to phy ed class our senior year. If you spot those two dancing, tap 'em on the shoulder and let 'em know when the music stops!"

A few minutes later the disc jockey turned on his strobe lights and cranked up the music.

Dan yelled at Kathy, "Why don't you guys who organize these things tell the DJs to keep the sound down so people can *talk*?"

She shouted back, "*What?*"

When the DJ spun *Moon River*, Dan led Kathy to the dance floor. "I requested this one."

She moved in tight. "How can it be thirty years? We were seventeen when we danced in phy ed." They moved slowly to the music, and this time didn't say a word. When the music stopped, she stepped back. "Your friend seems nice. Pretty quiet, though. I don't suppose he'll ask me to dance."

"Probably not."

"Think I could ask him?"

"Sure."

"Is he married?"

"No."

"Mm. What does he do?"

Pat should tell her this stuff, not him. "He teaches." It wasn't a lie, but it was far from the whole truth, and that wasn't fair to her.

But Kathy seemed to guess. "There's something you're not telling me. Is he an ex-priest like you?"

Good, she was wary. "Hey, all you two have to talk about is each other. Get him to dance and you can ask him all the questions you want."

When the theme to *Doctor Zhivago* started, Kathy reached for Pat's hand. "Dance?"

He jumped slightly, but didn't pull back. "I really don't know how."

She tugged at his hand. "I'll show you. Just move to the music. It's easy."

Pat's eyes begged Dan to step in.

"Go," Dan said, and he watched Kathy Sherman lead his girl-shy friend to the dance floor.

"Yeah, I told her," Pat said on the way to Dan's car after the party. "It was the first time ever that I didn't want to tell somebody I'm a priest. I wanted to see how she'd react to me as a man, without the difference that comes from knowing what I am."

"Nothing wrong with that," Dan said.

"Yes, there is. I shouldn't hide it. But this was the first time I've danced since that godforsaken prom. And the first time I danced more than once in an evening."

Dan grinned. "Three times, right? I'm glad you danced with her."

"Me, too, I guess. But I didn't tell her I was a priest until the start of the last dance. And by then I didn't want to."

Chapter 37

Three years later, in May 1994, Mike was ordained a priest in Minneapolis. The next day, Jessica and Dan watched their son trail a short procession down the church aisle after his first solemn Mass.

"He looks happy," she said.

"I hope he is. This is what he wanted."

Jessica studied Dan's face. "You're not upset?"

"I still wish he'd chosen something else, but you're right: he has to decide for himself."

Mike had asked Pat to be the deacon at his first Mass, and Pat showed up in Minneapolis ten pounds lighter than he was at Christmas. He'd been losing weight for several years, and that day he looked as fit as he did the last time Dan saw him on a basketball court.

Outside the modern wood, stone and glass church, Jessica and Dan joined Pat and Mike in the reception line. Dan whispered into Jessica's ear, "I wonder if there's a little you in this line who's going to give Mike a peck on the cheek."

She grinned. "And I wonder how many people know we're nonbelievers at our priest-son's first Mass."

"I haven't heard any alarms," he said. "Mike must have gotten 'em to turn off the atheist sensors." He watched Mike visit with an old couple, appearing to have nothing better to do that afternoon than to talk and thank them for joining him on his big day.

May you always be as happy as you are today, Dan silently wished his son.

Mike's good mood didn't last, of course. In late fall, Dan stopped at Mike's parish in Minnetonka to drop off a winter coat Jessica found in a closet. They stood in the entryway of the rectory, and Mike complained there were too few priests to handle the work.

"I know," Dan said. "Pat and I have said for years they should ordain married men. Women, too. Lots of 'em want to be priests and they'd make good ones."

Mike nodded. "But it's not going to happen. Not under this pope."

"Which means your problem won't get solved. Pat's seen the whole cycle, from our years when the seminary grounds crawled with guys in black cassocks, to today's closing of parishes the bishops can't find guys to staff. You could end up riding a circuit of several churches before you're done."

"Why would you care? It won't affect you."

"But it will affect you. And Pat. And other Catholic friends who suffer when their churches close. But, damn it, the Church is bringing this on itself."

"You sound like Uncle Pat. I keep reminding him he used to tell me the Holy Spirit speaks to us through Rome."

"If that's true, Rome's filtering the message to suit its own needs. The Council gave us a lot of hope, but now the Vatican has lost faith with the people it claims to serve. Pat hasn't, though, and I hope you don't either."

Mike smiled. "Jeez, you are one weird atheist, you know?"

"You should've heard him, Jess," Dan said the following week. "*You are one weird atheist, you know?* What does a guy say to that?"

Jessica set their plates in the dishwasher and shut the door. "You could have explained secular humanism to him—I suspect he doesn't know." She grinned. "You *are* a bit weird, you know, so I'm not surprised he noticed. But at least he's talking to you again."

They headed for the art museum. In the photography gallery, Dan said, "Pat's shot better stuff than this. Who decides what's good, anyway?"

"Not you, obviously. Enjoy the ones you like and forget the rest."

He followed her through Medieval Paintings into Greek and Roman Sculpture.

"I like the nudes best," she said.

"Me, too."

Her eyebrow went up. "Boy, have you changed."

"But I'm still not comfortable admitting it."

"You've come a long way though. You're not even blushing." She looked closer, then giggled. "Much."

A while later, Dan stood in the doorway of a gallery and watched Jessica gaze at a Dutch seascape. The independent girl he'd fallen in love with in high school had grown up and stayed independent, so autonomous that she didn't need him or anyone else to perfect her life. He would tell Corinne she was wrong, that Jessica wasn't punishing him, just living her life as she chose, free and self-reliant. She may have gone too far, but it had nothing to do with him. He'd kept loving her despite her apparent rejection, so perhaps at some level he'd known all along what she was doing.

And he'd keep trying to accept it. If she was happy this way, and he loved her, shouldn't he be happy too?

No. How could he be? They still spent too little time together. Whenever he visited her, like today, they enjoyed each other's company for a few hours. But all it did was give him another taste of what he was missing.

And in the end, he always had to leave.

The next weekend, Dan drove to Milwaukee to see Pat.

"Let's head for the lake," Pat said. "Seems the only time I get down there is when you visit."

As they strolled in the wet sand close to the water, Dan told Pat what he had decided about Jessica.

"I feel great when I'm with her, but when I leave I feel sorry for myself again. What good is it to love her if the only way I make her happy is to live a hundred miles downriver?"

"What's your alternative?"

Dan shrugged. "I haven't come up with one."

Pat stared out at the lake. "I think what you figured out at the museum is right."

Dan flung a stone as far as he could into the water, then grabbed his arm. "Ouch."

"Take it easy," Pat said. "How long has it been since you threw anything?"

Dan rubbed his shoulder. "Too long, obviously."

"Anyway," Pat said, "it might take a while for you to accept it, but it seems you loved her independence until it got in the way of her becoming dependent on you."

"I don't want her dependent, I want us to share our lives, a lot more than we are now. That's different."

"I know, but obviously you two have different ideas. Try to … oh, hell, I'm preaching again. But, hey, that's how I make my living, isn't it! So, try to love her the way she is and accept your place in her life. That's important, I think, for both of you, because she loves you, too."

Dan turned a small piece of driftwood with his foot. "I don't think so."

Pat tossed stones into the soft waves. "We've talked of how the seminary's repression left a lifelong imprint on us. Have you ever considered Jessie could have had something similar happen to her?"

"Like that night at the lake."

"Perhaps."

"She's too cool for that."

"Don't be so sure. I've envied *your* so-called cool at times, then had you tell me you were scared shitless. You're good at hiding it. I think she is too."

"But if she loves me, why hide it?"

Pat tossed several stones before he answered. "I've wondered the same thing about God. I know, you don't believe in him. I do, but I think he's unlike anything we were taught. I've told you before, I believe all love comes from him, and Christ's law of love is the only one we need to follow. It sounds simple, but trying to decide what we should or shouldn't do can get difficult. The moral issues of this world aren't black and white the way some people want us to think."

"Your ideas aren't even close to what they taught us at the seminary."

Pat grinned. "I know. I'm not even convinced the Bible is God's word. All religions' sacred books offer some good advice but contradict themselves at the same time. I see them as pieces in the puzzle of man's attempt to find God, and I figure it's a puzzle we're a long way from putting together."

"That's 'cause he isn't there."

Pat tossed another stone. "But the puzzle is. In the meantime, the love people show each other is an indication of God's presence. Remember that stamp I mailed my ordination announcements with, the one with the photo of Earth from the moon?"

"Mm-hmm. Always wished I'd thought of it."

"Well, I always believed that image would help people realize we have to find a way to get along. I thought it would make a difference in how we treated each other."

Dan reached back to fling a stone sidearm, but stopped and tossed it instead. "I thought so too, but it hasn't."

"Not enough, anyway. But I see that picture as another part of our search, the way great literature and music and human love are parts. That probably sounds strange."

"I see 'em as ways to survive on this planet, not as part of any answer about a god. Other than that, I think we're still pretty close in how we look at things."

The following summer, Dan phoned Pat. "Remember that class reunion we went to in Willow Run five years ago?"

"It's been five years?"

"You must be having fun if the time's gone by so quick. Listen, that woman you danced with—Kathy, remember her?—she's on the committee again, and the invitation to their 1996 reunion came today. I'm asking you *first* this time, since you had such a good time at the last one."

"I can't go. Besides, I remember her saying you're supposed to bring Jessie."

"She won't go. And how do you know you can't? I haven't told you when it is."

"When is it?"

"June 29."

"I can't go."

"But you had fun. And it was good for you. You've lost more weight and you get out more. Look at it as a refresher course on health. Kinda like a retreat."

Pat laughed. "You should have stayed a preacher. You've all but converted me."

"Great! I'll sign you up for chicken again. And no peas."

"'All but,' I said. I'll be thinking of you."

"Seriously, Pat, You should come. One, it's great therapy. Two, I enjoy your company. I'll have a better time if you come along."

"I can't, Danny. Someday … well, I just can't. But we'll get together again soon, okay?"

At the reunion, Dan and Kathy Sherman sat with Eddie Schmertz and his wife, Connie.

"You came alone this time," Eddie said.

Dan nodded. "Couldn't get anyone to come. Everybody's busy."

After dinner, Dan held Kathy close on the dance floor as the disc jockey spun *Moon River*. "My request again," he said. "An every-five-year tradition."

She smiled. "Maybe we should have annual reunions."

"I'd come," he said.

When the music stopped, he led her back to their table. "As much as I enjoyed that, I kept remembering Pat dancing with you last time. You looked good together."

She stared at him briefly but didn't say anything. He worried that he'd offended her. He offered to buy her another drink. When he returned, Kathy smiled and pulled back his chair. Connie Schmertz asked if they knew the cannery was closing. Eddie said he wished he didn't have to spend so much time away from home with his trucking business.

At midnight, the DJ said good night, and Kathy and Dan headed for the parking lot.

"Five years doesn't seem very long anymore," she said, "though the next reunion, in two thousand one, sounds awfully far away. Still, it's no longer than this one was from the last one. Maybe I'll retire by then."

"Don't," Dan said. "The kids love you. I've heard that from a lot of people."

"Thanks. We'll see."

"I don't know if I should tell you," he said, "but I came tonight mostly to see you."

"That's nice to hear. Thank you."

"But this is kind of odd, I guess: I still wish Pat had come."

She pulled her keys from her purse. "Do you think he'll ever quit being a priest?"

Dan laughed. "Odds are higher I'll go back." Dan glanced across the parking lot and saw no one nearby, but he kept his voice just above a whisper. "Kath, don't be offended. You know I've liked you for a long time. I have a nice room in Madison overlooking Lake Mendota and I wondered—"

She put her fingers to his mouth. "I'm not offended, but I can't. I'd feel guilty, more so than I could handle. I can't explain all the reasons, but you have no idea how good it makes me feel that you asked."

"Well," he said, "it was ask or kick myself all night for chickening out."

"Do you still see your Popcorn Girl?"

"Now and then."

"Still in love with her?"

He studied Kathy's face. "Yes. And now I suppose you'll ask why I invited you to my room."

"Danny Bates, I'm old enough to know people can love more than one person at a time. You're not the only one who's talked with Aggie Reuter, you know."

"I dropped by her house before dinner. She wasn't home."

"She fell last week. She's at the nursing home."

"So, in the meantime, there are no cookies for the kids."

"No."

"I'll stop by to see her tomorrow before I head back."

Kathy put her hand on his arm. "Maybe it's time you take *her* some cookies. She likes chocolate-covered mints, says they stimulate her blood. As though Aggie needs her blood stimulated."

"I'll take her some and run before the staff finds out who gave 'em to her."

"Aggie won't tattle."

"It's been a great night, Kath." He reached out and she came into his arms.

"Yes, it has." She squeezed him. "Please don't feel bad 'cause I won't stay with you. I came tonight to see you, too." She kissed his cheek, broke away and ducked into her red convertible.

"Till two thousand one, kiddo. Stay young!"

Chapter 38

Winter came, hung around, and finally started to leave. Dan drove home for a quick lunch on the first decent day of spring. Green shoots were popping up along the foundation of the house across the street, and soon the tulips would bloom. He considered taking the kids outside for his afternoon classes, but the air was still too cool. The phone rang.

"Danny, Meer Mohrical. Glad I caught you."

"Meer! How are you?"

"I'm fine, but I have bad news."

"What is it?"

"You might want to sit down for this one."

"Go ahead."

"It's Pat, Danny. Pat Fernettan. He … well, he died this morning. They think a heart attack."

Shivers went up Dan's spine. "Pat? Are you sure?" *Stupid. Of course he's sure.*

"He didn't show for Mass this morning. They found him in his bedroom. Common time for heart attacks, right after getting up, they said. Looked as though he collapsed and died right away."

"I just saw him a few weeks ago. He looked good."

"I'm really sorry. I know you guys were close. I thought I'd make sure you knew. The funeral's Friday at ten, at Pat's church."

"Thanks, Meer. I'll be there."

Dan dropped onto the couch and stared out his front window. Temple Street was out there, and his car and the neighbors' cars and their houses, and the people and cats and dogs and squirrels and birds. A blue sky peeked through green buds on the huge maple across the street. Everything was where it was supposed to be; nothing had changed.

Except his *life* had changed. Pat, poor Pat, all alone … shit. Dan stared at the phone. He should call Jessica. Was this her day off? He couldn't remember.

She answered on the third ring. Her voice was raspy.

"I know," she said. "Mike called a little while ago. I told him I'd call you but I couldn't say the words. I still can't." She turned from the phone and sobbed.

"Jess, I'm so sorry." God, that sounded trite. He'd said the same thing every time someone died. But this was *Pat*. He should say more, much more. But no words came.

"I feel like an idiot," she said. "I've helped so many people through this, but now I can't think of what to do next."

"I'll cut out early. Where do you want to meet?"

"At Pat's, I guess. Mike's going to drive. We're leaving in an hour, figure we should get there by seven."

"Don't speed." *Why did he say that?* "How is Mike doing?" *He didn't want them in a wreck, that's why. He couldn't handle that.*

"They called him, then he called me. He's shook."

"Do you think he's up to driving all that way? You could come here and I'll drive the rest. Or I could pick you up there."

"No, we'll be all right. We'll see you there."

After he hung up, he walked across the room, then stared back at the black phone. Had he actually spoken with Meer and Jessica, or had his mind retrieved a terrible dream? Pat had lost weight the last few years, had found time for friends and joking around. The sparkle had come back. The old Pat. But he had stayed too busy.

Still, Pat *dead*? No way. Dan ran a calendar check through his head: birthdays, anniversaries, holidays. Nothing this week. But the Fernettan twins had to be setting him up, drawing him to Milwaukee for some reason. A picnic or a play perhaps. A fancy dinner. Pat would be there, dear Pat, laughing his head off at Dan's shock.

No. Jessie wasn't acting. Neither was Meer. He'd never heard their voices so flat.

Pat was dead.

Dan got to Milwaukee first. He waited inside his car until Mike's rolled to a stop behind him. Jessica rushed into his arms and started crying. He eased her out of the street onto the terrace, and Mike came up behind her, head down, waiting. Dan put out an arm, and Mike joined his parents' embrace.

That night, in a small guest room above Pat's office, Dan pulled his journal from between the shirts in his suitcase. He lifted a pen from his left pocket. "Tuesday, March 25, 1997. My best friend, Patrick William Fernettan, died this morning. He was only 53." Dan stared at the page, closed his eyes and shook his head as though the motion might rub away the words. But the letters lay black against the white paper, and he flung the pen and his journal against the wall above the bed. He watched them fall to the floor, then stepped to the window to gaze at the cream-city-brick walls of Pat's old church, where the people who loved him would gather on Friday to say goodbye. Dan crossed the room, stooped behind the bed to retrieve his pen and journal, then headed downstairs to help Jessica and Mike plan the funeral.

Mrs. Hendrick, the housekeeper, stopped him, and Dan followed her into Pat's office.

"I checked for names in Father's card file," she said, "for people we should notify. Mostly numbers for priests and parishioners, but I came across an odd one. A serial number, like from a car. Or maybe that portable CD player he bought last week. But why would he put it in with his phone numbers?" She handed Dan a small yellow card with Pat's writing: KAS6085551313.

"I'll hang onto it," Dan said. "Maybe we'll find what it's for when we go through his things."

But there'd be nothing to find. The card had confused him for a second, then he recognized a Willow Run phone number and the initials: Kathryn Ann Sherman.

Pat and Kathy? No. Pat didn't even go to the reunion last year. Maybe he'd considered calling her someday for dinner, to talk again the way they did at the '91 reunion, the night Dan introduced them.

He nudged the office door shut and studied the number, not sure he should call. Maybe don't tell her about the card, just be an old friend sharing sad news about someone she danced with years ago.

He sat down at Pat's desk. On the wall above it, Pat had tacked a thirty-inch poster of *Earthrise*, the photo he loved so much: Earth from Apollo 8 in orbit over the moon. From their last year at the seminary. At the bottom, Pat had taped part of a conversation:

"We'd better learn to get along. We're all in this together." (Me)

"Actually, we're all ON it together—that little bitty ball out there in deep space." (Danny Bates)

—January 1969, five months before ordination.

Dan dialed the number on the card.

Kathy answered on the first ring. "Pat, you're early!"

Dan started to hang up, held the receiver in midair, then eased it back to his ear. "Kathy, it's Dan Bates."

"Danny? But my caller ID … where's Pat?"

"I have bad news, Kath." He could hear her breathing, and she started to say something, but it came out a whimper. Something was going on between them, but he didn't care, except it made this tougher. *Get it over with.*

"Kathy, Pat died this morning. He had a heart attack."

"No. Oh God no." She started crying, then suddenly stopped. "How did you know? How many people—"

"No one knows anything, including me. Pat had your number in a code, like a serial number for something he bought."

"Oh, God. I don't believe this. Are you sure? I mean … I don't believe it. A heart attack?"

"This morning, before Mass."

"Is there … I mean, I'd like to come for his service, but …"

"Of course you should come. You can sit with me and Jessie.… Kath? I have to tell you: Pat seemed happier than ever the past few years."

She started crying again. "He had chest pains. They kept coming, but he wouldn't get them checked. We argued about it. 'When I have time,' he'd say. But he never … I should have called you. You could've—"

"He didn't always listen to me either. Pat did what Pat wanted."

She spoke between sobs. "After that reunion when you introduced us, Pat and I met one day for lunch. Then we started getting together on his days off. He felt bad about not seeing you more. Oh, and turning you down for the reunion, but he was so afraid people might get suspicious … though we were just friends. That's the truth, Danny. We weren't lovers … I'm sorry, I shouldn't be telling—"

"I'm not going to think any less of him, Kathy … or of you."

"I know, but … can I tell you this? One night we were making out—just kissing, that's all—and Pat pulled away. I said something about I must be losing it, and he said no, he liked it but he felt guilty."

"I guess I'd expect that."

"Yes, I did too, but one time I thought he was going to give in. We were necking, and we ... well, we were rubbing our hands all over each other's backs. Our *backs*, Danny, that's all we were doing—five, ten minutes, longer than ever—but all of a sudden Pat jumped all the way to the other end of the couch and bent over and started crying. God, he just cried and cried and cried.... I knew it was 'cause of me, and I didn't know what to do."

"It wasn't your fault. His either. It—"

"I cried too. I felt so bad for him. But I was mad, too. I had—I still have—no idea how he could think what we were doing ... even what I *wanted* to do, was a sin."

Dan thought of the swimming party. Fifteen years old, forbidden to kiss. *Shall not descend to the common plane of the layman.* "You'd understand if you knew the seminary. It taught us—hell, it *condemned* us—to feel guilty about anything sexual. Not only doing, but thinking and feeling too. *Everything.* Those of us who believed it ... hell, it's with us for life."

"He told me some of it, but I didn't understand how bad ..."

"And maybe that night it wasn't only guilt. Maybe it was despair, too ... Pat finally getting a hint of what he gave up."

Kathy let out a deep breath. "I don't know. But I was afraid he wouldn't come back ... and when he did, I never tried anything like that again. Short hugs hello and goodbye ... little kisses now and then to say I loved him, but that was all."

Dan pushed the nap of Pat's maroon rug back and forth with his foot. "I probably shouldn't say this, but I was hoping you two *had* made love. Eventually he would have realized it was good. He'd have gotten over his guilt."

Her voice was so soft he could hardly hear. "No, I don't think he would have."

His wasn't much louder. "I don't either, Kath. I was just wishing."

Mrs. Hendrick went home and Mike left to meet with somebody from the archdiocese. Dan and Jessica faced each other across Pat's kitchen table. How many times had Pat eaten here alone, staring at the single red candle in the silver centerpiece? Dan had joined him a few times. Once they had brats. Pat fried them dry, then they washed them down with a dark beer from one of those new microbreweries. But Pat seldom used the table, and Mrs. Hendrick complained for years that he always ate on the run.

"Um," Dan said, "I made a decision a few minutes ago that I should have shared with you."

Jessica looked up.

"Pat had a friend … a woman friend I introduced him to several years ago. He—"

She raised a hand to stop him. "Kathy?"

"Yes. You—"

"Pat told me. God, how he told me, all embarrassed and stumbling over the words like an adolescent going to confession. When I finally figured out what he was trying to say, that he had a girlfriend, I was so happy for him. He really liked her, and most of the time he pushed aside the guilt and enjoyed being with her…. But you said you made a decision."

"I invited her to sit with us."

"Good. Pat loved her…. God, that seems strange to say." She stared toward the dining room. "But damn it, why should it? He was entitled to love … to be loved, too. And from things he told me, she loved him. So, yeah, she should be there with us. I'll tell Mom and Dad. They may not totally understand, but he mentioned Kathy a few times when we were with them, so having her there shouldn't come as a complete shock."

"You're sure?" Dan recalled her parents wanting nothing to do with him.

"They've gotten more … accepting, I guess is the word. But I wish I'd met her sooner, when Pat was alive." She shivered and wrapped her arms around herself. "He died so damned young, yet today I feel old. How can I be old the same day my twin brother died young?"

"We are getting older, Jess. But you're right, it's not time to die."

"It never is, but we will someday, just like Pat." She tugged at the sleeve of her teal jacket. "Jeez, I'm cold. And I do feel old … old enough to wish I'd done a lot of things differently."

"You don't have to be old for that. I've wished it for years."

She wiped her eyes. "I've heard people say that if they got to live their lives over they wouldn't change a thing."

"Liars. Or stupid. Or maybe their decisions worked out. Mine didn't."

"What was your worst one, becoming a priest?"

"I've made a lot of 'worst' ones. One was not moving to Minneapolis twenty years ago, no matter who told me not to."

"You still wish you had?"

"Yes."

She walked to the window and fiddled with a half-dead vine that had long overgrown its pot. "My worst was putting a wall between us. 'You're going to be sorry,' Pat said whenever I reminded him not to tell you where I was. He kept bringing it up every time he saw me, even after I threatened to quit talking to him if he asked again."

She stared out the window. "I kept the wall up, an emotional wall I built over a long time to stop getting hurt, by you or other men or my patients dying. When you became a priest I decided I couldn't depend on anyone and by God I wouldn't. I mean, part of it was knowing I couldn't keep going to pieces when my kids died." She turned to face him. "So I guess I developed this ... what, this crust, this wall, to protect myself. I blocked out everything. That's why Dick left. I wouldn't open up."

"I'm sorry," Dan said. "But you've helped so many kids."

She put up a hand. "Let me finish. By the time you showed up I'd gotten very good at hiding behind my wall. That's what my work became, in a way, a wall. Sometimes when you came I tried to crack it, but I'd get scared and put you off again. I couldn't even talk about it. *Damn!* I couldn't make myself tell you what was going on."

"You've told me now."

"But it's too late."

"It's a start. We can change."

"No. That wall is a part of me as much as guilt is a part of you guys."

"But now you've told me about it. You've already changed. Piece by piece you can knock it down. Not all of it. But you don't need to destroy it, just cut it down to where it helps instead of hurts you."

She looked at him. "You make it sound easy, but it's not."

"I know. But you can do it."

"I've changed. I'm not the Jessie you knew."

"Deep inside you are. When you laugh ... that comes from the you I knew. The you I've always loved. It's still there."

She looked away. "It's too late. I'm sorry."

Dan stared at her hair, cut short and combed back. Strands of gray were settling into the familiar light brown, and lines he'd never noticed before etched the smooth skin at the edges of her eyes and mouth.

Damn, it could have been different. They could have married and raised Mike together. If she had been less stubborn. If he had been more assertive.

Twenty years they could have lived together, sharing stories about their work each night, watching Mike grow, laughing and crying and fighting and making up. Making love. They'd done all that—except make love—for a few hours on his visits. A day here, a couple there. How many days over the years, maybe a thousand? A thousand days out of what, *ten* thousand?

She was staring out the window again. "We've gotten too old—"

"No, we haven't." He wrapped his arms around her and she turned and he brought his cheek to hers. Both were wet, and the tears weren't all hers.

"It's too late, Danny. It's too damned late."

Chapter 39

▼

Mourners who arrived after nine forty-five for Pat's ten-o'clock funeral had no hope of finding a seat in the old church.

Funeral director Lars Thorsson met Dan and Jessica, her parents, and Kathy at the church door. Inside, the organist started a slow, sad song Dan didn't recognize. Mike stepped from the rectory with priests from the Resurrection Seminary class of 1969. Pat's class, and Dan's. They wore matching chasubles, white cloth with full-length, metallic-gold-thread crosses glinting in the speckled sunlight that made it through the trees.

Dan hurried over to greet them. Pete Parensky was there, and Steve Towan, Meer Mohrical and Go-Go Gogarin. He had last seen them at the '86 reunion. So joyous then, so somber now. One of their class had died already, and Dan recalled Neil Diamond's song "Done Too Soon." But all of them were graying, and Steve's beard looked as though his hair had slipped from his bald head and settled along his jaw.

They shook hands and embraced—no one said much—then Dan returned to the church steps. Jessica took his arm. "You miss being part of that group, don't you."

"Yes." But the idea seemed so absurd that he thought any second she'd shake her head or roll her eyes or, if it hadn't been a funeral, laugh out loud. Instead, Jessica nodded, and Dan realized she hadn't asked a question, she had made a statement.

Kathy said, "Those guys, the priests. They're the ones in Pat's stories, aren't they? It's unreal, seeing them together like this." She studied them. "I wish he were here with them."

An usher led Mr. and Mrs. Fernettan down the center aisle to the first pew, a few feet from Pat's casket. Jessica, Dan and Kathy followed. As they sat, the old wooden pew creaked. Dan couldn't take his eyes off the casket. He recalled Corliss Lamont's words in *A Humanist Funeral Service*: "Those who feel deeply will grieve deeply. No philosophy or religion ever taught can prevent this wholly natural reaction of the human heart."

Jessica's hand squeezed his arm, and he put it around her and felt her sobs. The church was already warm. It would feel uncomfortable before the service was over.

The smell of incense preceded a procession of bishops and priests and acolytes marching to the front of the church. The organist played louder and the congregation rose to sing a song of alleluias. These people had hopes of eternal life. Dan didn't, but his throat had swelled so he couldn't sing anyway. Instead he wept, for poor dead Pat, for Jessica, for Kathy, for himself and for his class, all with more days behind them than ahead.

Jessica stood close, and Dan kept his arm around her.

Ushers squeezed past people standing in the aisles, announcing they could watch the service on closed-circuit television downstairs in the air-conditioned church hall.

"No," a woman in a dark-blue hat told a friend sitting behind Dan. "I want to see Father Pat's funeral here, where I heard him preach."

"We can trade off," the friend said. "Tell me when you get tired."

Dan stared at the casket. The sadness he understood. It was his anger that surprised him. Shitshitshitshit. I *told* you to take care of yourself, Pat, to let up a bit. You agreed we'd bike the Elroy-Sparta Trail, but you kept putting it off and we never did. Somebody needed you, you said. Well, somebody *always* needed you, and a lot of us need you now, too, but where the hell are you?

He glared at the archbishop. You stupid son of a bitch. Look what's happening to your men. Can't you pound away at this poor excuse of a pope until he agrees to ordain women and married men? You need them. Your people need them. But no, poor old Holy Father can't stand opposition to his decrees, so he demands you stay silent. You obey, and people suffer.

Dan shook his head. Pat's death was so unnecessary, so correctable. But Pat wouldn't appreciate his anger. The grief, yes. He'd understand their sense of loss.

Mike stood before the altar surrounded by Pat's classmates, and they began the prayers of the Mass for the Dead. Dan surveyed the packed church. Too bad Pat never got to retire, to have a huge party, to see how these people loved him.

From the sanctuary the archbishop, too, gazed at the crowd. His eyes were sad. He knew what he'd lost. He knew what they'd all lost.

The congregation sat while a young man from the parish read from Lamentations: "My soul is shut out from peace; I have forgotten happiness. Yahweh is good to those who trust him, to the soul that searches for him."

Jessica rested her head on Dan's shoulder.

Another reader recited from Paul's first letter to the Corinthians, a passage that Lamont had included in his humanist service. It fit Pat so well: "Though I have the gift of prophecy, and understand all mysteries and all knowledge; and though I have all faith, so that I could remove mountains, and have not love, I am nothing.... There is faith, hope, and love, these three, but the greatest of these is love."

Yeah, that was Pat.

Mike walked to the lectern to read from the Gospel according to John: "Do not let your hearts be troubled. Trust in God still, and trust in me. I am going now to prepare a place for you, and after I have gone and prepared you a place, I shall return to take you with me, so that where I am you may be too."

Damn it, Pat, I wish that were true. But wishing doesn't make it so. An image flashed into his mind: He, Daniel John Bates II, former priest and classmate of the deceased Patrick William Fernettan, was ascending the altar steps and telling the assembled mourners—bishops, priests, and faithful, and a very shocked Jessica—that this day he was returning to the priesthood to carry on the work of their dear friend, Father Pat.

But that was impossible. To be a priest, you had to believe in God, and he no longer did. Still, Pat's life of sacrifice held an appeal that Dan couldn't deny. And, he realized as he stood with her, so did Jessica's.

Mike was speaking. "To offer us a few words about Father Pat, let me introduce his best friend and classmate, Dan Bates."

Dan stepped to the varnished podium from which Pat had preached just last Sunday. He gripped the polished wood and felt at home, though it had been years since he stood behind one of these. Perhaps preaching was like riding a bike. Once you learn …

"I met Pat Fernettan the day we started high school at Resurrection Seminary, forty years ago. We were fourteen years old. Pat helped me feel comfortable that first day and many times after that, the way he helped many of you over the years. He never did stop offering his help. He gave us his heart until his heart gave out."

People were fanning themselves, but they were listening. "Father Pat believed a priest should be there for his people, and he was always there, even on days I tried to drag him away for a little R and R. For his physical and psychological health, I told him."

Dan glanced toward the archbishop. *You've got to do more for your priests. Will you now?*

"But Pat didn't seem concerned about his health, nor about the stress from today's shortage of priests. He believed that was just how things were, and went on with his ministry. Father Pat was the priest I always wanted to be."

He stared at Jessica, and she stared back. *Remember that first day? I've always wondered if I became friends with Pat more because I liked him or because I wanted to meet you.*

"The times I tried to get him out of here on his days off, I told him it was for his own good, but I knew it was mostly for me. I loved the guy's company. Didn't we all. That was because Father Pat accepted us even when he felt we were wrong. He told us what he believed, but always in a way that let us know he would never abandon us."

Dan turned toward Mike. *You're my son, but you bonded with Pat. How could I ever have felt that was bad?*

"It was Father Pat's influence, through the life he led, that persuaded the celebrant of today's Mass to follow him into the priesthood. He'll speak to us next: Father Pat's nephew, Father Michael Patrick Fernettan."

After the service, Dan nibbled a sandwich at the reception in the school hall. He left most of it on his plate, stopped for a few words with each of his classmates, then told Jessica, "I'm going outside for a while."

He sat alone on the cut-stone steps outside the old church's modern glass doors. Parishioners walked slowly to their cars, finished with their goodbyes to Pat and each other.

The memories kept coming, of classes, basketball games, and walks to the lake.

Pat kicking Dan's chair while Dan argued with Herkimer: "This isn't a proof. I believe in God, but I have friends who don't, and they'll laugh me out of the room if I say this is how Aquinas 'proved' a God. So, can we prove it or not?"

They never did prove it, but Pat's faith stayed solid.

Pat with a high-arching jump shot that swished through the net at the final horn. It happened several times, but one day their team pulled an upset over some upper classmen and everyone but Dan carried a nickname to the locker room.

Pat became "Nothin'-But-Net" Fernettan, then just "Net." Billy Gogarin had raced around the court like a kid possessed, harassing the opposing players into bad passes and missed baskets. "Go-Go." Before Pat's winning basket, Matt Mohrical stole the ball when hope seemed lost. It was a miracle, so he became "Miracle" Mohrical, "Meer" for short. Joe Trainer came to Resurrection as "Freight Train" and hated it—he said it made him sound fat—but settled for "Train." Dear Train. He'd dropped out of sight. No one had been able to find him.

The church door opened and Jessica stepped out. "You all right?"

He nodded. "Thinking of old times. They don't seem so old, though."

"The crowd is thinning. If you're okay, I'll go back inside for a while." She reached for the door, but it opened again.

Mike said, "You two all right?"

Jessica gave him a hug. "Mm-hmm. I was coming back in."

Dan nodded. "You?"

"I'm okay."

"Thank you for saying the Mass. I know it was hard, but there was no one more appropriate."

"Thanks."

Dan turned to Jessica. "Thought I'd run down to Southport, walk through the seminary, reminisce a bit."

Mike stepped closer. "Would you care for company?"

Dan stared at the church door. He preferred to be alone.

"Good idea," Jessica said. "You guys go. I'll see you later."

Dan shot her a look, but she disappeared into the church without glancing back.

Mike was studying him. "If you'd rather be by yourself, it's okay. I understand."

Dan looked into his son's eyes. Hell, Mike was grieving, too. He dug into his pocket for his keys. "C'mon. Let's go."

Chapter 40

Dan followed the I-94 freeway through downtown Milwaukee, then through the suburbs and countryside to the Southport exit.

"I wanted to tell you," Mike said, "that was a nice eulogy for Uncle Pat."

Dan kept his eyes on the road. "Thanks. I'd like to have said more, but it was warm and people were standing in the aisles."

"It was fine."

"Yours too."

"Even with God in it?"

"Of course with God in it. Pat believed, you believe, probably everyone in church except your mother and I believed. It would have seemed odd if you *hadn't* mentioned God."

They rode in silence along Shoreline Road. Dan swung a U-turn at the seminary gate and parked in front of a large wooden sign for Bay View Park. Jessica had driven away from this spot—away from *him*—more than twenty years before. He counted. Twenty-*nine*. Almost thirty. He hadn't been to the park since.

"Let's walk up the seminary drive," he said.

They waited for three cars to clear, then crossed the road and walked along the blacktop driveway under the twin rows of maple trees.

"There are so few guys here now, it seems like a ghost school," Dan said. "In the sixties we all dressed in black. From planes flying overhead we must have looked like ants crawling over the place."

Mike laughed. "That's how Uncle Pat described it. I wish I could have seen it."

"It was kinda odd."

Mike stopped. "If you feel that way, why come back?"

"I'm not sure. Maybe 'cause, despite all the crap, we felt secure here. We were a group of guys who shared one great goal. We thought we were gonna save the world."

In front of Kleissman Hall, Mike pointed to the southeast wing's third floor. "Fourth from the left: my room all the years I was here."

"Lucky. It took me till deacon year to get a room overlooking the lake." He studied the dome. "They taught us that if we disciplined ourselves, we'd be invincible against the wickedness of the world. We'd fix it, make it perfect. Did you feel that way when you were here?"

"No."

"Didn't think so. You went to a regular high school first, got a more realistic view of things. I still hate how damned naive we were."

Mike led the way toward the north side of the building. "You really think my going to a regular high school helped?"

"Oh, yeah, though the night you told us you were coming here I wondered if you'd learned anything at all."

"I begged Mom not to make me tell you, but that night I decided I would. I wanted to shock you. And then I hated you for being shocked."

"You shocked both of us, but your mom handled it and I didn't. I was glad to hear the seminary had changed, though. It doesn't work, raising kids like plants in a hothouse, sheltering them the way they did us. We need to accept reality, but first we have to learn what it is. We didn't till we were older, and it was a lot harder then."

"But now your reality says there is no God."

"Yes."

"Where do you think Uncle Pat is now?"

"Nowhere. He's gone."

Mike's voice took on an edge. "Like he never existed."

"No. That's not true. Don't even say that ... not here. Pat was so alive all those years. He still lives in our memories—and in the ways we're different because of him."

"But we'll die, too. *Then* it'll be as if he didn't exist."

"No," Dan said. "Pat's influence—ours, too—will continue even if no one's aware of it. Sure, the memories of him—the memories of all of us—die with those who knew us. But our goodness, our compassion or kindness or whatever, passes from one generation to another. And that's a long way from not having existed." He laughed. "Oh, man. Pat would tease me that I'm preaching again. He said I never lost the knack."

"He was right."

They paused in the parking lot between Kleissman and the old gym. "Here's where I first saw your mom and Pat, forty years ago this September."

"What did you say to them?"

"Nothing, till we met inside the dorm. Your mom and I just stood here staring at each other."

Mike laughed. "But you became friends. That was nice."

"No, that was hard. We weren't supposed to have girl friends. That meant not only girlfriends, but friends who were girls too."

"I'm still glad you did."

Along the south side, Mike kept glancing back toward the parking lot. In front, they stared once more at Kleissman Hall, then walked down the drive toward the lake.

At the seminary gate, Mike stopped. "Mom has a picture from here."

"Who of?"

"Nobody, just the park across the street. An eight by ten, with a deep blue sky and bright green trees and a row of forsythia bushes all yellow. I found it when I was little, peeking into one of the boxes she kept in her room."

"You peeked?"

Mike grinned. "Never told her, of course. A summer or two later I came home early from a baseball game 'cause I'd turned my ankle. Mom was at the kitchen table, crying, holding a piece of paper. I figured another one of her kids died 'cause she always cried when that happened. I went to give her a hug and she was looking at that picture."

"What did she say?"

"Nothing at first. Then, when she realized I was staring at it, she said, 'This is a very special place … from when I was younger.' That's all she said. She slipped the picture into an envelope and took it back to her room. I never saw it again, but sometimes I wondered where the place was. I pretty much forgot about it till my first morning at the seminary. We were walking down here after breakfast—we used to do that, like you guys did—and I stopped right here. I couldn't believe it. That park across the road was the scene in Mom's picture. It looked different, of course, 'cause it was late summer, not spring, but I knew right away it was the place. She'd said it was special, so I always felt close to her whenever I came here.… I suppose that sounds pretty weird."

"Unh-uh," Dan said. "Special things happen to us, and those places stay sacred, if I can use that word. Especially when we grow older, after we learn truly special things don't happen very often. Sometimes we visit those places. It becomes a sort of pilgrimage, but it doesn't have to be religious, just personal, like our coming here today to reminisce about Pat. I don't think it's weird at all."

"I never told anyone about it—the picture, I mean. One day I came here alone. I circled every tree in the park looking for initials. I knew I looked kinda crazy so I hoped no one saw me. I found a lot of 'em, but not a JF or a PF ... or a DB."

"I don't think we ever carved ours. It seemed like vandalism."

"I wanted to ask Mom why this place was special, but I was afraid to after how she cried the day I caught her with the picture."

"Pat probably took that photograph during one of our walks. Color film was new then, and it cost more than black and white, but he liked to catch the color in things."

"Well, he caught the forsythias in that one." Mike glanced across the road into the park. "Looks like they're done for this year. Did Mom ever meet you guys here?"

"Mm-hmm. Sometimes the three of us walked the beach together."

"That's probably why the picture's special."

"Probably."

Mike studied Dan's face. "Something happened here, didn't it?"

Dan didn't answer. He led Mike across Shoreline Road into the park. A stiff breeze whipped the waves into whitecaps and carried the scent of weeds and wet sand across the park. White gulls squealed overhead and two kids whipped by on rollerblades.

Should he tell him? Jessica didn't share it when she had the chance: Perhaps she wanted their story to stay a secret. Still, he'd want to know if it was a part of *his* life.

"I don't know how your mother will feel about me telling you, but I think you should know what made that picture—this place—so special. If you want to."

Mike nodded.

Dan looked out at the lake, then at his son. "The night before I became a subdeacon and took the vow of celibacy, I sneaked out of Kleissman at midnight and met your mother here. We stayed on the beach together till the sun came up. Except for her coming through my reception line after my first Mass, that was the last time I saw her till the day I met you. It was also the last time I came here, till now."

Mike didn't say anything. He stared at Dan as though he knew that wasn't the whole story.

"That was the night we created you."

Mike blinked. "So that's why. Jeez." He shook his head. "Man, I'd have never guessed."

"No, I suppose not. I'm sorry if it's more than you wanted to know."

"It's okay. It certainly answers my questions about Mom and that picture. Wow. I'd have never guessed."

Dan's gaze swept the park. "It's changed a lot. Some of the trees I remember are gone, and those trees and bushes on the side of the bluff weren't so tall. You could see the lake from here, even the beach down below. We used to slide down on the grass."

"There's a path to the beach over this way," Mike said. He turned south along the asphalt trail until the line of bushes came to an end and another trail broke off to the left toward the beach. The late afternoon sun gilded the rocks of the breakwater and the sails of the few boats out on the lake.

On the beach, Dan studied the bluff where it met the sand. It all looked different. Somewhere there'd been a clump of small trees …

Jessie's pale pink skin glistened against the brown blanket. And then she was dressed and running from him, up the bluff, and he was too slow to catch her, and her back tires spit gravel as she sped away.

Mike was kicking off his shoes. "Mom always said you should go barefoot across the sand. Did she do that here?"

I do when I'm with people I trust. Right now I don't feel that way about you.

"Yeah, she did." Dan took off his shoes and pushed his toes deep into the sand. "Did your mother ever tell you she cut herself running barefoot one spring and had to get a tetanus shot?"

"She showed me her scar. She never stopped, though. She used to embarrass the hell out of me at grade-school picnics. Every other mom flitted around all prissy and proper, but *mine* chased us kids around all day in her bare feet." He picked up a flat white stone and curled his index finger around it. "Uncle Pat said he skipped a stone six times one day when you guys came here."

"Your uncle Pat lied. I got five skips, two different times. He never got more than four."

"He told me you'd say that."

"He knew I'd tell you the truth."

Mike whipped the stone sidearm. It landed flat between two waves, skipped once, twice, then disappeared. "Haven't done that in years." He rubbed his shoulder. "Too many years, I guess." He crouched and fiddled with some rocks still wet and shiny from the last wave. "I told Mom not to let you live with us. I was scared you'd to try to make me be an atheist like you. That's why she never let you move in."

"Did she tell you that?"

"No, but—"

"Your mom had—still has, I guess—her own reasons. If she'd wanted me to move in, your vote wouldn't have counted. It wasn't because of you."

They stepped across the sand away from the water and lay against the grass on the side of the bluff. The last time Dan was here he'd been with Jessica, now he was with their son.

"I always liked coming here," Mike said. "You can see the city, but it's far enough away to feel apart from it.... Was it pretty that night ... the one you spent here with Mom?"

"Oh, yes."

"Not spooky?"

"No. At least not with her. I suppose it was after she left. But even then it was pretty. Lots of stars and the lighthouse reflecting off the water across the bay. It was very pretty."

Mike rolled over, pulled a blade of grass and rubbed it between his fingers. "One afternoon the whooshing of the waves lulled me to sleep here. I was late for dinner."

"In our day, they'd have campused us for weeks. What happened to you?"

"Everyone laughed ... and I had to fix my own dinner."

"Remember what you made?"

"A peanut butter and jelly sandwich."

"For *dinner*?"

Mike grinned. "Well, I found some apple jelly, my favorite."

They watched the clouds. The sun was going down, and the light high in the sky was turning red.

"I had a tough time not crying during Mass," Mike said.

"I know. I cried."

"I saw you. It made it harder for me not to."

"Sorry."

Mike pulled another blade of grass. "Know what? I believed everything Uncle Pat ever told me, except two things. The first was not to become a priest."

"He told me he didn't want you to, but I didn't believe him. Actually, I blamed him for it."

"He was upset when I told him I was coming here. Not like you were, but bad enough. 'You can do more good in other professions,' he kept telling me. Once I asked him how. 'Lots of ways,' he said. 'Use your imagination. In medicine like your mom, or by teaching like your dad, or by becoming an honest politician.' I laughed at that, and he got mad, so I apologized. But I liked what I saw him doing as a priest, so I went against his advice. I think he forgave me."

"He was proud of you. Your mom and I are, too."

Mike raised an eyebrow.

"We are. We don't share your beliefs, but we don't begrudge you them. And you can do a lot of good as a priest. I'm not going to try to make you an agnostic."

Mike flicked the grass onto the sand. "I should tell you: I am aware of the contradictions, things that make no sense in some of the Church's positions. There are times I do wonder."

He drew circles in the sand with his fingers. "The second thing I didn't believe from Uncle Pat was about you. Whenever he talked to me, he said, 'Have you seen your dad?' Or, 'Call your dad. He'd love to hear from you.' He got angry when Mom told him I stayed away from the house when you came. One day I said I wanted to be *his* son, not yours, and he yelled at me, said you'd be a great dad if I gave you half a chance and, if I didn't, I'd be sorry. I never saw him as angry as he got that day. From then on I pretended you and I were buddies, but I still stayed away from you."

Dan tossed a stone into the lake. "And I let you. Except for a few times like coming to the game you pitched, I pretty much gave up trying to be a dad."

The sun was gone, and blue shadows brought a damp chill to the air. The smell off the water and the sand took Dan back twenty-nine years to the March night he spent here with Jessica. A few gulls made their last pass of the day, heading south. Dan followed their flight and spotted someone standing on the bluff at the top of the path he and Mike had taken to the beach.

A woman in a teal jacket, watching them.

Jessica.

"Do you think you'll ever get together with Mom?" Mike hadn't seen her.

"I don't know. I'd still like to."

She was walking down the path toward them.

Mike touched Dan's arm. "I really hope you do … Dad. It would be great for you both."

Jessica had reached the edge of the beach where the asphalt path disappeared beneath the sand. She bent over, and started taking off her shoes.

978-0-595-44713-8
0-595-44713-9